THE BASTILLE SPY

C. S. Quinn is a travel and lifestyle journalist for *The Times*, the *Guardian* and the *Mirror*, alongside many magazines. Prior to this, Quinn's background in historic research won prestigious postgraduate funding from the British Arts Council. Quinn pooled these resources, combining historical research with first-hand experiences in far-flung places to create her bestselling The Thief Taker Series.

Also by C. S. Quinn

The Thief Taker Series

The Thief Taker

Fire Catcher

Dark Stars

The Changeling Murders

Death Magic (short story)

THE BASTILLE SPY

C. S. QUINN

First published in hardback in Great Britain in 2019 by Corvus, an imprint of Atlantic Books Ltd.

This paperback edition published in 2020.

10 9 8 7 6 5 4 3 2 1

A CIP catalogue record for this book is available from the British Library.

Paperback ISBN: 978 1 78649 843 4
E-book ISBN: 978 1 78649 844 1

Corvus
An imprint of Atlantic Books Ltd
Ormond House
26–27 Boswell Street
London
WC1N 3JZ

www.corvus-books.co.uk

Printed and bound by CPI Group (UK) Ltd, Croydon CR0 4YY

Inspired by true events

CHAPTER 1

St Petersburg, The Winter Palace, 1789

THE DAY I KILLED THE COSSACK WAS WHEN IT ALL BEGAN. If I think carefully, I can trace everything back to that slave market in St Petersburg – an illegal affair trafficking mostly Persians and Kurds foolish enough to cross the badlands of Khiva.

The dusty square bore a resemblance to other livestock markets in Russia. There were enclosures, merchants shouting their wares and buyers haggling, examining the goods. A good deal of vodka was being drunk and a few traders were filling their bowls from a cauldron of cabbage soup bubbling over a wood fire. Despite the sultry heat of the St Petersburg summer, most buyers wore thick fur-lined leather coats and boots.

In contrast, I was dressed in Turkoman rags that barely covered my body, with a metal cuff heavy around my neck and chains at my wrists and ankles.

The fellow slaves in my consignment were similarly clothed and bound, heads bowed low with the discomfort of their bonds, bodies wasted from their weeks dragged starving through the Russian countryside.

In the middle distance stood the fate of many people trafficked here. The magnificent Winter Palace was being extended for Catherine the Great; the boxy Hermitage annexe wrought brick by brick from the sliding marsh. Her Imperial Majesty had ended slavery. But she doesn't involve herself in building works. This square palace, with its endless gold columns and bride-cake green-white façade, was built on the bones of spent slaves, flung carelessly into the foundations.

Even now if I close my eyes I can see and feel that fateful day as if it's happening all over again. A bushy-bearded man steps forward and ushers our little group into a fenced enclosure. He wears a tricorn hat with red fur edging, jammed down low over his greasy dark hair. This is the man who bought us, the unseen buyer who paid the dead-eyed Khiva tribesman who herded us to the city gates. At his side stands a giant Cossack with a plumed turban, a studded-leather jerkin and a whip in his hand.

'Let's see what we have,' says the fur-hatted merchant in heavy St Petersburg Russian, with a humourless grin, 'in our Kurdish soup.' This is a derogatory term for a job lot of slaves bought cut-price from Khiva – like the cheap stew made in Kurdistan, where each ladle holds differing amounts of miscellaneous meat.

The slave merchant shoots a dark smile at his Cossack henchman.

'Those pig-ignorant slave-hunters wouldn't know if they caught Empress Ekaterina herself,' opines our owner with a sneer. 'My last batch had two Russians, worth fifty roubles each.' He eyes us greedily, assessing, whilst the Cossack stares stoically at the Winter Palace. 'Mostly Kurds,' he decides, disappointed. 'Perhaps some Persians if we're lucky.' He points. 'Separate those at the back.'

The Cossack moves among us, driving the slaves apart. He looks resigned and I wonder how he came to this position, hired muscle for a slave buyer.

Our owner's eyes land on me.

'Well, well,' he says, licking his lips. 'What have we here?'

I've tried my best to disguise myself, spreading mud over my skin, matting my long dark hair and arranging it over my face, but there's no hiding my height.

The owner lifts a chunk of tangled hair and I blink, scowling.

'Could be something,' he decides, turning to his hired thug. 'See the eyes? Blue-grey.' He spits on his finger and rubs away a little of the dirt on my upper arm.

'Dark, but not too dark,' he says. 'What think you? An African half-breed?'

'Too light. Maybe Moorish,' says the Cossack. 'The eyes are too savage to be Russian.'

'Maybe,' decides the owner. He prods his sharp stick into my chest.

'You,' he barks. 'Where from?'

I mutter a few words of frightened Kurdish. He shakes his head.

'Kurdish,' he says contemptuously. 'Hardly worth the chains that hold her. She's only good for the street brothels.' He indicates towards the back of the market. 'Put her in with the other whores.'

They drag me along, the chain weighing around my neck, my hands bound, to a stinking shack partially roofed with mouldering reeds. A door of sticks is dragged open and the stench of despair wafts out. A huddle of frightened girls look up as I'm pushed to the ground and fastened to a metal hoop on the floor.

The door shuts and I begin to free myself, working fast. I reach up, tugging a hidden lock-pick from my filthy hair. I unlock my chains and the manacle at my neck, rubbing my wrists in relief as the restraints fall.

The other slaves are watching me shed my bonds, their eyes like saucers. I scan the little hut and my eyes land on a single scrawny man, huddled in the corner. Without his rigid aristocratic clothing, he reminds me of a soft pink crab slipped from its shell. His head was once close-cropped for a wig, but now his hair grows out untidily in clumps of black and grey, to match his unshaven face. Bare knees are drawn up to his chin, the naked legs ageing and liver-spotted. There is a deep bruise on his cheek just below his haunted eyes. My heart aches for him.

I drop to the ground near where he sits.

'You are Gaspard de Mayenne?' I ask. He flinches, features twisted between confusion and fear.

'Who are you?' he whispers, his gaze trying to reconcile my light-coloured eyes to skin that isn't white enough to fit, in that way Europeans do.

'My name is Attica Morgan,' I say, speaking in French. 'I'm an English spy. I'm here to rescue you.'

CHAPTER 2

IN MY EXPERIENCE, MEN OFFERED RESCUE BY A WOMAN FALL in two camps: those who refuse the possibility and those who try to take command of the escape themselves. To my relief, Gaspard is in the first group; these are the ones who cause the least trouble.

He makes a little half-laugh, then stops when he sees my expression.

'You have the wrong person,' he says. 'I was exiled here by King Louis XVI. I'm of no use to the English.'

'Revolution is in England's interest,' I explain. 'We like what you're doing in France. Your pictures. We want you to keep doing it.'

Gaspard considers this. I wonder how much of his spirit has been broken in his hard months of slavery.

I move to unlock his chains but he pulls away, eyes furious.

'No!' he hisses. 'I don't need your kind of help. They will blind me and worse.' My thoughts flick back to the mutilated people in the market. Slaves who tried to run. Gaspard's eyes burn with boundless terror.

'Even if I could return to Paris,' says Gaspard, 'the King would boil me alive as a warning to others who seek democracy.'

It's then I notice a raised ring of branded flesh on his ribcage, ill concealed by tattered slave garments. The Bastille guards must have tortured him before sending him to Russia. He sees me looking and rearranges his rags.

I grip his thin wrists tightly and look straight in his eyes.

'France is closer to change than its King wants you to think,' I say steadily. 'Your rescue will show the French people they needn't be afraid. I give you my word as an Englishwoman. You will be free and you will be safe. I have done this many times.'

I've been unlocking his chains as I speak and they fall to the dusty ground. His mistrust fades and he starts shaking, tears running down his cheeks.

'It's true?' he whispers. 'The French people might have liberty?'

I nod.

'What about the others?' he manages, swallowing a sob. 'The other slaves. The things they do to them ...' He is trembling. I hold his shoulders.

'Every last one of you,' I promise, 'will have your freedom today.' Quickly I start unchaining the other girls, careful of their injured wrists and bruised necks. They are Kurdish and I speak to them softly in their own language. Without chains they seem even more vulnerable.

I snatch a glance at the low sunlight slicing through the rickety door. Our means of escape will come soon. I work faster. There are more slaves here than I thought possible. But at last each sits unbound on the dirt floor.

There's a sudden flare in the far distance, visible even through the slats of our wooden door. Flames, the sound of gunfire. It's time.

I throw open the door. The slave merchants have been thrown into panic, believing their illegal trade is being raided.

We've worked to give the illusion our limited troops are from the Palace and large in number.

I kneel and move aside a little dirt on the ground. My knife is where I buried it last night, before I hid myself in the wagon of kidnapped Kurds disguised as a slave.

I grip the dark-wood handle and pull the curved blade free. This is a Mangbetu knife, smooth black and deadly, awarded only to the deadliest fighters of the African Congo. I feel its reassuring weight in my hand and slide it into the back of my rags.

The traders are wildly freeing their captives, anxious to avoid arrest. Chains and manacles fall to the ground with a heavy clanking. Ropes are cut, fences kicked down. Unshackled slaves are staring around themselves, unable to comprehend what's happening.

Behind me the slave girls are watching the chaos.

'This is your chance,' I tell them, pointing to a building at the top of the hill. 'Go. Any slave who gets inside that church is promised sanctuary. Her Imperial Majesty decreed an end to servitude. By tomorrow night I'll get you on a fur-trade boat bound for Hamburg.'

There's a fraction of a pause. Then Gaspard remembers something of his revolutionary self. He grabs hold of two girls by either hand.

'*Vite! Vite!*' he cries, dragging them forth. As soon as they exit the hut, something changes. Their faces become determined, their movements certain. They flee as a pack, heading for freedom. It's like a dam breaking. Every slave is running hard, like a tidal wave moving uphill in the direction of the church.

I hear a cry. One of the girls has fallen, her leg caught tight in a slave-snare. It's only a simple rope-trap, but she's panicking. Other slaves are stampeding near where she lies.

I run to her. Falling at her side, I begin slicing through the trap.

Suddenly strong fingers seize my upper arm. I stagger as I'm pulled around to see a familiar face: the outsized Cossack guard from the slave sorting. I twist, breaking from his grip, step back into a low fighting stance, my long black blade in my hand.

The Cossack grins, revealing large white teeth. He tilts his head appraisingly, closing in. 'I knew there was something different about you,' he says in Russian, moving forward. 'We heard tales about a girl spy. I didn't believe it until now. You're going to fetch a fine price in Moscow.'

Out of the corner of my eye I can see the girl pulling at the half-cut rope around her ankle. I bring the blade low, pointing upwards as the Cossack closes in.

He taps his thick studded armour.

'Blades don't pierce military leather,' he says, lunging to take a heavy hold of my arm again.

Suddenly his face twists in shock. He lets out a strange strangled cough.

'Mangbetu knives do,' I say, turning the blade to slice his lung as his eyes bulge.

The Cossack drops silently to the floor, blood filling his airways. I look back to the slave girl sprawled in the dirt, mouth open in silent horror.

I move back to her side, slash free the snare, pull her up and give her a hard shove.

Her ankle is twisted and she gasps in pain.

'I can't do it.' The girl's starved and battered body is giving way. Her eyes are fixed on my bloody knife. 'I can't fight like you. They'll find me ...'

I take her face in my hands.

'Look at me,' I say, speaking in Kurdish. 'Do you believe me when I say I don't break my promises?'

She glances at my blood-soaked hands.

'Yes.' She swallows.

'You will survive this,' I tell her. 'I promise. I see it in you. Get to the church at the top of the hill and your freedom awaits.' I spin the gore-flecked knife. 'I will cut down anyone who tries to stop you.'

She runs, limping towards salvation.

I shield my eyes and see Gaspard has reached the safety of the church door. He turns, sees me and shouts something. I can't hear the words but his expression is unmistakable.

Hope, that emotion he'd so carefully guarded against, was in full bloom. I live for that look. It's what keeps me going through all the hard business of spying for the English.

Little did I know, in under two weeks, his face would look very different.

Gaspard would be lying dead in the Bastille prison, a diamond between his lips.

CHAPTER 3

London, two weeks later

IT'S GOOD TO BE BACK IN LONDON. THE TREES SURROUNDING King's Cross are in blossom. I can smell the sweet-grass meadows that lead to Camden Village. My family's town residence, a great red-brick hall awarded to my ancestors by Henry VIII, is resplendent in the sun.

Today I'm dressed for a wedding: a white silk dress embroidered with dainty violets. Beneath a little purple hat, secured at a tilt, my curled dark hair is elaborately styled with jewelled pins. My shoes are satin, pointed, with a small heel. Strings of pearls conceal yellow ghosts of manacle bruising to my wrists and neck.

I made the hour's walk here from the squalid Wapping docks, drinking in the lively industry of blacksmiths and papermakers, the press of girls with baskets of wares on their heads, a scent of fresh bread and pies in the air. So, unlike the other wedding guests, I haven't arrived in a gilded carriage. As I ascend the grand steps to the house an unfamiliar servant in gold-frogged livery is in the hallway making space on the portrait wall.

He's straightening an oil painting of my stepmother, the first Lady Morgan – a rapacious socialite who died many years ago.

Next in line is the picture of my mother. A bright turban frames her dark-skinned face and she holds a narrow spear. Mamma never did get to England, but my father made sketches and had her commemorated in oils.

Hearing my approach, the servant looks down from his half-ladder.

'A sad story there, I'll be bound,' he says, noticing me looking at my mother's portrait. 'They say she's why Lord Morgan drinks the laudanum. You are here for one of Lord Morgan's wedding guests?' he adds.

Of course, he assumes me a courtesan. It's hard for the English to see an unaccompanied woman in finery and come to any other conclusion.

'I'm Attica Morgan,' I reply. 'Lord Morgan's daughter.'

The servant overbalances slightly then rights himself, pulling my mother's portrait askew. He looks from her to me. A wild blush creeps up his neck and across his face. He tries to bow and the ladder jerks dangerously.

'Please,' I say, moving towards him, 'don't fall on my account.'

'My apologies,' he says. 'Miss Attica. I didn't know ...'

He pronounces it A-ttica, the way the English do, which could be correct for all I know. My name means 'of Africa' – perhaps an attempt to connect me with my heritage. I've never minded my mixed blood because I can look like many different people. I could be, say, a Jewess or a Spanish dancer or an Italian heiress or a coal-eyed beggar girl. This is a great advantage for a woman who travels in disguise.

'It's a common mistake.' I smile at the servant. 'No one can quite agree if I'm illegitimate and I never could sit still for portraits. That's the only one of me.' I point to a mischievous-looking girl sat on my father's lap.

This discomforts him worse than before. He begins leaning from foot to foot.

'Your shoes are the new Lady Morgan's choice?' I observe, taking in the little gold heels.

'Yes.' He smiles in relief, having found a better subject than my scandalous existence.

'I'll see if I can't put in a word,' I say, 'to get you something for standing about in.' I wink at him as I walk past, and through the main doors.

The dark interior closes around me as if I'd never left. The smell of beeswax polish, the richly coloured walls and oil paintings, the feeling of never belonging.

Garlands of flowers are festooned all around today and there's a hum of modernity. Servants are polishing glassware rather than tarnished old chalices. The wedding breakfast is fashionably understated. No huge sides of game or suckling pigs. The new Lady Morgan's influence is like a breath of fresh air.

I'm eyeing the small crowd, trying not to listen to the whispers about my father's new wife – an American slave-abolitionist, who has already scandalized London with her lack of English decorum.

'Attica!' I hear a high-pitched voice and realize the Spencer sisters have seen me. It's too late to beat a retreat. They close in, ribbons and bows flapping.

The older and younger siblings are almost identical, with fish-like blue eyes and mousy hair, sculpted upwards into precipitous waxy towers. As usual they are dressed for determined husband-hunting. Single men are giving them a wide birth.

'We have someone who is mad to meet you,' enthuses the older sister.

I scan the room for a way out. Likely one of their greasy cousins has come of age.

The younger Spencer sister makes some frantic beckoning into the crowd. A rather silly-looking blonde girl is the target of her wild gesticulating.

'This is her!' announces the elder, proudly, stepping back so her friend might get a full view of me. 'Attica Morgan, the escaped slave.'

CHAPTER 4

LONDON SOCIETY CAN BARELY BREATHE IN THE FETID AIR of its own stale gossip, yet I'm perpetually surprised by how resistant everyone is to forgetting my origins. If you believe the rumours, my brilliant father, Lord Morgan, sailed away from his acrimonious marriage into the arms of an African princess. She was captured by slavers whilst pregnant with me and my father was tricked into thinking her dead. His laudanum haze followed. Then some years later I docked at Bristol, a glowering little beast, so they tell it, who refused to speak a word of English and bit the first Lady Morgan's jewelled hand.

My recollection is rather less straightforward. Nevertheless, it's true I arrived in England as a small girl, to an estate of horrified relations and servants.

I have a similar sensation now, as a girl with solid blonde curls pasted to her forehead makes towards me, cooing as though I'm a monkey in a cage.

'Amelia is *mad* to meet you,' says the older Spencer sister, taking the blonde girl's arm. 'We've told her all about your daring getaway.'

'I thought she'd be darker,' says Amelia, sounding

disappointed. 'She could pass for Spanish. Do you speak any English words?' she asks, speaking slow and loud.

'Attica is frightfully clever,' says the oldest Spencer quickly. 'You would hardly know her mother was a savage. She is a translator of languages, isn't that right? You were helping the Russian ambassador.'

She glances around the room. Several young men look away in panic.

'I don't know how you can stand such dry work,' she says. 'How do you find time to embroider?'

'It's not as dull as it sounds.' I keep my tone impassive. 'Though I must admit my needlework has suffered.'

'You must apply yourself,' cautions the younger Spencer, her blue eyes wide. 'You will *never* catch a husband if your sewing is poor.'

Her sister elbows her in the ribs and the younger reddens, realizing her blunder. 'Very sad,' she ventures, in a strange babyish voice, 'that your wedding didn't go ahead?'

'No,' I say, 'I cannot say that it was.' The relief, the sheer relief, of escaping the bonds of wedlock. I can still call it to mind now, like a waterfall of gold washing me clean. 'I thought England had no slavery,' I tell them, 'until I learned about marriage.'

They all laugh a little too loudly. The new Lady Morgan has, after all, just become my father's legal property.

'Very good,' says the blonde girl approvingly. 'Don't get glum about it.' She gestures to a table where the remains of hot buttered rolls, tongue, eggs and ham are being cleared away. A large bridal pie with cornice-like fluting is being brought forth.

'Perhaps you will get the slice with the glass ring in it.' She holds up two crossed fingers inches from my head, her features scrunched earnestly.

'What good fortune that would be.' I keep my face perfectly neutral.

'You know you really are rather pretty,' she continues, encouraged. 'Those grey eyes are quite striking and not all men would mind such a tall woman. Perhaps another suitor can be found.'

'Unfortunately, we African brides eat our husbands on the wedding night,' I say. 'So it is a hard match to make. Would you excuse me?'

I make them a brilliant smile, curtsey and vanish into the crowd, leaving them wide-eyed in shock. I'm making my way to the servants' door when a hand tightens on my arm.

I turn around and find myself looking directly into the dark brown eyes of Lord Pole. I feel as though the warmth has been sucked out of the room.

How much does my scheming uncle know about what I did in Russia? I wonder.

Lord Pole is dressed in the clothes he wears to Whitehall: a bear-fur collar, long black robes, and a square felt hat, like a scribe might wear.

A thousand thoughts race through my head. 'No dress coat,' I ask, 'for your own brother's wedding?'

'I've come from urgent business,' he replies, watching the wedding crowd with a thoughtful expression. He frowns as a servant hands us each a dainty glass of red wine and a plate of bridal pie.

Besides being my uncle, Lord Pole is one of the most important men in English intelligence. He is keenly aware that, matched to the right husband, I could get into all kinds of drawing rooms and bedrooms. But so far his plans to have me married to the enemy have been averted. His dark eyes are surveying the room again. We are all outcasts, us in the low business of espionage, and Lord Pole is no exception. His long nose and swarthy features are courtesy of his German father – a Bavarian count whose scandalous lineage Lord Pole dedicates his life to nullifying. The rest of his time is spent plotting, an activity at which he is masterly.

'As if your father's African wife wasn't scandal enough for one family,' he says, more to himself than to me, 'now he weds an American heiress and it isn't even for her money.'

'Be sure not to follow his example, Uncle,' I say. 'You risk a happy marriage.' I take a small mouthful of pie. It is made of the traditional offal and oysters and loud with expensive spices, a nod to my father's generation, whose artifice and grandeur are now out of favour.

'I think the new Lady Morgan will be good for him,' I conclude. 'Less laudanum.'

Lord Pole hands his untouched plate impatiently to a passing servant.

'It's bad luck not to eat the pie,' I say.

'I don't believe in luck.'

There's a girlish shriek in the corner. One of the Spencer sisters is holding up a grubby glass ring, a symbol she'll be next to marry. Lord Pole's expression clouds in disapproval.

'I imagine you're looking forward to your own wedding one day soon,' he says, returning his attention to me.

'I hadn't considered it,' I say, careful to stop the tremble in my hands. 'I am told I provide a useful service to my country.'

'Yes.' He lifts his glass and swallows the contents. 'Become indispensable in the active spy network. That has been your game, has it not?'

'It isn't a game.'

Lord Pole locks eyes with me suddenly. It's an arresting, disconcerting sensation to be the sole focus of that calculating gaze.

'Don't think I don't know of the plots that were made to abort your wedding last summer,' he says. 'Very convenient that a mysterious fortune came into the hands of the bride who took your place.'

'I don't know what you're talking about.'

His dark brows knit together. 'Do not forget the service this country did for you, Attica. You arrived as legal property of a plantation. We turned a blind eye.'

'Because you saw my potential to marry the right man and spy on him,' I fill in. 'Or is it usual to train English girls in code-breaking and lock-picking?'

Lord Pole smiles but I see his fingers curl tighter. He hates for anyone to see his machinations at play.

'We only capitalized on your father's irresponsible beginnings,' he says, 'letting you into the cigar rooms, allowing you to cavort with his maps and instruments. I took the chance to gain you an advantage. Yet you squander it.'

He gives me a long look. 'The reprieve your father negotiated for you was supposed to end with one mission. It's true your abilities are exceptional, but we never meant you to become a *crusader*.' He waves his hands to signal the inexplicability of it all.

'You are afraid your pawn is not behaving as you expect,' I observe. 'I have been proving too useful in the field.'

'You have surpassed expectations,' he admits. 'Yet I've been hearing things. Your obsession with breaking up slave rings has compromised your neutrality. You were supposed to bring Gaspard back to France, not release two hundred Kurds into the bargain.'

I have a sudden queasy feeling that he's been waiting for me to slip up.

'What does it matter?' I say. 'I brought Gaspard to a safe house, as was asked of me.'

'A woman's usefulness will always be different to a man's. You are a year from spinsterhood, at which point your value will plummet. It's time your more *female* qualities were put into service.'

'What of my feelings on the subject?' I manage to keep my voice perfectly steady.

I've a terrible prescience Lord Pole is formulating something that will be difficult to evade.

'Ah! Feelings,' says Lord Pole. 'Yes. You young people seem to have so very many of them.'

CHAPTER 5

MY HEART LIFTS AS I SEE THE FAMILIAR HOTCHPOTCH buildings of Whitehall. Barefoot children with baskets of quill pens and reeds of cheap ink are pestering the wigged and waistcoated men entering parliament. Street stalls fry pancakes and sell pea soup by the pint from a cluster of tankards swinging on chains. A bird-catcher sits, emptying a net of chirping goldfinches into a small wooden enclosure.

I approach him, dip a hand in my purse and hand over a shining guinea. His eyes widen and his hand stretches out uncertainly.

'Let them all fly away,' I say, closing his hands around the coin.

He nods rapidly, opening the cage with a disbelieving grin. Clutching the money tight to his chest, he walks away, unable to stop smiling.

The birds take flight. They streak past me, black, red and gold, as I turn my attention back to the grand Whitehall buildings.

Tacked against the turreted wall of Westminster Palace is a threadbare canopy over a cauldron of hot green peas. A man with one eye and a single tooth stirs it with a long stick.

I move towards him, smiling.

'Hello, Peter,' I say.

'Attica!' He beams, treating me to the full view of his sole tooth. 'Those lyin' bastards said you was dead. Where've ya bin then, girl?' Peter leans over his tepid wares and grasps both my hands in his wizened old claws.

'Russia.' I grip his hands in return.

'Ah.' His eye lifts skyward, considering. 'That's north of Oxford, is it?'

I hide a smile. 'Yes.'

He tilts his head, taking in the new scar, running deep, just below my jawline.

'Robber got ya?' he suggests.

I touch it with my fingers, feeling the long track of raised red. It feels like it belongs to someone else.

'Something like that,' I say.

He leans back, assessing.

'Well, you've looked worse,' he concludes. 'Least you've some meat on your bones.'

He's referring to my training in Sicily, in preparation for which I'd spent far too long running in forests with logs on my back, so as to pass for a boy.

In the months that followed, my knife was so rarely from my hand, the palm muscles began to atrophy in the shape of the handle. By the end, those still alive could slash five different arteries in thirty seconds – abdomen, wrist, throat, thigh, chest – and no one ever deduced why a boot to the groin affected me so much less than my fellows. The final test was two sleepless weeks, hunted by assassins. Then fighting blind-fold, waist-deep in cold water. Two of us graduated – that is to say, lived.

Peter had been the first familiar person on my return. I'd lost so much weight my jaw jutted. My face held the burning gaze of what the Italians call 'blood on the soul'.

'I'm different now,' I remember telling Peter, looking at him with pupils blown wide from exhaustion.

He'd considered this for a long moment before heaping a ladle of peas into a tankard and pushing it into my hands.

'Drink this,' he'd said, looking at me steadily. 'Nothing's happened to you, girl, that hot peas and a good night's sleep won't fix.'

I still think about that sometimes.

'Good to have you back,' Peter says now. 'They're a savage lot Scotland way, so I hear.' He sniffs and wipes his nose on his sleeve. 'It's not the same without you here,' he continues, with a glance at Whitehall. 'They bin sayin' I can't empty me slops into the gutter.'

'I'll talk to them,' I promise. 'Is Atherton inside?'

'Yes.' His face turns wary at the name. Peter holds up a warning finger, eyeing the surging parliament men behind me.

Peter waits for his moment before stepping aside, motioning me behind his smoking cauldron. At the back of his stall is a hessian curtain; to all appearances it covers nothing but wall, but as I lift it, immediately beneath me is a set of old stone steps.

Whitehall's secret entrance. Once used by the King to smuggle in his mistresses, in these times of espionage it is employed for a different purpose. I descend into torchlit gloom, turn a corner and open another curtain into an underground room. The dark explodes into light.

This is the society of the Sealed Knot. We lie, steal, deceive and risk summary execution so upstanding soldiers and generals might win wars and medals publicly. They are the closest thing I have to a family.

And after almost a year in Russia, I've come home.

CHAPTER 6

In the Sealed Knot's labyrinthine headquarters, candelabras and candles burn along every wall, illuminating the carved wood-panelled ceilings. Large tables are lined with men, maps and papers of every kind.

The familiar bubbling chatter of plans and schemes surrounds me. Servants move about, pouring wine and brandy punch, putting down plates of meat and bread. The air is fuggy with pipe smoke and intrigue.

Naturally, the dirty underhand war of intelligence is staffed by those whom polite society shun. There's no one here without a scandal to tell, a price on his head or a court martial to run from. Though no recruitment was more shocking to our sensible German King than mine, so I'm told.

I pass through and a few faces turn to me, eyes wide. I raise my finger to my lips and head to a corner where a little knot of men are huddled over a large book. As I approach I can hear them arguing loudly about a wager that should be paid out.

I put my hand on the shoulder of the nearest – a dark-haired man with nut-brown skin and an expensive fencing sword at his hip.

'You should have bet higher, Emile,' I say.

He whips around. His face makes a strange contortion.

'Attica!' He grabs me in a bear-embrace. I wince. Emile fled from France to England after a fight with the wrong man; his upper-body strength is vicelike. Like me, he grew up with a gypsy camp, so we share a common language and have always been favourites to one another.

The other gamblers are welcoming me home now, delight on their faces. These are my friends, my comrades. Besides fencing champion Emile, there's a highwayman, an excommunicated young priest and a playwright-turned-forger. Like me – the tawny-skinned illegitimate daughter of an English lord – they are all outcasts with extraordinary talents useful to England's underground secret service.

'I thought you were dead!' Emile admonishes. 'The last German ship docked on Thursday.'

'I knew you bloody Hellfires would run a bet,' I say, 'so I spent a night in Southwark instead of coming straight. Only narrowly made it to my own father's wedding.'

I eye the open book over his shoulder.

'Congratulations, Emile,' I grin, 'I knew you'd take the longest odds.' I wag my finger at the rest of them. 'And you all should have more faith,' I admonish, smiling. 'Since when did some cold water stop me getting home?'

The assembled spies laugh, enjoying the joke.

I look to a tapestry hanging at the back which everyone is pretending a little too hard isn't there. The way to Atherton's door.

'He's in there?' I ask, nodding to it. The mood instantly changes.

'Ye-es,' ventures Emile. 'But he's in a foul temper. Something's happening in France. Missing diamonds or some such. People are turning on the Queen. You'd think Atherton would be happy,' he adds with a confused shrug. 'We've spent a lot of manpower trying to bring King Louis down.'

I glance at the tapestry. The power of life and death lies beyond. No one goes through without good reason. Or, more likely, bad reason.

'Best I find out more,' I decide, breaking away from the group. 'You can buy me brandy from your winnings later,' I toss over my shoulder to Emile.

I slip underneath the tapestry. A spiral staircase is on the other side and I ascend to another part of Whitehall. Atherton's office is the clandestine bridge between secret spying and public politics.

His door is at the top of the stairs and I turn the handle without knocking.

As it opens, I'm greeted by the familiar sharp smell of sealing wax. This is the heart of it all, where it all happens.

The most illegal of legal things in England.

Forged pardons, authorizations, safe passage in every language are issued from here. Maps and city plans, stolen and duplicated from the four corners of the earth, are rolled and filed.

The room is filled with smoke and at first I can't see Atherton. My heart beats faster. It's been almost a year since I saw him last. We wrote to one another whenever we could, but I know there are things he wouldn't tell me by letter.

The haze clears and there he is.

Atherton. Sitting behind the same desk. Wearing the same blue and gold naval coat, his thick brown hair just as unruly.

A rush of emotions hit me.

His shaggy head is lowered, deep in concentration, fiddling with a tiny brazier of burning coals. Floating before him, like dancing angels, are three paper lanterns, bobbing in the air. Each belches a trail of black smoke, rather ruining the celestial effect.

I watch him reach out a long finger and tap one of the hovering lanterns. It lifts gracefully, propelled by the heat of the brazier burning on his desk. Atherton's lanky frame is twisted awkwardly on his chair and twin walking canes rest against his withered legs.

'If you must play with fire, Atherton,' I say, 'you should find an office with higher ceilings.'

He looks up confused, then his face changes.

'Attica?' He stands with effort, his light green eyes lit with joy, a smile stretched across his narrow face. 'Those bloody French have mastered the hot air balloon,' he explains. 'King Louis tests them with convicts. They got one halfway across the English Channel before it mercifully combusted.'

Something like relief catches in my throat to find him so unchanged. I half-run at him and we hug tightly and for too long because there's no one watching.

'I thought you were dead,' he says.

'How could I be?' I say. 'I promised you I would return.'

'You'll stay?' He slides his hands from my shoulders, takes my hands in his. 'Longer than a week this time?'

I feel my heart squeeze. My eyes settle on his wedding ring.

'I can't,' I say, shaking my head.

'For a few days, at least.' Atherton makes the disarming smile I love, his green eyes tilted up, straight mouth drawn wide.

We're staring into one another's eyes, my hands still on his shoulders and his on mine. If we were reunited lovers, we would kiss now, I think.

Could we? Just once? I picture Atherton drawing closer, see myself doing nothing to stop him.

A blaze of flame behind us shocks me into my senses. One of his lanterns has caught on fire.

'Your flying balloons need more work,' I tell him, moving to extinguish the flames. 'Shouldn't you use silk, instead of paper?'

CHAPTER 7

Once I've extinguished Atherton's air balloon experiment, I take in his office.

It's different to how I remember it. It was once full of fashionable furniture, Chinois style, all red and gold and looping shapes. But things have been cut down, altered, removed. His old desk is still here, though – heavy black, with a scattering of different-sized drawers at the front, painted with gold-lacquered flying birds, willow trees and rivers from a far-flung land he'll never see. But bolted solidly to the top are two wooden handles, rough-hewn things for a cripple to grip at.

On the wall is a portrait of him five years ago in the Navy, before his illness began, standing tall in his admiral's uniform and tricorn hat. I wonder how he can bear to have it here still.

'Your office looks awful.' I grin, knowing he'll appreciate my honesty. 'Couldn't you have kept your limbs working a little longer?'

He laughs. 'It's been a long time since you decorated,' he says, smiling back at me. 'I became bored of good taste.' The smile fades away. 'You've been gone a long time, Attica,' he says. I see in his face a little snatch of how it must feel to be stuck here with someone you care for far away.

'That doesn't change things,' I say, squeezing his fingers.

I drop my hands down to hold his, reluctant to move apart.

'How are you?' I ask.

'Good and bad,' he admits, shifting his twisted legs. 'The rubber stoppers you got me come in useful on Whitehall's waxed floors. Fortunate those Caribbean pirates never found you.'

He gives me a mischievous glance.

'How did you ...?'

'How did I know you risked your life to steal them? Let's just say it's my job to know things.' He taps his nose.

Atherton plants his palms on his walking sticks and shuffles with difficulty to his desk. When his condition first deteriorated he told me in no uncertain terms not to treat him like a cripple. I've always respected his wishes, but it's not always easy.

I wander around the office, taking in the changes. I reach up to a little cabinet, all little-gold-leafed drawers. It bears all the markings of one of Atherton's puzzle boxes.

'You've altered the pattern?' I guess, reaching up and pressing on a gold-leaf. It recedes into the wood.

'I've made a few improvements.'

I nod, pushing in a few other sections in sequence. I only just duck in time, as a drawer shoots free, sending a whirling blade winging across the room.

'Very good,' I enthuse, noting how far it has lodged in the wall.

'The spring is a great deal stronger,' agrees Atherton, pleased.

I move to the opposite side of the room, where the blade has embedded, twanging menacingly with the impact.

'Anything else?' I ask, prodding it.

'Oh yes!' Atherton's schoolboy energy always lights him up when speaking of his inventions. He opens a drawer and then another, hidden inside.

After a moment's frowning search, he removes what look like some little pieces of wood. Their tips are coated in a yellow substance.

I look closer, then grin at him.

'They work?'

Atherton sits back proudly. He lifts one.

'Self-lighting fire-sticks,' he says. 'Drag them against any rough surface and they will fire on their own.' He picks one up carefully and drags it against the edge of his desk. It flares. 'Instant flame, and you can hide them in all kinds of places you couldn't fit a tinderbox.'

I stare at the fire, transfixed. 'I don't believe it.'

'They fail if you get them wet, mind,' says Atherton, blowing it out. 'I'm still working on how to fix that. Perhaps a different mix of chemicals at the tip.'

We share a smile; two strange people who love ciphers and mechanics.

I didn't realize quite how much I'd missed Atherton.

'You must at least stay long enough to drink with me,' he decides. He manoeuvres himself to his desk with impressive dexterity and using the wooden handles he opens the largest of his drawers.

'Sailor's finest,' he beams, lifting out a battered bottle. Atherton's vice is the filthiest of cheap naval rum, a throwback to his days warring at sea with common sailors.

I lift a chair and seat myself next to him. I lean forward and collect two glasses from inside his drawer and fill them both much too full. The sugary tang of strong alcohol fills the air.

Atherton takes one appreciatively and we sit side by side, our chairs touching. Through his large first-floor window I can see the pale stone of Whitehall streets and buildings and down below the wigged men hurrying to court.

He swigs deeply. 'Ah,' he says happily, 'the taste of the seven seas.'

I sip, shaking my head. The dark rum is as terrible as it ever was.

'This is why sailors die so young,' I say, my eyes burning from the fumes tunnelling up my nose.

'You'll appreciate it when you're older,' he adds, enjoying my wincing expression. His favourite thing is to joke about the age gap between us, which seemed very great when we first met. Atherton tutored me in code-breaking and lock-picking talents ten years ago when I was thirteen and he was twenty-two.

I feel suddenly choked with emotions and take a clumsy mouthful of rum to hide my expression. I want to tell him how I dreamed of the moment I'd see him again, almost daily, in Russia, gathering information for the Crown. That even though he was far away, I knew he was doing everything he could, helping me, keeping me safe, and that knowledge made me happy. But somehow the words don't come.

Instead, I say: 'I always liked this view,' in a cold little voice that doesn't sound like me.

Atherton eyes me sideways and I wonder if he knows what I'm thinking.

'So what brings you back to England? King and country?' he suggests.

'The usual reason. I've come to ask for your help,' I say, sipping rum. I feel the alcohol burn my stomach, a warm comfortable glow. 'I need papers. I uncovered a trail of slave trading leading to Madrid. I think there's a big market hidden there.'

He hesitates. 'You've already been assigned. It's not my decision. Lord Pole's office has higher authority.'

My eyes flick to his.

'Since when did Lord Pole involve himself in Sealed Knot business?'

'The man you rescued from Russia, Gaspard de Mayenne, we think he's in danger,' he says quietly. 'Lord Pole needs you to get him to Versailles.'

I'm looking hard at Atherton, wondering what it is he isn't telling me.

'What business could Gaspard de Mayenne have in Versailles?' I say. 'What did you bloody schemers do?'

I'd forgotten, in English intelligence there's no such thing as a simple rescue.

'Thanks to you, Gaspard owes us a favour,' says Atherton. 'His daughter has a position in the Palace, close enough to get to the Queen.'

'So you want this girl to smuggle something in?' I deduce, sipping the bad rum. 'What?'

Atherton hesitates.

'Have you heard about the lost diamonds of Marie Antoinette?'

CHAPTER 8

THE LOST DIAMONDS OF MARIE ANTOINETTE. I'M TURNING Atherton's words over in my head. An image forms in my mind: a newspaper sketch of extravagantly looped and tasselled gems. The description comes back to me.

'Constructed from two million francs' worth of diamonds and commissioned by the late French King for his working-class mistress,' I say, reciting from memory. 'When he died, his son wouldn't honour the debt. Marie Antoinette refused a necklace of such vulgar provenance. It was stolen, four years ago.'

'You've a good recall,' Atherton says. 'A confidence trickster convinced the jeweller that Marie Antoinette had changed her mind, disguised a prostitute as the Queen and stole the jewels. The thief was caught and the ensuing court trial became a national scandal.'

'*Lèse-majesté,*' I say, it was all flooding back now. 'The Queen tried to convict not just the thief but the jeweller, too. She accused him of disrespect for daring to believe she would have met a man alone and at night. But she lost the case.'

'It was all but decreed by law that Marie Antoinette was debauched,' agrees Atherton. 'After that, the gossip was unstoppable. The ripples of real discontent began back then. People thought that Marie Antoinette was venal, vengeful. The jewels vanished. Rumours started up that the Queen had taken them.'

'They're something of a legend now, aren't they?'

'So people have been led to believe,' he says. 'But whilst you've been in Russia, we've been working to find the missing jewellery. We got hold of it in London, before it was to be broken up and sold.'

'Impressive,' I admit. 'You tracked the necklace for all that time, through all the smugglers and shadowy jewellers whose hands it must have passed through. Wait until everyone thought it lost for ever. Then pounce. So,' I pour him more rum, 'I imagine you plan to smuggle it back into Versailles? Make it appear the Queen kept it all along.'

'I'd forgotten how clever you are at guessing plots.' He smiles at me over his glass. 'The French King and Queen are hated. It will take only the slightest push for the French people to revolt. A scandalous diamond necklace appearing in Versailles,' finishes Atherton, 'is just the pressure needed. Put the diamonds back, let the right servants see it ...' He waves his glass to suggest the ease with which this could take place.

'This is Lord Pole's doing?' I say. 'He's still trying to stop the French King sending troops to America.'

I can always smell my uncle's schemes a mile away; they have a distinctly cold-blooded reek to them. I picture Lord Pole, a spider in his web of intrigue, making plans, weaving futures for the unwitting.

'He has a genius for plots of this kind.' Atherton's tone is as disapproving as mine.

'It all sounds very interesting,' I admit, 'but I've saved Gaspard once. And there's a slave-trading ship docked off Portugal that needs my attention.'

Atherton rubs his face in the way he does when he's exasperated.

'I don't have a choice in this, Attica. Lord Pole has the highest authority in the Sealed Knot.' He says it in a way that means: '*You* don't have a choice.'

'This is apprenticeship level,' I protest. Humiliation is blooming.

'We didn't mean for you to vanish into Russia and start organizing our embedded men without permission,' he continues.

'I saw an opportunity. I took it.'

'It was a daring and brilliant mission,' says Atherton, 'in many ways a great success. But there is more to freeing slaves than fieldwork. And if you can't take orders ...'

I glare at him. I am so tired of hearing how people should wait a little longer in servitude whilst well-fed men decide their fates by warm fires.

Atherton sighs. 'It's Lagos slave docks all over again, Attica. You can't just go in burning things down for your own agenda.'

'A youthful grudge, now behind me.' I try for a winning smile.

'I took a chance on you, Attica. Everyone knows women aren't suitable for active service. You're proving them right.' He takes my glass, fills it, pushes it back into my hands. 'If you complete this mission, they'll let you back at the slave rings. Just prove you're willing to do as you're told.'

'You'd have me playing bodyguard? Those people in Russia have their eyes gouged out for looking at the wrong person.'

I toss the rum back in one, grab the bottle and pour myself another measure.

'I won't do it,' I say, as the alcohol burns. 'It's taken years to get inside those slave rings. I know Lord Pole. This is his way of putting me in my place, making sure Lord Morgan's daughter doesn't get above herself.'

'Maybe,' admits Atherton. 'But you know how clever he is.' There's a warning in his green eyes that makes me snap to attention.

'He knows I'll refuse,' I say, tracking Lord Pole's likely thought processes. 'I'll bet he's put some penalty in place.' I drink more rum, feeling suddenly confident. 'There's nothing he can do to make me go to France.'

Atherton has a strange expression on his face, almost as though he's wincing.

'What?' I demand.

'If you don't go to Paris and deliver this necklace,' says Atherton, 'Lord Pole will have you married off.'

I'm absorbing this when something else occurs to me.

'The unrest in Paris,' I say. 'Customs gates are on high alert. Lord Pole would have needed someone trustworthy to smuggle the diamonds into France.'

'I don't know who was sent,' says Atherton. 'Why do you ask?'

A horrible feeling slides into my stomach.

'Atherton,' I say, 'do you remember my cousin Grace?'

'The chubby girl who won't stop talking about politics? Small-pox scars?' He gestures around the eyes. 'How could I forget?' His expression darkens. 'The pair of you were absolute savages, digging forts in the tennis lawns and stuffing that old cannon with goose feathers. Wasn't it Grace that had you both using mud as warpaint?'

'She was absolutely fearless,' I say, grinning. I'd forgotten Atherton had been around back then. 'Grace kicked my slave terrors right out of me. I think my father must have known she would. We were kindred spirits.'

'Fortunate she grew out of it all,' says Atherton with feeling. 'It's far harder, nowadays, to bribe prison officials.'

'Grace is from a poorer branch of the family,' I say, 'so perhaps she considered she didn't have a choice. Her lack of nobility also makes her a natural target for Lord Pole's nefarious schemes,' I add pointedly. 'Grace wasn't at my father's wedding; I was told she was shopping for her wedding trousseau ... In Paris.'

I feel suddenly uneasy for my clever cousin.

'Grace does as she's told now,' I say. 'If you had absolutely no conscience, you might consider her an excellent choice to smuggle diamonds.'

We look at each other for a long moment.

'No.' Atherton is shaking his head. 'He wouldn't have. Not even Lord Pole would stoop to that.'

CHAPTER 9

JUST OFF THE COBBLES OF RUE PIGALLE IN PARIS IS A LITTLE dirt track, culminating in a clutch of rickety wooden shacks. In the twilight, candlelight glows through the gaps in the ill-fitted planks.

Inside one of the shacks sits Grace Elliott, speaking animatedly to Gaspard de Mayenne, her face alive in the soft flame.

Gaspard's face is now shaved, his greying head once again topped with a wig. He has exchanged the aristocratic clothing of his past life for more muted tastes: a black coat, fawn breeches and leather boots.

He watches the fair-haired English girl in her floating muslin dress, a simple ribbon beneath the bust. She hasn't stopped talking since she arrived.

'… and Attica shouted, "Run!"' Grace explains happily. 'And it just *exploded*! The groundkeeper was furious with us. Of course I am not at all wild now,' she counters quickly. 'I shall write all my husband's speeches. He is an aristocrat like you, who speaks against the old order. Did I tell you, I will wed Godwin only next week? That is why I am come to Paris …'

Gaspard looks to his small table. It is strewn with sketches in pencil and pen and ink. Some depict his time as a slave in Russia. A few show a tall woman, a honey hue to her skin. His rescuer. Her features are so strikingly similar to this chattering girl, Gaspard can scarcely believe the resemblance.

'You are Attica Morgan's cousin?' he says in his accented English, looking from the picture to the girl and the girl to the picture.

'Grace Elliott,' she agrees. 'My grandmother fell in love with a sailor, so I am a commoner. We took Attica in for a time when she landed in Bristol from the plantation. I was the only one she'd trust to pick lice from her hair. It took days!' Grace grins from ear to ear, dimples appearing in her chubby cheeks. 'She still teases me because I was more savage than any slave, but grew to be the most rule-abiding of either of us.'

'Incredible.' Gaspard touches the picture.

'Attica paid me back,' says Grace loyally. 'She insisted I share her private tutors instead of the penny school my father scraped to send me to. That's why I am betrothed to a lord. I met him riding on the Morgan estate.'

Gaspard notices Grace has smallpox scars around both her eyes, like a pitted masquerade mask, but she hasn't tried to fill them with paint, as a lady would. She has the rounded limbs of someone who grew up hungry and now eats at fine tables. If he were to draw her, it would be as a girl caught between two worlds.

'Do you have the contraband?' he asks.

'Oh, yes!' Grace removes a pouch from her dress and passes it across the table. 'Lord Pole told me not to look inside,' she says with an earnest frown. 'So you can be very sure I didn't.'

A wave of pity sweeps over Gaspard as he takes the pouch. It's suddenly clear to him that this poor girl doesn't know what she has been asked to deliver.

Gaspard opens the leather purse. Two million francs' worth of diamonds beam out at him.

The Queen's necklace.

He closes it.

'I brought you food, too,' Grace adds, taking a small loaf from her hanging pocket. 'I thought you might be hungry. Uncle Pole says you are too unwell to get out very much.'

'Thank you, my dear.' He is suddenly sickened to the stomach by all the scheming and duplicity, most of all how this innocent girl has been duped by her own relative. Gaspard touches his neck where the manacle once was, a reflex he can't yet seem to shift.

'It is a good thing you do for my country,' he concludes, 'but you are in great danger.'

Grace beams. 'My future husband will not mind that I am here,' she says. 'He believes France should be free from tyranny as I do. Everyone must pay tax, not just the poor.'

'I don't mean that,' says Gaspard. 'Your life is at risk. What you have been asked to deliver—'

He stops speaking, holding up a warning hand. Footsteps approach.

'You must hide,' hisses Gaspard.

Grace's face is a picture of shock as Gaspard gets to his knees and pulls up a floorboard as silently as he can.

He points mutely. Grace looks into the space. Several spiders run out. She closes her eyes, cursing her obedient nature, then sees the fear on Gaspard's face and moves quickly.

As she lowers herself into the gap, there is a kind of knock from outside, dissipated by the thin construction of the door.

'Who is out there?' demands Gaspard loudly, to hide the sound of Grace wedging herself sideways in the cobwebby space. The door begins to shake. Someone is pulling it open by force.

'God's blood!' shouts Gaspard. 'Have patience, won't you?'

He scoops up the pouch from the table and flings it atop Grace. Then he settles the plank gently over her terrified face.

'No need to break my door!' he adds, moving towards it. Gaspard lays hands on the makeshift bolt – a flimsy thing of stick and wicker.

When Gaspard opens the door, he staggers back slightly.

It is a musketeer. Or was. Beneath his broad-brimmed hat, half of his face is peppered in strange scars. A blood-red eye sits sightless in one socket.

'You are the Marquis de Mayenne?' asks the stranger.

Gaspard knows, in this moment, he is going to die. He thinks of Grace under the floor.

'Come in,' he says.

The stranger has a metal hand, Gaspard notices, elegantly made, with silver, skeletal fingers. He has a sudden awful prescience of what those fingers could do.

Gaspard sits, picks up the bottle, swigs deeply.

'How did you find me?' he asks.

'Your candle-glow was too yellow,' says the stranger. 'Beeswax. Most people in this part can only afford lamb-fat tapers.'

'Ah.' Gaspard drinks some more. 'But how did you know to come to this street?'

'Not all your friends are friends, monsieur.' He speaks with a country accent. Not native to Paris.

Gaspard accepts this. Beneath his booted feet, he can hear Grace's trembling breath.

He picks up a few sketches with shaking hands.

'Did you hear what is happening at Versailles?' says Gaspard.

'Commoners went to demand justice. They refuse to leave and the King has not force enough to make them.'

Gaspard pushes forward a pencil drawing of the two hundred animated men who have besieged themselves inside a covered tennis court in Versailles.

'I imagine you regret swearing your oath as His Majesty's musketeer now,' says Gaspard. 'You fools worked unpaid whilst the King spent your wages on American troops.'

The stranger's flesh hand curls slowly into a fist.

Beneath the floorboard, Grace tries to slow her breathing. A spider crawls over her face. She closes her eyes and prays.

'Know what Parisians say about musketeers?' concludes Gaspard. 'We say even the stupidest cunt in Paris gets paid for his work.'

There's a silence. From her place under the floor, Grace sees a flash of movement. There comes a sound like when one of the tin gutters at the Bristol docks becomes clogged. A steady *gugh gugh gugh.*

She strains to place it. The pouch weighs heavily on her chest.

Unexpectedly, warm liquid begins to stream through the floorboards, running down her cheek. A bottle of wine, Grace hopes. It has been spilled. But the flow goes on and on, in spurts, pooling under her head.

It isn't wine. Grace feels her body explode in a single, silent scream.

CHAPTER 10

HERE'S A FUNNY STORY. ON HIS WEDDING DAY, ATHERTON confessed he had wanted to ask for my hand but thought the Sealed Knot would never allow it. There was a strangely beautiful moment, perhaps a few seconds, when we knew we loved each other. But Atherton's marriage-of-convenience wife was waiting in his carriage and neither of us are the kind of people who break promises. As soon as I knew I loved him, I knew I must let him go.

Besides, Atherton had already saved me from one marriage and, knowing my feelings on the subject, knew better than to suggest I be his wife.

'I was born a slave,' I remember telling him, 'I do not mean to die as one.'

So it's perhaps not surprising that Atherton cannot meet my eye at the painful topic of my arranged wedding. But my feeling is there is something stranger at play.

'Why have me married off?' I demand, appalled, thinking back to Lord Pole's thinly veiled threat. 'I was the only person to bring direct intelligence from Russian slavers.'

'Because of those Kurdish slaves.' Atherton shakes his

head. 'You're not as good as you think, Attica,' he admonishes. 'You're young and you rush into things. You make short-term decisions based on emotion.'

'You think I should have left those people there, in chains?' I protest.

'If you had,' replies Atherton gently, 'if you'd only freed Gaspard as we asked, we might have got information on other slave rings. Now the market is destroyed, that information is gone.'

This silences me. An icy feeling of failure fills my gut.

'It was always your weak point, Attica,' says Atherton, 'to do it all alone. Now you've made enemies. Your right-to-travel documents, royal seals and weapons are all curtailed. They'll only issue you papers for France.'

'They? Or you?' I'm glaring.

Atherton rests his sticks and stretches out to put a hand on my arm. 'Attica, you know I couldn't care less who your mother was.'

I'm slightly pacified. Atherton is the only person who can do this.

'But *they* do.' He begins manoeuvring himself back down on his chair. 'There's no doubt of your bravery or talent,' he says, 'but no one in Whitehall wants you to succeed. You make a mockery of aristocratic privilege. They want you safely wed.'

He pauses.

'*I* want you safely wed,' he adds. 'Attica, do you know how many times I've planned your funeral?'

'Amongst the noble men, there's an acceptance that I'm not a real person,' I say. 'That I can be passed around, bought and sold.' I'm shouting, but I don't care. 'I expect it from them. I never expected it from *you*.'

'I only want to protect you.' Atherton is shaking his head. 'France is a tinderbox. They'll be militia on the streets in less than a week. Aristocrats will be lynched and you're noble enough to be a target. You can't rather die than marry.' There's something in his face I can't quite understand.

I lower my voice. 'I mean to get back to my work freeing slaves. If getting Gaspard to Versailles is the only way, then so be it.' My eyes meet his. 'But I can't do it without your help,' I admit. 'Without your contacts and papers I won't make it out of Dover.'

Atherton sits back in his large seat. His long face looks pained.

'Why must you always chase danger?' he mutters. 'Do you have any idea—' He stops himself.

'I'm sorry,' I say quietly, 'it's who I am.'

For a long moment I think he will refuse. He looks at me as though trying to commit me to memory.

He pulls a concealed lever on his dark-wood desk. My heart leaps. A compartment I've come to call the treasure drawer slides out silently. Inside are blank papers, awaiting a Crown stamp and signature. Slotted beside them is an array of charred sealing wax stubs arranged in a muted rainbow. These are royal seals, illicitly obtained from all over Europe. I stole several of them for Atherton myself.

Atherton's long fingers begin gathering the tools of his trade. He hesitates. Then he extracts papers, shuffles them, pauses again and finally picks up an ink-stained quill.

'These are French documents of safe passage,' he said, inking letters at speed. 'Forgeries, of course, but they'll get you into high places.'

I don't trust myself to reply.

'France's constitution changes daily,' he says. 'These permissions will be valid for a few days at best. After that, we'll deny all knowledge. We won't risk an open war with France.'

I nod, taking a reflexive sip of naval rum. It really is bad. I can feel my tongue curling at the edges.

Atherton slides out blue wax for France and holds it in the candle. With his other hand he pulls forth a cluster of rings hanging on a loop of ribbon from inside his coat. I watch as he sorts them dexterously, selects a House of Bourbon crest, smudges hot wax and presses the ring.

I let out a breath I didn't know I'd been holding.

'You'll need a code name.' He thinks for a moment. 'Mouron,' he says, rolling his French Rs. 'Should serve.'

I roll my eyes, translating.

'Little flower?'

'Pimpernel,' he corrects. 'A particularly poisonous species of primrose, capable of inducing nausea, headache and death. We've used the cxtract in several successful assassinations.'

I'm liking the name more.

'I suppose it will serve,' I say begrudgingly, thinking of the dynamic code names given to our male spies.

He looks at me for a moment then unexpectedly takes my hand.

'Be careful. France is about to get bloody. King Louis has lost control. The country is on a knife edge.' He swallows. 'Every day, for the past year,' he says, 'I have expected a letter telling me you've died.'

I hesitate. Perhaps in another life I might have boldly promised Atherton that he would never open such a letter. But I know the truth. Heroes fall, unbreakable promises are broken and no one can be trusted to stay alive.

So I say instead: 'When I do die, Atherton, know my only regret will be drinking your terrible rum.'

He smiles.

'You should get aboard the ship at Dover by nightfall. After that, you have one week, Attica. If you don't get those diamonds inside Versailles you must return to England and marry.'

CHAPTER 11

Grace emerges from under the floor, white with shock, red with blood. With shaking hands, she picks up the bottle of wine still on the table and drinks deeply. Her eyes take in the room vacantly. She is trembling with cold. Her teeth are chattering.

Gaspard is not here. She tries to imagine him taken to a place of greater safety but she knows this is not the case. Grace heard something heavy being dragged across where she lay, the grunt of exertion from the stranger. She glimpsed what looked like a metal hand, sparkling with blood, through a crack in the floor.

Gaspard's pictures have been taken, she notices. The tennis court at Versailles, where people demanded the King give them equal votes.

Feeling numb, she takes the pouch from her dress. Grace considers for a moment, wondering if she is now allowed to open it.

'I gave it to the man as I was asked,' she decides, speaking aloud to affirm it as fact. 'He gave it back to me.'

Inside is a necklace. She holds it for a long time.

Grace knows a great deal about politics. She reads pamphlets, writes essays. This diamond necklace is familiar. Grace imagines the particular style of jewellery is known to almost every literate person in Paris.

A necklace to surpass all others.

She blinks at the image for a moment and finds herself looking around, as if she's being watched.

Her hands are shaking again. She read the court case, as did a thousand Parisians. Queen Marie Antoinette had taken the stand to swear she had no knowledge of the jewels. No one had believed her. The public has not trusted the Queen since the trial. That was when all the lewd images started up. The cruel nicknames. Almost overnight it was indisputable fact: Marie Antoinette's profligacy was the reason Parisians starved.

Grace cannot get the man with the silver hand from her mind. And now she imagines she is responsible for ensuring the necklace is given safely back to Lord Pole.

The only place she can think of is the Rue du Faubourg Saint-Honoré, where the English Ambassador's house is. She stands, wondering if she is brave enough, and also thinking that she has no choice.

As Grace opens the door, a cluster of beggars eye her from over the street. Paris has changed, even in the few days she has been here. An army of dispossessed farmers now surround the city and have been filtering in, one by one, swelling the populace of vagabonds tenfold.

The price of bread has doubled. Things have reached breaking point.

There were parties last night. Grace heard people celebrating. They believe the men who besiege themselves in Versailles will be victorious. The King must grant them the right to vote by head. Many ordinary people are jubilant. They think a tide has turned. Democracy, such as the English have, surely is not far away.

She can hear a man's voice. 'No longer will the clergy and nobles pay no tax!' he is shouting. 'An end to the thirty days' unpaid labour commoners must annually give, repairing roads ...'

Grace is uncertain where this will lead. Versailles is a long way from Paris. She fears the King will not let this affront go unpunished.

As she slips out of Gaspard's house into the bright dawn of the Paris day, a man in a musketeer's hat moves silently from the shadows and follows after.

CHAPTER 12

DOVER IS A GRISLY SORT OF PORT, THE KIND OF PLACE I'D like if I didn't have to meet a pirate.

Muddy alleys are filled with malodorous taverns, houses of ill repute and down-on-their-luck women hoping to snare a sailor-husband. Tumble-down half-timbered buildings stand cheek by jowl. And everywhere are services to tempt sailors to part with their pay. Swinging signs advertise tooth removal, wedding licences and cheap tailors.

He's not here yet – the privateer I've arranged to meet. This is making me uneasy, since the sun is creeping to midday. If I miss this boat, there's no other way to get to Paris. Borders to France have clanged shut.

I've dressed myself as the kind of girl nice men avoid. My dress is tattered cotton, low-cut, with a grubby blue apron tied under the bust. I've no bonnet, no shoes and I've applied dirt and water to my face to make it appear I was crying yesterday and haven't washed since. It's a well-honed combination that allows me to sit alone in taverns without undue attention.

The meeting place is a meandering shack of an alehouse with bottle-glass windows and smoke-stained timber walls. It's cosy, with a little smoking fire and low dark-wood benches and stools. I've ordered a jugged hare and risked a red wine – a good decision as it transpires. They've got hold of some smuggled French stock.

I take a gulp of Burgundy and drum my fingers on the table distractedly. I've never done well at disguising my contempt for privateers. Legal pirates seem the worst hypocrisy to me. I eye the motley drinkers: a few dead-drunk sailors, a group of dockers ready for the night shift and two threadbare prostitutes doing the rounds.

I run through what I know. Atherton told me he'd be wearing a black leather coat and a tricorn hat – something of a uniform for murderous brigands at sea.

'We've a man at Dover,' Atherton had told me. 'He's a privateer, a rough sort, ill bred, untrustworthy.'

'Is there any other kind?' I've hated pirates ever since I was a small girl.

Atherton had smiled. 'It might take a bit of persuasion for him to get you aboard for the next tide. I'll get a trunk loaded with whatever you need.'

Atherton's eyes had clouded, apparently considering the nature of the man I would be meeting.

'This ... mercenary,' he'd said, 'he's the only one getting in. God knows how. He's not as bad as some.'

'That isn't saying much.'

I allow myself to imagine how it would be if Atherton was here with me. It was harder than I thought, leaving him after such a brief return.

I first met Atherton when I was twelve, sitting on the wall of my father's estate. I was barefoot. My hair was in rat's tails and I was firing stones into a nearby tree with a sling, *put put put*.

Atherton had won me over by failing to comment on my feral appearance or my predilection for playing with gypsy children – I even had scars from our blood-brother oaths.

I'd shown off to him, hitting only red leaves on the tree with my slingshot.

Atherton had watched for a time then revealed he was to be my new tutor.

'The work your uncle has given you copying accents,' he'd explained, as I scowled at the idea of being educated. 'I believe it is too easy for you. That is why you keep running off. How would it be if I taught you how to pick a lock?'

It was the nicest thing anyone had ever said to me.

I had turned back to the tree, pretending to consider and appear nonchalant. But when I let the next stone fly, it went wider than I intended, taking only the corner of the leaf.

'Think about it,' Atherton had said with a small smile. 'You know where to find me.'

My thoughts are interrupted by a young man entering the tavern; I'd guess him to be late twenties. He's got curling dark hair tied in a ponytail and is wearing a black linen shirt and the type of expensively buckled leather boots you don't wear lightly in a port town. My eyes stray to his belt, where a full compliment of good weaponry is arrayed. There's a dagger and sword I recognize as Spanish steel and a duelling pistol, English made, showy. The kind hot-headed unmarried men buy.

At first I assume he's lost his way, then a few old sea dogs slap him on the back and I realize he's well known here.

He produces a little bundle of tobacco leaves and slips it into the coat of a toothless old man, who grins gratefully. The sour-faced woman serving drinks cracks her first smile of the evening and pours him rum in a grubby glass.

He throws it back in one, surveys the tavern, sees me. Turning back to the landlady, he says something I don't hear. She passes him a dusty bottle of wine and he begins making for my table.

I frown in annoyance, trying to decide how best to put him off. But as it transpires there's no need.

'Mademoiselle Mouron,' he says, putting the bottle on the table. 'Or should I call you Miss Primrose?'

CHAPTER 13

'I LIKE YOUR DRESS,' HE SAYS, NODDING TO MY DOCKSIDE prostitute attire, 'but I'd recommend a bonnet,' he adds, tilting his head to take in my long black curls. 'Your hair is too shiny for what you pretend to be.'

I try not to let my surprise show. No one has ever seen through any of my disguises before.

'Your captain couldn't come ashore?' I say, guessing him to be bosun's mate or some other expendable person. He's in much too good condition to have been at sea for long. 'Is the brave pirate frightened of arrest?' I can't keep the contempt from my voice.

'Oh, we all are,' he says easily. He has a trace of an accent I can't quite place – Irish or something like it. 'Dover isn't a friendly port for pirates, even legal ones.'

His eyes are green, with a pinkish coloration at the corner of the left – a burn or a birth mark. It runs down about an inch, like a teardrop.

'I'm Jemmy Avery.' He extends a hand with a single battered-tin ring on the index finger.

I hesitate and stand. We're almost the same height, I notice, as I shake his hand, which must make him some way under six foot. Nor is he especially broad or muscular. Pirates are usually large men. I wonder what horrors he's done to supplement his average stature.

'I'm told your captain sails to France,' I say.

Jemmy pulls himself a stool and sits, legs spread wide in front of him.

'That he does. And I'm told you're in need of safe passage.' He pats the table and lifts the bottle. 'Will ye join me for a drink?' Jemmy draws the cork with his teeth and upends a generous measure into my tankard without asking, sloshing wine.

'I must be sure you are who you say you are,' he adds, 'before I can take you aboard.'

I swallow my annoyance and reseat myself on the opposite stool.

'If you make too sure of it,' I say, 'your captain will sail without us.'

'We've a little time to get to know one another. Have you finished eating?'

I nod, expecting with relief that this is the reason he's not yet escorted me to the ship. But to my surprise Jemmy leans forward, helps himself to a meat bone and gnaws away at the last morsels of flesh.

'Shall I get you a knife and fork?' I ask icily.

'Please, don't trouble yourself,' he replies, clearly enjoying his food.

'You're from the colonies?' I deduce, noting his lack of table manners.

'Very good.' He swallows the last bite. 'I'm Irish. But I grew up in New York.'

This explains the accent. Jemmy fills his own empty tankard

and looks up at me. 'You? Where were you raised?'

'Virginia for five years,' I say. 'Then England.'

He's taking me in more fully now.

'Is that so,' he says, letting out a whistling breath. 'Your father a plantation owner, was he?'

'My father fell in love with my mother, in Africa. She was betrayed into slavery and he knew nothing of a daughter, until I arrived in Bristol. The Morgans refuse to acknowledge me, but my parents were legally wed according to the customs of my Mother's tribe ...' I notice his concentration has drifted. 'You don't care,' I conclude.

'In New York,' says Jemmy, 'we're less concerned with whose mammy got a ring and whose didn't. Breeding, or whatever you call it. Not like you English. Couldn't even tell you for certain who my father was.' He grins. 'Me mammy says he was a famous pirate, but she says all kinda things.'

This is refreshing to me. As slaves we were all equal. But in my adult life I have had to learn who is the daughter or son of who, what that means and what it's worth. Still, I think with a frown, his etiquette is appalling and his attitude of sitting splay-legged downright rude.

'What of my father?' I ask. 'Do you care who he is?'

I'm wondering what a New Yorker might have heard of the brilliant, erratic Lord Morgan, a code-breaker whose searing intelligence is complicated by a weakness for narcotics.

'Can't say as I do.' Jemmy looks me in the eye. 'But what I should like to know,' he says, drinking more wine, 'is why a clever girl should want to get into Paris,' he replaces his tankard, 'when people are paying a fortune to get out.'

I look right back at him.

'I'm sure a clever man would know that already.'

'Paris is dangerous,' he says. 'What have you heard about France?'

'King Louis has been spending money unwisely on foreign wars,' I say slowly, careful not to paint myself as too knowledgeable. 'The price of bread has risen preposterously. There've been ugly scenes, protestors shot at.'

Jemmy is nodding.

'You know more than the propaganda that reaches most English people,' he says, 'but not enough. The nobles have ruled with a bloody fist. Commoners opposing the ancient regime are boiled alive, broken on wheels, have their skin pulled off with red-hot tongs. Now the common people have a chance to turn the tables.'

'Can you get me in or not?' I reply.

He sucks his lip and sits a little more upright, frowning.

'They told me you were the daughter of a noble,' he says. 'A translator of foreign words. I can tell from your fancy manners you're expensively reared, despite your not being pale enough for English gentry. But in my experience, fine families don't send their daughters into the care of pirates. Nor do spymasters take charge of their travel plans. So I can only assume you are a courtesan or a spy.'

'A woman spy? Now you really are ridiculous.'

He eyes me, then appears to accept this.

'Very well.' He stands. 'Very well.' He finishes his wine and looks me up and down. 'I can get you in. But it won't be the fine quarters you're used to. We're a working ship. You'll be either on deck getting showered in cold salt water or below with the reek of the boat bilge.'

I smile at this. 'I'm tougher than I look. Shall we go now? It's midday.'

Jemmy glances through the window at the sunny sky.

'They won't set sail without their captain,' he says.

I stare at him.

'You? You're the captain? But you were to be wearing a leather coat,' I reply. He is nothing like the roughened old salt Atherton described.

'A pirate habit I can't seem to shake,' he says. 'I don't like to meet with government folk unawares. Though now I am all legal, of course.' He flashes me a brief smile.

I'm staring at his hazel eyes and even features in a completely different light. He's so cleanly dressed, so *young* to have maimed and butchered. Besides the teardrop stain at his eye, there's not a mark on him. How did he manage it?

'But you *were* a pirate.'

'Aye.' He grins proudly. 'Best on the seven seas. Why d'you think your King hired me to rob Spaniards for his Navy?'

CHAPTER 14

THE SHIP IS NOT NEARLY AS ROUGH AS JEMMY MADE OUT AND his quiet pride for the vessel is obvious as he walks ahead of me on the narrow gangway. He's replaced his long black coat and is wearing a tricorn hat, which, along with his stubbled chin and dark hair tied in a ribbon, makes him look even more like a highwayman.

Men are hauling the heavier provisions aboard with ropes. Above us, canvas sails are tight in the breeze and the timbers creak as though straining to be free of the dock bollards. The air is sour with hot tar fumes from recently caulked deck seams.

'Welcome to the *Esmerelda,*' Jemmy says, waving a hand to a red-lipped carved woman fixed to the prow.

'You're the first pirate vessel I've seen to sail with a fully clothed figurehead,' I say, noticing painted clothes on the once-naked torso. 'Did someone lose a bet? Or is she your wife?'

'A girl of mine,' says Jemmy. I'm surprised. I'd been joking. He seems too carefree for the kind of relationship that comes with sentiment. 'She had a fierce temper,' he adds, nodding to the thickly painted clothing.

'Is that how you got that mark on your eye?'

He touches it. 'This? This is just an old burn. One of me mammy's fellas turned nasty. I made the mistake of getting in the way. I was fast enough to duck the saucepan, but the boiling water took me by surprise.'

'You've a fine ship,' I say as we cross the well-scrubbed deck. I've sailed with pirates before and the decks are usually tumble-down affairs, loaded with rusting cannons and stinking-drunk sailors. This boat is neat and clean with a sober crew hard at work unfurling sails and making ready to cast off. Everywhere is the air of industry.

'Aye.' He says it tersely, but I can tell Jemmy is pleased. 'She's not so well armed as some, but she's the fastest. We won her in the Caribbean and no one's caught us since. Ain't that right, Bailey?' He raises his voice and a broad-shouldered muscular man with jet-black skin looks down at us from beneath a broad-brimmed hat.

'Aye,' he agrees, his eyes sweeping my face for a moment before returning to his work.

'We rescued Bailey from an English slaving ship,' says Jemmy. 'You'll never meet a cleverer navigator. He's smarter than I am, but I don't let it bother me.' He lets loose that disarming grin again.

Bailey is watching me and I can see him wondering. Likely he has a better eye for mixed blood than most.

I've been inside slave hulls, with the stench of dead bodies and the moan of the sick and dying. Bailey has overcome his terrible ordeal and returned to sea at his own choosing. I wonder if he sees my admiration for him.

The wind catches the sails and the *Esmerelda* floats serenely out of Dover, taking my dark thoughts of slave plantations with it.

Jemmy leads me to a captain's cabin at the stern of the ship, with a hammock and a small wooden bed. A spectacular sweep of salt-encrusted paned glass forms the upper back wall, looking out on the ocean. Including the double door, that makes two escape routes. I like this room already.

'This is where you'll be,' he says, 'for most of the journey. Could be some bad weather coming, so best you keep out of our way.' He catches my expression. 'I wasn't serious about the boat bilge and the salt-water spray,' he says. 'I wouldn't put a woman in those conditions.'

'You were testing me?'

'Something like that.'

He heads to a large desk where a wooden box holds a shiny brass instrument, round with hands like a clock. Jemmy glances at it and turns his head to a chart on the wall.

'You can read longitude?' I say, realizing this is a chronometer – one of the latest tools of marine navigation.

'You assumed me an ignorant pirate.' There's the ghost of a smile on his face. 'Careful with the dial there,' he adds, as I move to the clock-like device. 'It's delicate.'

'I'm setting it for the right meridian,' I tell him, moving the hand. 'You assumed me an ignorant woman?'

Jemmy smiles. 'You've sailed?'

'A little. I thought longitude was for explorers,' I add. 'What use could you have for it?' Unexpectedly, his smile broadens further.

'On land, the petty thieves lurk in dark alleys,' says Jemmy. 'It is the same at sea. Most pirates hunt the coastal trade routes – near to shore, easy to navigate.' He smiles at me. 'I decided to hunt the open ocean. Why be a robber when you can be a highwayman?' He gives a flash of alarmingly white teeth.

I'm building an idea of how he came to be a privateer so young. He reminds me of my Sealed Knot colleagues: brilliant but with a reckless disregard for rules.

'Is that why you dress like a lord on his wedding night?' I ask, nodding to his frilled black shirt and coat. 'Apart from the boots, of course.'

His footwear is the most nautical part of his clothing: heavy-duty leather, rolled over at the top, ending below the knee in expensive buckles. The kind worn by naval captains.

'You don't want to know how I got these boots,' he replies.

'And what of that fancy duelling pistol?' I say, nodding to his flamboyant weapon. 'You'd be better with another sword. Those things misfire more than they fire.'

'Only if you shoot them in anger,' he says, patting his belt.

'So this is your cabin,' I say, taking in the tidy desk and rolled maps. 'You sleep in a hammock?'

'Never liked to sleep flat when my sailors are swinging in hammocks,' he says. 'But there's a bed for you, should you need it.'

'I can't take your cabin.'

'When you're on my ship, you'll follow my orders,' says Jemmy mildly. 'Besides, your spymaster sent supplies here.' He's testing my reaction, watching me as my eyes fix on a large trunk.

'I'm sure you wouldn't want to forfeit it,' he continues. 'Contains all manner of secret things, I shouldn't wonder.'

'See for yourself,' I say, striding over and opening it. Inside are three folded silk dresses: one blue, one green and one black and violet pinstriped.

'Don't be disappointed,' I tell Jemmy, seeing his expression. 'Perhaps there'll be an exciting woman spy to take on the next voyage.'

'If you're not a spy, what are you?'

'I'm a translator.'

'One of those dried-up women who follow diplomats to foreign courts?'

I smile. 'Exactly so.'

CHAPTER 15

GRACE IS IN A BACK ROOM AT THE ENGLISH EMBASSY ON THE Rue du Faubourg. The Ambassador is not here, but servants have allowed her to change her blood-soaked clothes for a rather inappropriate satin party dress.

She perches on the edge of a chaise longue wondering what will happen next. She moves a hand to her chest, feeling for the hard, lumpy presence under her clothing.

The Queen's diamonds.

She knows how dangerous a thing she carries – priceless and worthless all at once.

Hunger and exhaustion are making her dizzy. Last night she slept – or rather didn't sleep – on the streets of Paris. She'd had little time to think.

Grace spent the dark hours walking, acutely aware her bloodied clothing was a badge of wealth. The irony of this was not lost on her. Before Attica had brought her to be educated on the Morgan estate, Grace grew up poor by the Bristol docks, clawing and scraping to dress fashionably whilst her belly rumbled.

A maid in the French custom of black silk skirts and white apron arrives at the door and curtseys.

'This way,' she says, 'we have a little room for you. It is simple but I hope will suffice.'

She speaks in English, which Grace is grateful for. Having learned late, her French is rather basic.

What Grace really wants is food. She is so hungry she boils with it. But it has been ingrained from a young age that it is ill mannered to ask for things and she is not sure of the rules or hours of eating in this house.

The maid takes her up a wide staircase and to a room at the back of the house.

'In here,' she says.

The room is plain, with a cot bed and wool blanket. Grace enters.

'It is lovely,' she says. 'Thank you, so much, I—'

She stops speaking. Behind the maid is an apparition. She never heard him approach. A scarred face and a single red eye beneath a broad-brimmed musketeer's hat.

Grace opens her mouth to shout a warning, but nothing comes out.

The ghoulishly skeletal silver hand is curved into a hook. The maid is pulled backwards by her shoulders. Her eyes open wide, as cold metal slices her throat. Blood runs fast down, soaking her snowy apron.

When Grace speaks of this later, she will say how quickly it seemed to happen. The maid's glassy-eyed body dropping to the floor. The musketeer's soft boots padding towards her. She will say she couldn't tell you how she picked up the candelabra and threw it. That it was sheer luck that the hot wax hit her assailant's face and a flame set his ribbon sash ablaze.

All she really remembers is racing out into the hallway to see bodies of footmen and guards propped neatly against walls. And as she ran, she thought the blood pounding in her ears had turned her stone deaf. That was until she heard the musketeer call from the window as she reached the Embassy gardens.

'Run, little rabbit,' he had growled. 'Wherever you go, I will catch you.'

CHAPTER 16

AS SOON AS JEMMY LEAVES TO SUPERVISE OUR DEPARTURE, I fall to my travelling trunk with its folded clothes. I select pinstripes for Paris. It's fashionable in a distinctly French way, with a few more ruffles and bows than an Englishwoman would favour. But the grey and purple pattern has a pleasing sobriety about it and I'm eager not to seem frivolous. There are matching velvet gloves, a hanging pocket and pointed half-boots of soft-grey leather. All the better for running in.

I divest myself of my ragged Dover-tavern disguise, splash water to wash my face and pull the dress over my head, shrugging the upper part over my shoulders. The striped sleeves end at the elbow with a frill of lace, the neckline is low with dangling ribbons. I push the safe-passage papers Atherton gave me deep beneath the violet pinstripe.

The bodice is set with flash boning and I slide out a hollow tube with a top that unscrews. Inside is Atherton's recent breakthrough: three fire-sticks.

I resist the urge to strike one and watch it flame like magic. Smiling, I drop them back in their hiding place, screw on the lid and replace the hollow bone, sliding it the length of my torso and taking in my reflection.

There's no looking-glass, but I can just about make out my appearance in the large cabin window. I look decidedly aristocratic, despite my dark curls falling free.

Under the other dresses are more useful items. I lift a hidden compartment.

To my great delight, I see Atherton has left me his latest lock-pick. A thin, hooked blade, with the capacity to open even one of Mr Bramah's famous new locks. I put it into my hanging purse.

There is also a fan showing a map of Paris streets when unfurled and a list of important houses and names. Next to that is a bag of gold coins and a box filled with jewellery, arranged by worth in francs, should I need to sell them. I slide on a few rings, ordering them least valuable on my little fingers and most expensive on my indexes.

Last in the array of items is a little black pouch. Inside is an ivory hair comb, the carved tusk shaped like a 'y'. Beside it is a strip of rubber with a square patch attached.

I'm puzzling over it and suddenly I understand. I think it's a kind of slingshot. This is Atherton's little joke. But it isn't like the sling I whirled in the air as a girl.

I put the pieces where I think they should go, lift a gold coin from the bag and fit it into the sling. I stretch the rubber back. I can feel the tension loaded there. I extend fully, fixing on a tankard on the far side of the room. I launch the projectile and though the aim is imperfect, the coin topples it. My face breaks into a wide grin.

The power!

Atherton must have known how much I'd like this.

I'm contemplating how best to test the range when the planked floor gives a sudden unnatural lurch. I stagger and catch my balance. Something is happening.

I push the ivory slingshot into my hair. I can hear a distant cannon – a warning shot from another ship to stay our course.

We're being boarded.

Nightmares crowd in on me. I shut my eyes and mutter a strange little poem my mother taught me, to calm myself.

The door flies open and Jemmy enters. He takes in the greenish terror on my face.

'You mustn't fear,' he says. 'No harm will come to you on this ship. Bailey had the same for a time,' he adds, moving closer and taking my arm. 'You were transported?'

I nod.

'I'd like to see the pirates to board us,' he says with grim certainty. 'No one gets aboard without my permission. Just put one foot in front of the other, you'll stop shaking when we get out on deck.'

I let him lead me out and the terror abates.

'If not pirates, then who?' I ask, relief making my voice sharper than I intend.

Jemmy's face clouds. 'Royal Navy. I have to afford 'em certain courtesies. Part of staying legal.' He tries for a smile but can't hide his annoyance. 'We're barely an hour out of Dover,' he says. 'They'd have been better docking than stealing our supplies.'

A different fear pours back in on me now. I have an inkling of what this could be.

'What do they want?' I say, trying to keep my tone light. I'm desperate to catch sight of the boarding party, but there's a sail between us and I don't want to appear concerned.

Jemmy shrugs his narrow shoulders.

'Provisions, most likely. Wine. We're in France enough to maintain a good stock.'

This sounds reasonable. Perhaps I'm thinking too deeply. A gust of wind catches the sail obscuring my view and lifts it. And I see my instincts were all too correct.

The ship drawn up alongside us is the *Vulcan*, an English naval vessel of sorts. The sides are fitted out with gleaming cannons and the men boarding are well trained, uniformed and armed. In their centre, like a great black crow, is an all-too-familiar figure.

Lord Pole.

He's clad in his usual black long robes and priest-like square-felt hat.

What is he doing here?

I feel my stomach tightening.

If he's boarding the *Esmerelda* it can only mean one thing. He has come for me.

CHAPTER 17

I WATCH AS LORD POLE'S MEN FILE ON DECK. I MOMENTARILY consider hiding, but of course I can't. Jemmy might be suspected of sheltering me and Lord Pole wouldn't hesitate to tear his ship apart.

Lord Pole is looking at Jemmy now and I can see him processing, the same way I did. He is wondering how this man with his unbroken nose and enamelled pistol could be a murderous pirate. He looks more like the kind of third-born son who bets all or nothing on the turn of a card.

I walk clear out on the deck. Lord Pole's small dark eyes settle on me. He doesn't smile. Lord Pole always reminds me of a raven, silent, with an air of death.

Behind him, his men are throwing ropes, tethering the *Vulcan* to the *Esmerelda.* His vessel is black and gold with an understated Royal crest at the prow – he need not advertise his importance.

'Lord Pole.' I curtsey, not bothering to hide my displeasure. My eyes rest on the ropes joining our two vessels.

Lord Pole manages the briefest of bows. 'Attica,' he says, glancing at his ship, 'if you'd be kind enough to join us aboard.'

'What do you want?' I demand.

Lord Pole's lips press tight. 'I bring information,' he says, 'concerning Lord Morgan.'

A dread grips me. What news can Lord Pole have of my father? A horrible, terrible memory comes back.

Father, not breathing, little stinking bottles of laudanum scattered all around.

But that was a lifetime ago. Surely nothing could have happened with his happy new marriage? My mind won't stop conjuring horrors.

Lord Pole turns abruptly, dark furs swinging, and snaps his fingers high. Men arrange themselves rapidly to follow in line.

Several of his men crowd around me. I don't know what they've been told, but the language of their bodies is clear. They take me by means of a row-boat aboard Lord Pole's tastefully decorated ship. We enter a dark little room at the back, thick-walled, thick-doored, the kind of place you imprison captives who might be of political importance. This must be his room, I think. Ebony-clad and neatly filed papers written in Lord Pole's endless cramped script. No maps here, no spinning globes, no bed. Perhaps he doesn't sleep.

Lord Pole is already sitting at a desk. He's only a few years younger than my father and he's aged well for a man who has seen what he's seen. His head is bowed, so only the bridge of his long nose and black eyebrows are visible.

'What news?' I ask.

Lord Pole lifts his head, brooding brown eyes fixing on mine, and extends a hand to the chair facing him, gesturing I should sit. I pause and then I do. The faintly animal smell, born of Lord Pole's layers of heavy dark furs, encloses me.

Whether a human heart beats beneath is a mystery he will take to the grave.

'Tell me,' I demand, still working possibilities. I can get a fast horse at Dover. If I ride through the night I'll be by my father's side at dawn.

'Your hanging purse,' he says flatly. 'Might I see inside?'

I pass it over, too agitated to question the strangeness of the request.

Lord Pole parts the velvet fabric and extracts my lock-pick. He pushes it inside his coat, then raises his dark eyes to mine.

'Your father is in good health and sends his regards,' he says smoothly.

The relief flooding through me is tinged with dull fury as I realize he's tricked me. Lord Pole has taken my means of escape so he can imprison me in this secure little cabin and sail me back to Dover.

'Have you no shame?' I feel suddenly exhausted, torn between relief for my father and anger at Lord Pole's subterfuge.

Lord Pole leans closer. 'I would stoop to any deceit to protect our great nation. I have plans for you, plans that will not be altered.' He sits back. 'Everyone has their weak point, Attica, you mustn't dwell on it. It's my job to know such things. Yours is your father. And Atherton.' He frowns at this. He's always been uncertain what to make of my friendship with Atherton and Lord Pole needs to understand everything.

He reaches for a crystal decanter of whisky and pours two glass, slides one to me with his expensively ringed fingers. He plays the diplomat now, extending courtesies.

I pick it up, knowing before I even take a sip that this will be some excellent smuggled vintage that Lord Pole has acquired for his personal use.

'Forgive the deception,' he says, with a wave of his thickly jewelled hand, to suggest he thinks nothing of it himself. 'Only you wouldn't have come aboard if I'd told you the truth.'

'Which is?' My mind is whirling, wondering what possible reason he could have for tricking me on to his ship.

'The situation in France has changed.'

'Oh.'

'It is a great deal more dangerous. And ... our need to see you married has become more pressing.'

I jerk back without meaning to.

'Didn't I warn you, Attica, you would not escape another wedding?'

Lord Pole makes a smile that isn't a smile.

'Your husband is a lord,' he says, wincing with effort. 'Or he will be when his father dies. Not an ancient family,' he continues, 'but considered a high match for ...' He waves a hand in my direction.

'For someone illegitimate.' I fill in.

'People like us must work harder to be accepted,' he says. 'There's no shame in it.'

I sometimes forget that Lord Pole isn't a true noble. His title came courtesy of a famously acrimonious marriage.

'Even so,' I'm still reeling, 'what kind of lord-in-waiting would stoop to me for a bride?'

'Your husband-to-be is a parliament man,' says Lord Pole, 'active in abolishing slavery.'

'His name?' I demand, tight-lipped.

Lord Pole looks up into a corner of the room as he searches for the right words.

'There's no right way to put this,' he says. 'It's Godwin.'

'But that cannot be.' A sick feeling of fear is washing over me. 'Godwin is betrothed to Grace.'

I feel a flush of affection to think of my clever cousin. I sometimes think Grace is what I might have been had I ever learned to follow the rules.

'I'm afraid Grace has gone missing,' says Lord Pole. 'She journeyed to Paris and didn't return.'

CHAPTER 18

LORD POLE'S CLOSE CABIN IS SUDDENLY SUFFOCATING. I feel the world falling away.

Grace is missing?

'Grace may have become mixed up in some political thing,' says Lord Pole. The flash of guilt on his face confirms my worst fears.

'You used Grace to smuggle in the diamonds,' I say, appalled. Lord Pole doesn't even blink.

'We needed someone above suspicion. A young English bride, come for her wedding trousseau.'

'You sent my cousin to Paris,' I say, my words tight and furious, 'so you could steal away her husband and marry him to me?'

'If only it were so simple.' There's a distant look in his eyes. 'I worked hard to ensure the marriage between Grace and Godwin went ahead. Do you think his family agreed to such a preposterous arrangement without my help?'

I try to collect my thoughts. Now I'm truly frightened for Grace.

What has he done?

'Where is she?' I demand. 'Where is Grace?'

'Don't get any ideas, Attica. It's too dangerous. Besides, Godwin can't be left unwed. It's imperative he's married to a Morgan girl before those bloody Spencers get their women lined up.'

I have the same awful, trapped feeling I remember as a girl. The silent rage of being property to be passed around.

'Does Godwin have any feelings on his new bride?' I ask. 'He loves Grace!'

'Godwin is sensible enough to listen to his family, who will want him married before the gossip of an aborted wedding begins. In his shock and grief, I'm sure he'll be fairly pliable on the subject.'

Lord Pole appears to see something in my expression. 'France has changed overnight,' he says. 'A pack of commoners finally stood up to their tyrant King. A group of lawyers went for a meeting at Versailles,' he continues. 'When the King locked them out, they refused to leave. They besieged themselves in his tennis court and made an oath not to part ways until France had a constitution.'

My eyes widen. 'Did he have them all executed?'

'No. He's spent all his money. Can't even afford his musketeers. He had to agree to the terms to get the men out of his Palace. The King gave over a great deal of power to the French people yesterday.'

I sit back, absorbing the magnitude of this.

'The implications are bigger than you can ever imagine,' says Lord Pole. 'No one is getting in or out of Paris.' He looks at me. 'We've lost a lot of good men in the last few days.'

But I'm thinking, all the same. My eyes flick to his.

'What if I were to go to France,' I suggest, ignoring the

slight, 'and bring Grace home?' I'm having the butterflies-in-the-stomach that come before doing something completely reckless. 'You'd still have your Morgan wife.'

'It was a misplaced charity of your father's,' he sighs, 'to allow Grace to be tutored with you, gave her all kinds of political ideas above her station. It's astounding you didn't both grow beards. Not to mention the damage the two of you did to the grounds of the estate. And now you're letting emotion get the better of you.'

'You've always hated me.' I don't know what compels me to say it aloud. Only my mind is buzzing with fear for my cousin.

To my surprise, Lord Pole looks shocked. For a moment, I think, even a little hurt, but I dismiss this idea as ridiculous.

'I don't hate you, Attica,' he says quietly. He looks at his hands, frowning. 'To cause a person you have great regard for to dislike you, for their own protection ...' He spreads his hands. 'It is the curse of men in my position to be hated. There is a nobility in it, I suppose. You know I see you more often than I visit my own daughters?' He looks suddenly very tired.

It's such a strange outburst that I hardly know how to respond. Before I can, Lord Pole collects himself. I can almost see the formal façade locking back into place.

He takes a deep breath, rubbing his hand across his lined lower face.

'I am going to credit you with the same intelligence as a man,' he says graciously, 'and avail you of all the facts. I hope when I am finished you will understand why you cannot go to Paris.'

He breathes in deeply through his long nostrils.

'Gaspard de Mayenne has been murdered.'

There's a long pause whilst I absorb this.

'Royalists got him?' I say finally.

Lord Pole frowns. 'We don't know,' he admits, and this in itself is a shock. Lord Pole knows everything.

'Someone well known to Gaspard revealed his whereabouts,' he adds. 'A person he trusted.'

'How did he die?' The promise I made to Gaspard is ringing in my ears.

'Gaspard was tortured,' says Lord Pole briskly, 'and his body placed in the Bastille mortuary.'

My mind is working over the details.

'Royalists would have delivered Gaspard to the King,' I say, meeting Lord Pole's eye. 'It must have been a revolutionary. Some kind of threat, perhaps?'

'You have it exactly right. Gaspard's death was a warning to the Sealed Knot to stay out of French affairs. Whoever left Gaspard's body pushed a diamond between his lips.'

CHAPTER 19

LORD POLE LEANS OVER HIS DARK-WOOD DESK AND REFILLS the glass of whisky I hadn't realized I'd emptied.

'You told me Gaspard's rescue was to bolster the morale of the rebels,' I accuse, taking a long draft.

Lord Pole steeples his fingers.

'In part it was. The point is someone powerful got to Gaspard, someone we know next to nothing about. Considering the extent of our intelligence in France, this is significant. Their influence is everywhere. They are involved in deep intrigues and implicated in the assassination of several of our best men.'

'Implicated,' I demand, 'involved? Since when did you deal in anything other than absolutes.'

The strangest expression crosses Lord Pole's face, as though he's trying to grasp something just beyond his reach.

'There is an *organisation*,' he says. 'Or a rebel faction ... They are called *Le Société des Amis*.'

I translate. 'The Society of Friends? The name gives no indication which side they favour.'

'They could be royalists. Their opposition is split. Some want to keep their King, with democratic checks. Others,

Gaspard being one, wanted the monarch deposed and replaced.'

'What of the third option? No King at all?'

'The Society of Friends are unlikely to be extremists,' says Lord Pole, looking pained at his inability to say this for certain. 'This is not America. The French have had a King for eight hundred years.'

If I wasn't so frightened for my cousin, I'd be reeling at the existence of a group that intimidates the emotionally bulwarked Lord Pole.

'Whoever they are, they are powerful. We only know one thing about them for certain. They use a man named Oliver Janssen. He was a musketeer. Lost a hand in service and had a silversmith make him a prosthetic capable of cutting and worse.'

To my surprise, Lord Pole shuts his eyes for a long moment, then opens them again, the dark pools giving nothing away.

'Janssen gained a reputation as a man who gets confessions by whatever means necessary,' he explains.

A desperate need to see my cousin safe grips me. Grace was the first white person who ever smiled at me. When I landed in Bristol, stinking and lice-ridden, she had folded her fingers around my ulcerated hand. I remember her gap-toothed urchin grin as she enfolded me in her unruly games, almost all of which involved breaking things. 'Grandpappy says so long as you don't get caught it doesn't signify,' she'd told me, beaming. I'd been in awe of her outrageous incaution.

'Let me find Grace,' I say. 'Please. Just two days—'

'Atherton has let you get away with your crusades for too long now. He's sentimental about you, on account of ...' Lord Pole waves a hand to encompass and dismiss the Virginian uprising, near-death imprisonment in the hull of a ship and the eventual escape that led to the death of my mother. 'Your background,' he concludes.

'You have shown time and time again that you will pursue your own aims and squander resources freeing captives when there are more material gains to be made. That galleon you stole from Haiti had to be reimbursed to avoid a war. The Indian prison for deserters that we *did not* ask to be blown to pieces. Not to mention the relations we must now repair with the Russian Empress, whose goodwill is not easily won.'

I'm silent.

'I didn't know you knew about the galleon in Haiti,' I admit finally.

He takes a sip of whisky, hesitates, then speaks. 'We have reports from Paris that an English girl sold a ruby and amethyst hair comb to a coach driver yesterday,' he says slowly.

I steady my breathing. That hair comb was Grace's favourite.

'She wanted passage to the Salon des Princes,' concludes Lord Pole.

I close my eyes. Of course it would make perfect sense that Grace would go there. She would only have heard what is written about it in English pamphlets. The debates held amongst women there are often written up and circulated. My innocent cousin would have no idea what really happens at the infamous salon.

Lord Pole's dark eyes meet mine.

'Do you see now why there is no sense going after your cousin?' he asks pointedly. 'Grace might enter the salon as a fresh-faced bride-to-be, but she's unlikely to leave that way.' He steeples his fingers. 'In any case, the message of Gaspard's death is clear. The Society of Friends will come for Grace next.'

CHAPTER 20

SOMEWHERE IN THE BACK STREETS OF PARIS, A MAN SITS AT a plain desk. He straightens his already straight clothing: a lawyer's white shirt and black coat, leather shoes with a buckle. Nothing showy, but pin-neat and immaculate all the same.

The man has been watching the English girl, Grace Elliott. He watches everything. Information and the orderly assimilation thereof is what he believes to be the heart of true power. The Society of Friends is run on information.

His name is Maximilien Robespierre. Despite humble beginnings, he enjoys modest success practising law in Paris. He is told he should be grateful, but he cannot unsee what he saw as a poorer man. In his free hours he has begun to write political speeches. They are well received in the coffee houses and clubs. One day he hopes to speak to crowds of thousands.

A new letter is on his desk and he lifts it with long ink-stained fingers. It is secured with a blue wax seal used by a company of foreign villains and thieves known as the Sealed Knot.

This correspondence has been secretly intercepted from a fishing boat, docked in a harbour at Porte de Saint-Cloud, just outside the city limits. Hidden below deck, behind swathes of seaweed-scabbed nets, are cages of homing pigeons and materials for the manufacture of secret messages. It has been calculated, with the right messengers and horses in place, messages could travel from London's Whitehall to Paris in around ten hours and perhaps as little as six.

Robespierre breaks open this newest interception, reads, considers. He lifts a quill, hesitates and looks deeper. The code is more challenging than the last. This pleases him. Though immediately he is able to discern that the correspondence concerns Gaspard de Mayenne.

He reads again, turns the unfolded paper, taps it. Crumbs of sealing wax fall free. He frowns and sweeps them into a tidy pile.

Gaspard de Mayenne's daughter has a position at the Palace of Versailles. He believes this to be significant, but as yet he is not sure why. This makes him unhappy. He has the strangest feeling he is missing something important. That someone is laughing at him.

Robespierre stands and draws out a sheet of legal paper, written in a neat hand, from a fastidiously organized bookcase. It's his own report. A document he has been steadily adding to, following the English involvement in France. He has plans for how the future of France will be. It doesn't include interference.

His thoughts drift back to Grace Elliott, running like a little mouse through the dark streets of Paris. With no idea she was being toyed with.

She was seen getting into a carriage and Robespierre should have little difficulty discovering where the vehicle went. Regrettably, Grace will have to die. Someone always does.

Now Robespierre turns over some more papers. Amongst them is Gaspard's sketch brought to him by Janssen. A tall woman holding a knife. It disturbs him greatly, in a way he cannot define.

CHAPTER 21

THE *VULCAN* DRIFTS GENTLY ON THE SWELL AS I CONSIDER the implications of Lord Pole's words. In the creaking dark wood-panelled cabin, the rest of the ship feels far away.

'I think I've made sufficiently clear what is at stake,' concludes Lord Pole. 'Safest to leave Grace where she is and hope the necklace disappears with her.'

I tap the whisky glass against my lips. 'Find Grace and you could inadvertently fling some priceless reward into the hands of this mysterious organization. The Society of Friends are inhumanly careful,' he admits. 'I've never come across anyone more adept at covering their tracks. If they have a leader, he isn't inured with sentiment or mortal weaknesses. They seem to know everything and have ears everywhere. We simply cannot risk it.'

'You mean to just abandon her? It's *wrong*.'

'Valour is a privilege of the young,' says Lord Pole. 'I keep people alive by making hard decisions, not right ones. Your talents are more usefully deployed in the safe confines of a useful marriage. I have always said so.'

'How generous of you to let a girl die so I might infiltrate bedchambers the rest of you can't,' I say, anger getting the better of my judgement.

'It is the curse of men like me to play the longer game,' says Lord Pole, sounding tired. 'You might not understand it, Attica, but I have the greater good in mind. France is split. If the wrong people get those diamonds the death of every English resident in France won't be the half of it.'

'Don't pretend that is your principle concern,' I say bitterly. 'You hope to depose the French King and see someone more amenable to your politics on the throne.'

'This latest Louis is the silliest excuse for a king that ever lived,' says Lord Pole, annoyance surfacing suddenly. 'His people are starving, badly, awfully so.' He scowls at some distant image and I wonder if there is a glimmer of humanity at the heart of him after all. Or perhaps he just doesn't like untidiness.

'Louis and his idiot Austrian Queen are taking bread from the mouths of their own subjects,' he goes on, 'to buy guns for rebels in the colonies.'

Aha. So we come to the real reason. England losing America.

'The people are close to hanging their chubby King and gilded Queen from the nearest lamp-post,' concludes Lord Pole, his hand is stretched out as though to grasp the possibility.

'At the expense of my cousin.'

'Your cousin will be irrelevant in days,' he says. 'Certainly, she'll no longer be marriage material. Save your emotions.'

My fingers move to my hidden Mangbetu blade. His eyes register the gesture with mild interest.

'Irrelevant?' I feel anger rise.

He has the decency to look away.

'Would you have made the same assessment had Grace Elliott been noble born?' I say, my voice brimming with scorn.

'If my aunt hadn't made the unfortunate choices she had, would Grace be so dispensable?'

Lord Pole's lips press thin. 'You have so many unbecoming qualities for a woman,' he says. 'I remember being angry, as you are now,' he says. 'Life taught me not to rage against the things I cannot control. I advise you to learn the same lesson.' The ringed fingers roll his whisky glass. '*C'est la vie,*' he says in expert French, without smiling.

There's a weighed-down look about Lord Pole, I think, as though he hasn't slept well in a long time.

'This is a good opportunity for you, Attica,' he says. 'Far better than I might have hoped. Your duties to the Sealed Knot as Godwin's wife would be minor. You could live almost a normal life.'

Our eyes meet and I see something of his own hopes and disappointments reflected back.

'And if I don't wish to lead a normal life?' I ask.

'Marriage might agree with you.' He waves a finger infuriatingly. 'You won't be the first little shrew to be tamed by wedlock.'

I hurl myself at him, launching full force across the table. He is quicker than I would expect, turning sideways and slamming my outstretched arm to the wall. I twist away, breaking the hold, and grab a fistful of his fur collar. I feel the oily material in my hands, inhale a breath of Lord Pole's leather and animal tang. Then there is something at my throat. A knife. I look down to see him holding the blade. His face is hard, calculating.

'So you learned more at the Sicilian Assassins' Academy than the hardened steel formula,' he says. 'I always wondered.'

He withdraws his hand and seats himself, rearranging his ruffled furs. I'm breathing fast.

I wonder what Lord Pole assumes of my training. If he knows my hand still sometimes twitches in my sleep for want of a weapon. How I learned in an abattoir of beef carcasses – *jugular, aorta, radial, femoral* – like a mantra. That I can pick up a blade with my feet, fight left-handed and I still own a man-shaped sandbag, lacerated with practice marks.

Lord Pole looks up at me and there's something unexpectedly compassionate in his dark eyes.

'No matter how good you are,' he says, 'you will only ever be a woman. It was cruel of Atherton to set you up for defeat.' He exhales hard. 'War will always have casualties,' he says. 'A woman's usefulness is different to a man's. One day you will see. It's a noble thing I require of you, Attica, even if you do not see it now.'

'You are wicked,' I say quietly.

Lord Pole nods as if expecting this. He straightens his clothing and makes for the door.

'Your future husband is a sensible, measured man,' he replies, 'in many ways your exact opposite. I think you will make a good marriage.

'It's too late to dock back in Dover now,' he says. 'We'll sail in the morning. You'll be brought dinner here, wine if you like. I'll be sure you're comfortable.' He hesitates in the doorway. 'I shan't attend your wedding if you do not wish it,' he says. 'I'm not a monster.'

I sit very still. He looks as though he might say more then thinks better of it. He shuts the heavy door. It's only when I hear the key turn I permit myself a small smile of victory.

Whilst I was pretending to let him restrain me, I stole back my lock-pick, right from inside his coat.

CHAPTER 22

IT'S DARK, WITH ONLY A LITTLE MOONLIGHT, AND I'M CLIMBING with difficulty up the side of the *Esmeralda.* I'm sopping wet from my short swim between the two ships to a mooring rope. I pull up, hand over hand, willing my burning muscles to last. There's a lot of black water below.

A shadow appears above suddenly and looms over me. Then a hand extends from the dark.

'Let me lend you a hand there, Attica,' says a familiar voice. 'I was wonderin' when you'd join us.'

Dumbstruck I take the hand and let Jemmy pull me up on deck.

'If you mean to stowaway,' he says helpfully, 'the best way is to get in amongst the cargo. Have the dockers load you up and slip them a few coins if they spot yer.' He winks at me. 'Less conspicuous than scaling a rope.'

I straighten my clothes, trying to reinstate some semblance of dignity.

'Don't be embarrassed,' he adds, enjoying himself, 'a lot of women have been fooled by the way a ship is arranged.'

'I imagine Lord Pole has spoken with you—' I begin. Jemmy

holds up a hand.

'He's a very persuasive man,' he says. 'Met a few like him in my time. Don't take no for an answer. Wrote the book on bribes and threats. Best not to tell 'em no, in my experience.'

I realize I'm holding my breath.

'Lucky for you,' he says, 'I'm not easily persuaded. And you seem an interesting sort of character to have aboard.'

He frowns at me. 'How d'yer get so a man like that is chasin' you?'

I hesitate. 'Lord Pole is my uncle,' I admit.

There's a long pause.

'Is he so?' Jemmy is enormously amused by this. 'Your uncle.' He whistles. 'Determined kinda fellow.' He looks to the starlit horizon. 'Wouldn't put it past him to search my ship,' he decides.

I nod, not daring to speak.

'Best we raise anchor now, then,' he says.

'You can do that?' I ask. 'I thought sailing in the dark was dangerous.'

Jemmy grins his white-toothed grin. 'We're pirates,' he says, 'we love a little danger. And my men and this ship can go anywhere there's water.'

I like his strange accent now I'm not trying to decipher its origins. A hotchpotch of everything, I think: a bit of Irish, an American colonial twang and a few others besides. I suppose he must have travelled widely. And then I think, it's not his accent I like, it's him. Which is not necessarily good. People I like have a habit of getting themselves killed.

'Jemmy,' I say, 'Lord Pole isn't a man to annoy. If he discovers you've aided my escape, he could retract your licence.'

'You think I became a pirate because I love doing what fine

men say?' asks Jemmy. 'I told your man Atherton I'd get you into Paris. So long as you want to go there, our arrangement holds, no matter what your uncle has to say on it.'

He considers for a moment. 'My only condition,' he adds, 'is that you tell me your real reason for travelling to France.'

'Agreed.'

'Very well, you can start now.' He puts his fingers into his mouth and whistles. The bulky figure of Bailey rises up from somewhere in the gloom.

'Rouse the men,' he says. 'We're sailing by night.'

Bailey watches me, but he says nothing, only vanishes below deck. In moments there are sleepy men everywhere, pulling ropes, trimming sails. They seem to know not to make noise and the whole business has the eerie feel of a ghost ship.

As the yardarm turns, wind bites the sail and pushes us slowly away from the slumbering *Vulcan*, still bobbing limply on the water.

CHAPTER 23

Dawn is breaking as we begin sailing up the Seine. I'm watching the countryside from the deck, enjoying the different shapes to the haystacks and till of the fields. I let the rising sun warm my face. People are beginning to emerge from their homes now, fires are being lit, food prepared for a day's farming. There is a morning chill, so it surprises me to see so many bare legs and arms. I look closer and see the truth. The farmers wear rags. Less than rags. And their meagre clothing hangs on limbs no broader than broomsticks. Their eyes are too large for their pinched faces, their ribs pressed through paper-thin skin.

Jemmy is at my side suddenly.

'Breakfast,' he says, pushing a ship's biscuit into my hand. I mutter thanks, realizing I'm starving hungry and he follows the line of my gaze.

'You've not been to France recently?' he asks after a moment.

'Not for seven years.'

'Ah.'

I notice my hands are gripping the prow, the hard biscuit digging into my palm. It's a nightmare vision, all these poor people. I feel black anger rise. In England, Marie Antoinette's frivolity is a joke, how she sends for a fresh ten yards of ribbon a day for her shoes. But there's nothing funny about this.

'I heard things, of course,' I say, watching the people. 'The King and Queen were squandering money. The price of bread had risen ...'

I'm trying to drag my eyes from the half-dead people, but I can't.

'Nothing prepares you for seeing it,' says Jemmy philosophically, 'and you never get used to it. I thought you nobles learned how not to look,' he adds, his eyes sliding to my face.

'Our farmers don't look like that,' I say, stung. I'm remembering the strong-limbed and cleanly dressed families who work our estate.

Several bone-thin children have waded out into the shallows, staring mutely at the *Esmerelda* as we drift by. I pull back my hand, ready to hurl them my breakfast. To my surprise, Jemmy grabs my arm.

'Don't,' he says.

I turn to him, outraged.

'They're starving—' I begin. But he cuts me off.

'Throw it if you like,' he says. 'Watch those poor souls fight each other to death for it.'

I hesitate. Jemmy's hand is still holding me. I look at it pointedly and he draws it away. I curl the biscuit into my palm.

'Why aren't English ships sending food?' I ask.

'Because men like your pappy and grandpappy are too busy starving their own peasant folk,' says Jemmy. He laughs at my angry expression. 'Oh, I imagine you're one of the good families, are ye? Do you swan around the little poor homes in your silks and give out candied nuts at Christmas? Believe me, Your Ladyship, all you fine people think the same.'

I feel my face grow hot. He's right and I never saw it that way before.

Jemmy's eyes drift back to the shore. 'You mustn't fret; it won't last,' he says. 'I've seen it before, in the colonies.' He narrows his eyes, looking at the peasants.

'These people have nothing to lose,' he says. 'When they recognize it, their revenge will be terrible.' He eyes the waters ahead.

There's a pause as we're both lost in our thoughts.

'Was New York like this?' I ask, realizing Jemmy must have seen revolution in America.

'No. It's an exciting place,' he says. 'Brutal. Lawless, to be sure. A man can do very well there if he keeps his wits and a loaded pistol about him.'

'Why didn't you stay?'

'I like the ocean. No rules at all.' He grins. 'Talking of which, we're sailing into the heart of it. The place where they tax the bread and hold the money. Paris.'

The vista is changing now. There are tall buildings coming into view. Muddy riverside has given over to cobblestones. Dawn sun is giving way to a morning summer heat.

The houses are ornate with delicately wrought-iron balconies and washed in pastel hues. As we glide up the river I'm reminded why I like this city so much.

'Pretty, ain't she?' says Jemmy. 'You not arrived by boat before?'

'Only by road.'

We pass the Bastille, a glowering fortress on the horizon, and I see Jemmy's expression change.

'A thousand poor souls chained up underground without trial or justice, at the whim of a tyrant King.' He removes his hat and crosses himself, watching the building with a dark look on his face.

'That's just talk, isn't it?' I say. 'People manacled to the walls for thirty years. Ghosts of those tortured to death haunting the dungeons.'

My eyes slide to his face to share the joke, but he isn't smiling.

'So what's your plan?' he asks, leaning back and biting at a hard ship's biscuit. 'Disguise yourself as a serving maid? Slip in unnoticed and find this lost cousin of yours?'

I smile at his tone.

'Grace may have been headed to the Salon des Princes.'

Jemmy's eyebrows rise at the mention of the infamous salon, but he says nothing.

'I have a friend in Paris who can get me in,' I add.

Jemmy nods approvingly.

'Then your plan is already better than the others.' He rolls the biscuit in his hand. 'What's her name, this friend?'

'Angelina Mazarin. She lives in Montmartre. The bad part of town,' I say with a little smile, thinking of the little district with its heady mix of labourers, artists and good-time girls.

Jemmy hesitates. 'You mean La Mazarin, the courtesan?' he sounds surprised. I sometimes forget Angelina is famous, in her way. She's one of a handful of select mistresses who wealthy men fight to have at their side.

'You've met her,' I deduce, reading his expression as Atherton has taught me to do. I'm fairly certain Jemmy has done more than just meet Angelina.

'You could say that,' he says, trying for breezy. 'How well do you know her?'

'As well as you do, I think,' I say.

Jemmy starts to laugh, then does a peculiar kind of double-take when he sees I'm serious.

'You and La Mazarin?' he says, voice caught in a perfect storm between hope and disbelief.

'We were at finishing school together, outside Paris,' I say, waving my hand to dismiss any sentiment he might be attaching to our relationship. 'All girls. No boys. We were young and bored. It was innocent, nothing really.'

I can see his eyes sliding back and forth, picturing.

'The last I heard from her, she was a kept mistress to a bishop,' I say.

'You must be careful,' says Jemmy. 'The days of King-appointed clergy are numbered. In any case, La Mazarin might not be as welcoming as you hope,' says Jemmy. 'Paris nobles are low on charity nowadays. And I judge you have a week at best,' he says, 'before things get very dark. When they turn they will turn fast.'

CHAPTER 24

GRACE IS STANDING NERVOUSLY IN THE SUBTERRANEAN kitchen of the Salon des Princes. Her plan is to find a friendly woman, an intellectual. Such a person, she feels, will help her get back to England. But the footman who directed her here has vanished and she has been waiting for what seems like for ever.

Grace had arrived at the grand gold gates and simply stared. She never realized that chateaus looked like this. You might pick up London and shake all the money from every rich pocket, yet still not afford this grandeur.

Steeling her courage, Grace had stepped on to the sweep of manicured lawns. Despite the early hour, there were a great deal of people about. The dregs of a party, she had deduced. A surge of fatigue had made her sway.

This isn't the first time you've been hungry and tired, she had told herself sternly, *stand up straight.*

That was when she'd seen the footman. He'd been serving roasted songbirds to a group of silk-clad girls in heavy make-up who were staring dreamily at the dawn. Grace had waited as the guests took them indifferently, with plump fingers, crunching on the small bones. One had pushed a tiny beaked head into the mouth of a lapdog, laughing encouragingly as the pink tongue investigated.

'Excuse me,' Grace had announced in her best French, when the footman was finished. 'This is the Salon des Princes? Where women debate politics?'

She might have said it wrong, because he had smirked, then eyed her rather simple muslin dress, tied under the bust with a ribbon. But to her relief, he'd replied: 'Come with me,' and beckoned her towards the house.

Following obediently behind, Grace's attention had fixed suddenly on something shocking. Barely concealed behind a sculpted hedge, a woman was rolling, almost naked, with two men, her petticoats torn and stockings fallen to her ankles.

Grace had looked to the footman, but he hadn't indicated anything unusual was taking place. Growing up near Bristol docks, Grace had seen her share of scandalous things, but never in silk and lace on a green lawn.

Her eyes had settled on some half-dressed men and women making an untidy attempt to swap clothing, playing cards scattered at their feet.

Grace had been seized with a sudden certainty that something was wrong. This was a dangerous place.

That's the dockside-girl talking, she had told herself. *This is a fine household, there is nothing to fear.*

Her stomach had growled loudly, causing the footman to turn.

'You're hungry?' he had asked.

She had nodded, shame-faced.

'Come,' he'd said, 'I'll take you inside. They waste enough food to feed the whole of Paris. We'll find you something. You'll be earning your keep soon enough.'

Grace had been pondering this remark when the footman had placed a possessive hand on the small of her back.

'We must write your name in the book,' he'd said. 'Madame Roland likes to know everyone who comes.'

Grace waits now, in the vast kitchen where the footman deposited her. She has watched breakfast come and go; the hot rolls and chocolate were served fashionably late.

Cooks are now preparing for the evening meal, forcing meat through sieves, adding champagne to sauces. Cauldrons bubble, spits turn, sweating boys race to and from the icehouse and the orangery.

Grace watches it all happen through a screen of copper pans, which hang seemingly everywhere. Lack of food is making her light-headed, but she has not been brought up to ask for things, especially not food. That is begging. She chews a fingernail, wondering how much longer she can stand here without fainting from hunger.

Manners. She reminds herself, thinking of Godwin.

Suddenly the familiar footman appears. Grace lets out a breath she didn't realize she'd been holding.

'This way,' he says. 'The servants' table.'

He leads her to the far side of the sweltering kitchen, past three cavernous fires. There is a table groaning with leftovers: half-eaten cakes, torn bread, scraps of ham and beef.

'Here,' he says, 'take what you will. I'll come back for you nearer the time.'

Grace sits, taking in the vast selection with round eyes. She lifts a piece of cake and takes a cautious bite. Next she chews a crust, swallows a mouthful of meat, tastes some cheese. She finds she can't stop.

In the buttery air, Grace eats and eats.

CHAPTER 25

As WE FLOAT TOWARDS THE HEART OF PARIS, AN UGLY noise rifts the sky.

Jemmy points to where the river narrows. There are sets of steps, like in London, for ships to dock. Beyond that is a great high stone gateway, carved and official-looking. It's the height of two men and broad, with a crowd of people all around it.

'The Barrière du Trône,' says Jemmy, 'where they tax goods coming into Paris. Popular with both sailors and farmers,' he adds, in an ironic tone, 'as you might imagine. We'll drop you there.'

'Thank you,' I say, wondering how I might repay the risk he's taken for me. 'I'll write to Lord Pole,' I promise. 'Tell him I stowed away. You're not to blame.'

'So long as I'm useful to men in high places, I've no fear,' says Jemmy. 'And I've still a time to be useful yet ...' His words drift off. Jemmy is frowning. He holds up a hand.

'I don't like the look of those steps.'

Now we're sailing nearer, we can see the crowd at the customs gate are unruly. A rising cloud of dust comes from fast-moving feet.

'Something's not right,' Jemmy says, narrowing his eyes to the view ahead. 'Take us to the shallower waters over there,' he instructs his helmsmen. 'Arm the men', he shouts to Bailey.

He takes my hand and leads me to the other side of the ship.

I'm taking in the full scene: people are destroying the customs gate, screaming shouts of protest against taxes and the price of bread. Any attempt to guard the structure has completely fallen apart. Men have climbed the brick entry and are chipping away at it with hammers and chisels.

This is no unplanned attack, I realize, watching their methodical labours and their workmanlike tools. Those are stonemasons. They strike steadily, marking blocks of stone, hammering and letting pieces fall in an explosion of dust to great cheers. But the protestors have attracted a rough crowd of troublemakers, pillaging the docks.

I have a sudden prescience that Jemmy's horrors will begin even sooner than predicted.

'Best we land you on the south side,' he decides. 'There looks to be a skirmish. More protests about the tax on bread, I shouldn't wonder.'

But even from here it looks like more than a skirmish. I'd call it a war. Men are attacking, flailing, punching. Guards are firing weapons into the crowd. The boom of gunfire and ugly shouts float on the breeze.

We drop anchor across-river and Jemmy helps me board a small boat, which his men lower with ropes into the water.

'The tide will rest you up over there,' he says, pointing to a grassy bank with a few cows. 'You can cross the bridge by foot and avoid whatever's happening at the gate. Be careful,' he says, with sudden feeling. 'Paris ... It's no longer safe to be out of doors. Get inside before dusk.'

I nod my thanks and set my oars.

'I'll be here at dusk two days from now,' he says. 'I've an order to fulfil. If you're here, I'll take you.'

I catch the subtext. He won't wait if I don't arrive before sunset.

'Thank you,' I say, pulling back and rowing away from the ship.

He tips his tricorn hat but he doesn't wave. A blast booms all around.

As I'm trying to determine the direction of the threat I see Jemmy race to the prow and cup his hands to his mouth.

'Row!' comes his voice. 'Row!'

Confused, I tighten my grip on the oars and plunge them downwards. But before I can gain a hold, a volley of musket fire from the shore forces me to take cover. I duck clumsily, losing both oars to the river. And as I stagger to my feet, another wave hits, tumbling me back again. This time I fall more heavily, knocking my head on the little wooden seat.

It's probably a grenade, I hear myself thinking. *Someone has dropped a grenade into the river. Keep down.*

I stay down for a long moment, as residual waves batter and rock my tiny boat. When the force has passed I risk sitting up. The first thing I see is that my oars are long gone. The second is that Jemmy's ship is vacating. I see the tips of his sails beating a retreat around a bend in the river. Of course I wouldn't want him to endanger his crew trying to rescue me, but I feel a shade of betrayal all the same.

You can't expect gallantry from a pirate.

Whilst I'm considering this, I notice the explosion has turned my boat in the opposite direction and the tide is taking me away from the riverside I meant to bank at.

I paddle with my hands, but it's useless. I'm being pulled inextricably towards the shore and the chaos of the gates.

CHAPTER 26

ONCE AGAIN GRACE IS WAITING, THIS TIME IN A SUMPTUOUS upstairs drawing room of the Salon des Princes. It is finely decorated, with silk curtains framing the long windows and expensive deep-green wallpaper reaching to the high corniced ceiling. There are no other guests.

Now it is dark outside. She can see through the glass that torches have been lit in the vast grounds. Wafts of cooked meat drift from somewhere. There's a noise on the stairs, female voices. Grace's heart lifts but her hope turns to confusion. Five young girls enter the bare room. Some are seventeen or so – almost the same age as Grace, but two of them can't be older than twelve.

All are extremely thin, but dressed in the kind of aspiring bright printed dresses Grace recognizes well. Not so long ago, she was one of these girls, attending penny-school, buying her calico from smuggler taverns, sewing modish patterns by candlelight until her eyes burned.

The arrivals don't look at her, but Grace is used to social exclusion. A table is brought in and set with elaborate pastries and patisserie. Grace notices the girls' eyes grow big. She feels as though she is looking in a mirror, seeing herself five years ago.

A man in fine clothing arrives. Not a low servant, Grace decides, but she can't see him to be noble either. He wears no wig, leaving his greasy dark hair curling around his ears. Perhaps he is a butler who has inherited clothes from a fond master.

Grace has never felt so tired. Her mother used to speak of being bone tired and now she knows what it means.

The man begins to talk in a voice so grating and high-pitched that Grace misses part of the meaning, wondering at the strangeness of it. Something about midnight.

Grace works backwards, willing her mind to keep hold of the words.

They will come at midnight.

This must be it, decides Grace with relief. The house will hold its debates at twelve. She will listen carefully and try to identify a sympathetic ear.

A traitorous voice whispers that something untoward is happening, but she drives it down. Grace lives with the daily memory of her London social blunders; Godwin masking his mortification. She won't embarrass herself again in front of fine people. Best to stay silent.

Exhaustion sweeps over her in a great wave. She forces her eyes wide open. Surely midnight cannot be too far away.

She notices something else about the girls now. They don't talk to her, but they don't talk to one another, either. They stand, shuffling uncomfortably, chewing fingernails, biting lips.

Now that she considers it, Grace realizes, they all look frightened.

CHAPTER 27

MY LANDING IN THE LITTLE ROWING BOAT NEAR THE customs gate was eventful. It cost me every gold ring to bribe my way past some drunken officials, but I gauged it more sensible than attracting attention to myself by killing them. I left as a dedicated pack of stone masons began work on the stone gate, chiselling away the images of monarchy.

I made my way to Montmartre easily enough. But now I look at the half-timbered buildings and accept that I'm lost. I've been walking around for an hour and none of the streets are named. I can't understand it. Even in this down-at-heel part of the town I'd thought there would be signs bearing the street names. But they seem to have gone.

I came here by way of the grand houses that characterize Paris. They dropped away to ramshackle wooden dwellings, leaning into one another for support, jumbled in with the *pieds-à-terre* of wealthy men-about-town – the Montmartre district I knew well ten years ago. Music drifts out, violins, soulful singing. Through candlelit windows I catch snatches of naked flesh, laughing faces, wine being poured.

I notice many shop signs swinging overhead. The shaped

kind are now illegal in London – the huge plaster tooth for the dentist, a great iron key for the locksmith, a barrel for the cooper. Too many heads have been broken from falling signs.

I guess in Montmartre this wouldn't be a problem since a disproportionate number are hanging coffins and trios of gold spheres: pawnbrokers for the poor to raise capital; funeral houses where they can loan accessories to bury their dead – a rough-woven pall to cover the body, perhaps handles for the coffin.

A little group of table-dancing girls walk by in corsets and stockings, swinging their collection bucket as they decide the next inn to try. Somewhere I can hear a play being performed.

From deeper in the city, shouts rift the air. Something began happening as darkness descended, something violent, and I've a bad feeling it's headed to the unconventional area I'm currently failing to navigate.

I ask a maid scurrying to work where I might find the Place Louis XVI. But she only looks at me blankly and runs on, muttering something about it being dangerous to speak of the King. My address is for Rue Monsieur-le-Prince but I can't find it anywhere.

The shouts have become noticeably louder now. Light on the near horizon has taken on a peculiarly luminous hue, as though a lot of torches were assembling only a few streets away.

I pass a large white-stone house with a plaster crest above the wide wood door and something draws my attention. The surname has been painted over. I can still make out the gold letters beneath. *Artois* – one of the wealthiest houses in France.

I stop for a moment and stare, trying to tune out the ominous growing crowd noise which comes from every direction.

It's not vandalism. The painting-over is neat, as though the family themselves have paid for this to be done.

A drumbeat starts up and with it a great round of ugly cheers. I hear the sound of glass shattering and a boisterous drunken sort of melody. It can only be a street or so away.

I force myself to concentrate. Why should the Artois family paint out their own name? There's a nameless threat here, floating on the air.

I can hear the song now – near, too near. I listen. They're singing the same two words over and over. '*Ca ira!*' they shout. '*Ca ira!*'

I translate the meaning: 'It'll be fine.'

This itself is bizarrely threatening. A mob raging the streets, breaking glass, chanting at the top of their lungs that all will be well.

Once again I regret my choice of dress. The silk pinstripe marks me out as noble. And just as I'm thinking this there's a rumble that is no longer on the distance. The drumming is joined by screams and shouts. I need to get inside.

A school memory floats back to me from my time in the French convent, a bawdy sort of joke song that the local merchants sometimes sang. About the King's lack of virility and Marie Antoinette's sexual proclivities.

> *The roads of Paris*
> *Are a Hanover Royal marriage*
> *The Queen joins the King,*
> *The Prince comes a long time after!*

Something occurs to me. I take out my fan and follow the streets with my finger. Just as in the song, the Rue de la Reine spirals out from the Place Louis XVI and Rue Monsieur-le-Prince runs beneath that. The shapes of the roads match the ones I've walked down, I'm certain.

I think back to the defaced noble home. Could it be that the streets themselves have received the same treatment? The royal names painted out?

Quickly I look back at my fan. If I'm right, I'm almost on Angelina's street. I run for it, just as torchlight spills around the corner. More glass shatters and I hear a door being beaten in.

'This way!' shouts a man with a rough voice. 'There's a lady out of doors!'

I turn to see a tall figure is pointing in my direction.

'Make 'er pay 'er taxes!' decides an unseen drunk voice behind him that could be male or female.

I break into a run. I think I can see Angelina's house now: four storeys, with a view across the rooftops. But I see it's all wrong, just as a mob bursts on to the street.

My heart sinks. Angelina wrote to me as a kept mistress in a fine townhouse. She must have moved without telling me. This residence is a huge, gaudy brothel.

CHAPTER 28

I'M STARING AT WHAT USED TO BE ANGELINA'S HOUSE, barely able to believe what I'm seeing.

Someone has caked the outside of this large building in a strange three-dimensional sculpture, made from plaster of Paris. A great yawning devil-mouth encompasses the bottom storey and the door I stand at. Angels and devils flutter upwards. The modelling works along the full façade, as though the structure below has been gobbled up by demonic forces.

It's the most shameless brothel I've ever seen. Candles wink in the windows and the high strain of pretend laughter drifts forth.

The first of the group round the corner and I feel rough hands seize me from behind. I'm too surprised even to swing my blade. Instead, I'm dragged backwards, my boots kicking impotently in front of me.

'Stop struggling,' says a woman's voice, with a strong Parisian accent. 'You'll rip your nice dress.'

I'm being bundled into a huge immaculate hallway, lit with more candles than I've ever seen in one place. The door closes behind me. The firelight of the mob vanishes.

I feel myself released and turn to see a girl wearing an outrageous outfit and the slightly dead-eyed expression common to brothel workers.

'It's dangerous out of doors,' she admonishes.

'I'm looking for someone,' I say. 'Angelina Mazarin.'

The girl picks up a crate of candles from the hallway and hefts it.

'She's the mistress here,' she says. 'Come on. I'll take you to her.'

I'm absorbing my surroundings and what they mean as I follow the half-dressed girl along the corridor. Angelina became a kept mistress in Paris. She never told me anything about a brothel.

We break into a cosy cavern-like room filled with young Parisian men – artists and writers, if their eccentric dress is anything to go by. Candle-holders are fastened into the walls, giving low warm lighting. And floating over it all is the unmistakable strains of Angelina singing.

It's a sound of pure emotion and the memory of it leaves me breathless. She's sat behind a battered pianoforte, atop of which is a squat candelabra, which hides her face. Peeking above is her auburn hair arranged in two whirls on her forehead, with exquisitely detailed silk flowers holding it in place. As always, everyone in the room is transfixed.

When Angelina sings, it's as though there's a silver pool of light around her.

She stops mid-line and the spell is broken.

'Attica?' Her eyes are fixed on me. She is small, Angelina, for such a heavy voice. Her eyes are large and fairy-like, blue pools in the perfectly white oval of her leaded face. The generous lips I remember are shrunk to an inch-wide bee-sting of vermillion lip-paint. A tiny moon of black felt is stuck to the pronounced apex of her upper cheek.

My breath catches. There's a lump in my throat I wasn't expecting. The memory of us stealing the nun's sour white wine, drinking it with feet dangling into the river outside our convent school. I hadn't realized it, until now: I'd been happy.

How could I have told Jemmy this was nothing? She was everything.

She leans forward and blows out the candelabra. Greasy smoke rises.

Angelina stands, sways, catching herself against the side of the pianoforte and resting a hand to support herself. She's drunk, of course. I'd forgotten that. You can never tell when she sings.

'Gentlemen,' says Angelina, her consonants blurring a little, 'here she is. The girl who broke my heart.'

CHAPTER 29

THE ATMOSPHERE IN ANGELINA'S LOW-LIT ROOM IS AS thick as the candle smoke. Faces switch back to me with interest. I cross the room towards her. Angelina's face ripples with a hundred different expressions as I near.

She is dressed in a gauzy white dress that is almost completely transparent. It ends mid-thigh and her white stockings are tied above the knee with red ribbon.

'Do you remember,' she says loudly as I draw close, eyes locked on me, 'what we did on this pianoforte?'

Behind us, I sense a little ripple of expectation travel around the room. Angelina always did play to her audience. They're wondering if things will erupt.

'I remember everything,' I say, kissing her lightly on either side of the face. 'I even remember how beautiful you are,' I add, 'without all this paint.'

I draw back a little, absorbing her face, taking a light grip of her forearms.

'Do you really think I would forget my first love?' I say.

Her twisted mouth softens. She tilts her head, animosity melting away.

'*You* were always in love with Atherton,' she mutters. But she looks pleased, all the same. 'My friend from England,' says Angelina, raising her voice to the crowd. 'Shall we toast in her honour? Some English drink? Whisky?'

She catches my expression.

'Don't be like that, Attica. Spirits sober me up. I have cognac with my morning rolls nowadays.'

The knot of drunken men, disappointed now, are drifting away to have more drama. Now the song is finished, they peel away on the arms of half-naked girls, heading either up the gilded stairwell or back out into the hallway.

'Ah, but it's good to see you,' Angelina enthuses in her soft little voice. She kisses me hard on both cheeks. 'I wish you had never left.' She lifts her eyes to mine and there is the Angelina I remember. The vulnerability I always wanted to enfold in my arms and defend.

'I didn't want to leave,' I say.

Angelina pouts a little. 'Oh, him,' she says. 'It was only jealousy made me do it.' She looks at me again. 'Did you marry Atherton?'

I shake my head. Her eyes widen.

'But you were like two fingers in a glove. Chattering away about things no one else understood. All those letters he wrote ...'

'He married someone else.'

I must have said it more bluntly than I intended. Angelina flinches.

'I'm sorry,' she says softly. 'Not even an affair?' she adds hopefully.

'Neither of us would compromise the other.' How can I explain? I was different when she knew me. It was before I'd killed anyone.

Angelina notices my taking in the gaudy decorations and lurid candlelight and smiles.

'Of course my old protector became bored,' she explains with a brittle laugh. 'It was nice while it lasted.' She gives a little shrug of her narrow shoulders. 'My house falls somewhere between an entertainment hall and a brothel, I suppose.' She looks wistful as she says this, as though this distinction represents the death of some dream of hers. 'It's a little game, you see. Heaven and hell. Various rooms for different tastes. And different purses, of course.'

I make out a staircase towards the back, ostentatiously styled with gilding and white feathers as a stairway to heaven.

'The cheap seats are downstairs?' I guess.

'Dancers, a little theatre and a flash of something you shouldn't see if you're lucky,' she agrees. 'Really it's nothing more than a damp little cellar with false fire and brimstone. Upstairs is luxury. Heaven.' She smiles to suggest this also is the barest of illusions. 'We had local artists make the front for us cheaply. They haul plaster up from beneath the city for a few centimes a sack,' she adds. 'Montmartre is so riddled with gypsum mines now it's amazing we don't all collapse underground.'

I'm picturing the plaster of Paris excavations, running like a honeycomb under our feet, when we're interrupted by the arrival of two men, young and laughing.

'What about her?' one of them asks Angelina, looking at me. 'Is she downstairs or upstairs?'

Angelina is greatly amused by this.

'Oh, you mustn't trouble Attica,' she says with a laugh. 'She'd have you both for breakfast.'

She turns back to me as they stagger down into the cellar.

'Come with me,' she says, taking my hand. And she leads me up the shallow steps of the broad gilded staircase to Heaven.

CHAPTER 30

Women dressed in gauzy celestial dresses are waiting to greet patrons on the first floor. They nod to Angelina as she passes.

Arrayed on plump cushions are several bored-looking girls. They are naked apart from Grecian sandals and angel wings of white goose-feather strapped under their breasts. A few stand at the windows to lure men. Sheep-gut condoms float in a gold bowl on a table, soaking in warm milk. Another dish contains honey and cedar oil – a pox-stultifying mixture for internal application.

The air hangs with the same fetid smell I always associate with brothels. Somehow, no matter how many fine fabrics and furnishings, the scent of male lust pervades.

There is a chamber pot in the corner and Angelina lifts it up and moves to the nearest window.

'You must keep these empty,' she tells the girls, opening the casement and heaving the contents of the pot into the street below.

'My private room is down the hall,' she says, setting it down. 'This way.'

We pass braziers burning scented oils and an ornately legged table laid with fruit, marzipans and huge tiered cakes.

Angelina turns the handle of a grand door and leads us both inside.

'This used to be my music room,' she explains, looking at the frenzied decadence of gold and silk furnishings. I smile. Angelina never did quite master the noble art of less is more. She can't help but show she has money. For her, it is evidence she is loved.

'So tell me—' Angelina begins, then stops suddenly, her face wary. 'It is nothing,' she decides.

'Angelina,' I say, 'I'm looking for an English girl. Her name is Grace. She's my cousin.'

'I think I remember you speaking of Grace,' says Angelina. 'Wasn't it her idea to put firecrackers in that copper pan?'

'She's much better behaved nowadays, more's the pity. I think she may have gone to the Salon des Princes, expecting a debating chamber.'

Angelina moves to the door and puts her finger to her lips. Having checked there's no one listening outside she heaves it shut with her slender arms. She trips lightly back to where I stand and lowers her voice.

'The Salon des Princes is different now,' she advises. 'Madame Roland ... She holds her own little court there, amongst the debauchery. Even last week, I might have got you inside. But it is all changing. The King has granted a constitution to the people. The nobles are less certain of things.'

This is an unexpected setback. I'd been sure Angelina could get me access to the infamous salon.

We're interrupted by a fanfare from the street. Angelina gasps. 'He is here,' she whispers, horrified. 'I didn't think it was so late ...'

'Who is it?' I move to the window, frowning. Outside a ludicrously decadent carriage has pulled up. It is flanked by a number of armed men. Someone is taking no chances in this district.

'Why, my keeper, of course,' she says.

'I thought ...' I glance again at the street below. I had assumed she ran the house independently. 'Who is keeping you now?'

'Foulon,' she whispers, looking sick. 'Foulon keeps me.'

'The royalist finance minister?' I'm frowning, scrolling through my knowledge of French politics.

Angelina is nodding.

'But he is an old man,' I say, a cold feeling in the pit of my stomach. 'Ancient.'

'Foulon came with his guards one night,' says Angelina, her eyes sliding to the door. 'He told me if I didn't ...' She swallows. 'If I didn't do what he liked, he would have me thrown in the Bastille.'

'He cannot threaten to imprison you for no crime!' A fierce, powerless fury burns in me. I can't stand to think of Angelina in the stale embrace of this ancient lecher.

'This is not England, Attica,' says Angelina. 'Our King can lock away anyone without trial.'

A heavy door bangs downstairs and we hear Foulon's guards enter the house. The sound sparks a new note of panic in Angelina.

'Attica, he is so dangerous,' she says. 'If he doesn't like you, he could have you tortured and worse—'

She's interrupted by a loud knock on the door. Angelina blanches. I've never seen her look so afraid.

'That's him,' she whispers. 'It's Foulon. Foulon is here.'

CHAPTER 31

IN HIS SMALL OFFICE, ROBESPIERRE SITS HUNCHED OVER his plain desk.

The light begins to flicker. He looks to see his candle has burned to a stub. Outside, the sun is rising.

Papers are piled neatly. One is written in English and annotated in French. It bears the words, *Queen's diamonds.*

He moves a pile of documents and searches.

The diamonds.

It's an image of the lost necklace of Marie Antoinette. He holds up the picture: drooping swags of jewels.

'Two million francs,' says Robespierre aloud, 'that can be fitted into the palm of a hand. A trinket that could buy the King all the weapons and troops he needs,' he concludes, 'to rule with an iron fist.'

Robespierre pinches at his long mouth with thin fingers. He had suspected all along that the English had got hold of them.

He can't be certain, but Robespierre guesses the diamonds are back in France. Gaspard de Mayenne was involved somehow.

There is an idea to depose the King and put the Duc d'Orléans on the throne. Orléan's sexual indiscretions and flashy clothing are surpassed only by his strange obsession with English manners and democracy.

Robespierre moves some papers towards him, shuffles them, racks them perfectly straight and then slides free the top document.

He stands and walks to a locked bureau. Robespierre is a collector, a connoisseur. Here, neatly filed, are his favourites.

Two are in German, in such elegant, pleasing cipher they were almost impossible to break.

Four letters were written by an Englishman named Atherton, a retired naval officer of exceptional intelligence with a gift for inventing, lock-picking and ciphers. His battalion of hand-picked spies are assigned to all corners of the globe.

Robespierre's hand falls to his greatest prize, perfectly preserved between sheets of card.

This is *The Letter.* From Him. The unknown man. The man whose code has so far been unbreakable. Robespierre has been edging away at it for over a year. Sometimes he thinks he has made headway. But these have been only false dawns.

What he has had better success with is the provenance of the letter. It is from someone Atherton writes to. Someone *important.* A person who has a genius for coding that is entirely unique. He believes the prodigy is English, but operated in Russia until recently.

Robespierre decides it reasonable to assume this code-breaker must have been instrumental in Gaspard's escape and return to Paris.

He lifts The Letter reverently. It is worn and folded from so much study. The failure to solve the code and identify the coder haunts Robespierre. It keeps him awake at night. But in some strange counter way it makes him feel alive.

CHAPTER 32

I REMEMBER, AS A GIRL, THE FIRST TIME I WENT TO A play, seeing the actors in their thick paint and painted cheeks. And as Foulon throws open the door of Angelina's parlour, for a moment, I think he is an actor, fresh from stage.

Reality slots into place. And after that, horror. Because Foulon is at least seventy years of age. Ancient, thin and sinewy, his aged face is thickly coated in white make-up. His sunken cheeks are rouged like an English prostitute and his preposterously frilled and ribboned clothing reeks of heavy perfume.

I have an awful image of him pawing at Angelina. I'm so transfixed by the yellowed fang-like teeth poking through the purple-painted lips.

'Angelina, you've brought me a little morsel,' he's saying with a vulpine grin.

Foulon uses a jewelled walking stick, which I assume is an affectation until I realize he needs it to prevent himself tripping on the enormous ruffled ribbons of his silk shoes.

My face must give me away, because Angelina gives an imperceptible shake of her head. *No, Attica, don't.*

'My coat,' he tells her, frowning. 'Angelina, you seem quick to forget how you are protected.' He looks at me. 'Did she tell you about our outing?'

Angelina bites her lip. 'Monsieur Foulon was good enough to allow me to see a punishment at the Bastille,' she says, not meeting my eye. 'A young boy.' Her eyes are filled with tears at the memory.

I think of Gaspard de Mayenne. Perhaps he was already lying in the mortuary as Foulon flaunted his powerful associations.

She helps Foulon off with his lace-trimmed coat, forcing a smile as he pushes a hand inside her dress. Foulon lowers his creaking limbs into a velvet armchair.

'And whom have you brought for my amusement?' he asks, eyeing me up and down.

Angelina lifts a decanter, almost stumbling to get in between us. I think she's worried I'll do something rash. With clumsy hands she pours wine and hands a drink to each of us.

'This is Attica Morgan, an old friend from Convent School,' she says.

I curtsey with deliberate formality.

'Monsieur Foulon,' I say, keeping my expression polite and my accent flawless country-French, 'I am enchanted to meet you.'

'You have heard I am the King's appointed finance minister?' he demands.

'I have told Attica how active you have been, maintaining the old order,' says Angelina quickly.

'The peasants hate me for speaking the truth,' explains Foulon proudly. 'The people say they are starving. Those rascals always claim to be deprived. So I say eat the grass if you are hungry.'

I wait uncertainly, watching for the cue I should laugh. I catch Angelina's expression and I realize he isn't joking. This disgusting old man really does believe it.

'Monsieur Foulon,' I say, fighting to keep my voice even, 'people cannot eat grass.'

'You or I could not,' agrees Foulon, 'our constitutions are too fine. But peasant people can. They have become entitled and impertinent, eating bread. I've told the King I think it best we cut their wheat supplies completely.'

'Attica has had a long journey and is greatly fatigued,' says Angelina quickly, moving to my side. 'I must take her to my room to get some rest.' She begins to pull me away from Foulon.

Her elderly protector smiles his dark-lipped smile. 'Not yet, my darling.' His small eyes narrow as he considers, receding into his aged face. 'I think I should get better aquatinted with your guest.' There's a snake-like quality to him now. A cunning.

'Go upstairs,' he says to Angelina after a moment, 'put on the dress I like.'

I feel a flash of pure hatred for him, showing off now, lauding his power over Angelina. She nods wordlessly and leaves the room.

Now it's just him and me. My heart beats faster. I wonder what he means by getting me alone. In an English house this would be an unthinkable discourtesy; but we're not in England and French nobles have a much looser notion of entitlement.

I notice my knuckles are white around the stem of my wine glass. Deliberately I relax my fingers.

'Engleesh,' says Foulon, speaking the word in a strong French accent, 'are you not?'

'You are very clever to have discerned it,' I say. 'I spent many years in France. I'm told my French is flawless.'

'It was not your voice that gave you away,' says Foulon. He's looking alert now. 'It's your demeanour. The way you carry yourself.' He taps his nose, causing powder to fall. 'I notice such things.'

Foulon sips wine through his darkly pursed lips. He knocks on the floor with his walking stick. The door opens and a dour-looking servant appears.

'Tell my guards to wait outside Angelina's bedchamber,' he says, not taking his eyes from me. 'My little songstress is not to leave.' The servant vanishes.

Not a question. Foulon regards me thoughtfully.

My heart is pounding, a slow, steady beat.

'You've come because of the diamonds.' He says it flatly.

'Why should you think that?' I ask, sipping wine.

'Why,' Foulon concludes, 'because Monsieur Robespierre told me.'

CHAPTER 33

THE CANDLES IN ANGELINA'S ELEGANT ROOM BURN LOW and the air feels warm. Any pretence of guest and host has vanished and I'm wondering desperately what Foulon knows. The thought overtaking all others is that I need to protect Angelina. My usual rational mindset is jumping and sliding.

Foulon watches me, assessing. The flame throws shadows on his painted face, making him look like a dead-eyed puppet.

'A man was found dead in the Bastille with a diamond in his mouth,' says Foulon, rolling his wine glass around his hand. 'A rebel named Gaspard de Mayenne.' He's watching for my reaction.

'The rebels were sending us a message,' he says. 'Someone powerful. They were telling us: we can go anywhere we please, even inside the unbreakable prison. We have money enough that a priceless diamond is nothing. And we can even kill one of yours, an aristocrat.'

I gauge it safest to say nothing and there's a tense pause as I wait for Foulon to continue.

'No foreigners are getting in or out of Paris,' he goes on, 'yet you arrive here, days after Monsieur Robespierre warns us of an English diamond smuggler. A woman. Angelina will pay for her treachery,' he adds spitefully. 'You shall watch. France is no place for rebels, Mademoiselle Morgan, no matter what you might have been led to believe.'

'Who is Monsieur Robespierre?' I ask, playing for time. I've never heard that name, which is unusual. I thought I knew every significant name in Paris, even those no one else knows are important.

'Robespierre is a lawyer,' says Foulon with a slight smile. 'A very intelligent man.'

There is something guarded about his tone. I'm sure I detect a spark of fear in his eyes.

'How can you be so sure his information is accurate?' I enquire, my heart beating fast. This Robespierre, whoever he is, has acquired dangerous intelligence. It occurs to me there could be a link between the elusive Society of Friends and this mysterious lawyer.

'Robespierre is never wrong,' says Foulon, looking down. 'And he is a wolf dressed as a sheep – is that not how you English say it? Such a *humane* man.' He rolls the word in his mouth disgustedly. 'Frightened of blood. Has made speeches against the death penalty. But cowards do the worst horrors, you may be sure of it. Already he winds himself tight into the heart of it all. He makes himself indispensable to all of us.'

Foulon looks at me. 'Robespierre says the English are plotting. They mean to use the Queen's long-lost necklace to undermine the Crown. And now an Englishwoman arrives in my house pretending to be French, a woman who is not who she claims to be. I tell you again,' he leans forward, 'you've come because of the diamonds.'

'I have no idea what you mean.'

His eyes lock on mine. 'Make no mistake, this is a war now,' he says. 'Those commoners invaded the King's Palace. Can you imagine,' he says, 'what two million francs could do in the hands of the enemy?'

'By enemy,' I say, my voice thick with contempt, 'do you refer to the people of France?'

'Those who stand against the King are traitors!' Foulon smashes a fist into his hand. 'If some rebel faction gets those diamonds they could buy an army!' He grips his walking cane, consumed by this fearful scenario.

'No more talking,' he decides. 'Let us call for Angelina. I'm sure my guards can persuade her to talk.'

I'm pushing down my fears for Angelina, searching for a solution. Something else occurs to me: an obvious way to use Monsieur Foulon to my own advantage.

'I don't have the diamonds,' I say. 'You have the wrong Englishwoman.'

Foulon lifts his stick to rap on the floor.

'But I know the person whom Robespierre refers to,' I continue, looking him dead in the eye. 'And I can show you where to find her. But first, you must take me to the Salon des Princes.'

CHAPTER 34

At the Salon des Princes, midnight approaches.

Wine is served and Grace finds herself drinking glass after glass without meaning to.

Emboldened by drink, she looks at the other girls from the corner of her eye. She has the feeling they are doing the same to her, assessing the mask of smallpox scars around her eyes, her dress, her shoes.

Grace notices the girls seem only preoccupied with their appearance, straightening caps, adjusting petticoats. A troop of drunk men file into the room and her heartbeat increases. There is a look of venal expectation on the men's faces.

A servant arrives with a tray on which rests several covered dishes. One of the girls moves forward, takes a dish, lifts the lid and breathes in the contents.

The girl coughs, then turns to Grace, her eyes slightly glassy, weaving a little.

'Take some,' she suggests. 'It will help you.' Her breath has a strange sour note to it.

Grace looks to see other girls taking dishes. She takes one, a ceramic dish in the Chinois style, no doubt worth some preposterous sum. Her main thought is not to drop it. The lid makes a tinkling sound as she lifts it. Grace frowns. Underneath is a sponge. She sees the other girls are lowering their heads, sniffing. Grace does the same. She has learned the hard way, it is better to do as others do, in polite company.

'Ether,' she hears someone say as the smell hits her nose. She's seized by a sensation of warm well-being.

Nothing matters, she realizes with a surging sense of detachment. Grace takes another deep inhale. Euphoria swells. She looks up to see the other girls smiling, laughing with her.

'It is good?' asks one in halting English, her mouth soft like a plum.

Grace giggles in reply.

That's when Grace sees the men pointing. The weasel-butler-man arrives at her side. He pulls her roughly, in a way she has seen men do with whores at the dockside.

His eyes fall to her betrothal ring.

'Take that off,' he hisses, moving his hand to pull it from her finger. 'No one will believe you're a virgin if you wear that.'

Shock and fear resound somewhere deep and far away in Grace. It is muffled, buffered by the warm clouds of ether.

Grace feels the man take her ring and push it into her palm, but it is as though it were happening to someone else.

'Spotless pure,' the butler is saying. 'Bidding.'

Men have begun cheering, gathering in. Grace dimly notices they hold raised purses. The butler reaches in front and pulls down the top of her dress in one rough movement.

There is a thump. Grace looks down. The pouch with the diamonds has fallen from inside her dress and lies on the wooden floor.

Grace stands in complete shock, exposed to the crowd. Leering men eyeing her nakedness, others waving money. The haze begins to lift. Her scattered thoughts are gaining solidity and form.

A middle-aged man in a white wig takes her hand to more cheers. He raises it in triumph.

'You are mine now,' he tells Grace, fingers closing on hers. 'I bought you.'

He leads her from the room and it is only when he drags her inside a bedroom that she begins to protest, pulling against him.

The man's grip is immediately vicelike.

'You'll be paid after,' he says. 'No sense changing your mind now.'

His hold on her intensifies as he pulls her towards the bed, bringing his other hand to pin her arms to her side.

'No ...' says Grace. But he pushes her down. He is surprisingly heavy.

Grace is too shocked to scream. And then she begins shouting, in English at first and then she switches to French.

He lifts a hand off her arm, to pull up her skirts. Grace takes the chance to flail her free hand, smacking and hitting at him. It's embarrassingly futile, glancing off him.

Grace knows with a sickening certainty that this is how it's going to happen. Not on her wedding bed, with the man she loves, under the coverlet she stitched herself. But here, in this strange house, with this wine-soaked stranger. With a kind of detachment she feels him wedge his knee between her legs, the silken cloth of his breeches on her bare skin.

A great wave of exhaustion overtakes her. It's the first time she's lain down in days. Her bones are sinking against her tired muscles. She wonders if perhaps she might just fall asleep, spiral into unconsciousness and let this terrible thing happen in a realm she's not part of. Grace is floating, dreamlike images coming to her.

She sees her docker grandpappy in their small Bristol house.

'If anyone gives yer trouble, Gracey, stick it to 'em with a hairpin,' he would tell her with a wicked grin. She had laughed, knowing she would never need his advice.

Then Grace remembers: she has a hairpin securing what is left of her hair arrangement.

Grace frees the three-inch pin and insinuates it under her assailant. The pins twists around jabbing him briefly in the thigh. He yelps and pulls back slightly. His expression darkens. He slaps her forcefully enough to make her head spin, then moves to grab at her weapon, his weight still pushing her into the bed.

Grace stabs the pin deep and hard, exactly in the place her grandpappy advised.

The man makes a noise she has never heard before, an animal cry of despair. Grace wriggles free, her pin still buried to the hilt in her attacker.

Grace breaks from the room and runs headlong into the corridor, her only thought to get out from this dreadful house. She collides with a wall of perfumed silk, then realizes she has crashed into a woman.

'You poor child!' says the woman, taking in Grace's ripped dress and crazed expression. 'Come with me.'

CHAPTER 35

I TELL FOULON'S GUARDS THEY ARE NO LONGER NEEDED outside Angelina's door. They peel away uncertainly.

When I knock on the door, she opens it just a crack, her pale frightened face appearing in the gap.

'Thank God,' she says. 'I thought Foulon would have his men arrest you.'

'He's asleep.' She sags in relief against the doorframe.

'What happened?'

'Foulon agreed to take me to the Salon des Princes tomorrow,' I tell her, smiling. 'He even boasted how the owner's wife, Madame Roland, was once a great lover of his.'

Angelina rolls her eyes.

'And then?' she asks.

'Then he unwisely tried to outdrink me.'

Angelina smiles. She looks ten years younger.

'That's my Attica,' she says.

'Angelina,' I say, 'have you heard of a man named Robespierre? A lawyer?'

'Of course. Robespierre is a lawyer who makes speeches against tyranny. He even believes in equality of the sexes. The women line up to hear him. He is exceptionally clever. And a hoarder of information,' she adds. 'Those who speak against him will find contradictory things they said five years ago thrown back at them, word perfect.'

I absorb this.

'Something about how Foulon spoke of him wasn't right,' I say. 'Foulon seemed ... frightened of him.'

'No,' says Angelina, 'Foulon is frightened of no one. Like you.' She tilts her head, smiles.

'Has Foulon ever spoken of a man named Gaspard de Mayenne?'

'The man who makes pictures against the old order?'

'That's him.'

'Foulon has said nothing to me,' says Angelina, 'but it's all over Paris: Gaspard was found dead in the Bastille. The governor claims he had nothing to do with it but rumour has it that the King had Gaspard tortured to death for returning to Paris.'

'My uncle believes the murder was a warning to the English,' I say grimly, 'of what is planned for Grace. There was a plot and she was involved in smuggling diamonds.'

Angelina's eyebrows lift slightly at the mention of the famous jewels.

'Might Robespierre have reason to kill Gaspard de Mayenne?' I ask, thinking through possibilities.

'Oh, never! They were friends, very much in support of one another's opinions. Besides, Robespierre is an idealist and against the death penalty. He would hardly resort to murder, even if Gaspard was his strongest opponent.'

'Wouldn't he want the diamonds to further the rebel cause?' I suggest.

Angelina laughs at this, but it's a nervous laugh. 'Oh, Monsieur Robespierre cannot be bought,' she says, 'not for any price. He is *incorruptible*.'

I consider this.

'I think whoever killed Gaspard is looking for the Queen's diamonds,' I say, 'which means they are looking for Grace.'

Angelina's expression darkens.

'Then you are looking for royalists,' says Angelina with certainty. 'No rebel would want Gaspard dead, you can be sure of it.'

Angelina is looking at me expectantly, her hand on the doorframe.

'Come with me tomorrow,' I say impulsively. 'It's not safe here.'

She smiles. 'Oh, Attica, you may not see it yet, but we are at war and must all fight for what we believe.'

'There is nothing you can do about a grain shortage,' I say. 'No amount of fighting will put bread in those people's bellies.'

She takes hold of my wrist affectionately.

'I thought you of all people would understand,' she says quietly. 'This isn't about food. It's about freedom.'

A feeling of loss passes between us. For the first time ever I have a sense that she is French and I English. That we are on different sides.

'I never did know what was happening in that clever head of yours.' Angelina reaches a hand and taps the side of my face.

I look into the room behind her, to the large four-poster swagged with red silk.

'I'm thinking,' I say, 'that bed looks more comfortable than your pianoforte. Aren't you going to invite me in?'

CHAPTER 36

It's morning in Paris as Foulon and I roll along in the carriage. Traders are out in force: milkmaids leading their cows from door to door, coffee-sellers ladling from their rolling cauldrons, fish girls with baskets on their heads.

With every second that passes, my dislike for Foulon grows. It began when his leering driver fitted the horses with heavy leather straps to reduce their speed, so 'his master might have a better view of any pretty girls'.

Then Foulon himself arrived, after two hours of primping, his ghost-white face slashed with deep vermillion lip-paint, eyes red rings from where his make-up has irritated. His outfit was all leaf-green and lace, from his silk shoes and suede gloves to the curling feather in his tall hat.

Foulon wedged his ancient limbs so close to me on the velvet seats he'd shed powder on my dress and begun incessantly boasting about his ridiculous carriage, an activity he hasn't yet ceased, despite my pointedly silent responses.

'I imagine you have nothing so high-wheeled in London,' he crows. 'And these glass-paned windows would be large for many homes. It took four months to have the gold frames carved and gold-leafed.'

The vehicle would indeed earn acclaim in London, but not of the kind Foulon imagines. The ornamentation is so ludicrous we could have driven straight out of fairyland. Every wooden inch from wheel to roof carries gilded carvings of flowers and fruit, ribbons and bows. Side panels have been painted rococo style with turquoise enamel. It all but drips with opulence as we roll along, like a fat little over-iced pudding.

A pamphleteer appears suddenly at the open window, waving some dog-eared booklets.

'Wanna hear what Marie Antoinette gets up to with her ladies-in-waiting?' he asks. 'There's pictures. All here, in the latest libelle.'

I eye the title he proffers: *The Austrian Bitch and the Royal Orgy*.

'Get back,' shouts Foulon, 'before I have my driver flog you!' He raps on the roof and a horsewhip is dangled menacingly down. The pamphleteer backs away, muttering furiously.

'This is because of that tennis court impudence,' rages Foulon as we jolt away from the scene. 'Those gutter rats never would have *dared* approach my carriage with their treasonous filth. Now they act as though they are equals!'

Through the glass I see the pamphleteer shouting, pointing at our gaudy vehicle. Faces on the street are turning towards us. Hungry people, angry people. Foulon doesn't seem to notice. He begins opening compartments, revealing little treasure boxes of jewel-bright candied fruit and nuts in a glossy caramel coating.

'These oranges were sugared in Seville,' he tells me, pushing one through his yellow teeth. He leans forward again and lifts white wine from a silver bucket. 'Chilled with Pyrenees snow, from my icehouse,' he explains, as frost slides from the sweating bottle. 'Usually there is a man to pour, but I thought it better just you and I.'

He gives me a lascivious grin and I realize in shock that he imagines I have some kind of designs on him that go beyond transport to the Salon des Princes.

We're being followed by pamphleteers now, I notice. The plodding pace of Foulon's plumed horses makes it easy for them to keep up with us as we near the east city gate.

Something ugly is building. The spectacular carriage is whipping up a frenzy of bad feeling and dragging it along behind us.

'No thank you.' I haven't taken my eyes off the Paris streets. Something is happening ahead of us, a problem at the city gate.

We are caught between a disgruntled mob and soldiers guarding the way out of Paris. Something tells me this is an explosive combination.

'Your outfit is very becoming.' Foulon has changed tack now, openly leering at the rather transparent layers of my dress.

Angelina has dressed me in a white calico with narrow red and blue stripes, a deep cherry-coloured silk scarf cinching my waist and a blousy sheaf of muslin in a low-cut collar at the neck. My hair is tied up with a few loose-falling curls and a jaunty little shepherdess hat tilted to one side. The dress is looser fitting than English fashions, but I've managed to slide in the false boning Atherton had made, in which my fire-sticks are hidden.

Foulon's gloved hand reaches across to stroke my leg, his mouth drawn into a leer.

'I have a purse of jewels just for you,' he says, smiling encouragingly. His face shifts, his smile falling away, brows drawing together. Puzzlement, then fear.

He has felt rather than seen my knife at his groin. Sensing danger, his red-rimmed eyes drop to where the dark blade rests between his legs.

Foulon makes a noise between a grunt and a squeak.

'Now it's just the two of us,' I say pleasantly, pressing the sharp metal where his breeches join, 'let's get some things very clear. *My* price is not worth your paying.'

'All I need do,' says Foulon, flushed anger peeking the edges of his white face paint, 'is knock on the ceiling for my driver. It won't trouble him that you're a woman. In fact, he'll likely enjoy it.'

I nod, keeping my hand in place.

'You have a thick artery here,' I explain, pushing my knife slightly against it. 'One fast cut and you'll bleed to death before you realize I've ruined your silk breeches.' I move the blade an inch inward. 'Here,' I say, 'your chances are better. Half of Italian eunuchs survive their castrations. How is your singing voice?'

Foulon smiles a rage-filled lipsticked smile.

'If I were a younger man ...' he begins.

'If you were a younger man, you'd be dead,' I say. 'I'd have cut your throat last night. It's only out of respect for Angelina that you're still alive.'

'Who *are* you?' splutters Foulon.

I glance out of the window. Something is happening up ahead. The libelle-sellers seem to have whipped up a frenzy of dislike for Foulon's gilt-wheeled opulence. People are swarming closer in now, a great pack of them. A clod of mud hits the carriage.

Trouble.

'Let's just say you have misjudged things, monsieur,' I say, glancing again at the amassing hoards, 'in more ways than one. This wasn't the day to drive a golden carriage amongst starving people.'

I sigh, lifting the knife and twirling it thoughtfully.

'If you keep quiet, Monsieur Foulon,' I say, 'and don't agitate me further, I may save your life.'

CHAPTER 37

ROBESPIERRE WALKS ALONG THE SEINE, OUTSIDE THE terraces of the Tuileries Palace. He makes this journey often, past the empty rooms – the King and Queen preferring to revel in preposterous splendour twelve miles away.

In the royal absence, starving women and their babies line the walkway. Robespierre gives no money. Charity sanctions inequality.

He turns things over as he walks. Reports of all kinds have been coming to him, things he has not yet made sense of. Something has been confusing him greatly and he cannot bear to feel confused. It brings back memories best forgotten.

He notices, whilst he has been considering this disturbing fact, that his fingernails have dug little grooves into the palms of his hands.

Someone has arrived in Paris, someone who could be useful in obtaining the diamonds. The woman is a translator – one of those roles the English nobles give to spinster daughters to keep them out of trouble. He pictures her, sipping wine in spectacular foreign courts, nodding earnestly.

She was raised an English noble. Yet by all accounts she was born a slave in a large cotton-farm in Virginia. He knows from documents acquired from the plantation that she was caught up in an ill-fated uprising in which a number of slaves were brutally put down. He calls to mind the list of punishments meted out. Many he didn't fully understand, but he could guess and the guessing made his finger tremble.

She was placed in a hotbox, several times. This makes her perhaps brave, more likely stupid. Though he will settle for stubborn. Robespierre has a bit of time for stubborn.

He tries to imagine the desperate close confines of the hotbox. The American sun beating down on the tiny grave-like container sunk into the ground. He finds he cannot easily picture it.

What happened next is unclear. How the mother died is unrecorded and the daughter's impossible voyage to England even less so. Robespierre doesn't like this lack of clarity. Not at all.

He reaches his planned location: a large tree with a hole in the trunk, blasted black by lightning nineteen years ago on the inauspicious wedding day of Marie Antoinette and Louis XVI.

During the same storm, talented schoolboy Robespierre had been honoured with addressing the newly weds. The King and Queen had arrived hours late, keeping him waiting in the pelting rain, then refused to exit their carriage.

Robespierre had spoken aloud to no one, water pasting his hair to his head, his school friends ranged behind him giggling. The monarchs had left without word or sign of thanks.

Remembering his boyhood humiliation, Robespierre leans down as though he is adjusting his shoe. When he is certain no one is watching, he stands and swiftly retrieves a sealed bottle from inside the trunk.

He pulls the cork and with a slim finger, slides out a message from the glass neck. Returning the bottle to the tree, he walks away.

At a safe distance, Robespierre unfolds the message and removes a snuff box from his coat. He opens it, loads a fingertip with dark snuff and smears the powdery substance on the paper. A single word is revealed.

Robespierre studies it for a long time.

After all the waiting for Him, the man of the unbreakable code.

He reads it again to be sure he is not mistaken. But there it is. At last, he has a name.

Le Mouron.

The Pimpernel.

CHAPTER 38

THE CRIES OF THE CROWD OUTSIDE FOULON'S CARRIAGE have escalated from insults to threats. And as the city gate comes into view it suddenly becomes clear why the atmosphere is so volatile.

Four men guard the gate in the unmistakable uniform of Swiss militia.

'The King has posted a foreign guard,' I say grimly. 'He has turned on his own people for daring to request justice.'

Foulon is in a semi-trance, letting the carriage jolt him along.

'Swiss troops,' he says, licking his painted lips. 'Ingenious. Those men will not hesitate to fire on Frenchmen as our own guard might. The King shows he cannot take this tennis court insult to his authority. A bold move.'

'A foolish move,' I say. 'No wonder these people are riled up to murder.'

The carriage creaks and groans, iron wheels striking the cobbles, leather suspension straps creaking as they absorb the impact, turning towards the city gate.

'You're not a popular man, Monsieur Foulon,' I say. 'You've abused your life of privilege.' I look out of the window. I place my Mangbetu blade on the seat between us.

He looks at me, then at the knife.

'I'm hoping you'll be fool enough to grab for it,' I explain, nodding to the curved black metal. 'Then I can kill you without conscience and getting out of Paris will be a great deal easier.' I look into his frightened eyes. 'Sadly for me, I don't imagine you will,' I deduce. 'But if you are seized by bravery,' I wink at him, 'the knife is there for the taking.'

I peer outside, trying to understand what's caused the change on the streets.

The pack of people closing in on Foulon's carriage have moved back slightly, assessing the foreign guard. There's a tension in the air; neither side knows which will strike first.

I've encountered this atmosphere before – just before the revolt in Virginia – and it never bodes well.

'You need to get us through that gate,' I advise Foulon. 'Quickly.'

Ahead of us a cart and rider is being stopped. The guards search the man roughly then turn him back.

Foulon lowers the window and pokes out his wigged head.

A uniformed man approaches the carriage and bows.

'No one is allowed out, monsieur,' says the soldier, 'beg your pardon. Better go back.'

'I don't take orders from a Swiss guard,' says Foulon. 'Bring me a French soldier, someone who knows who I am.'

'Your King replaced all the Frenchmen with us Swiss,' explains the soldier.

Foulon's rage is building. 'I'm an important man,' he says. 'If I can't travel by this gate, then which might I leave the city by?'

'None today,' says the guard. 'Come again tomorrow.'

'I mean to drive through that gate and if you try to stop me, I shall instruct my driver to use force.'

'You won't get far.' The soldier shrugs amiably. 'It's not just us guards. There's more soldiers beyond the gates. No one gets out or in.'

The blood drains from Foulon's face.

'We've been instructed to go all around the wall,' continues the man conversationally.

I turn to Foulon, furious. 'This is your great and magnanimous King?' I demand. 'A man who lays siege to his own capital with a foreign guard.'

'Likely, he only increases security for his own safety ...' manages Foulon.

'Versailles is twelve miles away!' I tell Foulon. 'Surely you are not such a fool as to imagine these troops have any other purpose than to kill every Republican in Paris?' And he pays the Swiss to do it. Because even the King understands that a French guard won't massacre their own people.'

Up in front, I can see the driver panicking, flailing his whip. He's making things worse, lashing at commoners and insulting them as low-borns. The horses are tossing their heads, unsure of their direction.

I make a decision, flipping up my knife from where it lays next to Foulon and levering out two of the bejewelled boxes of candies. Holstering my blade back in my dress, in a deft movement I open the door.

Foulon's mouth opens in an 'O' of horror as the cluster of furious Parisians are revealed. As a hand reaches towards me, I launch the sugared fruit and nuts from the carriage. They scatter in a bright spray, coffers smashing in smithereens of painted wood. The children are fastest, swooping to grab the candies from the floor. They are soon elbowed aside by adults, cramming handfuls of sweets into their pockets.

In the momentary disarray, I step out of the carriage. I lift myself next to the driver at the front, holding on to my little shepherdess hat.

'Excuse me,' I say in my politest voice. The driver turns around in confusion. Before he has a chance to object, I push him hard from the driver's seat. He goes flying, legs pedalling, and lands in the muddy street.

I reach forward and give the horses an encouraging pat, then slice the restraints, holding their forelegs. The effect is instant. The animals rear in joy to be free of their restrictions and break immediately into a canter.

We're gathering speed, aiming straight at the pack of Swiss guards defending the city gate.

A pistol blast whistles past my ear as Foulon's dislodged driver fires at me.

'Not very gentlemanly,' I mutter, adjusting my hat and taking the reins in one hand.

The gunshot silences the growing crowd of protestors momentarily. And then all hell breaks loose. Accusations and threats fly at the Swiss guard. People are shouting insults at the top of their lungs. Stones are thrown. The Swiss guard hold their weapons uneasily, exchanging glances.

Seeing my chance, I urge the horses faster. The carriage bounces wildly, metal-rimmed wheels sending sparks from the cobbles. There's a muffled moan from Foulon, somewhere in the back of the vehicle.

I narrow my eyes, concentrating on the target of the city gate. It is a thick-walled bastion, a medieval-style turret with a portcullis gatehouse.

I lean forward to touch the flank of the horses, murmuring encouragement, then flick the reins again. The carriage is gathering a speed it was never designed for and I hear a loud crack, behind me. The gold-carved decorations are coming apart.

We're less than twenty feet from the dark aperture of the gatehouse now, but one of the guards has evidently worked out how to lower the portcullis. It begins slowly, half a foot at a time.

I can hear Foulon knocking desperately on the roof.

'Stop!' he screams. 'The floor is breaking up.'

'I think we can get through,' I shout over my shoulder. I slap the reins again and we barrel for the doorway. I throw myself low as we go under, feeling the points of the portcullis touch my back.

The carved carriage roof smashes apart on contact with the unyielding iron, tossing broken bouquets of gilded roses and shining fruits on to the dirt.

We clear the gate, riding out into the green French countryside, beyond the Paris wall. An army of confused Swiss soldiers are milling about, but none is confident enough to halt our disintegrating carriage as we fly past.

Soon we're into fields and amongst sun-browned farmers bearing the same expressions of quiet confusion as the soldiers before.

I stop the horses, jump down and open what's left of the door.

Inside, Foulon has been thrown to one side, his wig askew, make-up smudged.

'I think I've bruised my hip,' he complains, righting himself with effort.

'Better if I go to the Salon des Princes alone,' I say. 'Your carriage will be useful to make the journey. But you have become a liability.'

He doesn't seem to understand my meaning, so I rephrase.

'Run, Monsieur Foulon,' I say. 'If those people catch you, they'll hang you from the nearest lamp-post. I won't stop them a second time.'

CHAPTER 39

GRACE AWAKES IN A SOFT, WARM BED. SHE IS CERTAIN SHE has never slept so deeply.

The first thing to hit her is the headache, which feels like it's shrinking her skull. She puts a hand to her head and scattered memories return. The men, the girls. Nothing else.

Quickly, Grace checks her clothing. Under the covers, she is fully dressed. The front of her dress is ripped, but has been mended.

The diamonds.

In a panic, she feels inside her clothing. They are gone. She remembers them falling to the ground and not caring very much to pick them up again.

She has a terrible feeling about this. Lord Pole gave her the pouch to pass on. Grace is not from the kind of background where girls can simply lose expensive jewels and apologize. They had been entrusted to her and the idea of failing in her responsibility makes Grace feel slightly ill.

Pulling herself up on her elbows, she takes in the room. It is lavishly decorated. A study: there are bookshelves and a desk. A long window looks out on to green grounds. The room reminds her of the library where she wrote Godwin's speeches. She remembers him, arriving drunk, late enough that her candles had burned low and she'd fallen asleep, quill in hand.

He'd kissed the top of her head and said what a wonderful wife she would make, rolling up the pages of close writing and tucking them in his jacket.

'Your time for politics will all change once you have children, of course,' he had added.

'Surely you don't want me to abandon my writings?' she'd said uneasily, not liking the direction of the conversation. He really was very drunk.

Godwin had laughed. 'The noble tradition is an heir and a spare. But we shall have a larger family. You will nurse and tend our children yourself, as enlightened people do.' And he'd patted her again, as if it were all decided.

Grace has already raised most of her brothers and sisters. She can still see her Mother's weary face, heavy with her sixth child, and knows Godwin has a romantic view of it all.

Grace remembers something else now. Her betrothal ring. The man had taken it from her finger and put it in her palm. Grace holds up her hand. It is bare.

She closes her eyes, trying to remember. But it is all so hazy.

There is a click, like a key turning in a lock. The door opens. Grace's heart begins to pound. But on the other side is not the man from last night. It is a woman. She is around forty. Sophisticated in an unmistakably French way. Dark hair, shot through with grey, handsome features and wearing a red dress. Unusually for someone of her obvious status, she carries a silver tray with a steaming bowl of broth.

'Hello,' says the woman in faintly accented English. 'How is your head?'

'It hurts,' admits Grace, sitting up.

'I brought you bouillon,' says the woman. 'It is the best thing.' She walks over to the bed and sits next to Grace. 'You poor creature,' she says. The woman has large, rather round brown eyes, drooping at the corners. 'Those men are rascals.'

Grace takes the broth and sips. It is wonderful. She can feel her head clearing.

'What happened?' she asks, feeling a rush of affection for the woman. 'Can I still be married?' she adds in a little mouse voice.

'No one touched you.' The woman's dark brows drop low over the drooping eyes. 'I came just in time. You were very drunk and addled, crying, your dress torn. And some predatory fellow had tried to trap you in a bedroom.'

She pats Grace's hands. 'I assume one of those young brutes mistook you for a girl from the town. They come to sell their virtue,' she adds, looking disapproving, 'and fetch a high price. It is their choice, I suppose. My husband allows such distasteful amusements, but he has gone to Paris now.'

The woman smiles. 'In any case,' she goes on, 'I saw your name written in the book and had come looking for you.'

'The book?'

'The footman writes the name of everyone who comes,' explains the lady, 'so I might know my guests.'

Grace blinks. 'You are Madame Roland?' she deduces. 'The owner of the salon.'

'Oh, I wouldn't say owner,' says Madame Roland with a wink. 'At least not in front of my husband. He likes to pretend he is in charge of things. Oh, I nearly forgot.'

Madame Roland removes a pouch from her purse. Grace recognizes it immediately.

The diamonds.

'This is yours?' confirms Madame Roland.

Grace nods, not daring to speak.

'It is very impressive. Paste jewellery – is that how you call it in England? False jewels?'

'Yes,' whispers Grace.

'Well, you must be careful,' says Madame Roland. 'It might be a joke to you English, but it is dangerous to wear a necklace in this style in France. You risk imprisonment. Keep it hidden.'

She pushes the pouch into Grace's unresisting hand then rises suddenly.

'Stay here,' she says. 'Sleep a little.' She hesitates. 'There is someone who would be very interested to meet you. A lawyer who is very invested in the plight of common people.'

She turns in a swirl of red silk skirts and makes for the door.

'Get some rest,' she says, exiting and closing the door.

Grace reflects on her good fortune, reaching for another draft of the wonderfully restorative bouillon.

Then she hears the unmistakable sound of a key turning in a lock.

CHAPTER 40

MONSIEUR FOULON SITS NEXT TO MONSIEUR ROBESPIERRE on a hard church bench in the Sainte Chapel. The magnificent building soars an impossible height above them, set with countless lozenges of jewel-bright stained glass and topped with an arcing sky of sparkling gilt stars on a deep blue. It makes Robespierre feel as though he is inside a lantern.

'This was the safest place I could think of,' mutters Foulon, 'but it is not safe.'

He is sweating, frightened, in ruffles and lace. His ancient powdered features dancing with fear. He glances to Robespierre.

The lawyer is as calm and still as the classical statues he admires. Now they are in close quarters, Foulon notices, there is something wrong with Monsieur Robespierre's eyes. Something missing.

Robespierre makes a smile that isn't a smile, more a twitch of the mouth.

'I didn't think you lowered yourself to meet commoners.'

Foulon swallows. 'Recollect how I helped you,' he whispers, 'got your common man into noble places.'

Foulon glances sideways, but Robespierre's expression is so icy he looks quickly away again.

'You were paid in full, Monsieur Foulon,' says Robespierre. 'A gentleman doesn't refer to a settlement as a debt.'

'No,' mumbles Foulon apologetically. He looks up at the altar, hands wrung in supplication. 'I need a safe place to hide,' he pleads, his eyes darting to the few scattered people sat in prayer. His tongue slides across his lipsticked mouth, choosing his next words. 'I beg you. Save me.'

'I?' Robespierre widens his eyes. 'How might a mere commoner help a great man such as Monsieur Foulon? A friend of the King, no less?'

Tears rise in Foulon's eyes.

'Monsieur Robespierre, please. I may be great, but I am also a man.'

Robespierre taps his fingers together. His face is pained, a man trying to understand.

'Of course. Of course. Yet. An angry mob wants your head. Might this be because you have been going around proclaiming the starving peasants might fill their bellies with grass?'

'I never said that,' said Foulon. 'It is lies, exaggeration.'

His voice rises to a hiss, attracting the attention of a fat bishop, plush in his red robes. He looks at them for a moment then goes back to lighting an enormous silver candlestick. One of eighteen, Robespierre notes, not to mention the hundredweight of gold, precious plate and jewel-encrusted cabinets containing various magical relics to awe the populace.

'And what of all the women?' asks Robespierre. 'You have a terrible reputation, Monsieur Foulon. Quite awful. There are several respectable men in this city who claim you have harmed their daughters. Naturally, since they are mere doctors or lawyers such as myself they have no recourse to justice.'

'It isn't true,' splutters Foulon. 'Girls of that class throw themselves at me. I give them trinkets and they leave happy. It is the pamphleteers who make up these stories that I trap innocents in my carriage.'

'Yes, yes.' Robespierre is frowning in understanding. 'I myself know how prone the libelles can be to mistruths.'

He drums his fingers lightly on the desk.

'So, what is to be done?'

'I will pay you,' says Foulon. 'Anything. Name your price.'

Robespierre's face darkens. 'I am not for sale, Monsieur Foulon.'

'I can give you more riches than you can imagine, Monsieur Robespierre. Castles, palaces. You could retire a wealthy man.'

Robespierre raises a pale finger. Foulon stops speaking instantly.

'Please, do not continue to insult me. Money is not an interest of mine. My conscience cannot be bought. If we are to make a new France, a democratic France, it must be one of ideals, of honesty, not the corruption and bribes of the old order.'

'I quite agree.' Foulon sags.

'But,' Robespierre raises his finger again, 'there is something that has a value beyond money. A value of conscience, if you will.'

Foulon is nodding, licking his painted lips, though his eyes suggest he is struggling to understand.

'*Le collier de la reine*,' says Robespierre, 'the Queen's necklace.'

'Yes!' Foulon all but bolts up from his bench. 'I know where it is!'

'You have it?' Robespierre's fists curl slowly into balls.

'I ... No. But, I can give you information ...'

Something closes in Robespierre's eyes. 'I see. How disappointing. As you know, I am well stocked with information.'

'But this is something you don't know. There is a girl. She is English – looks ordinary. But, but, she drew a knife in my carriage ...'

Foulon's eyes are desperately searching Robespierre's pale eyes for a reaction.

'Go on,' says Robespierre patiently.

'Attica Morgan,' says Foulon. 'That is what Angelina said her name was.'

'Angelina?'

'My courtesan.'

'I see.' Deep unease passes across Robespierre's face. 'You converse with this lady about our communications?'

'What does it matter?' Foulon frowns. 'She is a woman and understands nothing.'

'What is her connection to this Attica Morgan person?'

'They are old school friends, I think. But Mademoiselle Morgan told me a girl called Grace Elliott has the diamonds. Another English girl. She was at the Salon des Princes.'

Robespierre sits perfectly still. There is no indication this information has had any effect on him.

'Can you tell me anything else, Monsieur Foulon?' he asks quietly.

'The Morgan girl wields a knife, like a dockside cut-purse.'

'You have told me that, already.' The slightest rearrangement of Robespierre's features indicate he grows impatient.

'She threatened to castrate me.'

The corners of Robespierre's mouth twitch slightly. 'How terrible.'

Robespierre stands, seeming to have made a decision. 'Monsieur Foulon, I am moved to help you. You must first go to a less conspicuous chapel. If you can walk to the Church of All Saints, you can be assured of sanctuary. From there I will organize a group of sympathetic men to smuggle you from Paris. We will put it about you have died.'

'Yes.' Foulon is crying with relief. 'That is a good plan, a fine plan. I shall ready my guard.'

Robespierre appears to hesitate.

'What is it?' asks Foulon.

'Might it be best to go without your guard?' Robespierre suggests. 'You are a recognizable man; you will only draw attention to yourself.'

'Yes.' Foulon hesitates. He looks into Robespierre's eyes and is assured by what he sees.

'You are an honest man and a man of your word,' he decides. 'Not susceptible to bribery or corruption.'

'Yes.' Robespierre makes that unnerving expression again, not quite a smile.

Foulon stands, leaning on his jewel-encrusted walking cane. Robespierre quietly totals how many sacks of grain the gems might buy. Three hundred, he estimates, and Robespierre's estimates are more like facts.

Foulon staggers out, fear and relief making him clumsy. Robespierre watches the door close.

He lifts a little bell and rings it, a delicate tinkling.

A barefoot boy appears in ragged trousers.

'Monsieur.' He bows.

Robespierre produces a centime and holds it up.

'Go to Les Cours des Miracles,' he says. 'Explain to our friends, please, that Monsieur Foulon can be found at the

Church of All Saints on Rue de Honores. He is alone and unarmed.'

The boy leaves and Robespierre's mouth moves silently, making calculations.

A mob is already headed to the Salon des Princes. They will be there within a few hours. Though now, of course, the mob will arrive at Madame Roland's chateau by way of a detour, to where Monsieur Foulon believes himself hidden.

Everything is going as he'd hoped. What's more, he may have discovered a way to flush the Pimpernel into the open. This knife-wielding woman could be the link.

Later, back in his plain office, Robespierre hears the roar of the crowd. Screams.

He writes out one name, over and over, the sharpened feather driving deeper into the paper with every fresh line.

Attica Morgan, Attica Morgan, Attica Morgan.

CHAPTER 41

THE ROLANDS' GRAND CHATEAU IS SIMPLY SPECTACULAR, an enormous turreted castle of a building with endless slate rooftops, great glass windows and rows of perfectly sculpted poplar trees lining the broad approach.

I pass the large gates on foot, to see a strange kind of party has spilled out on to the grounds. Amongst drunk guests, a motley-looking circus has pitched up, trying to earn a few pennies. Tired-looking horses are being encouraged to rear up on their hind legs.

Nearby, several men are struggling with a great swathe of fabric. It's a globe aerostatic – a silk lantern that rises up in the sky like magic. The Rolands are so preposterously wealthy they've bought themselves a hot air balloon.

Currently it's being used as an entertainment for guests, rather than making flights of leisure around the countryside.

The limp material has begun to ripple, as though blown by a giant mouth. Two drunk aristocratic men attempt to climb into the balloon basket before it's ready, demanding to be floated up. One sets his jacket alight. He falls out, swearing and batting at the flames.

I walk past them, making some quick adjustments to my toilette. Since the French share the English affectation to clothe their maids in fine silk dresses, it's simple enough to adapt.

From my hanging pocket I remove a rolled lace-trimmed pinafore and a matching maid's cap, fitting the latter over my long hair and tucking the black curls underneath.

I pass by fruit trees and quickly pull down some low-hanging cherries, bundling them into my apron.

Servants bearing wheelbarrows of food are arriving on the grass, unpacking a vast spread. Cold meats, jellies, fruits, cheeses, bread and pastries are being laid artfully on lace cloths, dotted about the lawns. The delicacies keep emerging as I pass, a never-ending disgorgement of comestibles. On and on it comes, with fruit and cakes and marzipan sweets joining the savouries. Spectacular crockery is carried out: gilded dishes flashing like suns, solid gold cutlery.

But no one is really interested in filling the decorated plates, loading the fancy forks. The round-bellied people out on the lawn are too drunk to care for food. They signal only for wine. I pass a man drunkenly scratching at the wig-sores on his shaved head, his gigantic flowing wig lying at his feet like a pet dog.

There's a boating lake in the middle distance where a mock-battle is being staged by men so full of drink they can barely stand in their boats. Long-suffering servants row the painted vessels around, firecrackers are hurled.

I always viewed this kind of behaviour with disdain but here there's something desperate to it. Like adults clinging to childhood.

A familiar smell wafts on the air: opium. It hits me at the back of my nostrils, taking me to my father's little study where papers are scattered and curtains shut out the sun.

Everyone looks to have missed several nights' sleep, as though they have been at this exhausting business of decadence for days. It seems no one wants to go to bed for fear they will wake to find the festivities have vanished, never to return.

Angelina's warning floats back to me. 'Be careful,' she had cautioned me this morning, before I left her house. 'The nobles were careless before. Now they sense their world slipping away, they become cruel.'

I walk on, past gardeners who are shovelling up the messes from the dogs who pelt around the lawns. Ahead of me is the great house. If the gardens are the ragged edges of the party, where spent guests stumble, this is the burning heart of it.

As I near the large doors a footman in a gold-brocaded coat trips down the steps of the approach, his face drawn in puzzlement. He sees my apron, filled with cherries.

'Madame Roland wanted fresh fruit for the table,' I explain, walking as though in a rush.

He gives the tired nod of a man used to fielding whimsical requests and makes no mention of having never seen me before. As I'd hoped, there are so many servants in this household it's difficult for anyone to keep track.

I take the staff entrance and follow the smell of roasting meats to the kitchen. I pass a cook by a darkened birdcage. He reaches into the depths and throws fistfuls of cheeping finches into a boiling cauldron of Armagnac.

Further along there's a housekeeper's room, hardly more than a cupboard, with a lock on the door that I make short work of with my pick.

Once inside I locate the household ledger next to some well-used writing materials. I flick through the pages of food orders and staff wages and find the page listing party guests.

I lift a stubby quill, dip cheap ink and write my name, painstakingly emulating the housekeeper's primitive letters as I learned under Atherton's tutorage.

Since my name now looks too black and fresh, evidently added later than the others, I take a pouch from my purse. Inside is an invention Atherton and I came up with together. Gum sandarac, ground to fine dust, has the effect of both drying wet ink and giving it a passably aged appearance. I sprinkle and rub and the tell-tale deep black writing dulls to grey. At a glance it looks to have been written days ago.

A thought occurs. I leaf back through the pages, scanning the names of guests. My finger moves rapidly down the list, then stops at a name I've heard before.

Oliver Janssen.

The dangerous musketeer. Why should the Rolands let a killer and a torturer into their house? There's only one logical answer to that question and my stomach is churning as I investigate further into the book.

I stop. In the middle of the elegant curling script is an ugly black blot. A name has been crossed out.

My fingertips brush where the looping tops of a few letters can still be determined. I lift the page and let my fingers feel underneath, where the shape of the sharp quill pressing the letters is discernible.

I close my eyes, letting the shapes reveal themselves. There's a 'G', two 'l's and two 't's. It's a simple enough puzzle, though I wish very badly it wasn't.

Grace Elliott.

She was here. Grace was here.

I want to believe she is alive and in the house still, but I have to face facts. Someone has crossed my cousin off the list and invited a killer to their party. The implications of this are hitting me hard. There's a sound outside. Footsteps are coming down the corridor outside the room. I quickly shut the book.

I'm mulling this over as I slip quietly out of the housekeeper's room. My best hope is to get into the salon and find Madame Roland.

CHAPTER 42

INSIDE, THE ROLANDS' HOUSE IS EVEN MORE MAGNIFICENT than the exterior. A wide marble staircase with lacily carved ebony banisters winds up the centre of the cavernous entrance hall. Everywhere, I think, remembering some Mauritian slaves I rescued near Madagascar, are imports of slavery. The insidiousness of such goods across Europe sometimes overwhelms me.

The party is on the first floor. I follow the steps up, greeted by an expanse of long windows with far views of rolling green.

I slip off my maid's pinafore and announce myself to the footman. He is at first suspicious I have no written invitation, then returns, obsequious and apologetic, when he discovers my name in the housekeeper's book and leads me to the grand hall.

There's a strange squeaking sound as we approach, which gets louder. The doors open and I see the reason. It's an incredible sight. Every guest has a costume, most of them shocking. There are gauzily clad sultanas and men dressed as women. A great many people are masquerading as commoners, maximizing the chance to expose their plump limbs through meagre rags. There's more skin on display than in a Turkish harem and a flash of almost everything. I see comely milkmaids, farmer boys, shepherd girls and open-robed clergy.

Everyone wears a mask and now the squeaking sound is explained. Speech is made in high falsetto, to disguise voices.

My hopes of easily identifying Madame Roland are evaporating.

The footman hands me a plain black mask and exits.

Music starts up and I turn to see the orchestra have their backs to the room. It only takes me a moment to realize why. The half-dressed guests flood the floor, laughing, dancing outrageously close, sliding hands where they shouldn't.

I overhear a conversation nearby, a man and a woman talking.

'My husband says it's Robespierre who is the problem,' says the man airily. 'He *hates* all nobles.'

'At least men like Danton can be bought,' agrees the woman, nodding furiously. 'But this Robespierre ... He is *incorruptible*.' She sounds the word like the worse kind of insult.

'Over-kindness with the commoners is the reason for all this unrest,' opines the man. 'A public spectacle is the thing. Boil alive a whole pack of these parliament rogues. Put the fear of God in the others.'

I'm taking it all in when I hear a deep voice in my ear.

'They call them masquerades. Isn't it quite ridiculous?'

I twist around in shock to see a masked man standing behind me. The bottom half of his face looks different under the bright candlelight, a slight sheen to his olive skin and stubbled face, but I'd recognize his voice anywhere.

He removes his mask.

'Jemmy!' I'm so pleased to see him I throw my arms around his neck, kissing him on both cheeks in the French style. His hair is hanging loose, I notice, without the usual dark ribbon tying it back. It's wavy to just above his shoulders and he's tucked it behind his ears. A footpad robber, I decide, rather than a highwayman.

'Well,' he says, the teardrop blemish at his eye twitching upwards, 'so this is what it takes to make Lady Attica Morgan affectionate: a masquerade ball of false commoners.'

My delight at seeing him is cooling now. I'm remembering how he sailed away.

'You might have stayed to throw me some oars,' I admonish. 'You left me to the dogs.'

'The wind was against us,' says Jemmy, 'and the grenade that rattled your boat was meant for us. I couldn't risk thirty lives for one. Even a pretty one.' He grins.

I'm taking in his attire. He still wears a black shirt but with a deep-purple neckerchief, his outlandish boots have been polished to a high shine. I raise a hand above my eyes.

'What is it?' asks Jemmy, disconcerted.

'I'm shielding my eyes,' I say, 'from your cravat.'

'Jaunty, ain't she?' says Jemmy, pleased. 'Thought I'd bring a little life to the party.'

'And what of your unfortunate shoe-shine boy?' I ask, looking at the mirrored polish on his boots. 'Can he still use his arms?'

'I shine me own boots, Your Ladyship, 'specially for a spectacle like this one.' He gestures to my dress. 'I see you've gone all Frenchified. It well becomes you. The top part, in any case.' Jemmy gestures to the billow of transparent muslin at my décolletage. I hide a smile as he looks around the room.

A girl in a tatty sack barely covering her torso is pretending to beg, laughingly imploring other guests for food.

'Look at them,' he says, shaking his head in disgust, 'a party to show how much they love the new democracy, when last week they were buying their sons commissions in the clergy so they might never need pay tax. Dressing in rags for a lark. I tell you, Attica, I've seen things in this house to make a docker blush.'

'What brings you here,' I ask, 'if you dislike the affectation so strongly?'

'I was anxious for you in your fine dress, as it happens,' he adds. 'I even asked at the gatehouses.'

'Did you?' I feel rather flattered. 'How did you manage that?'

He reaches into his pocket and brandishes a tricolour cockade – a rosette in red, white and blue. 'Easy enough. I just showed this to any Republican guard and said, "*Vive la France*."'

I smile at him, knowing he's underplaying the danger. 'You did all that just for me?'

'Don't be getting any ideas about my having feelings for you, Your Ladyship,' says Jemmy. 'I've an idea you're searchin' for some famous diamonds. Marie Antoinette's necklace is something of a legend to us pirates. You know how we love lost treasure.'

He looks at me pointedly.

I consider him for a moment. I've never regretted my actions, but sometimes I badly wish I wasn't who I was. That I could just be normal. At the least, I wish I could tell Jemmy the truth: that I'm happier solving codes than choosing dresses, that I've killed people, that I never, ever want to be a wife.

Instead, I look out into the room.

'A diamond necklace worth two million francs?' I say. 'It's more myth than fact.'

'I've been talking to people. Lots of guests are drunk enough to be free with their words. Some say an English girl was here last night. I put two and two together. Reckon that girl might just have been this cousin you're lookin' for.'

'You know something of Grace?' I say. 'Where she is?'

Jemmy's face falls. 'There was talk of some scandalous auction. Men bid on her virginity. Probably just rumours,' he adds, seeing my expression.

'Can you tell me who Madame Roland is?' I ask, looking about the guests. 'I've a feeling she knows where Grace is.'

I'm thinking of the housekeeper's book, the name crossed out in black.

'Aye, I know her.' He cocks his head to one side. 'So it looks as though we must help each other, Mademoiselle Primrose. I will show you to Madame Roland but first you must agree to my price.'

The music ends and several dancers exit in pairs or threes, looking for bedrooms.

'Your price?'

'Dance with me,' he says. 'Nothing is what it seems at this party, Attica. Nothing at all.'

CHAPTER 43

'I'M NOT A GOOD DANCER,' I ADMIT AS JEMMY LEADS ME TO the floor. 'I'm too tall. At school they always made me dance the man's part.'

'It's a folk dance,' he says, 'informal. I'll lead you.' And without waiting for my assent he draws me against his body. The close contact is faintly shocking. I've never been pressed this tightly to a man in broad daylight.

People are watching us from the sidelines, the tall noble woman and the dashing stranger. I rearrange my face so a false smile shows beneath my masked upper-face. Jemmy holds my waist and whirls me sharply.

'I've been wondering about you since you got aboard my ship,' he accuses in a low voice as he pulls me close again. 'The way you moved wasn't quite right. And now I see you here I understand what I was missing. Some fancy daughter of a noble isn't the half of it.' He lowers his voice. 'I think you're an assassin.'

'And how do you imagine I should kill a man?' I answer. 'With my bare hands?'

He slides his hands around my ribs and lifts me with surprisingly little difficulty in time to the music.

'Perhaps with that blade hidden in the front of your dress,' says Jemmy, letting his thumb feel out the pointed shape.

'I shall never trust an invitation to dance with you again.' He's tricked me and, despite myself, I'm rather impressed.

'You shouldn't.' Jemmy takes both my hands in his. 'I always dance with bad intentions. I've spent time in Italy,' he concludes, 'I know how to identify an assassin. I've just never seen a female one, so it took a while for my mind to catch up with what my eyes knew.'

'I'm not an assassin,' I say. 'I only kill people when I must.'

'A spy!' says Jemmy, triumphant. 'I knew it. Women *always* make the best spies.'

'They're better at not announcing themselves to a party full of people,' I say, looking around to see if anyone is listening. 'Just tell me what it is you want,' I hiss, 'so I can find Madame Roland.'

'Gaspard de Mayenne ...' says Jemmy. 'How much do you know?'

I weigh up what to reveal. 'He was an aristocratic rebel,' I say. 'They found him dead in the Bastille. Most likely he was killed by royalists; the nobles thought him a traitor to his own kind.'

'Whoever murdered Gaspard was an executioner, a professional.' Jemmy's dark brows draw together. 'Tools had been used,' he says, 'devices that your average man doesn't just pick up and deploy. Both Gaspard's shoulders were dislocated. The bones in his legs had been shattered with heavy weights. His fingers—'

'I understand,' I say, cutting him off. 'Strappado, boots. Torture.'

'That's what someone wanted people to think. But I'd say he'd been killed before all the torture took place.'

'You saw the body?'

'It's for all to see. The Bastille mortuary displays its corpses publicly to deter rumours its prisoners are never seen again. There was no bruising to the shoulders,' says Jemmy. 'When you dislocate, the blood vessels rupture. Same with the legs. White as snow. Yet the throat was bruised where it was cut. Worse than cut. Mangled. If I was a betting man, I'd say everything had bled out of him before he reached the Bastille.'

'You're not a betting man?'

'Only on certainties.' Jemmy pulls me close as the music plays. 'I think you know more than you're lettin' on about our poor dead Gaspard. Tell me and I'll show you to Madame Roland.'

My hands are on his shoulders for this part of the dance. For some reason it's difficult to think straight with those green eyes on me. Something about Jemmy is muddling my thoughts.

'I'll tell you all I know,' I say, 'which isn't much. There's a powerful organization in Paris: the Society of Friends. It's likely they murdered Gaspard as a warning to the English and they mean to come for Grace next.'

Jemmy considers this.

'You're not certain?'

I consider. 'I was,' I say. 'But Foulon, the finance minister, believes Gaspard's death was a warning to royalists. I can see how it looks that way.'

'Interesting,' says Jemmy. 'Because the rebels think it's a message for them, the royalists proving their power.'

We both ponder this.

'Everyone thinks the death is significant to them,' I conclude. 'Yet someone somewhere knows what Gaspard's murder means for certain. Whosoever it is will also be able to identify the killer. If I know that, I have a better chance of keeping Grace safe.' I put the puzzle to one side. 'I've told you what I know,' I say, 'now show me Madame Roland.'

'Oh,' Jemmy appears distracted, 'she's the one in the black and red beatin' all those poor fools at Hazard.' He wheels me about so I catch sight of a middle-aged woman throwing dice with a determined expression. Unlike the other guests, Madame Roland has not troubled herself with a costume or a mask. Her dress is exactly the kind that English women admire in the French, all scalloped red hems and swoops of black lace.

I'm trying to listen whilst keeping track of what my feet are doing.

'You really are a bad dancer,' Jemmy observes mildly as I step jerkily in time to his movements.

'It's not a skill I've troubled myself to perfect.' I look directly at him, our faces a few inches apart, and to my satisfaction he flinches.

'Madame Roland is not at all like the usual decadent French aristocrats,' says Jemmy. 'She has a secret room somewhere in the house where she writes her letters. I think she's in some intrigue with Robespierre. They are all half in love with him, these clever wealthy women. I've been trying to find it. But she's not susceptible to my charms.' He smiles and dimples appear in his cheeks.

'You amaze me. The great pirate Avery.'

'Regrettably she thinks me a fool,' admits Jemmy. 'I've already lost twelve forfeits playing her at dice.' He nods in the direction of some gaming tables. 'She's the most dangerous woman here.'

'I find that hard to believe,' I reply, wondering if he can still feel my long knife, pressed against my ribs as we turn around the room.

I consider for a moment.

'Very well,' I say, 'what if I discover Madame Roland's room?'

'You won't.'

'If I do,' I say, 'I'm willing to trade information. But you must do something for me in return. Agree to get Grace out of Paris when I find her.'

'Not you as well?'

'I can get myself out.'

'You'll never get Madame Roland to tell you where her secret room is,' he says with certainty, watching where she sits throwing dice. 'The lady of the house takes after Robespierre: incorruptible, she cannot be manipulated or seduced.'

'Everyone can be seduced. You're not trying hard enough.'

He snorts at this. 'Not Madame Roland. Ask any man here. Don't waste your time,' he says. 'There'll be a Swiss army around Paris by sunset. If you tarry too long here the way back to Paris will become impassable.'

I'm looking harder at Madame Roland now. I slip my hand down into the tight pocket of Jemmy's breeches.

'On second thoughts,' he says, 'we can stay as long as you like.'

I hold up the tricolour Republican cockade. Jemmy's face falls.

'We'll see how incorruptible Madame Roland is,' I say, pinning it to my dress. 'Wait here.'

CHAPTER 44

GRACE IS RUNNING. HER PARTY DRESS IS TORN, HER SATIN shoes are bloody.

He is chasing her. He will catch her. It is only a matter of time.

Grace slows to a walk, trying not to draw attention to herself. She has got out of the chateau and limped in her soft footwear to a small village on the outskirts of the Rolands' grand estate.

Grace knows she is being followed again. The one who she had seen kill and worse. He wears the uniform of a King's musketeer.

After she heard the key turn in the lock, she went to the window. It wasn't long before she saw him striding across the ground.

She tries not to picture his hideous metal hand streaked with blood. Grace has no illusions. It's only a matter of time until he tracks her down. And she is so conspicuous out on the street, her English accent giving her away at every turn.

The village is tiny, more of a hamlet. Even so it is crowded with people, a crush of recently arrived farmers, shocking in their terrible rags, the barest skin on their bones.

For much of her life Grace has been poor, living eight people to a house, scraping for a toehold in respectable circles. And now, here she is, eyeing the peasant classes with faint terror because of the great treasure she has hidden.

But she *has* to get off the streets. Every pair of eyes looking could identify her to him. And if he finds her ... Grace walks faster, biting back the pain as blood slides between her toes.

She stops. A carriage with black windows is rolling along the cobbles. A dark, shuttered thing, doing the rounds. People's heads turn in terror. It is a Bastille carriage, Grace realizes, come to make an arrest.

Its purpose is to remind the people of Paris that the terrible prison is only a letter away.

She watches, mute, as people duck inside their homes, close shutters.

This is how the King controls his people. Fear.

Her heart sinks, when she sees the musketeer. He holds up his metal hand in a half-salute, as though they are old friends who have arranged to meet.

The musketeer has followed her from the house as she knew he would. He had been toying with her all along.

His single eye is fixed on her and even from this distance she can see he expects her to crumble, perhaps to collapse in terrorized defeat.

A steely anger burns in Grace. Ever since she met Godwin, she has been acting a part, being no trouble to anyone. She remembers, with sudden boiling rage, how she was tricked into smuggling a priceless necklace. How the men in the Rolands' house tried to auction her like a sheep in a marketplace.

Grace feels the fear that paralysed her ebbing. She thinks: *I am not some perfumed girl to be toyed with. I did not grow up in drawing rooms, learning pianoforte. I was raised in the Bristol docks and I know a thing or two about the streets.*

I've had enough of you, she decides savagely, looking at Janssen. *There's worse than you who sleep in the gutter outside my mother's house.*

She turns, watching wagons and riders trot past. Her eyes settle on the prison carriage. Grace approaches the vehicle. She waves down the driver and mutters something urgent, her face earnest.

He signals his thanks and spurs the horses. And Grace steps behind whilst his back is turned and enters the blacked-out vehicle.

It is dark inside, there are iron plates securing the doors. Grace breathes a sigh of relief. She peaks through a crack in the boarded window and feels a peculiar satisfaction to see the musketeer standing with his mouth open. She has found the only place in Paris he cannot possibly get to her.

Grace leans back on the hard bench. She is being driven to the Bastille.

CHAPTER 45

As I move nearer to Madame Roland's little group of gamblers, Jemmy vanishes away into the crowd. Her dice table is small and wooden, the kind you find in the local wine shows. The chairs too are humble and hard looking.

People in this part of the room are less concerned with debauching themselves. It's an oasis of serious gaming in the wider frivolity.

Since the winner holds the table and chooses their opponent, men are standing in line, waiting to be called. None of them looks like they are relishing the opportunity to lose.

Teresa Roland is a plain woman who I can imagine having a youthful prettiness. Her brown hair is soft with a few strands of grey, twisted up in curls and painstakingly dressed with rubies. She is holding court, speaking in a confident, rasping voice, a torrent of clever words weaving around a small audience of ardent listeners. Her fashionable dress falls loosely around her shoulders. The matching red-velvet gloves wave in time to her conversation, their deep amber-musk perfume scenting the play.

I hover at the sidelines, watching the dice fly. It's a game similar to the English Hazard, but more complicated. Players must keep a running mental tally of complex mathematical percentages with every throw and simultaneously try to distract the opposition from calculating correctly.

I watch for a few minutes as Madame Roland roundly defeats every player. She's impressive, hurling the dice with graceful speed whilst her opponents sweat and twitch and bow out one by one; she throws personal observations like daggers. No one can keep up.

I insinuate myself into the line of men, making certain my Republican cockade is clearly visible.

Teresa's brown eyes have a kind of puppy-dog droopiness about them, I notice, which is at odds with her intellectual way of speaking. She tilts her head, taking me in.

The downturned eyes observe the cockade then lift to my face.

'I presume you haven't met my husband,' she says, 'if you dare wear that in his house.'

'I have not had the misfortunate,' I reply, 'of meeting him.'

I tilt my head and give her an insouciant half-curtsey.

'I'll play her,' she says, pointing a finger.

The men are giving me their full attention now, grumbling.

'Come now, Teresa,' complains one, 'we must see something of a game. We all know you're the only woman for Hazard.'

Teresa doesn't deign to reply, watching me with interest as I sit, my gauzy dress rustling. She takes in my indeterminate origins but doesn't ask where I'm from.

'That's a dangerous symbol you wear to this party,' she observes, looking to the cockade once more. 'Republican colours.'

I pick up the dice cup. 'Perhaps I like a little danger.'

She looks amused by this, as though I've said something rather childish.

'I can see you're new to us,' she says. 'I must warn you, I never lose.'

'Neither do I.'

Teresa laughs. 'Unless you are hiding a genius for sums beneath that lovely face, I fear you have been playing duller gamers than you realize.'

I smile at this, but don't reply. Ever since I can remember I've had an affinity with numbers. In the code-breaking of my youth, I deciphered algebra like others read letters.

'Of course, you know I am Madame Roland.' She says this in the expectation I'll know of her famed salon. 'But who might you be?'

'Attica Morgan.'

'Oh.' She looks hard at my face. 'I believe I know Lord Morgan. He was in Paris perhaps fifteen years ago. Is he a relative of yours?'

I wonder in what circumstances she encountered him. By my understanding, my father's limping journey from southern Spain back to England was in the worst depths of his laudanum depravity. It was shortly after he'd been told my mother was dead.

'Lord Morgan is my father.'

'Is that so?' She's looking at me more deeply now, in the way people do when they've met my father. 'A brilliant and unhappy man, your father,' continues Teresa with a slight frown. She extends her hand in the English style of introduction. 'I didn't know he had a daughter.'

'No,' I say, 'I'm not generally acknowledged.'

It takes a moment for realization to dawn. Lord Morgan's scandalous liaison with an African princess was the talk of society and the arrival of his half-breed offspring to England news enough to reach French nobles.

'The slave daughter,' she says. 'I have heard of you, of course. There are tall tales of your daring escape from Virginia in every noble house in Europe. You look nothing like I expected. Do you take more after your father, do you think?'

'In some ways.'

She's staring into my face.

'I think I see the resemblance,' she decides. 'You are darker, but those green-grey eyes are his. Or maybe the expression of them.'

This takes me aback. When I first met my father I thought his eyes were the saddest I'd ever seen.

'Perhaps we shall have some sport after all.' Teresa sweeps a magnanimous hand. 'Please do favour us with the first roll of the dice.'

'What shall we play for?' I ask.

'Oh, I never play for money,' says Teresa, 'it's a tawdry business.'

'If not for money, then you must play for love,' I say.

She hesitates, looking into my face, wondering, I suppose, how much I know about her.

'I don't play for that either,' she says, swallowing slightly. 'I've no idea how such a thing might be won,' she adds with a forced laugh.

'Perhaps you'll find out when I win,' I reply, smiling at her challengingly.

'Gambling is a depravity of the old order,' she replies primly. 'You should hear Monsieur Robespierre speak on the subject, he is quite compelling.' She smiles to her gentleman watchers, but I notice she is breathing faster.

'If you never lose,' I say lightly, 'what does it matter?'

The assembled men enjoy this hugely, laughing and teasing Teresa for her cowardice.

'Have you finally met your match, Teresa,' grins one. 'A challenge from the fairer sex too strong for your marrow?'

Teresa's expression is stony. 'Then here are my terms,' she says thoughtfully, 'Monsieur Robespierre is interested in an Englishman. Someone he believes has recently arrived in Paris.' She holds my gaze. 'His name is Le Mouron: the Pimpernel, in English.'

My heart beats faster. How can she know this?

'Paris has emptied of *les Anglais*,' she adds, 'yet here you are. A new arrival. Rather a coincidence, don't you think?'

'I can only imagine you have a great deal of spare time to dwell on such things.'

Madame Roland smiles. 'Us women have always been adept at listening, don't you agree? And you seem to me a good listener.'

Her eyes fix on mine. 'Lose and you must tell me what you know about Le Mouron.'

I look back into her eyes and give the smallest nod of acceptance.

She raises a hand and a servant appears.

'You'll take something to drink?' she asks me.

'Brandy. With a little water.'

'Very good. A brandy for Mademoiselle Morgan.'

'Nothing for you?'

'Oh, I never drink when I'm gaming. Perhaps a little Champagne to wake me up if it's after midnight.'

She picks up the dice, playing to her audience.

'I've a nose for scandal, gentleman,' says Teresa, eyeing the assembled men. 'This lovely little creature didn't come all the way to Paris for a new dress.' I notice people appear a little afraid of Madame Roland. Her eyebrows lift. 'I look forward to earning Monsieur Robespierre something more valuable than love.'

'We shall see,' I reply. 'But first you will need to roll better than an eight.'

CHAPTER 46

IN ROBESPIERRE'S QUIET OFFICE IN LES COURS DES MIRACLES, the door bangs open.

Without looking up, Robespierre knows it is his old friend Georges Danton. The man enters every room as though he is arriving in a brothel by way of a tavern.

A hot-blooded revolutionary, Danton has become famous all over Paris. Every freedom fighter recognizes the booming voice and solid barrel chest, his giant head like a malformed potato and his scarred and pockmarked face.

Robespierre stands.

'Maximilien.' Danton embraces his old friend, kissing him on both cheeks. His usually jubilant manner is subdued. Danton is not noticeably drunk, therefore Robespierre deduces he must be hungover.

It has been thus since they attended law school together, Robespierre spinning his high ideals, the inebriated Danton considerately thumping anyone who mocked skinny little Max. Robespierre loves him dearly, yet still can't quite bring himself to trust him.

'How was Versailles?' enquires Robespierre, his face puckered in distaste.

'Ah,' Danton opens his wide hands, 'larger than life, more golden than gold.' He smiles. 'The Queen has had herself a little peasant village built in the grounds so she can pretend to be common.'

Robespierre picks up a pen, shaking his head, and jots a note for his next speech. The preposterous wealth never fails to stagger him. He occasionally makes the twelve-mile journey in his mind, past hollow-cheeked farmers on parched fields to the golden-gated land of clipped lawns and splashing fountains.

'And it still stinks,' adds Danton, wrinkling his nose. 'The King has nobles wait, hours and hours, sometimes days, for an audience. People shit behind curtains, in stairwells. Everywhere!'

Robespierre has heard this before, but enjoys it all the same.

'And here we are,' concludes Robespierre, 'the common people who pay for all their splendour, with the audacity to desire our own vote.' He makes a small, humourless smile.

'Well,' Danton seats himself, throwing up the tails of his black lawyer coat, 'I have bad news on that front, I am afraid.'

'Oh?' Robespierre's face is perfectly neutral.

'I have it from our friend at Versailles that the Paris weapons cache is better hidden than we thought.' Danton watches Robespierre's reaction. When there is none, he presses. 'If we don't know where the gunpowder and guns are, there is no way of raiding them. I'm afraid His Majesty has outwitted us, Max.'

The quill between Robespierre's fingers bends in two with an audible snap.

'You have a secondary plan,' decides Danton, looking at the broken pen. 'You always do.'

Robespierre nods. He glances absently at his hand.

'I have been cultivating certain friendships,' he concedes. 'But I have been preoccupied of late.'

'Still hunting those mythic diamonds?' Danton smiles indulgently. 'Imagine if the necklace existed. There'd be some better horses on your carriage, eh?' He winks.

Robespierre's mouth presses to a thin line. 'You think I want diamonds, to buy horses?'

'Stop being so proper.' Danton waves a hand. 'Of course the necklace would arm the men, feed hungry mouths, help move things along, as we all want.' He tilts his big head. 'But if a few small gems should fall off, who would notice?'

'Your avarice will be your undoing,' Robespierre says disapprovingly.

'Whores will have their trinkets, men will have their wine,' replies Danton, un-offended. 'Admit it, Max. It's not even the diamonds you want. You're obsessed with besting the English. It's all about this mysterious spy-fellow, isn't it? The one whose codes you can't crack.'

'The Pimpernel.'

Danton's eyebrows rise.

'The *little flower*?' He shakes his head, appalled. 'Leave it alone, Max. You do battle with a man who names himself after a hedgerow plant; you'll come off the worst.'

He assesses Robespierre's face for a moment, hoping he might get even this one joke. But his friend's pale face is thoughtful.

'It's a sad thing, Gaspard's end,' sighs Danton, changing the subject. 'I know he was a great supporter of yours. It seems a compromise with the nobles is necessary, Max. They show their ruthlessness.'

Robespierre's eyes flash. 'Nobles would have us model France on England,' he says. 'A King with some unspecified role. Merging old and new laws like a patchwork quilt.' His nose wrinkles. 'Messy. *Untidy.*' His eyelid twitches. 'We shall create a new France. A true democracy, with the best of the ancients and enlightened thinking.'

'Yes, yes.' Danton's eyes have glazed slightly. 'No need to practise your speeches on me, Max.' He slaps his broad thighs. 'Well! Look to the future. There's no denying Gaspard's demise has galvanized the troops, eh? A few more men willing to go to death and glory now they know the aristos will stoop to murder.'

'Fear is not always bad,' agrees Robespierre.

Danton narrows his rather piggy eyes, considering Robespierre. 'If you want your perfect France, free from corruption,' he says, choosing his words, 'you must be certain to go about things the right way in the beginning. Start with terror, we will end with terror.'

'You think I favour bloodshed?' Robespierre speaks deliberately. 'Violent means?'

'Of course not,' says Danton, 'we all know you don't have the balls for that kind of thing.'

He glances at Robespierre. If he is offended by the observation of his cowardice he gives no sign of it.

'Just be careful,' says Danton. 'That is all.'

Robespierre picks up a fresh quill. 'I always am.'

CHAPTER 47

THE DICE WHIRL AS TERESA ROLAND AND I PLAY. IT IS A dizzying, exciting game. I am enjoying the challenge. I also notice how Teresa's eyes light for just a little too long on my mouth, my hands as they throw.

I take the cup. When I let my fingers linger on hers, she makes no move to pull away.

'Four and a six,' I say. 'I pick a main of two, so my probability of winning is five over three. I make that a disadvantage of one and a half per cent to the castor.'

I hand back the dice shaker with a polite smile. Teresa's drooping eyes widen in admiration.

'Well, well,' she says, 'a worthy opponent. Look you this, gentleman. It isn't only men who can make numbers. Some of the great Lord Morgan's talents have been conferred to his pretty daughter.'

She's looking at me differently now, as though I've tricked her. Teresa's need to win is competing with other desires.

She shakes the dice pot, throws and lifts her hands in a happy gesture.

'Six and four,' she says. 'I make that my advantage.'

I pick up the cup and shake it thoughtfully, watching her face.

'How did an old goat like Foulon ensnare a mistress so much younger than he?' I ask, remembering the elderly minister's boast that they'd once been lovers.

She laughs and watches my dice roll. Three and two. We are level pegging.

'Flattery does not work with me,' she says, retrieving the dice from the table.

'I mean no flattery,' I say as she throws. 'I heard Foulon made his fortune off the backs of the poor, stealing their taxes. I wondered if you were attracted to his great wealth.'

Her drooping eyes fix on mine.

'Be a little careful, Mademoiselle Morgan,' she decides, searching my face. 'I know something of your family,' she adds meaningfully. 'Three and twelve,' she says with a happy clap of her hands. 'If you were hoping to distract me, you have not succeeded.' She shakes her head as I take back the dice.

I try another tack. 'The death of Gaspard de Mayenne,' I say, watching her carefully. 'What do you make of it?'

Madame Roland's drooping eyes lift. Nothing in their expression suggests anything other than mild interest. 'My opinion is Gaspard's murder was a threat to moderates such as myself,' she says. 'We who believe King Louis XVI should rule with a constitution.'

'Not everyone wants a King with a constitution?'

'Some want a different monarch. You English, for example.' She smiles faintly.

'You seem very sure of the murderer's motive.'

'Of course.' She gives a light little shrug. 'Who but a royalist could have got inside the Bastille? A person cannot simply walk through the doors. You need a letter from the King himself.'

She assesses me for a moment.

'You really do take after your father,' she says. 'I wonder, how does someone such as yourself feel about France's political situation?'

'I have little interest in it,' I admit. 'My attentions are directed to abolishing slavery through more active means. But now I am here and I see your people,' I conclude, 'I realize not all slaves wear chains.'

The truth of this surprises me, even as I say it.

Teresa calls numbers, then throws.

'Then you are for equality,' she decides, 'as I am.'

'I am for revolution,' I say, taking back the dice cup.

'A revolution of ideas, certainly,' agrees Madame Roland. 'We must draw up papers, use the ideals of Voltaire and Rousseau to shape our new France.'

'No,' I reply. 'This talk of social philosophy is no more than a fashion for you, a game. You play at enlightenment, Madame Roland. The people are not playing. They are dying.'

Madame Roland gives a slightly high-pitched laugh.

'We've all seen the sad scenes on the Paris streets. But we cannot let sentiment forgo caution. Things must be done properly, without violence.'

I shake my head, impatiently. 'You had your constitution in that tennis court.' I uncurl my fingers. 'You held it in the palm of your hand. All your King needed do was accept that his power comes from his people and not from God. He would not and I am sorry for it. It is too long and too late to avoid bloodshed now. The people have woken up.'

I lean in a little closer, looking her straight in the eye.

'It is over, Madame Roland, all of this. Everything you see is already gone.'

She shakes her head, but her smile is not quite genuine. There's a fear in her eyes that she's trying to hide. I see my chance and I take it.

'But you,' I whisper, leaning close, 'are not like other women. You are different, are you not?'

'I ...' Teresa's mouth opens and shuts. Her brown eyes are fixed on mine, confused.

'All those years,' I say, 'labouring behind your silly husband. Playing clever cards. Taking lovers as a politician counts votes. You are so bored with it all, I can tell. I think you are more interesting than all of that.'

Teresa is frowning, meeting my eye then looking away. She rallies, but barely.

'I don't know what you mean.' She tries for a smile.

'Then let me show you.'

Something changes in her face. A yearning suddenly exposed.

I throw fast, tot up the odds and put the cup back into her grasp before she can follow the calculations.

Her fingers shake slightly as the dice fall and her mouth moves uncertainly as she watches the numbers. 'Fifteen,' she says too quickly, her usual unflappable logic in disarray. But even the drunken gentlemen know her to be wrong.

'You didn't calculate the main,' I say.

'Well, well, Teresa,' says her last defeated opponent. 'You have lost at last.'

Before she can reply, I seize my moment, leaning smoothly over the small table and bringing my hand to cup her chin. I look into Teresa's eyes long enough for a glimmer of curiosity to shine through her apprehension. I lean forward and kiss her on the mouth, winding my fingers behind her neck.

The men roar with appreciation. I can feel Teresa's body softening through the creaking structure of her formal dress. There's a deep perfume to her, a rich scent that matches her low voice.

When I'm certain of the right moment, I break away, drawing back to consider her face. I bring my mouth to Teresa's ear, so only she can hear what I say.

'Tell me where we can be alone,' I whisper. 'I will wait for you there.'

She hesitates for just a moment, then swallows and inclines her head in acquiescence, eyes slightly unfocused.

'The second floor,' she says, 'third chamber on the left. It's my private study.'

I stand, bow to the company and move to leave the room, giving Jemmy a quick glance of victory as I vacate.

CHAPTER 48

THE ROOM IS DARK AND MUSTY AS I SLIDE THE FOOT-DEEP brass catch of the mahogany door. So much so, that for a moment I think perhaps this isn't the right place. I see new candles, white wax, a variety only perfected in the last few years. I lift up a stub and light it, using a burning taper set for the purpose in the doorway.

The first thing I see is a large bed. A table by it. Lying atop is a familiar piece of jewellery. I'm drawn to it, wondering where I've seen it before.

It's only when I pick it up, realization floods me. This is Grace's engagement ring. I recognize Godwin's family crest.

Was she here? I scan around the room but see no other evidence. Quickly, I begin searching the room, looking for more clues.

There is a space for correspondence. A large desk with writing materials and a little tray filled with yellowing papers. I look closer to see them inked with the political ideals of Monsieur Roland. An ideal place to leave a letter, I decide, hidden amongst dull panegyrics to France's ancient monarchy. No one would start reading this pile of simpering King-worship voluntarily.

I lift a few and notice crumbs of brittle red wax – the kind dropped when a seal is broken. I press my finger on them and put the residue to my mouth. Atherton and I used to spend hours testing one another on the different tastes of sealing wax. He was better than me, but we could both tell the difference between the expensive variety dyed with cochineal or a cheaper cinnabar and we knew the texture of a lawyer's sealing wax – high lacquer content for security but low colour compounds for cost-effectiveness.

This is a lawyer's sealing wax. And since Robespierre is a lawyer, I now look for a letter with a matching seal. I find it easily enough, tucked under the others.

It's written in tiny, neat script. My eyes swoop straight to the small signature at the bottom: *Maximilien Robespierre.*

I begin reading, but to my disappointment there is nothing incriminating. The letter pontificates on the possibility of King Louis XVI being removed from power.

'If King Louis is deposed,' writes Robespierre, 'his heir is too young to rule. The Duc d'Orléans would rule as Regent – a man with an English mistress and a love of England's constitution.'

Robespierre is greatly opposed to this notion, believing France to be too corrupt to adopt a system of compromise.

I'm turning over the blandness of the content when I notice something, something only a code-breaker would see. Some of the letters are formed differently to the others, but the difference is so small it is almost impossible to discern.

I sit, holding the letter, compelled by the puzzle of it. It's a system I've never come across before, blending numbers and alphabet. I haven't met a challenge of this complexity in a long time. My fingers search for a quill and ink and I begin scratching out some workings on a piece of paper. I jot some long equations and shapes, completely absorbed.

I'm so in the thrall of this exceptionally clever letter, I hardly hear the door softly open.

Candlelight spills into the room. I hear soft footsteps and a waft of perfume glides into the air.

I've not had enough time. As the flame swells into the room, I see Madame Roland is already here.

CHAPTER 49

ROBESPIERRE'S FAVOURED GLOVE-PERFUMER IS ON A cobbled street in a fashionable part of Paris. Unlike the bakers and candlestick-makers of lowlier areas, these shops have kept a steady trade, catering to the wildly rich.

Robespierre knocks and the shopkeeper – a woman in a high white wig and silken swaying skirts – comes to open the door.

'Monsieur Robespierre.' She is both unsettled and excited to see him. 'We have new perfumes,' she says in hushed tones, 'from Versailles.'

This is the code. In her supply of perfumed gloves to royalty, Madame Caron is privy to very sensitive information.

She beckons him inside, to a world of thick aromas. The walls are lined with bottles and vials. A carved countertop is set with plump mounds of leather, suede and butter-soft kid, a muted rainbow palette, awaiting the hand to dictate their glove.

A huge glass perfume flask, fatter than a clergyman, boils rose petals in the fireplace, belching puffs of scented steam.

Robespierre looks around the shop. 'Your Marquis has now paid his debt?'

Madame Caron's face darkens.

'*Au contraire,* monsieur. The taste in Versailles is now for brushed suede, so he now owes me a hundred more. Marie Antoinette's fashions bankrupt us shopkeepers.'

As she speaks, Madame Caron steps on to a short ladder that allows her to pluck bottles from the higher shelves. She tucks several under her arm and descends.

Slowly she lays them out. Robespierre leans forward and lifts one at random. He uncorks and inhales. Lavender.

'A little feminine for monsieur,' advises Madame Caron. 'Perhaps one of these?'

She pushes four bottle forwards. Cassia, musk, frankincense and juniper.

Robespierre keeps his breathing steady.

'The juniper,' she says, meeting his eye, 'would suit monsieur very well.'

She lifts the perfume, waves it so that the scent wends upwards.

Robespierre permits himself a silent moment of victory. Madame Caron has independently confirmed where the King intends to hide forty thousand muskets and two hundred barrels of gunpowder.

L'Hôpital des Invalides.

Having cross-checked Madame Roland's information, Robespierre can now be certain. None of his compatriots would stoop to using a woman for the supply of intelligence, but he has found their sex the most reliable, the most cunning and, if it comes to it, the most able to tolerate pain.

'I am greatly obliged for your advice,' he says.

Feeling a little giddy with success, he approaches the large flask of perfume, bubbling away.

'A re-purposed brandy still?' he confirms.

'You are familiar with distillation, monsieur?'

'I was raised in the countryside and our local monks made *eau de vie.* They paid my school scholarship, so naturally had their pound of flesh, working me in their brewery. They refused me their secret formula, though I must say their coded recipe was almost laughably easy to work out.'

Now he thinks about it, this may have been the first cipher he broke.

Madame Caron's face confirms what Robespierre is testing – she will not be moved on matters of religion. He logs this for future use, returning his attention to the glass still.

A cork stopper has been removed, allowing rising vapour to escape. It dangles on a chain.

Robespierre lifts the cork and replaces it, watching the contents of the flask.

'Monsieur Robespierre,' says Madame Caron uncomfortably, 'that is very dangerous. If the steam builds ...'

'When I was a boy,' says Robespierre, 'local famers challenged the noble who owned the land. The braver ones attacked his chateau, raided his cellar.'

He watches the liquid boil for a moment more, then removes the cork. Steam hisses free. Madame Caron sags with relief.

'After their little victory the heat went out,' explains Robespierre. 'They drank on the streets, crowed of their great glory. Months later, when it was all forgotten, the ringleaders mysteriously disappeared. The noble had been sitting tight, making plans, just as our King does now.'

Robespierre adjusts his glasses and looks at Madame Caron.

'It always struck me,' he says, speaking with deliberate care, 'it should have been better if there had been no early victory.

If tensions had been allowed to build.'

Madame Caron nods but looks confused. Robespierre pushes the cork back in. This time he waits a good deal longer as the perfume swells to an angry boil.

'What might have happened had those brave farmers been crushed?' muses Robespierre, watching the rolling fragrance sputter and hiss. 'Had there been a *massacre*, then would the people have found their courage. There would have been the true uprising. Sometimes sacrifice is necessary, wouldn't you agree? For the greater good?'

The perfume is bubbling high on the sides of the flask now, more froth than liquid. Steam is hissing wetly at the cork.

Robespierre closes his eyes and his nostril flare.

'Imagine a great many people lawfully gathered to gain access to weaponry they are entitled to. It is enshrined in law that the people may bear arms when under threat from a foreign enemy. What is the Swiss guard if not a foreign aggressor? The death of such innocents would be simply *awful*.'

'Monsieur Robespierre,' Madame Caron spreads her hands helplessly, 'you will crack the flask.'

'No,' he says, 'the container will not break. Pressure will collect behind the point of least resistance.' Robespierre stretches a finger and touches the cork with the lightest of taps. It shoots from the neck of the still with a loud pop, hissing steam shrieking into the room.

'Observe,' Robespierre watches as the stopper falls back, limp on its chain, 'the tyrant is cast aside.'

He looks up at Madame Caron and gives her a pleasant smile. 'I shall return to choose the glove leather.'

She curtsies uncertainly. 'Very good, monsieur. I wish you God's speed in all your endeavours.'

Robespierre doesn't believe in God, he believes in France. But he has established it would be imprudent to share this with Madame Caron.

He lets himself out silently, the new information simmering in his mind. It is unbelievable, Robespierre notes to himself, what people will tell their glove-makers.

CHAPTER 50

IN MY YEARS OF SPY WORK I HAVE BECOME EXPERT AT foreseeing how people will behave when cornered. Some cower, others fight and, as I predicted, Teresa is a fighter.

Her lined face is rigid with fury as she sees the letter in my hand.

'How dare you!' she glowers, stalking over and making to snatch the paper.

I take hold of her and push her back into the room, ignoring the shout of outrage this elicits. She is tall, though shorter than I, but no match for my strength.

'Make no more noise,' I warn her, 'or all of Paris's fashionable intellectuals will know you for what you are.'

Teresa's mouth shuts at this threat. The fight is gone from her now, but her clever mind is whirring away, looking for ways out. She's still breathing heavily from the shock of my manhandling her, one long-fingered hand touching the shoulder I restrained her by, unable to believe it.

'What happened to Grace Elliott?' I demand.

Teresa's lips press tightly together but she collects herself, her cleverness sliding smoothly to the rescue.

'That is nothing,' she says, 'only correspondence between myself and someone I might welcome to my salon.'

'And why would the wife of a royalist invite a revolutionary into her Paris home?'

Teresa switches tack. 'Us women have to always hide behind men. Monsieur Robespierre promises a new future.'

'An innocent girl has gone missing,' I say. 'I know you played a part in Grace's disappearance. She is my cousin,' I add. 'Don't think I won't take extreme measures to find her.'

Her puppyish eyes flash guilt and I know she knows who I mean. Then her gaze drops to the letter.

'You think no one could break Monsieur Robespierre's code?' I suggest.

Trepidation plays on her features but she speaks with the quiet confidence of a woman who thinks she's being bluffed. She's perfectly assured that I couldn't detangle Robespierre's genius in the few moments I've been alone in this room.

'I have done nothing wrong,' she says haughtily, 'only corresponded with perfect proprietary to a politically minded man.'

'You've been telling Robespierre that the King hides enough weapons for an army at the Hôpital des Invalides in Paris.'

Teresa's face reddens. Her eyes dart around the room, as though looking for an escape.

'You were an inspired choice of informer,' I add. 'A clever woman bored of her gilded cage, hating her royalist husband. He woos you with talk of equality, flatters your opinions on government.'

'It's not about that,' says Teresa. 'It's an ideology. We want a democracy, a good and fair leadership.'

'So you tell Robespierre where the weapons are. He relays

the information to his favoured faction of revolutionaries. They raid the guns and suddenly Robespierre has an army.'

'Sometimes extreme measures must be taken.' But Teresa sounds less certain.

'And what of his request that you spy on my cousin?' I suggest. 'Written in code, of course, but I have abilities in that regard. A girl whom you plotted to have placed in the hands of a murderous torturer. Do you believe that to be perfectly proper?'

She flinches.

'How did you ...?' She's reaching for the letter. I hand it to her.

'I haven't deciphered all of it, I admit; it really is a wonderful code. Monsieur Robespierre is to be commended. I'll leave it to you to decide if I know enough to prove you led a killer named Oliver Janssen to Grace Elliott. And that your principled Monsieur Robespierre had Gaspard de Mayenne murdered.'

I let this threat settle around us. She hesitates perhaps to insist on the details of what I know.

I seize her by the shoulders.

'Tell me where Grace is!' I demand. 'Tell me what you did with my cousin.'

Teresa's eyes widen in alarm. But there is something in the depths. An excitement. I have a sudden image of a clever women so intensely bored by her formal lifestyle she'll do anything to break the ennui.

'She's on her way to the Bastille,' says Teresa. 'I'm sorry for it. As soon as she passes inside there is no hope for her.'

A thousand thoughts overwhelm me.

'You had Grace arrested?'

'No! I would never be responsible for putting a living soul in that dreadful place.'

I release Teresa's arms. A glimmer of disappointment resounds in her eyes.

'Tell me everything,' I say, my mind racing. I'm turning over how I can possibly free Grace from the impenetrable prison.

'Very well,' she says, with a sigh. 'I'll tell you the truth. I ... I am not the monster you think, Mademoiselle Morgan.'

CHAPTER 51

The candles in Teresa's study seem like glowering eyes as I absorb what she's telling me. A killer came looking for Grace. Grace is gone.

Madame Roland is frowning, choosing her words. 'It's true I found Grace,' she says slowly. 'Monsieur Robespierre asked me to watch for anyone of that name. But I helped her. Some of my husband's rogue friends had mistaken her for one of the harlots who come here for profit.'

Teresa's brown eyes flick to mine. 'I ran into her just in time. Dress torn, sobbing uncontrollably. She was so drunk as to hardly be able to stand and they'd given her ether. I dread to think what might have happened had I not got to her.'

'You think yourself virtuous for taking her out of the frying pan and into the fire?' I don't bother to hide my contempt.

'I never meant for it.' Teresa looks down. 'She was in my bedchamber. Then she vanished. Just after I gave her back the necklace.' She sees something in my expression. 'She had a piece of paste jewellery – Robespierre had already told me it was how I might identify her.'

'Was this glass necklace styled on *le collier de la reine*?' I know the answer, even before she speaks.

'Why, yes. I imagine Grace didn't know what a dangerous thing it is, even to imitate. I avidly followed the trial of the jewel thief and Marie Antoinette. We debated it endlessly in my salon. I would go so far as to say it was those missing diamonds that started the first ripples of revolution.'

'So the first thing you did was send word to Robespierre that Grace was here?'

'Robespierre believes there is some English plot. He thought Grace should be arrested and returned to England and I agreed.'

I smile at her naivety.

'You didn't think,' I say slowly, 'that the necklace you saw might have been the real *collier de la reine*?'

'I ... But the diamonds were lost. Four years ago. In any case,' she shakes her head, assuring herself, 'Monsieur Robespierre is not motivated by money. He would never ...'

'Send someone to murder Grace and steal the diamonds to fund the rebel cause?'

Teresa blinks hard. 'I know Robespierre to be an ethical man. A good man. He means a new future for France.'

'Teresa,' I say, 'a man came to your house. A man named Oliver Janssen, known for torturing confessions from his victims. Do you know who he is?'

'He was a musketeer,' she agrees. 'The King disbanded them last year for lack of funds. Many have defected to the rebel cause.'

'Teresa,' I tell her gently, 'who else but Robespierre could have told this musketeer that Grace was here?'

Her eyes track back and forth sightlessly, searching for an explanation that could exonerate Robespierre.

Finally Madame Roland's shoulders sag. Utter devastation seizes her features. 'I didn't know,' she whispers. Her eyes lift to mine. 'Please believe me. I didn't know.' Her chest is rising and falling fast. She swallows and examines her fingernails guiltily.

'When I went back to the bedchamber, Grace was gone. Perhaps she saw him from the window and ran. Just before we played at Hazard, a messenger came from the village. Monsieur Janssen had seen Grace entering a Bastille carriage. He wanted me to inform Robespierre by carrier pigeon.'

'So you did.'

'It was never my intention to put the girl in danger,' says Teresa, her voice strained. 'I assumed she had fled and Robespierre might have the means to help ...' Her face has a tight flush to it and for once she has run out of words.

'You didn't realize what Robespierre was capable of?' I suggest. 'You've been playing at revolutionaries whilst real people have been dying?'

I can tell I've painted the picture well because Teresa can't meet my eye.

'So Grace is on her way to the Bastille.' It's such a terrible thought. 'When did this happen?' I ask. 'When did she get inside the carriage?'

'I can't say for sure,' says Madame Roland. 'This morning, I think. They like to make arrests in the countryside early.'

She looks so beaten down by the revelation of Robespierre's true nature, I feel sorry for her.

'You were doing your best for France,' I say, putting a hand on her shoulder.

She nods, wiping away a tear. She turns to leave, then hesitates.

'The prison guards don't always drive straight to Paris,' she says. 'They often stop at the countryside lock-ups to collect felons who the King deems criminal enough for the Bastille.'

Her eyes meet mine.

'You may still have time to save your cousin,' she says, 'the gaol-carriage is slow and won't travel the most direct route. If you go fast to Paris there's a chance ... Certainly, if your cousin enters the prison, there is no hope for her. People are rarely ever seen again.'

'Thank you,' I say, considering my next move. I think for a moment. 'You have carrier pigeons here?'

'Yes. Another affectation the poor hate us for,' she says. 'They're not allowed to eat them.'

'Can any fly to the east gate of the city?'

'Of course.'

'Then you might send a message for me.' I'm making calculations. The Sealed Knot have a man at the east gate trained to look for our codes. If I can get word that Grace is in a Bastille carriage, perhaps one of our men in Paris can intercept it and rescue her. The odds are not good, but it's worth trying.

'If you write it,' says Madame Roland, 'I will send it. You have my promise. I have made mistakes, I know, but I will try to make amends.'

I move to her desk, tear a small strip of paper and pen a note in code.

Teresa takes the message, places both hands firmly on my shoulders and kisses me on either cheek.

'I shall put it into the hands of my most trusted servant,' she promises. 'It will be at the east gate within the hour. Times are changing for women,' she adds. 'You are welcome in my salon, Mademoiselle Morgan, any time you choose. My time with Robespierre is done. But I am still hopeful there can be change in France, without bloodshed.'

I return to the party in a kind of daze, thinking through my next move.

Carrier pigeons are unreliable. I can't be sure my message will get to the right people in time. I need to get back into Paris and track Grace. I look up to see Jemmy striding towards me. He has a dark expression out of keeping with his usual easygoing nature.

'Attica.' He grabs my arm and moves me away from the elevated country views of the long windows.

I'm aware of a strange noise: a buzzing sound. Something I can't place. As though the hum of party conversation is backed by a lower, louder din somewhere else. The music stops. There's a scream.

We all turn in shock to see Teresa standing by the window, her face white, a high-pitched cry issuing from her thin lips.

At first I think I don't understand her French. But then I hear. She isn't saying words. It's a noise of pure animal anguish.

She steps back, her eyes glazed like a sleepwalker's and stumbles. A man catches her just before she falls, red ribbons fluttering.

The party is silent now. I'm suddenly aware of a strange noise at the glass of the fine long windows.

Tap tap tap.

The large apertures have the shutters open. But we're a full storey off the ground. How could anyone be knocking?

Tap tap tap.

It comes again and then I see it. We all do.

Tapping against the window is a severed man's head, stuck on a long pike.

Foulon. Or what's left of him. The mob has brought him here.

CHAPTER 52

FOULON'S HEAD BOBS CLUMSILY UP AND DOWN, PECKING AT the glass. His hair is still dressed perfectly in the courtly style but the corpse lips are glued shut in a rictus of pain. One eye is missing and the skin at the bloody neck is hacked and tattered.

More people are screaming now. The head wavers, one-eyed on his high pike, tapping against the window tauntingly, as though he's trying to get in.

Now I know what the other noise was. The strange humming is the roar of a mob clamouring in the grounds below.

There must be thousands out there.

There's a loud smashing sound and then the tinkling of glass hitting the wooden floor. The head, on its pike, has broken through. Foulon's single eye surveys the room like a macabre puppet.

I instinctively reach for my knife.

Shouts come up from the street.

'Teresa! Come kiss your lover!'

Now stones and missiles are pitched through the smashed glass. A dead cat thuds on the floor and slides unceremoniously across the shining boards.

'Attica.' A calm voice cuts through the shouting. 'Get away from the window.'

Jemmy's hand tightens on mine.

He drags me to stand flat against the wall. We both stare out at the chaos in the room. People are running around like headless chickens. A rain of stone and rocks sail through.

Jemmy and I exchange glances.

'The mob will come in the front door,' I say.

He casts a glance at my fashionable dress and removes a pistol from his belt. 'You won't get out without my help.'

'You have it the wrong way around,' I say, pulling out my knife in an easy movement. 'But I will do my best to protect you.'

'Holy Mary Mother of God!' says Jemmy, eyeing the curved blade with its dark wood handle and pointed back section. 'That's a Mangbetu blade. Where did you get that?'

'It was part of my mother's dowry.'

His eyes are glued to the knife.

'A story for another time,' I add.

I nod to the large double doors leading to the stairway. Between us and the exit are a run of long windows, several of which are now broken. Through them, projectiles fly. A hysterical woman dressed as a shepherdess makes a break for freedom. A gun-blast rings out and she goes down, a spray of shot shattering one side of her face. No one moves to mourn the dead woman. They're all too scared for their own lives.

'It's a gauntlet,' I say. 'Anyone who passes the windows is a target. The escape route is blocked.'

'A little organized for a rabid mob, don't you think?' says Jemmy.

I nod. 'Perhaps someone else heard the diamonds were here,' I say. 'Someone doesn't want survivors telling tales.' I look at the double doors, then at the pistol in Jemmy's hand. He understands immediately.

Jemmy pivots to the open window. He fires a loud shot downwards and flattens himself back against the wall. Shouting erupts from outside but the assault dies back.

'We have a few moments until they regroup,' mutters Jemmy. 'Think we can make it?'

'Only one way to find out.'

We set off at a sprint across the long ballroom, weaving through terrified aristocrats, reaching the doorway just as missiles start coming thick and fast again. Partygoers scatter as Jemmy and I make it into the hallway.

Together we scan a quick assessment. At the bottom of the wide staircase, the front door to the house is splintering. The mob is battering it from the outside.

'We've got time to get through the servants' entrance at the back,' says Jemmy.

I take hold of his arm.

'No,' I say. 'Those people got to the house with no alarm raised. We can't trust the servants. At least some of them are complicit.'

'Then the only way is up,' says Jemmy.

We race up to the second floor just as the doors below us burst open. A swell of pike-bearing men and women swarm into the ornate hallway. Jemmy ducks a head over the landing and switches back.

'We have to keep climbing,' he hisses, keeping an iron grip on my wrist. 'If they see us we're dead.' The staircase narrows as we reach the third floor.

'This is where the household staff live,' I say. 'We must be wary, if they've turned on the Rolands ...'

The words aren't out of my mouth when a footman with a sword emerges from a hidden corner of the stairs. He runs at us, blade held out. Jemmy dodges, drawing his own weapon so swiftly I could have sworn he was holding it all along. The footman advances and Jemmy parries his first swipe.

I duck between them and plunge my knife upwards, past Jemmy's cheek and driving it under the ear of his assailant. I feel the pointed section pierce brain and then the man's right eye fills with blood.

Someone is behind me, taking hold of my shoulder. A sword is coming towards my throat. I lift the hand, slash the wrist and turn, kicking back another surprised footman who stumbles and collapses, staring at the blood cascading from his severed artery.

I wipe the curved steel on my dress. 'Come on.'

Jemmy stands open-mouthed, sword still poised. 'You move fast,' he manages, 'for someone who dances like a wind-up toy.'

'Some moves are worth learning, others are not.'

Jemmy is strangely quiet as we reach the top. Through a small door is an empty attic room with a tiny cot bed and thin blankets.

'I never saw a Mangbetu knife in action,' he says as I shut the door. 'You could have killed me,' he adds, touching his cheek where the blade plunged past.

'I never learned from an African native,' I say, moving to look out the window. 'So I'm afraid I'm not using it as a Congo warrior might.' I glance at him. 'I won't tell your pirate crew you were saved by a woman.'

'You didn't *save* me. Only speeded the conclusion.'

'You can thank me later.'

'So these are the servants' quarters,' says Jemmy, changing

the subject, his lips a thin line. 'Very different to the grand rooms.'

The meagre room is cold, draughty and ill maintained, with mould flowering on the ceiling.

'There's nowhere to hide,' I say.

Jemmy's eyes cast about the room. There's a shout from the stairs.

'I think your dead man might be telling tales,' he observes. 'Best put that knife away.'

'I need it.' Many footsteps are pounding upwards now. The walls of the room are closing in on me.

Jemmy turns to look at me. 'Attica,' he takes my shoulders, 'there's no way out of this room. If you start fighting a mob, you'll end up worse than Foulon.'

My hand tightens on the blade. A dark panic is bearing down, something deep-seated and familiar.

'So I just wait and let them capture me?'

'You're reacting to being confined,' says Jemmy. 'I've seen it in a lot of people who've been enslaved. You're not thinking right.' He catches my uncertain expression. 'My mamma used to take in escapees in New York,' he explains. 'I can't pretend to understand everything, but I know a bit. I'm bettin' you're not keen on official papers with your name on either.'

This brings me up short. It's true; in Virginia this was our deepest dread. A named letter meant you belonged to someone else.

'What do you propose?' I ask tightly. 'I throw myself on their mercy, in my fine dress?' The see-through muslin outfit Angelina lent me is decadent and frivolous all at once.

'I've an idea to save us both,' says Jemmy, 'but you're not going to like it.'

'Because?' I'm looking at the door, knife in hand.

'You'll need to take your clothes off.'

CHAPTER 53

ROBESPIERRE IS CAREFULLY CROSSING A 'T' WHEN HIS door is flung open noisily, causing him to smudge the ink. He looks up, deeply annoyed, then his expression softens.

A heavily drunk Georges Danton sways in the doorway. His dark coat hangs unbuttoned untidily over his broad stomach. Robespierre's old friend wears a smile so wide it threatens to split his great pockmarked head.

'Georges,' Robespierre stands. 'Come take a chair before you fall.'

'Maximilien!' Danton crosses the squeaking floorboards and crushes Robespierre in a bear hug, kissing him heartily on both cheeks. 'What a day it is for France! That rogue Foulon is lynched by a crowd demanding justice!'

Danton's scarred face is alive with joy and strong drink. The tavern smell pours off him.

He sits on a hard stool opposite Robespierre's desk, great legs splayed. The seat emits a gunshot crack beneath Danton's bulk and Robespierre winces.

'Do you have wine?' Danton scratches under his lawyer's wig, a functional rather than decorative item acquired in the second-hand market outside Les Halles.

Silently, Robespierre removes a decanter and two small glasses from under his desk and pours Danton and himself a modest measure of pinkish-red liquid.

Danton takes it gratefully, the tiny vessel like a toy in his huge hand.

'So!' Danton slaps his broad thighs. 'Tell me this grand scheme of yours. From what I hear you are becoming a dangerous fellow, Max. Not the pale little runt I knew at law school.'

Robespierre stands, feeling very small, as he always does around Danton.

'I can trust you?' he confirms.

'How can you ask me such a thing?' Danton rises to his feet. 'Come, we are friends, are we not? If a man like you can be said to have friends. We have known each other many years.'

Robespierre notes that Danton has not answered directly.

'Madame Roland has revealed to me where the King is hiding the weapons.'

There is a pause. Danton's small blue eyes widen.

'*Mon Dieu,* she has *not*! You sneaky cat! I can scarce believe it.' Danton roars with laughter and knocks back his wine in one. 'I commend you heartily, old friend. No other man could have done it. Pretending you thought Madame Roland as intelligent as a man was inspired.'

'It was no pretence.' Robespierre frowns. 'Our new France must be one of true equals.'

'Yes, yes.' Danton waves a chubby hand. 'Of course you would say such things. You are not encumbered with the usual drives. For myself, I will have a few kept women and I'm sure they shall not mind!' He winks and helps himself to more wine.

'Well now, we must then disagree,' suggests Danton. 'You want a fresh start, no King at all. But I say such a thing cannot be done. Slowly, slowly, you cook the goose. We shall follow the English way.' He holds up his meaty hands. 'I know, I know, you loathe the English. But a King with the correct checks and balances is how it will be. Louis is a reasonable enough fellow to go along with such things. He is no Sun King to have us tortured to death in the Bastille.'

Robespierre raises a glass. 'To liberty and equality,' he says.

'And brotherhood! Do not forget the most important part.'

Robespierre smiles thinly. 'Of course.' He drinks.

'Holy saints, Max, I'd forgotten about your wine. Try spending more than a centime a bottle, it might even take that vinegary look off your face. The nobles don't get it all wrong, you know.' Danton puckers his mouth. 'You should live a little, Max. When was the last time you got tight with drink?'

Robespierre considers the question. 'Les Innocents Graveyard,' he admits.

Danton widens his eyes. 'When we were law students, clearing those graves for centimes?' Danton crosses himself. 'I still shudder when I pass the fountain at Les Halles. All those poor souls dug up, moved without prayer or headstone. Bones pulled out and wheeled away in carts, as if they were no more than turnips.'

Robespierre does not share how his grave-digging days had put pictures into his head he couldn't shake. His mother's body, clutching the cold baby. Dirty soil hitting dead faces.

'There were a great deal of candles in Versailles that year,' he says instead, 'made from corpse wax.'

'Ha ha! So there were! I had forgotten we did that.' Danton grins at the memory. 'Made a pretty penny selling candles and soap from those fatty grave deposits, didn't we?' Danton becomes serious. 'Well, out with it. Where does your pet *aristo* say we shall find these weapons?'

Robespierre leans back, savouring the moment.

'L'Hôpital des Invalides.'

CHAPTER 54

AS THE MEN ENTER THE ATTIC ROOM, THE FIRST THING they see is Jemmy's naked back. He is embracing me with a conviction I think excessive, breaking away only when the men take hold of his shoulder.

He turns, acting alarmed and then relieved. I grab up the bedsheet to cover myself.

'I thought you were the mistress,' says Jemmy with a grin. 'Come to claim the revolution at last, have you, boys? Good luck to you.'

The men stop in confusion. From underneath Jemmy I can see them considering my uncovered shoulders. We didn't have time to unclothe entirely. Below the threadbare bed sheets is all the evidence of our fine clothing the men need to rip us to shreds.

'You're English,' says one man.

'That I am,' says Jemmy, his accent twanging as he speaks in French. 'We've got our Republic and wish you God speed of yours. The only thing I love more than liberty is my girl here. This is her room. And you're in the wrong part of the house, citizens. As you can see, we're occupied.'

With the door open we can all hear the most awful noises drifting up from the main room. People are screaming, but it's not the screams of fear any more. There are dreadful thumps of flesh on flesh. Brutal killing sounds. I hear furniture overturned and shrieks as people are dragged out of hiding places.

'And you're wasting time in the top of the house,' continues Jemmy in a confidential tone. 'There are wine cellars.'

The men's faces light up.

'Filled with France's finest,' says Jemmy. 'Enough for ten barrels each,' he pauses for effect, 'unless your comrades have found them already.'

'Wine!' The men are gruff and exhilarated now.

'Best we search the cellar,' growls one. 'Be sure no fine folk hide themselves there.'

One turns to me.

'Give us one last look, sweetheart,' he says. 'I ain't never seen anything like you afore.'

'Leave off, Victor,' says another man. 'It's equality now. Robespierre says it.'

A little ripple goes through the group, as though the name alone sparks terror in this rough band of opportunist freedom fighters.

They retreat, the door banging shut behind them.

'You didn't have to be quite so convincing,' I complain, wriggling out from under him.

'Believe me,' says Jemmy, glancing to the door as I begin pulling up my clothing, 'I can be a great deal more convincing than that. Surely I haven't offended your honour?'

'Only my dignity,' I say, fitting my dress back into place.

We stand and move to the door.

'With luck they'll all head for the wine cellars,' says Jemmy. 'Now they've finished with the guests.'

I nod in agreement. Though the horror of what happened in the room below is milling around us, an unspoken atrocity. I push my knife back into my dress.

'That blade,' says Jemmy, watching me holster it. 'If your mother was a slave and you were born in Virginia, how did she manage to keep it?'

'It was given to my father,' I say, 'to trick him into thinking my mother was dead.'

'Can I touch it?'

'No.'

'Where did you train?'

'Sicily,' I admit. There's no point lying, I decide. He's cleverer than I gave him credit for.

'Expensive business, Sicilian Assassins' Academy,' muses Jemmy. 'Your pappy pay for your tutorage in knife skills, did he?' This idea seems to amuse him hugely.

'Yes. But he didn't know what he was paying for.' This is only half true. Atherton arranged it, but I suspect my father knew.

'Did you become expert in a particular fighting style?' asks Jemmy. 'Stiletto blades? Fencing?'

I smile at his naivety. 'My speciality was staying alive.'

Jemmy laughs. This is the first time I've admitted my strange shadow-world training to anyone but Atherton. It makes me feel strangely close to Jemmy.

'I've killed a few men,' says Jemmy thoughtfully. 'You're always smaller after, less of a person. I wouldn't wish that on a woman.'

I feel the sharp little nugget of self-disgust I always carry digging in below my ribs.

'What I'd like to know,' he adds, looking me up and down and moving to the door, 'is where you hide your pistol.'

'I don't shoot a pistol.'

'What?' he hisses, eyes flicking to the unseen danger beyond. 'Don't tease me. Every lady in London has one.'

'As you have cleverly discerned,' I whisper back, 'I work in secret for the English army. Do you know how many of our men were killed by their own pistols last year?'

He shrugs. Puts an ear to the door.

'One hundred and twenty-six,' I say. 'One hundred and twenty-six burned by their own powder, blasted by backfiring guns.'

Jemmy raises his eyebrows. 'There are always a few fools.'

'If you believe the reports,' I say, calling to mind Atherton's neat crabbed script and thc crossed-out names, 'you might think we recruit a very large number of fools for service. Or,' I lean across and tap the head of his pistol, 'you're so enamoured with the feel of that thing stashed against your thigh, that you're blind to the reality it's more likely to kill you than an armed attacker. Pistols misfire more often than not and it's impossible to do more than aim in the direction of a target.'

'So you don't carry a pistol.' Jemmy doesn't bother to hide his disappointment.

'Oh, I sometimes carry one. They can be a useful distraction from the knife.'

He opens the door. 'We'll see how your knife works out against whoever's still down there. Come on.'

We begin to go back down the stairs when Jemmy holds up a warning hand. He peers around the corner, then flattens himself back against the wall.

'Lot of armed men down there,' he whispers, drawing a gun from his belt. 'Still sure about that knife of yours?'

A voice drifts up on to the stairwell, low and gravelly.

In walks a man I have never seen before, except, perhaps, in nightmares. He's a horrifying sight. One eye is ringed with ferociously burned skin, shiny pink wheals clustered around a blood-red iris. His left hand and lower arm, too, are metal, but like no prosthetic I've ever seen. The replacement limb is silverwork with bony fingers, like a ghoulish skeleton.

'L'Hôpital des Invalides,' he is saying. 'Enough weapons for every man in Paris to hold a gun in his hand. The raid will take place at dawn.'

'Shit.' Jemmy's face falls. 'That's Oliver Janssen. Looks as though he's doing more than musketeering.'

I'm soaking in this information, deciding what it means, when I realize Jemmy stands rigid beside me. I turn to see soldiers emerge from either end of the corridor. Too many, all pointing guns.

One of them calls down the stairwell.

Janssen looks up and the temperature in the room seems to drop a few degrees as I take in the King's infamous torturer. He looks every inch a terror, his red eye hard and merciless.

'Come down, Monsieur Avery, and bring the girl with you. You're quite surrounded.'

CHAPTER 55

I LET JANSSEN'S GUARDS LEAD ME BACK THROUGH THE MAIN room, where the masquerade was being held less than an hour ago.

The floor is strewn with the evidence of a bloody battle: broken objects, scattered food, upended furniture, and everywhere the ominous stench of death and terror. A black mask lies in a pool of blood, its feathered plume bent and dirtied.

'The mob can be brutal,' observes Janssen.

His single brown eye flicks to my face, trying to discern what I'll make of it all.

'You are a musketeer?' I say, absorbing his uniform. He sports the signature red tabard with a stark white cross at the front and back, roll-top boots and a belt-full of weaponry. 'Yet you fight with the rebellion?'

'I'm still a musketeer,' grunts Janssen. 'I swore an oath for life to protect the King. But a King is no King who disbands his musketeers.'

'If you mean to serve his successor,' I say, 'you must be certain the Society of Friends shares your view. Some rebels want no King at all.'

Janssen makes no reply to this but I sense just the slightest unease in his face, as though something has just occurred to him.

I log that he has silently confirmed the Society of Friends instruct him.

We walk through to a smaller room, what was Teresa's salon. I'm thinking of the thick pile of documents I read on the French monarchy, the various rebel factions. I'm piecing things together.

There's a desk and chair, but Janssen doesn't sit, only paces back and forth. After a moment, he looks up, his burning red eye trained on me.

'So, mademoiselle,' he says, 'I must demand to know what you and the pirate do in France?'

'You have no right to do so,' I say coldly. 'I am a free woman according to the laws of your country. Is it your usual practice to hold foreigners against their will?'

I'm wondering where Jemmy is. Men took him in a different direction to me.

Janssen removes his broad-rimmed hat and places it on the desk. Beneath it, his hair is long, in straggling curls. Black mixed with grey.

'Foreign spies are rife. I only ask for your help in protecting France from her enemies.'

'In which case, tell me, how does a Dutchman become a French King's guard?'

The head tilts in a strange little movement. 'I am from Fontenay.'

I cycle through my studies of French wars.

'You were born Dutch,' I deduce, 'and the French besieged and won your town. Saint's blood,' I add, making the calculation, 'Fontenay's fall was brutal. You could have been no older than five. Is that how you came by your injuries?'

Janssen raises a metal hand to his damaged face.

'The wounds I sustained as a boy in Fontenay, you cannot see,' he says. 'Those you can are from an exploding cannon,' he explains, his good eye meeting mine. 'A battle against the English.' He pauses, to let this inference sink in. 'It reduced my ability to fire a musket. But gave me ... other talents His Majesty found useful.'

My eyes dwindle on the evil-looking metal hand. I feel a wave of pity for him. I have read about the monstrous things done to children in the French acquisition of Dutch lands. One day they were Dutch, the next French, with some terrible starving scenes in between to ensure any lingering patriots saw reason.

'I did not bring you here to exchange stories of my awful boyhood,' he says. 'I brought you here to give you a warning from the Society of Friends.'

He curls and uncurls his metal hand. I look at it for a long moment, facts slotting into place.

'Your society is rather too free with their warnings,' I say. 'Gaspard de Mayenne, for example. It was you who killed him, was it not?'

I look for some reaction but there is none.

'I assume your instructions were to stage the body so as to be significant to a particular rebel faction.' It's a guess but I'm hoping to bait him. 'Perhaps your new masters did not think you important enough to share this detail with. Or did you fail to follow exact orders, Monsieur Janssen?'

'I followed my orders ...' begins Janssen, anger mounting. He stops, checking himself. But not before I've inferred a great deal.

'The Society work for France. As does your pirate friend.' Janssen watches my face. I feel a flicker of unease.

'Anything else?' I say, not willing to let Janssen see this information has unsettled me.

'You are not welcome here,' says Janssen. 'You may soon find aristocrats of any kind are in danger.'

'And you hope, in return, for a new strong King who will restore his musketeers?'

Janssen looks at me. 'Our new country will have no place for weakness or for enemy foreigners. You must go from France, Mademoiselle Morgan.'

'That I cannot do.' I look into his single eye. 'I have business in the Bastille.'

'You will leave and not return,' he says, 'but before you do, you will tell me the identity of the English spy. The Pimpernel.'

I say nothing.

He frowns. 'Did you hear that Foulon was first lynched by the mob, but didn't die by hanging?' He leans forward suddenly. 'The rope broke. Several times.' He waits a moment for this image to sink in. 'So the people dragged the half-dead Foulon to a butcher's shop. They hacked off his head with a rusty knife. Stuck it on a pike. Then they found his son-in-law driving his carriage and made him kiss the dead lips.'

He's looking at me intently, hoping, I think, that I will flinch.

'If you think you can make me talk, you are mistaken.'

He looks at me.

'You imagine yourself resistant to pain?' he says. 'You forget there is more than one kind. Everyone can be broken. It's only a matter of using the correct technique.'

Before I understand what I'm seeing, Janssen vanishes and returns promptly, dragging with him a frightened-looking woman. It's Teresa Roland.

CHAPTER 56

IN THE SALON DES PRINCES, SOUNDS OF BREAKING AND pillaging echo all around. Oliver Janssen is watching me closely.

I try not to react as Teresa is manhandled into the room, her dress torn, the styled hair dishevelled. She's trying to appear calm, but there's a flash of real terror in her eyes.

Janssen looks at me.

'Madame Roland has not proved the ally Monsieur Robespierre was hoping for,' he says. 'It would be unfortunate for an aristocrat,' he spits the word, 'to end up in the hands of the mob.'

I glance at Teresa. Her expression is unreadable but her chest is rising and falling fast. The loathing on Janssen's face is clear. I'm guessing Teresa has never before been confronted with the hatred felt by men like Janssen for women of her class.

Janssen moves in close to Madame Roland and does something I can't see but I hear a strange moan escape her and she sags in horrible slow-motion, hands twitching.

Teresa straightens with difficulty, her face drained of blood. It takes every ounce of self-control not to run to her aid.

Janssen turns to me. He seems to have derived a particular satisfaction from his victim.

'I shall ask again,' he says, 'who is the Pimpernel?'

'Does Robespierre mean to torture his way to power?' I demand angrily. 'Is that a man you want to lead you?'

Janssen pulls Teresa upright. Tears are running down her cheeks. My stomach twists.

'I think you know the English plans,' he says. 'And I think you will tell me.'

Janssen moves again and Teresa cries out in pain. I force myself to stare into Janssen's eyes. I have met men like him before, in Virginia, in Russia; men for whom 'I don't know' can never be enough, even if it is the truth.

'I think you are all bluff,' I say. 'You cannot kill Madame Roland,' I continue. 'If she dies, the crime of the mob is no longer political,' I say, casting a gaze to Teresa's anxious face.

Janssen smiles. 'I can do what I like,' he says. 'As the people did with the unfortunate Foulon. They put a garland of nettles around his neck and a bushel of grass on his back, walked him barefoot for miles. They beat him, made him drink vinegar.'

Madame Roland looks pained. Janssen glances at her, enjoying her discomfort.

'When they tired of it, they conducted their own trial,' concludes Janssen. 'Tried Foulon for crimes against the French people, stuffed his mouth with grass and hung him from a lamp-post.'

'So the people had their revenge,' I say, 'for the cruelty they endured. Monsieur Foulon was a corrupt politician,' I say, 'the people performed a public trial. Madame Roland is an innocent woman who has been careful not to overstep her wifely boundaries, despite an unfortunate marriage.'

I pause to let my words take effect.

'If the justice for Foulon became high-spirited, well,' I open my palms. 'A severed head is unsavoury to be sure, but there is no law against what happens to the remains of convicted criminals.' I nod to Madame Roland. 'An aristocratic lady. That would give the events of today a very different flavour. No one would blame the King for raising a foreign army against Paris if a blood-thirsty mob were killing women indiscriminately.'

A glimmer of unease sparks in Janssen's single eye.

'I imagine Monsieur Robespierre would be *very unhappy* if his well-planned machinations fell apart,' I add. I'm taking a chance that Janssen is afraid of Robespierre.

Teresa says nothing, but I can see a fortitude blooming in her down-turned eyes. She knows I'm right and is switching a hopeful gaze between Janssen and his guard.

Janssen withdraws his metal hand.

'Take Madame Roland away,' he says without looking at me. 'Leave her at the gates of Versailles. Ensure she gets inside the Royal Palace grounds without harm.'

Teresa bites her lower lip and gives him a hard glare.

'I helped you people,' she says. 'How could you?'

Janssen doesn't even look at her as she's taken from the room. He turns to me.

'You will leave France tonight,' he says. 'My men will escort you outside and drive you straight to the port.' He smiles as though this is a courtesy, whilst we both know it to be the opposite.

'And if I refuse?'

Heavy hands take hold of my arms and I feel myself roughly escorted from the house where a coach and horses await.

Not a fine vehicle. This looks more like the black Hackney coaches of London. A dark wooden box set on unadorned wheels. There's a parcel shelf at the back, a perch for the driver at the front and oiled leather straps holding it all together.

The men are opening the door, gesturing I should step inside. Inside is much like outside: planked sides with a hard seat and plenty of gaps for the draughts to get in. The plain functionality of it is of small amusement to me.

Robespierre. The incorruptible.

Even as he rises to importance, he will not allow his men the vulgar trappings of the noble class. There's something to be admired in such conviction, I suppose.

I sit in the carriage, assessing my situation. There's a driver at the front and two heavy-set men standing on the back.

Too many men to drive one woman to the port.

So, the Society of Friends want me dead but will keep my murder secret from Janssen. I'm building a picture of ruthless compartmentalizing. An organization where one person alone knows everything.

I think for a moment. If I were planning an untraceable killing I would have me assassinated long before we reach the road to Paris. It would avoid the potential for witnesses and afford long tracts of countryside to dump a body.

Two men. Three if you count the driver. I log their weapons. One is holstering a dagger. They wear a sword each and a gun apiece they haven't troubled themselves to load.

I smile to myself. It's the great advantage of being a woman: to be always underestimated.

CHAPTER 57

JEMMY FINDS ME BY THE SIDE OF THE ROAD, SOOTHING THE frightened horse. He's still in all-black attire, the long coat and dark shirt. But now there are weapons loaded in his belt and his hair is tied back with a black ribbon.

He slides easily from his own steed and approaches, eyeing the dead men lying on the grass.

'I came to rescue you,' he says with an elaborate bow, 'but I am too late. You had all the fun without me, Madame Pimpernel. Ah, but you are pleased to see me at least,' he says, taking in my wide smile.

'I am,' I admit. 'I have never been happier to see a man in civilian clothes. Uniformed men in France are not as chivalrous as they appear.'

The horse breathes out heavily and I stroke her nose. Jemmy looks at the spinning wheel of the upturned carriage, the smashed front. His eyes cross to the corpses on the ground, each bearing a single knife wound under the ribs. He takes in the driver, the reins tight around his neck.

'You were showing off, Attica,' he admonishes.

'No,' I protest, 'I was saving my own life.'

'With unnecessary flair,' he says, looking at the scattered men disapprovingly. 'Now Robespierre knows what you're capable of.'

I open my mouth to disagree, but I see he's right. I was so sure Robespierre had underestimated me I never thought it might be the other way around.

'You've left Robespierre a message,' concludes Jemmy.

This pushes something to the forefront of my mind.

'Gaspard's death.' I shake my head, trying to dislodge a thought. 'Everyone thinks it is a message for them. Yet even his killer seemed to have no real idea of the purpose of it all.'

'Then it is a very bad message,' observes Jemmy, 'and an ill-considered murder.'

'It would appear so,' I agree. 'Yet all the evidence points to Robespierre – a lawyer who exercises great caution in all his affairs. Does it not seem wildly out of character for a man such as he to make some ill-planned assassination?'

'It does,' agrees Jemmy.

'Something is happening in Paris,' I say, 'something significant. Robespierre has discovered the whereabouts of a huge weapons cache at the Hôpital des Invalides.' I put my hands to my temples. 'It is all connected,' I say, 'I'm sure of it. Gaspard's death. The weapons. It feels like two halves of the same plan.'

'To be sure, you have your answer,' says Jemmy. 'Robespierre is for the rebels. Some faction or other will relieve the *hôpital* of its weaponry and our careful lawyer will have an army.'

'I don't think he wants an army. He wants ... power. Ideals.' The solution is just beyond my grasp, as though I could touch it with my fingertips.

'If I'm to rescue Grace, I must know what happens in the

city. Else I walk in blind. I'm certain Robespierre had Gaspard killed. I don't know why.'

Something else occurs to me. How does Jemmy know so much about Robespierre? Janssen's words come back.

The Society work for France. As does your pirate friend.

Jemmy sighs. 'We should double back,' he says. 'Go the opposite way to the city. Throw them off the scent. I've got some money, we can take shelter—' He catches my expression and stops.

'I'm going to Paris,' I explain. 'Grace was last seen in a carriage headed to the Bastille. She may be inside already.'

'The *Bastille*!' His tone says it all.

Jemmy passes a hand through his dark hair. 'Attica, it's a terrible plan. You want to walk into Paris as mobs are starting up, putting noble heads on sticks. Did anyone from this secret spy ring of yours warn you against impulsiveness?'

'Oh yes,' I agree, thinking of Atherton, 'all the time.'

'First you'll get past an army of Swiss troops,' he reminds me.

I absorb this information.

'Attica, it's too late,' says Jemmy. 'Robespierre has allies on every tollgate and guard house. You'll be arrested before you pass the first village.'

'How do you know that?' I glare at him. 'Tell me the truth. Who are you working for?'

'Myself. Same as you, as far as I can make out.'

'I work for England.'

'Do they know that? Attica,' Jemmy says patiently, 'did it ever occur to you that Atherton might have sent more than one person to retrieve this necklace?'

'Atherton hired you? He didn't trust a woman to make

the mission?' I'm cut to the quick. Everything Atherton ever asked of me I have done.

'Put down your pride, Attica, it's not about that. Your neutrality is compromised. If it came down to keeping Robespierre from those diamonds or saving Grace, which would you choose?'

I look away. 'You lied to me,' I accuse. 'I thought you were hunting treasure.'

'You didn't wonder why a privateer knows so much about the lost jewels of Marie Antoinette? Rather a political set of gems to be seeking out, don't you think?'

I am momentarily silent. He's a good actor, I realize, slightly stung. I believed him when he said he was hunting the necklace for treasure. Now I don't know what's true and what isn't.

'What's the problem, Lady Morgan,' asks Jemmy, 'did ye think secrets and lies were the sole talent of nobles?'

'No.' But this isn't quite correct. Mostly I work alongside people of a certain social class – misfits, miscreants, to be sure – but the majority highborn to one degree or another.

'Of course you did.' He rolls his eyes. 'We're on the same side, the only difference is I'm working for money and you're working for your country. To my mind that makes me the more trustworthy, since a country is such a slippery thing nowadays.'

'What are you saying,' I demand, 'that you'll help me find Grace?'

'I'll help you find the diamonds,' says Jemmy, 'and keep them out of Robespierre's hands. If a man like that finds them, there's no telling how this revolution will play out. He could end up directing it.'

There's a thunder of hooves in the distance. I stand, shielding my eyes from the sun.

'Seems you didn't miss the fun after all,' I say, releasing the horse from its carriage and heaving myself on its back. I nod at a body of armed riders on the horizon. 'Plenty of entertainment still to be had.'

'Robespierre's men,' says Jemmy grimly. 'I imagine he sent a larger group to murder your murderers after your body was buried. Cover his tracks.'

'Surely Robespierre doesn't fear the loyalty of his own guards?'

'Robespierre fears and plans for all eventualities,' says Jemmy. 'That is what makes him so dangerous.'

He points to the road to Paris. 'We cannot go straight. I could lead us a safe way, but it would take us days. If what you say is true, Grace will be deep within the bowels of the Bastille by then.'

My stomach lurches at the thought of my innocent cousin lost in the prison-of-no-return.

I shut my eyes, searching for possibilities. None are forthcoming. I imagine the great wall of troops ringing Paris. *No way in; no way out.*

I look around, looking for any means of escape. And then I see an unlikely possibility.

The gypsy camp in the Roland grounds, with their large circus tent and band of horses.

The globe aerostatic.

It's fixed to the ground by several strong ropes, its stitched silken structure billowing prettily above a burning coal brazier.

'So,' concludes Jemmy, hands on the hips of his black shirt, 'any notion of how we get past an army of Swiss soldiers.'

I point to the waving balloon.

'There,' I say to Jemmy. 'We fly.'

CHAPTER 58

'I DON'T LIKE THE LOOK OF THOSE CIRCUS MEN,' JEMMY says as we near the encampment.

'Let me talk to them,' I say. 'I spent part of my childhood with gypsies. Anyone who speaks Romany is a friend. You go and ready the globe aerostatic.'

'How do you propose I do that? I sail ships, remember?'

'It works on heat,' I explain, remembering Atherton's little lanterns. 'There'll be a brazier. Get it as hot as you can. The steering must be at least a little like a ship,' I add. 'It's like one large sail in the wind.'

Jemmy vanishes away. I approach the camp, running my hands through my dark curls and working my hair into a long gypsy-style plait. I'm still dressed for the Rolands' party, of course: the light muslin dress with flapping ribbons, satin shoes. Nevertheless, I'm confident my fluent Romany will soften any animosity.

There's a ring of little tents in the distance and two colourful caravans, large with arched fronts, that I remember helping make as a girl. Near to the road is a much larger tent for displays with horses and acrobat tricks.

But as I pick across the badly tied guy-ropes my mistake becomes apparent. This is no Romany camp. The caravans are pitched all wrong, one leaning at a bad angle. A large tent is barely standing and outside it is a barrel with circus equipment carelessly flung inside. Juggling batons, long ribbons on sticks – the kind a gypsy would never make.

There are no gypsies here any more. It's a stolen circus.

Of course. My stupidity hits me. Someone let the mob in through the gates.

My stomach tightens in anger. Horses are tethered to a single post, boggy mud and sawdust under their hooves. Beyond them, around a smoky fire, sits a group of feral-looking Frenchmen who I assume murdered the original owners.

They stand as I near, pulling knives from their belts. Seven muscled men, scarred and dirt-streaked. A knife whirls past my face. I turn and run.

As I flee, sawdust striking up beneath my feet, more blades pass me, narrowly missing my head. I aim for a tent, plunging through a gap in the canvas on the far side and back out of the grassy campsite. Three knives lodge in the fabric behind me.

I have a plan of sorts. I double back, making for the horses. I grab a stick with a long ribbon attached from the open barrel of circus equipment as I go.

I hear the men rip through the tent behind. I fall upon the rope holding the horses, draw out my blade and slice through.

Once the tethering slackens and drops, the animals mill uncertainly, in that way captive creatures do when given unexpected freedom.

The men are fanning out to surround me now, assured of their prize.

'Looks like a little aristo escaped the mob,' observes one.

I hold up the stick, letting the ribbon unfurl. It waves gracefully in the air as it circles to the ground.

One of them grins. 'You think you can wave us away with that?' He continues to advance.

I drop low and sweep the long ribbon around the horse's legs. And as I hoped, the effect is immediate. The snakelike motion spooks them, sending them startled in all directions. There's sudden chaos as they gallop blindly.

I fix my sights on one, run at it, grab hold and pull myself up. The horse skitters from side to side and for a moment I swing wildly. I manage to secure my hold, throwing my weight forward. I feel my thin skirt tear revealing lace-trimmed white cotton culottes beneath.

I see Jemmy looking at me in horror from his place at the globe aerostatic as I gallop at him with robber-men in pursuit.

I draw my knife, grab a tight fistful of mane and dig in my heels to steer the frightened horse at the largest badly erected marquee. Sliding low to one side, I hold out the curved blade and cut clean through the main guy-rope as we charge by.

The huge central pillar leans then slowly topples as we race away, taking with it the entire vast tent in a billow of heavy canvas. Beneath the collapsing structure I hear the shouts of the remaining robbers as they are felled by its weight, floundering inside.

I urge my horse forwards, gripping with my thighs as I learned to do as a girl. Relief at the unlikely escape begins to wash through me. But my celebration is short lived.

I hear Jemmy shout a warning. As we pass the last tent, a gunshot sounds. My horse's legs tangle suddenly in an unseen guy-rope and we both tumble to the ground.

I roll just in time to stop the animal crushing me and get to my feet. My horse makes a high, frightened cry. I look down to see a line of blood across its flank.

In the middle-distance is a guard, holding out a smoking gun. Behind him, seven more armed men. Robespierre's reinforcements are already here.

My eyes drop to the injured animal. The shot only grazed it, but there's no use trying to ride the frightened animal now. I stroke its nose, soothing it.

'You will be well,' I promise. 'It's only a scratch. Lie here and rest.'

The horse snorts in answer.

I scan around for an alternative steed, but the others are far back, running amok in the chaos of the circus.

'Attica!' I hear Jemmy shout. 'This way! I need help to make this thing fly!'

CHAPTER 59

I RUN TO THE BALLOON. IT'S A HUGE GLOBE OF SILK WITH A belt of rope pinching it all the way around the middle. Attached is a basket, hovering above the ground. Inside is red-hot fire, contained in a metal brazier, the size of a barrel and spotted with air holes. There are sacks of coal on the grass near by.

'We need to get it hotter,' says Jemmy, the teardrop burn by his eye a shade darker in the heat. 'It hasn't enough height to take us out of here.'

My earlier optimism is vanishing away now I'm nearing the balloon. There is little upwards trajectory. I glance behind me to the guards in the distance.

'Coal,' says Jemmy, 'as much as we can load.' He swings up a sack and upends it into the brazier. There's a swell of flame as the dust catches. Sweat is pouring from his dark hairline.

'Get inside,' urges Jemmy, throwing a leg over the balloon basket. We both climb in and the bobbing vessel sinks straight back to earth.

I notice a set of bellows, grab them up and start pumping at the base of the brazier. The fire burns redder and flames shoot from the top.

The smaller pieces of fuel blaze with a happy crackle and the balloon wobbles uncertainly, straining to a lift. We're hovering now, inches above the sawdust-scattered earth.

'It's working!' says Jemmy, looking over the edge. 'We're getting off the ground.'

He grabs the bellows and begins pumping hard.

'The coal isn't catching fast enough,' I say, looking at a line of large black pieces, resisting combustion. The guards have run out of ammunition at least, so no more shots are going off. Our balloon is now a few feet high, exactly the height most difficult to defend. It shows no signs of more upward propulsion.

Jemmy's dark hair is slick to his head. Despite his efforts we're not getting any higher.

'We need to get more air to the flame,' I say. And then I remember. Jemmy has gunpowder.

'Jemmy,' I say, 'your black powder.'

He stops pumping, wipes his brow. His highwayman coat is hanging open, his black shirt beneath soaked with sweat.

'Are you mad? You bore me half to death with your "don't trust guns" talk and now you want to load an explosive into a fire we're standing right next to?'

'The metal fire-basket.' I point. 'It's thick. You must have worked cannons aboard ship,' I add, 'you know about controlled explosions. Could it work?'

Jemmy is looking more analytically at the brazier now.

'It's a third of the thickness of a cannon,' he says. 'Punched with holes that would weaken it.' He picks out his bag of black powder. 'If I use one fifth of charge,' he decides, carefully pouring black grains into a measuring horn, 'half an ounce. It could work.'

'Half an ounce sounds like a lot,' I say uncertainly.

'Only to someone who doesn't like guns,' retorts Jemmy. 'You load for twenty-five per cent of the projectile weight,' he adds. 'I lifted you when we were dancing and you're heavier than you look.'

'Brain weighs more than brawn.'

I make a quick calculation.

'You need one-third of an ounce,' I say. 'One-fifth of a cannon charge adjusted for the catalyzing effect of the coal.'

'Am I to take it you've never fired a cannon?'

I nod. 'No. But detonation and combustion are my favourite studies. Grace and I used to bet on gun salutes.'

I glance across to the guards, getting closer every second.

'Trust me,' I say quickly, 'I was almost never wrong.'

'Almost?'

'It's not an exact science.'

Jemmy looks at the approaching men.

'See you on the other side,' he mutters.

I shut my eyes tight as Jemmy empties the measured powder into the brazier.

And all I remember next is an explosion and empty air beneath my feet.

CHAPTER 60

I'M TOLD LATER THAT A NUMBER OF PEOPLE SAW OUR balloon shooting up into the sky and thought it a sign that God approved of revolution. I don't recall myself, because as the gun powder exploded, two things happened. Firstly, as we'd theorized, the coal was ignited rapidly and the balloon lifted upwards, faster and higher than we could ever have hoped. Secondly, the power of the gunpowder blew out the top half of the brazier nearest to me, which hit me square in the chest and sent me flying backwards, over the edge of the basket.

Beneath us, the amazed guards were looking up as we rose from their reach. Then I came spilling out with such force I tipped full head over heels, plummeting feet first.

All this happened so fast, I couldn't tell you any of it for certain. But what I do remember is a painful jerk of my wrist and something cutting into my fingers.

Jemmy's head came over the side of the balloon, an expression of fierce determination on his face.

'I've pulled aboard more than one drowning man,' he says, 'you won't fall, I swear it.'

'It's hot,' I manage, coughing. Smoke is coming from somewhere.

'Your dress is on fire,' says Jemmy calmly. 'Don't let it worry you.'

He drops another hand around my forearm and wrenches me back inside. Jemmy rips away the burning bottom part of my skirt, which is so thin it has already frizzled up to almost nothing, and tosses it over the side. Then we're in the basket together, floating up, the circus growing smaller beneath us.

'Thank you,' I manage. I look down at my cotton culottes, smoke-stained but unburned. My feet have miraculously maintained their pointed shoes.

I look over the side, breathless, awestruck. My fingers grip the wicker side. Jemmy comes to stand next to me.

'Can you believe it?' he says. 'We're flying.'

For a moment, we just watch. And then we're both grinning, ear to ear. We turn to one another, unable to keep the smiles off our faces.

'It's all so small,' I say, looking down. 'Can you control our direction?'

'Not like on a ship,' says Jemmy. 'You pull ropes on either side and I can work with the wind. Paris is a big enough target,' he adds, 'we've a fair chance of clearing the city walls.'

'If it could take us all the way there,' I say excitedly, 'we might get to the Bastille before Grace?'

Jemmy points down.

'Judge for yourself.'

I squint in the direction he's pointing. Far below, are four tiny horses pulling a black carriage behind.

'That could be any carriage,' I say.

'Perhaps,' agrees Jemmy. 'But it's the only vehicle on the Paris road. Word's spread there's no way into the city. But that doesn't apply to His Majesty's prison cart, does it? That can come and go as it pleases.'

I watch the horses, dust from their striking hooves like sprinkled crumbs on a fallen ribbon.

'If you're right, we're outpacing them,' I say.

'As long as the weather holds,' says Jemmy. He grins again, white teeth glinting. 'What do ye think of it, Mrs Pimpernel? We're flying like birds.'

He turns his head to look out, the breeze ruffling his black hair. He ducks down into the basket of the balloon.

'What are you doing?'

'These balloons are used for nobles,' he says, sliding out a wicker hamper. 'I'll wager no French aristocrat engages in any leisure pursuit without victuals. Aha! I was right.'

He stands triumphantly, holding two bottles of wine and some cheese wrapped in paper.

'One bottle each,' he says, unwrapping the cheese and breaking me off a piece.

'Thank you,' I say, biting into it. 'Goes some way to making amends for your taking advantage of me in the Rolands' house,' I add wryly.

Confusion wrinkles his brow for a moment and then understanding dawns.

'The kiss? Oh, come now, little primrose, I saved us both. You're lucky I didn't kiss you for real,' he adds, raising his dark eyebrows. 'Women have died from less.'

I laugh. 'I'm glad to hear it. You currently rank beneath Madame Roland.'

CHAPTER 61

THE BALLOON IS DRIFTING TO PARIS ON THE BREEZE. Jemmy and I are drinking wine and eating cheese. It all feels very dreamlike.

'What happened to your girl in New York?' I ask, looking sideways at him.

Jemmy extends his arms, pushing back against the basket. 'Which one?'

'You know very well which one. The figurehead on your ship. The one you won't replace, though your crew wants it.'

'Ah, her. Well, we thought to be married once.' He examines his fingernails. 'But she was a religious girl. Jewish. I wouldn't convert and nor would she. Eventually it came between us.'

I consider this. 'Seems a silly thing to be parted over,' I opine, thinking how I would give anything for such a trifling issue between Atherton and I.

He nods good-naturedly. 'True enough,' he says, 'true enough.' His eyes connect with mine. 'And what about you, Attica Morgan? Why are you so frightened of marriage?'

'Who says so?'

Jemmy leans back, considering my face.

'You pick up a thing or two about people when you captain a pirate ship. It's important to see in a man's eyes if he has a past.' He looks at me closely. 'I'd say you have a few ghosts that gnaw at your soul. But in my experience, there's nothing so bad as heartache. It's none of my business, of course,' he adds with a shrug, 'but I'm a good listener if you care to tell me.'

I chew a fingernail.

'There's ... a man,' I admit, 'in London. I love him, he loves me. But we can't be together. You met him,' I add. 'It was he who arranged our first meeting. And briefed you to come out here and do my job for me.'

This still stings.

'Atherton?' Jemmy raises an eyebrow. 'The clever one with the long face and the sticks for walking? That's who you're tumbling the hay with?'

'He's married,' I say curtly. 'There's no tumbling.'

Jemmy pulls a face. 'That would make him the only man in England to keep faithful to a marriage made for political advancement.'

'Perhaps he's the only good man in England.'

Jemmy snorts. 'I'd bet my ship that Atherton would forget his vows at the slightest nod from you. Are you sure it's not his twisted legs botherin' you?'

I laugh. 'Of course not. Atherton is the best and bravest man I have ever known.' I hesitate, feeling Jemmy is gaining the wrong impression. 'I grew up semi-illegitimate in English society,' I say. 'I've seen into the little half-world of courtesans and mistresses. There's a great deal of pain in that place. It's better to keep things simple.'

Jemmy laughs.

'If only life were like that,' he said. 'Love is a messy business, Your Ladyship. If you're waiting for a painless relationship, you'll be waiting a long time.' He assesses me. 'It's a lot easier to be in love with someone when you can't have them,' he says. 'Saves awkward questions, too.'

I frown. 'It isn't only that,' I say, choosing my words. 'I've grown used to freedom.'

'Sounds like an excuse to me. Plenty men join my ship saying much the same. I'll tell you what I tell them: loneliness isn't a cure for anything.'

'Better, surely, than hurling myself into every heartbreak that looks my way,' I say pointedly.

'Ah,' says Jemmy happily. 'You have me to rights there, of course. Every mad girl within a mile of Hell's Kitchen. That's what me mama used to say.' He drums his fingers on his knees. 'Well,' he says after a moment, 'everyone feels that way one time or another, Attica. Loving someone we can't have. Time to grow up, move on, stop wallowing.' He pats my leg then stands to look over the edge of the balloon.

'So what else, then?' he says. 'Being as you're in a confessional mood. How did this friend of yours die?'

'Who says I had a friend who died?'

'I do,' he says easily. 'Unless you care to correct me.'

I lift the wine, drink.

'I've had a lot of friends die,' I say finally. 'The same as you, I imagine. Why don't you tell me,' I add, 'how you came to be a privateer?'

He moves to sit next to me on the floor of the balloon.

'Nothing much to tell,' he says and I have a feeling he's not being quite honest. 'Left America broken-hearted and your government thought my sailing might come in useful. After they arrested me for piracy. Flung me in a Bermuda lock-up then a London one.' He grins.

'Try the red,' he says, raising his bottle at me. I take it gratefully and exchange my bottle with his.

We drink and say nothing. It's cold and I huddle nearer.

So we sit like that for a long time, drifting through the calm French sky, with only the birds for company.

CHAPTER 62

ROBESPIERRE IS WALKING BACK AND FORTH, WIGGED HEAD bowed, hands clasped behind him. The wide floorboards of his study creak beneath his buckled leather shoes.

He stops and raises his head, round glasses catching the light.

'The guards were found on the road?' he says.

'Yes.' The messenger is still panting with the exertion of the horse ride back to Paris. Robespierre reminds him of a little bird, small shoulders back, chest puffed out, always alert.

'All gone?' confirms Robespierre.

'All.' The messenger coughs. 'They were seen ... They got inside the globe aerostatic. The wind is against them now, but if it changes there is a chance they will clear the city wall.'

Robespierre's neat eyebrows lift very slightly.

'Oh?' His voice is icy.

'They might well make it to Paris.'

Robespierre shows no obvious emotion at this, but if you looked hard enough you might see a slight strain to the face, a rigidity to the gait, and something dark and bottomless in the eyes.

Robespierre touches his neat white wig as though fearing an unravelled curl, then he holds out a hand. 'The letters, if you please.'

The messenger has them secured inside his leather satchel. He never ceases to be astounded at Robespierre's foresight. There are two, requested by carrier pigeon. He pushes them both into Robespierre's cold little fingers.

The first are the prison lists: inmates of the city's twenty-one prisons. He begins leafing through papers.

'Four new souls incarcerated in the Bastille,' Robespierre observes disapprovingly, 'without trial.'

He selects the hardest-looking chair in the room and sits, knees neatly touching as he reads.

'Elopement with a married member of the aristocracy. Can you even call this a crime?'

The messenger says nothing, feeling ill equipped to comment. He is a farmer's son.

Robespierre looks down, shaking his head, wishing for a more worldly companion.

'She is not there yet,' he says to himself. 'No English girl has been committed.'

Robespierre had been hoping Grace would be in the Bastille governor's custody by now. He has a secondary plan. He always has a secondary plan. Usually several, in fact.

'Foulon's whore, Angelina Mazarin,' he says in his high voice.

The messenger shuffles uncomfortably, not sure who this is.

'Someone must pay her a visit.'

Robespierre is speaking to himself, the messenger realizes, relieved. The lawyer looks up, surprised to see him still there, then signals curtly to dismiss him.

As the messenger exits, walking a little too quickly, Robespierre opens the second letter, breaking a seal from a house with an English name in Paris. He is pleased. His good foresight is paying dividends as usual.

Long before sending Janssen to Madame Roland's disgustingly indulgent chateau, he had the prescience to write to the English Embassy.

It informed the Head of Command that a traitorous pirate, Jemmy Avery, was active in Paris. Robespierre had been careful to give just enough detail of how their trusted privateer was also working for France. There really was only one course of action for the recipient of the letter.

Bring in Jemmy Avery, dead or alive.

Robespierre dashes out another message, informing the Embassy that the pirate may sail over the city walls in a stolen globe aerostatic. Avery has a female accomplice, Robespierre adds, who should be considered dangerous, insofar as a woman can be.

Robespierre permits himself a small smile as he imagines his bird outpacing the unwieldy flying basket. Villains falling from the sky.

CHAPTER 63

DAWN IS BREAKING AS I WAKE JEMMY. THE WIND BUFFERED us away from Paris all night and for a time we doubted if we would get over the wall. But now the bad weather has dropped away and though our fire is almost burned out we're headed straight for the city.

Jemmy blinks groggily. His hazel eyes look muddier against his tired face.

'Paris is close,' I say excitedly. 'We're going to make it. I can see the city wall!'

The fire has gone down a great deal, but even with the loss in height we'll clear the high fortification by six feet or more.

Jemmy rubs the stubble of his chin.

'Well, there's a thing,' he says, moving to the brim of the basket.

As we drift towards the deep wall that surrounds Paris, we see the full breadth of the King's treachery. Outside are camped thousands of foreign soldiers, stretching back half a mile. They are preparing for battle.

Jemmy peers over the edge.

'What a bastard their King is,' he opines. 'He's spent every centime he can stretch to on Swiss troops to punish his own people for the crime of asking for bread.'

He points to something inside the wall and frowns. 'What do you think is happening around that big building there?'

I look. A great crowd of people are converging.

'That's the Hôpital des Invalides,' says Jemmy. 'Nothing there but old and injured soldiers.'

'And around forty-thousand muskets,' I remind him, thinking of the letters in Madame Roland's study and Janssen's overheard words. 'The King hid his weapons there, in case the people tried to defend themselves. Looks like they got wind of it.'

There's shouting, the kind that never bodes well.

Our balloon is sinking faster now. We're at rooftop height, low enough to see broken-toothed women clutching limp babies, men in rags so tatty they barely qualify as clothing. There's an air of hopelessness to them, I think, as though they're waiting to die.

Jemmy looks over the side for a moment then ducks quickly back down.

'What is it?' I ask.

'Good and bad,' he admits. 'The bad part,' he goes on, 'is we've come by way of a guarded gate.' He bobs up again, risking another glance. 'People are mad with terror that those foreign guards will attack,' he says, 'and we've just sailed into Paris bearing the Swiss colours.'

I wince, remembering our silken balloon is black, red, blue and yellow, like the many-hued Swiss flag.

'They'll tear us to pieces,' I say. 'What's the good part?'

'I may get to see you running in those culottes,' he says, pointing to where my skirts have burned away.

'Lend me your shirt,' I say.

He takes it off and hands it over disappointedly, buttoning his coat back over his bare chest. I put on his long black shirt.

'We'll make a gentleman of you yet,' I say, letting it fall to mid-thigh with my culottes peaking beneath. I look quite Romany now, my black hair still plaited the way I used to wear it as a girl.

People are pointing and shouting now. Desperate-looking, furious people.

'We're by the fifth arrondissement,' I say. 'If we can get a little further in, we'll land by the wharves. Can you hide us there?'

A stone hits the side of our balloon. Then another.

'I can hide you in any dockside in the world,' says Jemmy proudly.

We're losing height and a crowd of people has formed, jogging along, pointing up at the globe aerostatic. More join them, coming from their houses and the gutters.

A constant patter of stones is striking at the balloon-silk. Something hits it hard and the loud exhale of air sounds all around us.

I look up to see an arrow sticking out of the colourful silk. Below a man with a crossbow is rearming, taking aim.

We begin falling faster out of the sky.

'We're never going to make the docks,' I say. We're touching the low rush rooftops of this poor district now, our basket jolts against a chimney. And then suddenly there's a great tug on the far side. A determined young man has climbed on to a roof and hurled himself at the basket. He hangs by his fingertips.

'*Vive la France!*' he bellows. 'Death to the Swiss!'

Jemmy grasps the ropes holding the failing balloon and

tugs them hard. The basket tilts sharply and the man dislodges, pedalling his legs as he crashes to the cobbles. A circle of people collect about him and suddenly the mood is murderous.

I pull out my knife. A gunshot sounds.

Jemmy and I exchange glances.

'I thought the people had no arms?' he says.

'They don't.' I'm looking in the direction of the shot. The people are drawing back now, running to their homes. 'Those are English dragoons.'

I watch with relief as the dragoons charge down the street, dispersing the angry people, heading for our balloon.

'What are English dragoons doing in Paris?' asks Jemmy.

'The English Embassy keeps a few deadly men for special purposes,' I explain, feeling my heart lift. 'Maybe word reached Atherton and they've been assigned to our protection.'

We're sinking lower now, only fifteen feet or so from the ground. The guards are huddled together, five of them, looking up. We're drifting straight for them.

I'm expecting them to help us down and offer us a protected escort. Instead, they open fire on our basket, now floating a few feet from the street.

I duck down, hearing several bullets puncture the silk balloon.

'Not as friendly as you thought?' suggests Jemmy.

More shots explode above our heads.

'No,' I say, trying to understand it.

'We've nothing to defend ourselves,' he adds, 'unless you count the cinders from the brazier. We're headed into the sights of those guards.'

I pull out my curved blade.

He frowns at me. 'Still think a knife is better than a pistol?'

I stand to look out over the edge, absorbing as many critical details as I can before ducking out of sight. There's a sturdy gatepost. I tug up the tethering rope. I tie the end to the handle of my knife, take aim and throw.

It flies rotating fast through the air and lodges in the gatepost. The balloon jerks, impeded by the stuck blade, it's trajectory towards the Dragoons halted.

'Pistols have their uses,' I say, 'knives are more versatile.'

The bottom butts against the cobbled street. I pull my knife back and unknot it.

Jemmy and I stand, both of the same mind. We leap from the basket just as the Dragoons close in on it and run.

CHAPTER 64

IT'S DAWN IN PARIS. GRACE PRESSES HER EYE TO THE window of the Bastille carriage as it rolls through the city gates.

It has been a long journey, winding through every outlying village settlement around Paris, solely for the purpose, so far as Grace can make out, of spreading terror.

The Paris streets, which had seemed so exotic, so compelling only days ago, look very different now. There are more poor people, Grace notes. Legions more. As though they wait for something.

Grace notices something in the air has changed. There is a metallic tang, as with the beginnings of a thunderstorm. She senses an excitement, a lifting of a great oppression, like a public festival has burst free from its allotted day and sprawled luxuriantly across the weeks.

She feels the ground shift beneath them as the dirt tracks leading into the city change to the cobbles of the streets.

Painted large on a wall is a hunched old peasant. On his bent back sit a plumed nobleman and chubby-legged clergyman, riding him like a horse.

But now it is over, Grace tells herself. *The King has agreed that the nobles and clergy pay taxes.*

She has a feeling she is missing something important.

As she watches, the Bastille carriage grinds to a halt. There's a conversation with the driver at the front and she strains to hear.

'Nothing this way,' a man is saying. 'The order has been given to restrict all movement.'

Grace holds her breath, wondering what this could mean.

'All the carts and wagons are being sent to the Place de Grève, outside the Hôtel de Ville,' adds the man. 'We're anticipating a battle.'

The driver says something Grace doesn't quite hear, something about the King.

'Because there's a fucking Swiss army surrounding the city,' replies the man loudly. 'What do you call that, if not a foreign attack? The lawyers tell us this is all perfectly legal. In a state of emergency, citizens may bear arms and stop all movement.'

Grace feels the carriage jolt and hears swearing.

She squints through the small hole, trying to see up ahead. She can make out casks and sacks, crates and bundles being flung into heaps by a steady stream of city guards. The goods vehicles are all being made to unload.

'You can try the east way,' says the man outside, 'but you may not get far. I warn you, friend, it is war. Citizens are handing out gunpowder and shot. I'd get to the Bastille before someone pulls your wheels off.'

The carriage trundles away, but they are barely a few streets further when it stops again. Hope and fear play at Grace in equal measure. She tries to see the reason, but nothing is clear. Has someone arrived to rescue her?

CHAPTER 65

JEMMY AND I RACE THROUGH THE STREETS. WE'VE LANDED in an arrondissement on the outskirts of Paris with a few brick houses and roaming pigs. People are coming out of their homes, lured by shouts and gunshots. I see several children fall on the sunken globe aerostatic and begin hacking themselves off portions of silk.

'I don't understand it,' I say. 'Why are they shooting at us?'

'I mightn't have been entirely straight with you,' admits Jemmy, looking left and right for a place to hide. 'It could be me your dragoons are after.'

'But you work for the English,' I say. 'They'll probably only be under instruction to make your arrest ...'

A gunshot blows past my cheek, ruffling my hair.

'Dead or alive,' concludes Jemmy. 'There's no way we can both outrun them,' he adds.

'I can't kill them,' I say.

'What?' Jemmy's face is stricken.

We've reached a cul-de-sac, a little street that runs to nowhere.

Jemmy is drawing his sword on the foreman. His face has changed. I have a frightening flash of how he might look, leading his crew in a charge.

'They're English dragoons,' I say. 'I'm sworn to protect the life of every person in England. I can't take down one of my own.'

Jemmy turns to look at me and the fierce demeanour melts away. He lowers his cutlass.

'Can't or won't?'

'Won't.'

'This patriot thing is getting rather tiring,' says Jemmy, eyeing the guards. 'You know countries are just fences put up by greedy men?'

'You're frightened for your own safety? How like a pirate. The docks are that way. Just follow the river. They'll be plenty of boats for you to sail out of France.'

'A pirate doesn't abandon his crew,' he mutters.

'Your crew aren't here.'

'I meant *you*.' His green eyes flash. 'I was foolish enough to credit you with the same loyalty as a man. But you don't work with others, do you?'

'Do you know what happens when I work with others?' I demand. 'They die. Horribly. You think I'm heartless because I won't put anyone in that position?'

Something has snapped between us. An easiness I realize I'd taken for granted. I don't know him as well as I think, I remind myself.

'You're free to run,' I say, keeping my eyes on the guards. 'I'm going to find out what they want.'

'Mademoiselle Morgan!' one of them cups his hands and shouts. 'We've come to bring you to the Hôtel de Ville.'

I turn to Jemmy. He holds his hands up to me. 'Absolutely not,' he says. 'I've a bad fear of government places.'

'Under whose orders?' I call back.

'Captain Atherton.'

'It could be a trap,' says Jemmy.

'No. That's Sealed Knot code. No one would know to use Atherton's name.'

Jemmy looks unconvinced.

'Trust me.' I take his hand. 'The English have a safe house at the Hôtel de Ville.'

Relief is flooding through me. My message arrived. Someone stopped the Bastille carriage and got Grace to safety.

CHAPTER 66

We allow the guards to escort us through the city streets until we reach the Place de Grève, outside the Hôtel de Ville. It's filled with confiscated carts and wagons.

'What's happening?' I ask the man acting as captain as we approach the Hôtel de Ville.

'All movement is restricted,' he says. 'Rule of war is in place. Best we get you to safety.' But I notice his glance doesn't include Jemmy.

The dragoons lead us inside the Hôtel de Ville and up a wide staircase. A few corridors later and the layout of the building changes entirely. What were colourful frescoes and marble staircase is now crumbling plaster and whitewashed floorboards.

'Why is it less grand?' asks Jemmy, looking at the barn-style exposed beams of the roof, the plain-plastered walls.

'This part was a merchant bank,' I explain. 'It was joined with the Hôtel de Ville eighty years ago after the finance bubble burst and the bank was abandoned. Since then the King has given the task of economics to sycophantic courtiers. Our safe house is in the old vault,' I add.

We've arrived at an ominous-looking door bolted with sheet metal.

Suddenly more guards pour in from either side and seize Jemmy. I watch, horrified.

'It's a trap,' he mutters. 'I knew it.'

I'm looking back and forth at the guards, not knowing what to make of it.

'I'm sorry, Mademoiselle Morgan,' says the captain apologetically, 'a little subterfuge for your own safety.' He points to Jemmy. 'This man is a turncoat, sells his services to the highest bidder.' There is a look of utter contempt on the captain's face.

I turn to Jemmy, expecting him to contradict the accusation.

'I imagine,' continues the captain, 'he painted a romantic picture to you. You've probably read about highwaymen and pirates in your lady's novels, Miss Morgan,' he adds sympathetically. 'I'm afraid in real life they are less heroic. Did this brave pirate tell you he shot a number of English troops in the back? There was a little skirmish in America. Crates of tea, thrown into the Boston river. Mr Avery was hunted down and captured in Bermuda, after having murdered a lot of my comrades.'

Shock rises up. I look at Jemmy, waiting for him to deny, to correct. But he says nothing. I feel suddenly rather sick.

'France's pet pirate,' continues the captain. 'But now we've caught up with him,' he concludes pointedly.

I try to tell myself I really shouldn't be surprised. There's no reason why a man from New York would be loyal to England. He is nothing but a mercenary. So why do I feel this betrayal?

Jemmy has a black look about him. Defeat doesn't suit him.

'What of my ship?' he asks the captain, his eyes hooded, glaring.

'Your vessel has been reported to the port guard. By now it will have been impounded, with all your crew of criminals.'

Jemmy bolts upwards, reaching for his sword, but the men hold him in place.

'What have you done with my boys?' demands Jemmy. I've never seen him like this, face taut in menace, eyes burning. He looks like a different person. A bad person. For the first time since we've met I see him as a pirate.

'I regret you had to see this,' says the captain, speaking to me.

Jemmy turns to me, stricken, his fierce demeanour vanished. I look away.

'I'm afraid we have instructions to secure you both,' says the captain, 'just while the correct people are summoned.' He gives me an apologetic smile. 'I'm sure it isn't necessary in your case,' he adds, 'but our orders are such. I believe your uncle fears you have become sentimental for the pirate and may try to escape. You are due to be married, are you not? You can be sure your future husband is a better man than this one.'

The door opens, revealing nothing but pitch black. The guards move us inside, pushing Jemmy roughly, leading me with polite care.

A great numbness has settled around me.

'Why is it so dark?' asks one of the guards.

'Someone has stolen the candles,' replies the captain, frowning. 'These bloody French will have the fur off a dead dog the moment your back is turned. No matter, we can see clear to the bench. Secure them there.' The captain points.

Hands take hold of me. I feel manacles bolt to my wrists and I sit heavily.

'It is a bad business,' says the captain, stooping so as to be level with my face. 'Truly. I hardly relish locking a lady up with this brute. He is well restrained, I promise you. I am quite certain it will not take long to have this misunderstanding put aside. You'll be on the next boat to Dover.'

'Surely you might bring more candles?' demands Jemmy, at my side. 'You can't leave the lady in the dark.'

'You will be brought some presently,' says the captain, addressing me. He turns disgustedly to Jemmy. 'I'm sure a man such as you might click his fingers and call a devil to light his way.'

They exit, footsteps making a quick march, with the thick vault door hanging open. Seemingly from nowhere, a flame appears in the corridor. As it nears, a little glow is cast into the cell.

There is a shape on the floor, something I didn't see before: a young girl lying on a wide raised bench.

My heart skips a beat. Strange thoughts play at me.

'Grace?' I whisper into the dark.

'Wait,' says Jemmy. I barely hear him. I'm realizing by slow degrees that the grime on the girl's skirts is not grime. She isn't breathing.

I look closer at the familiar dress. A terrible realization dawns.

I'm moving like a sleepwalker, drawing the full length of my manacled chain.

'Wait!' Jemmy's voice is louder now and he moves to take my arm, but I shake him off.

I'm standing next to the girl and I know for sure she is dead.

The beloved face is all too recognizable.

Blood is everywhere. For a moment I can't breathe. The lump in my throat is so painful.

'Oh,' I whisper. 'I'm sorry. I'm so sorry. I came too late.'

The body lies face up, long hair matted with blood, arms spread wide, as though trying to fly away.

It's Angelina. My eyes flood with tears as I take her hand.

'I was going to come for you,' I say. 'To put you safe.'

I feel myself tunnelling back to a dark place I thought I had forgotten. Anger rescues me. A great black whirling fury.

There's a noise at my ear. It's Jemmy. He's been saying something to me. I look at him, feeling strangely underwater.

'Attica,' says Jemmy. 'Attica.'

Thoughts are overwhelming me. The terrible truth is I kill people. Everyone I love dies.

'Keep yourself together,' Jemmy says urgently. 'This is deliberate. Someone wanted you to find her.'

It's then we hear a voice, thin and high, from the entrance. Candle-flame swells the room.

'You didn't heed my warning, Mademoiselle Morgan.'

I swallow, cold blood rushing to my head.

Something about the voice passes a wave of fear through me that is almost primal. Though I'm sure I've never met its owner.

A slight man steps calmly into view. He is fastidiously dressed in a snowy cravat, spotless black waistcoat, white-powdered wig and tiny round glasses.

'Forgive me,' he adds with exaggerated courtesy. 'You are English aristocracy, of course, and are wedded to the old manners of introduction.' He bends low, then raises his head.

'My name is Maximilien Robespierre.'

CHAPTER 67

At the Hôpital des Invalides, Oliver Janssen is carrying out his orders. As usual, the Society of Friends laid its plans seamlessly. Three letters was all it had taken to see the musketeer placed in command of a few thousand old soldier-pensioners whom no one cared very much about.

As Janssen understands it, a dangerous rebel faction is headed to take the weapons, a splinter group who mean to spread chaos and murder. His instructions are to put them down – a simple task for a King's soldier.

Janssen pictures the attackers: an ill-conceived, half-formed thing with no weaponry and no plan, hoping to lay hold of the secret arsenal.

They come to raid muskets and gunpowder. But thanks to judicious communication with the Bastille governor, all two hundred and fifty barrels of explosives were delivered safely to the infamous prison last night.

That still left some forty thousand muskets. But six hours ago Janssen set the elderly soldiers to work, dismantling guns. By the time the mob arrived, there would not be a single functioning weapon. When they cross the gate, Janssen will order the soldiers to turn cannons on the marauders. The threat to France will be obliterated.

Janssen can see, in the middle distance, a crowd of rebels. There are more than he might have imagined. Perhaps a thousand.

Something occurs to Janssen, just faintly. That if Robespierre had told him false – if these were innocent Frenchmen – there would be no recourse, nothing to link the strange little lawyer to Janssen at all.

There is a roar from the street. The approaching mob is calling for liberty and justice.

Janssen moves all doubts of Robespierre aside. The cannons are prepared, the guns will now be in pieces. It is all happening as the lawyer said. He is ready to dispatch the traitors.

CHAPTER 68

Robespierre walks quietly through the doorway, his neat clothing at odds with the dank prison cell. There's no silk, no lace to his attire, but his clothes are as immaculate as a Marquis's new suit.

I'm still watching Angelina's face, as though by some trick, she'll come back to life.

He stands for a moment, taking us both in, then he bobs a strange little lawyer's bow. 'Good day to you, Mademoiselle Morgan.'

He looks around the room, selects a hard wooden chair and seats himself. He crosses his legs rather awkwardly, as though trying to appear relaxed.

'You were something of a mystery to me,' he says. 'I have been wondering about your sudden appearance in Paris.'

I couldn't reply if I wanted to. I can't tear my eyes from the girl I loved.

Robespierre follows my gaze.

'Angelina Mazarin,' says Robespierre, his pale eyes settling on the lifeless face. 'Paris's famous courtesan. A traitor to France.'

He rises and crosses to where she lies, seeming fascinated by the corpse. 'A woman who prostituted herself for gold and jewels whilst mothers had no milk to feed their starving babes.'

Robespierre bends over and touches Angelina's tiny pointed chin. Her mouth falls open and Robespierre quickly retracts his hand. He steps away and wipes his fingers on a handkerchief, with the air of a boy who has failed to complete a dare.

Rage is burning in me, a dark, ragged thing.

'Regrettably, she chose the wrong side,' says Robespierre.

He lets his gaze settle on me.

'I have been hoping to meet you for some time. I assume,' he concludes, taking in my height, 'you are the product of a ... disgraceful liaison? The ravishment of a slave girl?'

He is so keen to lay the mystery of my origins to rest I almost feel sorry for him. His gaze is roving my black curling hair and broad mouth, the incongruously light green-grey eyes and slightly turned-up nose.

'The daughter of an English nobleman raised on a grand estate.' He lifts pale fingers and taps them against his thin lips. 'Yet you were born a slave. Are still legal property in America. People like you can be very dangerous. You present a grey area when there should be none.'

Robespierre uses his palms to make a perfect rectangle and I have a sudden flash of a man terrified by disorder, a man who must have things neat and clear.

'My father met my mother in Africa,' I say. 'She was fighting the English, successfully by all accounts. They fell in love and my father persuaded her to negotiate peace, but the slavers betrayed him and captured her.' I give him a slight smile. 'They gave my father her knife, so he would believe my mother dead, and he never forgave himself. She gave birth to me in captivity and later died so I might escape.'

Robespierre's eyes flick up to mine, mildly shocked.

'You must not weigh yourself down with thoughts such as these,' he remarks. 'I myself am an orphan. Things were done to me one does not speak of.' He shrugs his small shoulders. '*C'est la vie.*'

He runs a pale finger across his lips.

'I have been following the movements of an English spy.' There's a distant look in his eyes, a faint awe. 'The *Pimpernel,* is that how you say it in English? A deadly flower. You wouldn't happen to know anything about that person?'

I look him right in the eye.

'It's me,' I say, 'you're looking at her.'

CHAPTER 69

GRACE HAS HAD AMPLE TIME TO REPENT OF HER RASHNESS. But it is only now, when approaching the famous prison, that her courage begins to desert her.

She can hardly believe the scale of what she sees. Of course she knew the Bastille was large. She's seen it, looming in the distance, the entire time she's been in Paris. From her vantage point on the ground, she cannot see the top. It's like a giant's castle, its ramparts hidden in the clouds.

The size is such that a small town has sprung up around it, purely, Grace assumes, to cater to its inhabitants.

They roll through this makeshift assortment of stalls and market-traders, until the carriage comes to a stop.

Ahead of them is what appears to be a cliff edge. Grace sees a sheer drop as far as the eye can see. It's a dry moat, swampy at the depths.

'Lower the drawbridge!' the driver shouts.

In answer a booming shrieking sound echoes out. A slab of wood, broad as a house, tall as a tree, peels away from the stone walls and falls towards them.

It's only a drawbridge, thinks Grace. But she grips the hard seat as it thuds down, throwing up a cloud of loose earth. The carriage starts up. It takes a long time to cross the abyss.

There are, in fact, two drawbridges, Grace notices. Both join in the middle at a stone bridge. Once she has crossed the first it rises behind her, sealing the escape. Then she is over the second and into the fortress itself.

Darkness envelops them and she hears the final drawbridge raised behind them. With every crank, Grace feels her freedom slipping further away.

The only way back into the world now is if Grace can convince someone to set her free.

To her confusion, she sees that they are not yet inside an actual building. The carriage has come to a halt in a courtyard, stone-walled, with a section of shaded roof running along the edge. Barrels and sacks of what she imagines to be food are stacked untidily, bales of firewood lean against one another. A large half-butt filled with indeterminate liquid rests on iron legs.

There are guards, a great many of them, dressed in Swiss uniform. Foreign troops. They stand in a line, but as the carriage arrives they swivel and turn, so as not to watch her entry.

The driver opens the door and beckons Grace out.

'Why do they look away?' she asks, mesmerized by the strange view of twenty male backs.

The driver looks at her pityingly.

'This is the Bastille,' he says. 'The gate guards are not permitted to know who the King imprisons.'

Realization is dawning on Grace. Her mouth is dry.

'So the King might lock away anyone,' she says, 'and no one would ever know?'

'Prisoners are anonymous,' agrees the man.

'Might I speak with the prison governor?' Grace tries to stand tall.

The driver only laughs.

Grace is passed to a blindfolded man. It reminds her of a game she played back in England, blind man's bluff, only nobody is laughing.

A sickly dread is taking hold of her.

The blindfolded guard grasps her arm and walks her with deliberate care to a large wooden door. The vehicle and its driver begin to turn. One of the horses lifts its tail and soft balls of steaming manure drop on the flagstone floor, worn smooth from centuries of use. No one moves to sweep it away.

An outsized key is produced and fitted into an enormous lock. Every proportion is monstrous, hulking. Grace stands childlike against the massive scale.

She hears the door shut, the mighty lock turn. Now nothing of the outside world can be heard. All she can hear is the click of tumblers, a clang of closings. A damp smell coils around her. She feels suddenly, achingly alone. Her body rings with it.

A man in guard's uniform steps forward and gestures impatiently and Grace is handed forth.

The door shuts. The man peers at Grace, frowns again then says finally, 'This one doesn't have a letter.'

He looks her up and down.

'What's your name?'

'My name is Grace,' she says quickly. 'There has been a mistake—'

'English?' interrupts the guard.

She nods.

He considers. 'Put her in the Compte Tower,' he says. 'We'll think on it later.'

They pull her inside.

Grace hears a voice echoing along the wide corridor. The accent is aristocratic and French. She struggles to translate and then when the words become apparent, Grace wishes she hadn't.

'They're killing the prisoners!' a man is shouting. 'They're killing the prisoners!'

'That's the Marquis de Sade again,' one of the guards says, sounding annoyed.

He looks at Grace again and comes to a conclusion.

'Time he kept quiet,' says the guard. 'Put the girl in his cell.'

Horrible fear hits the pit of Grace's stomach. She has heard of the Marquis de Sade. Everyone has. He is an aristocrat who believes in complete freedom for those of noble birth. Specifically he believes in freedom to rape and murder – at the same time, if he feels the situation demands it.

'Wait,' says Grace, but the guard is pulling her along.

The voice comes again, reedy and strange.

'They're killing the prisoners!'

Little does Grace know that the cry is to be taken up by the district around the Bastille. It becomes a whisper and then a shout in the heady streets of Paris. People will later say that those four words started the revolution.

CHAPTER 70

IN THE HÔTEL DE VILLE'S OLD BANK VAULT, I SIT MOTIONLESS, waiting for Robespierre's response to my confession that I am his mysterious Pimpernel.

There's a long pause. His pale eyes flicker uncertainty. Robespierre relaxes his features with effort.

'Of course,' he says, 'a little joke, because of my views on the equality of the sexes.' His face darkens. 'I know you are working for the Pimpernel. Maybe you even imagine yourself in love.' He waves his little hand, painting a picture. 'This Mouron is perhaps handsome, charming.'

I sense Jemmy trying to catch my eye and refuse to meet it.

'You sound half in love with him yourself,' I say.

'I have an ... admiration for his work,' says Robespierre. 'Whoever this Mouron is, I must warn you, your own government has retracted any support for this villain. I have it here in writing.'

He reaches into his coat and extracts a piece of paper. I see, with a lurch to my stomach, it has my codename on it. It's from Atherton. I am overtaken by an animal urge to snatch it back.

I have only scattered memories of the plantation. But the terror of my name on a document has never quite left me.

'Perhaps you think helping a spy makes you of value to important men in England,' says Robespierre. 'I am afraid that is not so. I have it here. Monsieur *Atherton* – is that how you say it? He regards this Mouron as entirely expendable. Funds for his extraction from France have been reassigned.'

A sense of hot betrayal flushes through me. Most likely Atherton knew his correspondence was being intercepted. This letter is false. But cold fingers of doubt are tightening their grip.

'Has Mouron promised to find your errant cousin?' suggests Robespierre. 'But he hasn't told you that Grace Elliott will, by now, be deep within the Bastille prison. I fear the cause is hopeless.'

Robespierre studies my face then lifts a finger. 'Perhaps we could help each other. I am in want of a clever woman,' he says, 'to report on the French aristocracy. Someone who can get into drawing rooms, be trusted to deliver valuable messages.

'France is changing,' he goes on smoothly. 'I imagine you are an outcast in England. That would not be the case here. We are building a new Republic where women are equal to men. Join us.'

There's a long pause as I consider my response.

'My mother died a slave,' I say. 'I spent a great deal of time examining slavery transactions trying to find her.'

Robespierre brings his hands together, viewing me carefully over the top of his steepled fingers. The round spectacles reflect candle-flame, hiding his expression.

'When I eventually found her consignment, there was a strike through her number,' I say, 'as one makes with cattle. My mother was dead and no one had taken the trouble to record why.'

I meet his eye. 'Slave records are kept by people like you,' I say, 'men who hide behind ink and paper whilst others do their dirty work. I don't work for men like that.'

Robespierre's mouth draws thin. I sense a quiet fury. A leviathan beneath a calm ocean.

'How disappointing,' he says. 'There are different kinds of cleverness, Mademoiselle Morgan. I suppose we cannot all enjoy the superior kind. I had hoped you might be a progressive.'

'A progressive such as you are?' I can't keep the disdain from my voice. 'You imagine you are not a despot because you don't wear a crown?'

His thin upright body leans suddenly forward, eyes burning. 'Be careful, Mademoiselle Morgan,' he snaps, civility vanishing away. 'Dreadful things are being done, in the city, on the streets. A mob does not discriminate a woman from a man when they are tearing a body limb from limb.'

'You think by murdering those who oppose you your politics shall gain sway?' I demand, furious. 'You cannot kill ideals.'

His light-blue eyes assess me, bird-like. He appears disappointed.

'I quite agree,' he says. 'The people must come to the correct thinking of their own accord.'

And just like that, I see it clearly.

'So that is why you killed Gaspard de Mayenne,' I say. 'I had it wrong all this time.'

CHAPTER 71

ROBESPIERRE IS TAPPING HIS MOUTH AGAIN, WITH HIS fingers. He glances to the door and I detect a dash of deep-seated uncertainty, a boiling paranoia just under the surface.

'It was the diamond left with Gaspard's body that had me confused,' I say. 'I have to concede it was an expert touch. I was so certain that element would make sense to a particular faction.'

I breathe out, realization hitting me from all sides.

'In truth, the staging of Gaspard's death was the opposite,' I say. 'It was designed to make sense to no one. That is how you promote the most confusion, the most terror. Have everyone guessing who was behind it and why.'

Robespierre says nothing but in his face is the tiniest acceptance that I have paid him a compliment.

'You sent Janssen to murder Gaspard,' I say. 'A departure from your perfect morality, to be certain, but what is a single small crime for the greater good? And Gaspard was ideal, was he not? An aristocrat and a rebel, with links to the English. He could mean something to everyone.' I look Robespierre in the eye. 'Let the commoners blame the royalists and the royalists blame the commoners,' I deduce. 'The city is already on a knife edge. Create enough terror and you push the rebels to greater boldness.'

Robespierre is distant behind his round glasses. 'All kind of fancies are possible, I suppose,' he says. 'Certainly nothing you say can be proven.'

'Ah, Monsieur Robespierre,' I say with feeling, 'how I pity you. Is that what you thought it would all hinge on? One little murder for so much good and it would never be traced to you. Death is never so tidy. You pulled the thread, now it unravels.'

There is a faraway look in Robespierre's eyes, as if remembering something he'd rather forget.

'And how it runs,' I say, 'when first you let slip your fine principles. How distasteful it must have been to you to use Monsieur Foulon, a lipsticked old aristocratic of the worst kind, to gain access to the Bastille.'

Something flickers in Robespierre's face.

'How soon did your careful thoughts fall to eliminating that loose end?' I continue. 'One death can never be enough. Not for a thorough man, such as you. Foulon has a mistress.' I glance at Angelina, tears filling my eyes. 'Who knows what they discuss behind closed doors? The risk is too great.'

Robespierre stands, straightening his already straight clothing.

'An interesting story,' he says, 'but to no real purpose.'

'Aside from this,' I say. 'Now I understand what happened to Gaspard, I know your plan at the Hôpital des Invalides.'

Robespierre's face is peculiarly rigid.

'I commend your intelligence,' I say, 'but not your originality. The *hôpital* is nothing more than Gaspard on a larger scale.

The people go to raid the *hôpital*, but you have made certain they will fail and be massacred. Am I close to it? You believe their deaths will create a surge of rage and terror, enough hatred towards the monarchy to put your radical ideas in place. You hope to revolutionize the moderates. To bring about a republic, with no King at all.'

'All those innocent lives lost. Even if you succeed, how many more perfect deaths must now be composed? There is no way of stopping the thread. You begin to fear everything, doubt everyone. I should hate you. But my sincerest sympathy is yours, Monsieur. For now you cannot be at peace until the world lies dead at your feet.'

A void opens just behind Robespierre's blue eyes. For a moment I am staring into a yawning abyss. At its mouth stands a little schoolboy from the country, afraid of the big city and its important men. I am reminded of myself, landing at the Bristol docks all those years ago.

Robespierre's hand shakes as he adjusts the chair square to the wall.

'You are an aristocrat.' It isn't a question. 'Daughter of Lord Morgan. A family, whose fortune is forged off the sweat of the people.' His lips press tight. 'Your people would enslave us. Put your puppet on the throne. Dictate our constitution. You are, to my mind, the worst kind of traitor. Born with a choice and you chose to side with *them*.' He pauses for effect.

'I am not the only man in Paris with a distaste for the aristocracy,' he says. 'As it happens, there are rioters who are roving about the Hôtel de Ville. They have a bloodlust about them, after the severing of Monsieur Foulon's head.'

He tilts his head. 'It would be most unfortunate if someone were to advise this savage group that some traitors were under arrest in this room,' he says thoughtfully. 'And the pair of you appear inadvisably dressed.'

Robespierre looks pointedly at my lace-trimmed culottes and satin shoes, Jemmy's well-fitted black coat and boots. His eyes settle on Angelina's lifeless body.

'I am told she didn't suffer,' he says quietly. 'I shall give you your last moments without the distress of these remains. A guard will be brought to take them out.'

'You have broken every law of your own country and are a traitor,' I say.

Robespierre's grimace twists to a cold rage.

'Be careful, Monsieur Robespierre,' I say, 'of the manner in which your change will come, and how fast. When you rip apart a way of life with violence, a great ugly energy is cut adrift.'

I search my mind, trying to define that feeling, the nameless shapeless thing that seemed to bellow in the sultry Virginian night through our slave huts and straw beds.

'Such a thing unleashed will not be contained,' I tell him. 'It will lash its tail and do horrors.'

There's a flicker of unease in Robespierre's pale eyes.

'Perhaps best to leave La Mazarin here,' he says spitefully. 'You can explain your friendship to the people when they arrive.'

He steps towards the entrance. 'I would say *au revoir*,' he says, 'but you are English. So instead I will say goodbye.'

CHAPTER 72

GRACE IS LED THROUGH THE ENDLESS DARK CORRIDORS OF the Bastille. What she notices most is how empty the vast space is. She doesn't see a single other prisoner on the long walk to the Compte Tower.

'Where are all the prisoners?' she blurts, passing deserted rooms with bars for doors.

One of the guards looks at her as though wondering whether she is testing him.

'The Bastille only holds a handful of inmates nowadays,' he says.

There is something in his expression that makes Grace wonder. Were there legions of secret prisoners languishing in the dungeons? She'd heard tall tales of a man in an iron mask, of felons without names, held in manacles.

As the guard leads her up into the sweltering heat of the tower, she notices how lonely it feels. How this vast emptiness makes it feel more like a prison than anything she might have imagined.

'The King just keeps it to look intimidating,' adds the guard. 'He means to knock it down in a few months.'

They ascend a stone, then wooden staircase, into the top cell of the tall tower.

As the guard throws back the door, Grace prepares herself. She has been half-expecting the Marquis to leap out at her from the shadows.

Grace doesn't know what she'd been expecting as she steps on to the plain floorboards of the prison room. But it isn't this.

It's fashionably furnished with rugs and a comfortable bed. There's a writing desk with several pages crammed with untidy, tiny letters. The room is stiflingly hot but completely empty.

'Where is the Marquis?' asks Grace timidly.

The guard stares at her for a moment.

'Why, we took him elsewhere, of course,' he says. 'You don't think we would lock up a girl with him?' The guard shakes his head. 'He's a deviant of the worst kind. Daily, fathers come, begging for justice. We cannot give it. The Marquis was put here for his own protection. King's protection.'

The guard retreats back towards the door.

'Food will be brought,' he tells her. 'Good food they have in the Bastille. De Launay often dines with prisoners, for it's a lonely place.'

Relief and shock are hitting Grace in equal measure.

'The Marquis left his papers,' adds the guard. 'I wouldn't go reading anything.'

He shuts the door and locks it. Grace hears his footsteps go back down the tall turret. They resound for a long time.

Despite the warning, Grace moves to the writing desk. She lifts a page labelled 'One hundred and twenty days of Sodom' and drops it again sharply. There are a few sketches, thrown in the corner of the room, depicting disturbing scenes. She turns them face down.

Grace scans the rest of the cell. The ceiling is arched. There is a large fireplace and a small stove.

Now she notices carvings on the stone of her wall. A prisoner has drawn a crest, which looks, somehow, familiar. She peers at it but the answer won't come.

Below it, someone has carved: 'Man is born free and everywhere he is in chains.'

Grace recognizes this statement. It was written by a poet named Rousseau. Many of his ideas on democracy and politics caused a stir in France.

A sound startles her; heavy barrels being rolled.

Grace looks around uncertainly then realizes the noise is coming up her chimney.

She moves towards it. If she stands in the unlit fireplace she can hear something happening elsewhere in the prison.

The thunder of rolling barrels goes on and on, joined by what sounds like the dragging of stone on stone.

Voices drift up, rather ghostly, through the flue.

'Rocks to the top,' says a guard with a Swiss accent. 'Pile them near to the edge. The governor says if anyone gets close on the north side, throw them down. Don't await orders.'

'The gunpowder?' asks another voice.

'Take it to the dungeons,' comes the reply. 'There's two hundred more of these barrels to come from the *hôpital*.'

'S'all gonna end tonight, then,' says someone thoughtfully. 'Poor bastards. Governor de Launay is a ruthless bastard, ain't he?'

'He's afraid of losing the Bastille,' says another guard. 'Someone let slip where the King hid the muskets. There's a great crowd of people going to raid 'em.'

'Ah, but de Launay's taken measures, hasn't he?' says the

first. 'That little wiggy fellow with the glasses. Roberts-Pierre. He's been whispering in his ear, giving him advice.'

'God knows he needs it.'

'Roberts-Pierre told de Launay, leave the guns at the hospital.'

'Forty thousand muskets? Why should he do that?'

'He's clever, isn't he? Thinks ahead. There's a couple thousand old soldiers at the hospital. They've been put to work dismantling the guns. The mob will go there for the muskets and find loaded cannons pointed their way. De Launay has said all the rebels are traitors. Must be treated as such. He wants them all blown to bits.'

'Brutal. Lure them there, then kill 'em all.'

Grace can almost see the other guard wincing. She realizes she is balling her fists. It's all so *wrong*.

The men are retreating now. She can't hear them so well.

'Because I know the plan, if the mob ever arrives at the gates ...' a guard is saying in a disgusted voice.

Grace strains to listen, but the second guard's conversation is lost. The first guard replies loudly, 'First sniff of attack and we kill all the prisoners.'

CHAPTER 73

As Robespierre leaves, I allow myself a moment of utter despair.

Jemmy and I are sat side by side, chained to the wooden bench, but I've never felt further away from him.

'There there now, Attica,' Jemmy says uncertainly as I put my head in my hands. 'No sense in letting it get you down.'

I look up at him angrily, through bloodshot eyes.

'Angelina is *dead.* Grace is in the Bastille, about to be murdered. Thousands of innocent people are being massacred.'

I don't voice the other fear: that Atherton has given up on me.

I try to push hair out of my face but my wrists are jerked back by the manacles.

'I admit, things look bad,' says Jemmy, 'but there must be a way out of here.' He gives his chains a manful tug.

'There is,' I say, moving my foot to where Angelina lies on the hard floor. I slide my toes under the bottom of her dress and kick it nearer to my feet.

'This isn't the time to fall apart, Attica,' says Jemmy uneasily. 'She's dead. She can't help you.'

'Why do you think I insulted Robespierre?' I say. 'Angelina always hid a little pouch of gunpowder in the hem of her skirts.'

Jemmy stops pulling on his chains.

'That was why you goaded him? To have him leave the body?'

I nod, letting my fingers follow the bottom of Angelina's skirt.

My hands settle on a hard lump, sewn in place.

Angelina's gunpowder.

I feel a surge of pride to have known her so well after so many years.

'Thank you,' I whisper to her, my eyes filling with tears. 'You see? I always told you. It is you who saved me after all.' I sniff, wiping my face. 'Goodbye, *chérie*.' I bring my face close to hers. 'I am so sorry I couldn't keep you safe. I always thought ...' I swallow. 'I meant one day we should go back to that river. I will go for you, I promise, when all this is over.'

I untangle the last threads, disengaging her gunpowder and pull it free.

Everything of that old self is gone now, I realize, looking at Angelina. The girl I was, before Sicily. Before Lagos slave docks. Before everything. Something else occurs to me.

What I am now, Robespierre has made me.

'Attica!' Jemmy is clicking his fingers. 'Come back to me.'

I blink, forcing my mind back to the present.

'The gunpowder,' I say, holding it up. 'If I'm careful, I should be able to blow open the manacles.'

'A sound idea, to be sure,' says Jemmy, 'but where's your flame?'

'I've the means for fire inside my corsetry.' I'm remembering the flame-sticks Atherton developed, hidden in the hollow bones of my dress.

'You risk blowing our hands off,' says Jemmy uncertainly.

Far down the corridor are shouts, voices, a door beaten in and then blood-curdling screams.

My heart races faster. It sounds as though someone is being torn to pieces.

'It's a good plan,' says Jemmy hurriedly. 'Let's waste no more time discussing it.'

'I don't intend to open your manacles,' I retort haughtily. 'You're a traitor.' I'm remembering Robespierre's revelation.

'I don't set much store in that word,' says Jemmy. 'From where I'm sittin' "traitor" is just an idea bandied about by high-ups to make us all behave. There's no country I like well enough to nail my flag to.'

'Well, I am loyal to England,' I say, 'and you killed English troops.'

'You're loyal to England because you don't know any better. But you should,' says Jemmy. 'A country can become something different overnight, Attica. Believe me, I've seen it. The only thing you can be sure won't change is in here.' He pats his chest.

I glare at him. 'You haven't told me one piece of fact since I met you. You're for the English or the French or yourself. I lose track. Do you have even the tiniest scruple, or do you just work for the highest bidder?'

I'm reaching inside my dress when my victory dissipates. The manacles stop short. There's not enough length to reach down to where the fire-sticks are hidden.

I look up to the ceiling. Let out a long breath. The only way I can slide the boning out is if Jemmy does it for me.

He deduces this almost instantly, his dark brows lifting in amusement. 'Having problems?'

'Laugh and I'll kill you.'

'You might find that difficult, in your current situation. Here,' he sighs, 'let me help you.'

I flinch back, feeling the knife hard against my chest.

'I told you, I don't trust you.'

We hear a door slam open, not far away, and furious shouts.

'Attica,' says Jemmy, 'there is a bloodthirsty mob headed this way. Don't take your anger out on me. Your inventor fella in England has a job to do. He's a captain with a crew, that's all. He can't make decisions on personal feelings. It wouldn't be right.'

He sighs, seeing my unrelenting expression.

'Robespierre never told you why I killed those Englishmen,' he says. 'Your troops were massacring natives in their tepees. Women and children too. Butchering them like cattle. I stopped them as fast as I knew how and I'd do it again.'

There's another crash from outside. Jemmy holds out his hands then he moves them to the top of my dress.

'I tell you this, and I tell it only once,' he says, 'take it how you will: I have my own code that I live to. I have never broken it. Three rules only: be loyal to your crew, defend those who need defending and don't kill anyone you like.'

He slides out the hollow bone of my dress and passes it to me.

I unscrew the top wordlessly and tip out the fire-sticks.

Jemmy's face drops in disappointment.

'That's it?' he says incredulously. '*That's* what you think is going to make fire? They're just little pieces of wood.'

'They're dipped in a flammable paste,' I explain. 'With enough friction, it sets alight.'

'If you say so.' Jemmy looks entirely unconvinced.

'Only three,' I say. 'Should be enough for both of us, if they all work.'

'I've encountered many strange things at sea, to be sure,' says Jemmy. 'Mermaids, swimming unicorns. But a stick that flames itself? I'll believe it when I see it.'

CHAPTER 74

OLIVER JANSSEN IS ASSESSING THE HIGH-CEILINGED infirmary of the Hôpital des Invalides. Hundreds of ragged soldiers are sitting cross-legged, carrying out his orders to dismantle muskets.

He moves further into the main hall, where boxes of guns lay stacked. He sees an elderly man with a peg-leg. The man doesn't seem to be *actually* taking the musket apart. Rather, he is messing about with the trigger.

'What's your name, soldier?' Janssen demands.

'Jacques,' replies the man; Janssen believes there is a note of amusement in his voice.

'These are the dismantled guns?' Janssen asks, nodding to the nearest crate. 'The hammers have been unscrewed?'

Jacques passes a hand through his wispy hair.

'It's slow going,' he says unrepentantly.

Janssen takes a few seconds to absorb his meaning.

'You're telling me,' he says, with a creeping horror, 'these crates contain working muskets?'

'We're soldiers of France,' says Jacques. 'Our business is to defend the people from foreign attack not to disengage weaponry. Morale is low.'

Janssen looks about the elderly men. Many are wearing leaf cockades, he notices, symbols of the revolution. They have a defiant air to them.

'You've had six hours,' growls Janssen. 'There are a thousand of you. It only takes moments to unscrew a musket hammer. How many guns have you completed?'

Janssen stands tall, glaring from under his musketeer hat. He's used to his appearance having a certain effect on people. But these old men don't seem concerned in the slightest by his ghoulish red eye and sharp metal hand. It is disconcerting.

The pensioner looks up to the high ceiling, calculating. He addresses the nearest man.

''Ow many d'you think we done?' he asks.

The other man frowns. He spreads his fingers, counting. 'Maybe ... twenty,' he says.

The pensioner turns back to Janssen.

'Maybe twenty,' he says remorselessly.

'The mob is at the door,' rages Janssen. He turns to the man with the missing teeth. 'What is your name?' he demands. 'There will be penalties for those who disobey.'

The man sucks the space where his teeth had once been.

'I am also named Jacques,' he says.

Janssen looks left to right between the men.

'You are both called Jacques?' he says finally.

'I think you will find,' says the peg-leg man easily, 'a great many of us go by the name of Jacques today.'

Janssen's hand curls menacingly. 'Do not play games with me, old man.'

In the wider hall, old soldiers wordlessly raise themselves to standing, watching the exchange. Janssen's gaze flicks around the room. He has faced men in battle, run into cannon-fire, yet there is something unsettling about these silent pensioners that defies words.

'Why have you have done so little?' shouts Janssen.

'There's two more here,' Jacques-with-the-missing-teeth supplies helpfully. 'So that makes twenty-two.' He beams a toothy grin. 'Only 41,978 to go!'

Janssen tries to collect himself. 'You have defied orders,' he accuses. 'Give me your true name or you will have cause to regret it.'

Several soldiers shuffle in either side of their comrade.

'Trouble, Jacques?' enquires one pleasantly.

'Go back to your work,' commands Janssen. 'This is not your affair.'

No one moves.

'None of us have defied orders,' says Jacques-with-the-peg-leg. 'We did as we were asked. Every man here has been working, disarming muskets. I can give my word there is no insubordinate here, not one. Good men and true to France.' His eyes flash. 'We are but elderly soldiers. Our hands are slow.'

'I'll have you all imprisoned for this!' shouts Janssen. 'Every last one of you.'

'We're old men,' says Jacques-with-the-peg-leg calmly. 'We don't care very much what happens to us.'

They are interrupted by a roaring sound.

'That's the mob,' says Janssen, furious. 'Our orders are they must be put down.'

'Pardon me, sir,' says Jacques-with-the-missing-teeth politely, 'those are citizens of France.'

Janssen snatches the gun from the pensioner's hand and dashes it to the ground. The old man frowns.

'Leave the guns,' Janssen says. 'Line up outside. Turn the cannons on any who come within twenty yards of the musket store. That is an *order.* In the name of your King.'

Jacques and Jacques exchange glances.

'We are soldiers, sir,' says Jacques, standing firm on his peg-leg, 'we will not shoot French men and women.'

Janssen's good eye swivels around the pensioner-soldiers. There are so *many* of them, all now looking in his direction. He feels suddenly overwhelmed.

'I command you!' he rages. 'Defend His Majesty's weaponry. Fire on those people!'

'We heard you, musketeer,' says Jacques patiently, 'and our answer is no.'

CHAPTER 75

JEMMY GASPS AND CROSSES HIMSELF AS THE FIRST STICK bursts into flame.

'I told you,' I grin, holding the fire, 'Atherton's weapons always work.'

'It's magic,' breathes Jemmy. 'Incredible. Simply incredible.' He stretches out a finger then retracts it sharply. 'Real fire.'

I touch the stick to the bench, where our chains are joined. The gunpowder ignites with enough force to free us, blowing out the match as it combusts.

We stand, manacles still on our wrists, but able to move about the room.

Jemmy takes the bag of gunpowder and lays a thin line to act as a fuse. He wedges the pouch under the door.

I take out a second fire-stick and swipe it against the wall. This time there is nothing. I try again.

'It got damp,' I say uncertainly.

'Use the last one,' says Jemmy, fear in his voice. 'Quickly,' he adds.

The noise of smashing and riot has returned with full force, and sounds almost upon us.

I strike the last match, concentrating hard. It doesn't flame. I keep trying, but it's clear this isn't going to work.

Jemmy casts his eyes around the prison then his gaze moves to our manacles.

'Metal on metal,' he says. 'We create a spark.'

'What?' I back away.

'Put your manacles against the ground,' he says. 'I'll strike them with mine.'

'Absolutely not.'

'I've done it before,' says Jemmy. 'We did it all the time in New York. Most of us couldn't afford tinderboxes.'

'With manacles?'

Jemmy shrugs. 'There was always someone in Hell's Kitchen with a sawn-off manacle.'

'You want me to strike a spark, near a pouch of gunpowder, using metal cuffs around my hands?'

'I can make the spark jump. I promise.'

There's a horrible drunken roar from outside the prison. I can hear the door next to ours being smashed in.

'No one can predict gunpowder,' I say. 'You'll blow both our hands off.'

Jemmy fixes his eyes on mine. 'Attica,' he says, 'I can do it. Trust me. I like my hands too.'

I don't answer, only lay my manacled hands on the cold floor. I sense Jemmy come near and steel myself.

A sudden strange shriek echoes around the cell and my eyes snap open. Pushed up at the square of bars on the wooden door is an apparition: a bloodied, haggard face, with wide yellowed eyes and a mouthful of foul teeth.

A woman. A fish-seller I think, by the dirty striped handkerchief wrapped around her rat's tails of greying hair. The shriek comes again and now I make out words.

'Here they are!' she says, not taking her eyes from us. 'The two traitors!'

As she speaks, Jemmy brings his manacles high and strikes them hard on mine. I'm not ready and my hands jolt away, losing the force of the blow.

'Stay still,' says Jemmy, frowning in concentration. He raises his fists and strikes again. This time I keep my wrists firm on floor, but even so, there's no spark at all.

'They got black powder!' shrieks the woman at the door. 'Pass me some beer to dampen it.' Almost immediately a short man appears at her side, passing up a flask.

'Hurry,' I urge Jemmy as he makes for a third attempt.

'And here I was taking my time,' says Jemmy, his face set with grim determination. Lifting his hands, he brings them down. This time the manacles bend and a single spark skitters free, lighting the fuse.

My heart soars. I see the fishwife launching the flask contents. Warm beer arcs through the bars of the door. It falls in a spray, throwing the line of crackling gunpowder into scattered heaps that flare and die.

Hope goes out of me. The door begins to splinter. There's a rabble now, drawn by the fish-seller's raucous threats. I look to Jemmy, realizing we'll be dying together. But instead of readying himself for the fight, Jemmy has thrown himself prone on the cell floor.

I stare in disbelief. He's blowing on the scattered powder. The embers are ablaze.

'Attica,' he twists his head up, 'get back.'

And he blows a spark with incredible accuracy, straight into the heart of the gunpowder pouch.

The door bursts in on us just as the powder explodes. The blast flings our attackers backwards. In the aftershock, smoke fills the room, bodies are strewn.

Jemmy and I both run at the opening, stepping over the bloodied remains.

Out in the corridor, Jemmy stops short at an open door.

'Hold steady,' he says, folding the chain holding my manacled hands together into the door jamb. He opens it then slams it hard. My bindings spring apart.

'Bermuda gaol?' I say as he dangles his own fetters into the gap.

'London,' he admits, as I break the links between his wrists.

My eyes track back to the blasted bodies.

'We can use their clothes,' I say, pointing to some scattered remnants. 'Disguise ourselves.'

'This is the second time you've asked me to take my shirt off,' says Jemmy, eyeing me. 'If I didn't know better I'd say it was a preoccupation of yours.'

I wipe a little ash on my cheeks and slip off my shoes.

'How fortunate you know better.'

CHAPTER 76

As JEMMY AND I BREAK OUT OF THE HÔTEL DE VILLE, THE whole city is different.

'Look at that,' I point.

On the steps of the town hall Parisians have formed a collective. They're pooling gunpowder and shot, sharing them out.

Even more incredibly, a steady troop of animated people are pouring from the north side of the square. Each man carries armfuls of muskets.

Jemmy's eyes are wide.

'There must be hundreds,' he whispers. 'Where did they get all those guns?'

I shield my eyes from the sun and look up to the thick crowd stretching back as far as I can see.

'More like thousands,' I decide. 'If Robespierre wants panic and death, he doesn't have it. I don't know how they did it, but somehow the French people have raided enough guns for an army.'

Jemmy and I watch, open mouthed, as teams of people troop past the Hôtel de Ville. There is an atmosphere of focused camaraderie. The people share out guns and what little shot they have. Children pass out little leaf cockades. A steady war cry begins.

'To the Bastille! The Bastille!'

'Black powder for the muskets!'

I look at Jemmy.

'They've got muskets but no gunpowder,' I say, realization dawning. 'The explosives must have been moved to the Bastille. They're going to raid it.'

'They'll never get it,' says Jemmy. 'The whole of the French army couldn't storm the Bastille.'

He shakes his head sadly, watching the resolute people come together.

'Robespierre will be trying to get the diamonds,' I say. 'I think he's too bloodless to kill Grace himself. It would be too great a risk. Most likely he'll send a trusted professional.'

'Janssen?'

I nod, an idea forming. If a crowd has formed it might create enough of a distraction, for the mighty Bastille must have a way in, after all.

'So if you want to rescue your cousin,' says Jemmy wryly, 'all you have to do is cross the impossible drawbridge and storm the impenetrable fortress.'

'My thoughts exactly.'

'*What?*'

'I'm going to save my cousin,' I say, 'and perhaps help a few French freedom fighters along the way.'

'Attica,' says Jemmy, 'those people are all going to die. How do you think they know the gunpowder is in the Bastille?'

I pause, absorbing his meaning. Someone must have let slip this fact.

Robespierre.

'Has it occurred to you that Robespierre might be influencing the Bastille governor?' continues Jemmy patiently. 'What do you think he would advise his noble friend to do if civilians come for the gunpowder? He'll hardly open the doors and send them away peaceably.'

I'm silent, thinking of the heavy artillery at the Bastille.

'Even if you were to get inside, you'll never find Grace,' says Jemmy. 'It's a fortress. Prisoners can be buried so deep even the gaolers forget them. If you try to do this alone, you will fail and you will die.'

'I never fail.'

'Then this will be a first for you. No one can break into that prison without help. You'd need an army – a real one, not a ragged mob. And someone to lead them—' He stops, as if something has occurred to him.

Jemmy rubs a hand between his eyebrows.

'I can't believe I'm doing this,' he mutters. Jemmy looks at me. 'I might have an idea to help you.'

'You do?'

'We need to find Georges Danton.'

CHAPTER 77

DISCOVERING THE WHEREABOUTS OF GEORGES DANTON is remarkably easy. Everybody, it seems, is familiar with the outspoken lawyer and his preference for drinking all hours in the Café de Chevaleux. Getting to him is proving far more difficult.

Jemmy and I are forcing our way against the flow of people towards the wine shop, which is famous for attracting rebels and free thinkers.

'Georges Danton is a great speaker,' says Jemmy, 'legendary for his booming voice. I've met him: I once smuggled him some books on the English constitution through the border at Montmartre. If anyone can rally the people, it's him.'

'I know who he is.' I'm calling to mind the documents we hold on Georges Danton. To Sealed Knot intelligence he is a 'person of interest'.

Danton is a lawyer who makes long speeches on the rights of men and enlightened thinking. He is also a great rabble-rouser, drinker, womanizer and fighter. Our information has him as very large, with a country accent on account of his common upbringing and a fair deal of scarring on his face.

The crowd is getting denser and the way impossible.

'It's no good,' I say to Jemmy, 'we must have got fifty feet in the last ten minutes.'

Hope for Grace is slipping away. I try not to imagine Robespierre briefing Janssen on how to cleanly execute the English girl.

My eyes rove around the small Paris back streets, looking for a solution. There's a little shop selling wine by the glass, a large coach house with a courtyard of wooden balconies and a cooper's yard.

I see something else. A cart loaded with barrels marked with the sign for gypsum.

'There's a mine entrance nearby,' I say. 'If we can find it, I've an idea of how we could get there faster.'

'A mine?' Jemmy is looking at me as though I've turned lunatic.

'Plaster of Paris mines,' I explain. 'The city is riddled with them. They form a network under the streets. The only problem,' I admit, 'is many of them are illegal. I don't know where the entrance might be.'

Jemmy is casting about and his gaze lights on a laundry house with huge barrels of soaking clothes outside. He runs to a strong-armed washerwoman plunging red hands in soapy water and gives her a disarming smile.

'If I may, madame,' he says, raising her wet hand to kiss it and throwing a few coins on her table. And before she can protest, he seizes a tub of laundry and upends it over the dusty road. As she begins shouting in outrage, Jemmy does the same thing with four other washing butts, sending a river of water along the street.

'Something we do with leaky ships,' he explains, as I watch him, mystified. 'To find a hole in the hull, you follow the water.'

I'm wondering how this technique might translate to underground mines, when I see a shape appear in the cascade: where water is draining away.

'Straight line,' says Jemmy. 'So the entrance will be there, or there.' He points to each end of the disappearing water.

I'm seeing things now that I didn't notice before. The fact the barrels don't look new enough to have been made recently. That man turning the hoops doesn't have the usual humped shoulder.

'The cooper's yard,' I say, 'would be a good front for a gypsum mine. Coopers are notoriously corrupt.'

'My brother is a cooper,' says Jemmy.

We both make for the yard, to the surprised faces of the barrel-makers.

Inside, just as I'd hoped, is a large dusty shaft, hidden from sight from the main street. There's a wooden track, leading down into the depths. Men are dragging up wheeled trolleys loaded with gypsum.

The mine shaft is almost vertical. Next to the trolley track are craggy steps cut into the chalky side. They wind precariously down into the gloom.

'Come on,' I say, 'the last trolley!'

The miners operating the pulley are too surprised to stop us as we run for it and leap into the cart at the back of the convoy. We land on a rocky pile of dusty gypsum and the rickety plank sides of our makeshift vehicle squeak in protest.

I pull out my Mangbetu knife and rip through the cord securing us to the carts in front. With a lurch, we break away in the opposite direction.

We career along the precipitous winding track down into the gypsum mine.

CHAPTER 78

GRACE STARES THROUGH THE BARS OF HER WINDOW. SHE gives them an experimental tug, feeling slightly foolish as they move not an inch.

Below her, Paris's rooftops and streets are laid out. Notre Dame is on the horizon and in between a mass of movement. All of it headed this way.

A crowd has been steadily amassing outside the prison and Grace has no idea what it might mean. The people pack into the district of St Antoine – the marketplace village that has sprung up around the great island of the Bastille.

She hears footsteps now. Someone is climbing the stairs. Grace has only been here a matter of hours, but the promise of any kind of company in this lonely tower is more welcome than it is frightening.

As they become louder and nearer, however, sweat prickles under her arms. The memory of the guard's threat to kill the prisoners rattles around her mind.

The lock turns, the door opens and a man enters. The first thing Grace notices is that he holds the largest bunch of keys she has ever seen. He is dressed in what Grace now knows to be

Paris fashion. The black coat with gold edging and lacy cravat are flowery by English standards but, as she understands it, positively funereal for Versailles.

He wears an old-fashioned white wig and a jewelled sword, which Grace would bet her last penny has never been used in anger.

The man bows.

'I am Governor de Launay,' he says. 'You are something of a mystery.'

Grace's heart lifts. 'I am an Englishwoman. I made a mistake getting into the prison carriage. They look quite the same as Hanson cabs in London.' The words she carefully rehearsed come out as a nervous babble. Grace sounds guilty, even to herself.

She tries for a little laugh but her throat is dry. 'Can you imagine how my friends will tease me?'

De Launay considers.

'The Bastille is a very secret place,' he says. 'Prisoners are only released having signed promises that they will not tell the inner workings.'

'I am happy to do so,' says Grace, a little too quickly. 'I will not speak a word. I have hardly seen anything, in any case. I have been so confused.' She realizes she is saying too much and stops.

De Launay thinks some more. He looks to the cell wall.

'"Man is born free and everywhere he is in chains,"' he reads. 'Several *philosophes* were prisoners here, men who claim an absolute King on a throne is unjust. Voltaire was held in the dungeons for his opinions on monarchy.' His eyes land squarely on Grace. 'He fled to England to avoid second imprisonment. Tell me, is it as they say, in your country? Do jackal politicians dare to cross words with a King of the blood?'

'They do,' says Grace. 'I believe we have better laws because of it.'

De Launay smiles. 'You are young,' he says. 'You will learn. The King must rule his country as the head must rule the body. Perhaps you know of the famous diamonds?' he says. 'It was widely thought they were sold in England.' He toys with the hilt of his sword.

Grace can feel the necklace hard under her dress. She feels colour surge to her cheeks.

He knows.

Her armpits prickle with sweat. Better to confess now, than risk his anger. Grace opens her mouth, choosing her words. But de Launay speaks over her.

'She was a prisoner of mine,' he says. 'Jeanne de la Motte-Valois.'

The name sounds strangely familiar, but Grace can't immediately place it.

'The necklace thief,' de Launay adds. 'May I?' He points to one of the comfortable chairs belonging to the Marquis de Sade. De Launay sits.

'Jeanne was a difficult prisoner,' continues the governor, frowning. 'She was born into aristocracy but her family was dispossessed, leaving her penniless. Jeanne hoped her birthright would weigh in her favour; the Queen did not agree.'

Hope sparks in Grace's chest. Perhaps, de Launay is only lonely.

The governor frowns at the memory. 'Jeanne was beaten dreadfully, branded on either shoulder and thrown into a common prison.' He looks keenly at Grace. She wonders what expression is best advised.

Is it a coincidence, his talking about the necklace? Or is de Launay simply playing with her?

De Launay appears to come to a decision. He stands.

'There is some trouble outside,' he says. 'I'm hoping it will die down. But if not, you will be moved.'

'Oh,' says Grace, fear snaking its way through her limbs. 'Where?'

'A better place for you,' says the governor. 'The dungeon.'

CHAPTER 79

Jemmy and I are heading deep into the bowels of the earth. We're careering at speed down a mine shaft. Our wheeled cart twists and turns down dark passages, weaving us ever lower into the vast network of plaster mines beneath Paris.

'Look out!' shouts Jemmy, as we fly towards a trolley being loaded by unsuspecting miners. They look up in horror to see us coming at them and run for cover.

Our little cart smashes into a rocky wall in a cloud of tinder and gypsum. We are flung from our vehicle and land in a heap.

'You're certain this is a mine?' Jemmy is taking in the great scale of it as he stands, brushing pale dust from his dark clothes. 'I've never seen anything like this.'

The ceiling is vast, at least cathedral-high, but narrowing to a thin point, in a shape reminiscent of a ragged fang.

A damp chalky smell of gypsum sits heavy on the air. Every single wall and curved surface is chiselled with a thousand little pick marks, stretching away infinitely into the distance. It's like being inside a giant fossilized shell.

Jemmy shivers slightly, closing a few more small buttons on his frock-coat.

'We're under central Paris,' I say, 'but the mines go all the way to Montmartre.' I look to the ground, where trolleys have worn troughs in the soft floor. 'If we work out which way is south-west,' I decide, 'we can get there. The deepest tracks will take us west to where most of the plasterwork are,' I say, enjoying the puzzle of it, 'but there are also royal works south. They would require the finest plaster, perhaps leaving a trail of the whitest dust. If we intersect the two, we could discern which way is north ...'

I look up to see Jemmy shaking his head pityingly. He takes out a compass from inside his black coat.

'That way,' he says, his dark books kicking up plaster dust as he strides off.

We reach our underground destination in a few minutes, but the way out presents us with a new problem. Jemmy puts out a cautionary arm and we hang back, keeping out of sight.

A group of miners and their pulleys stand between us and the route above ground. Ranged around them are a few ragged men with cudgels and a battered old musket between them: guards to stop thieves getting into the mine.

'They'll think we're here to steal,' says Jemmy, eyeing the valuable barrels of plaster.

Jemmy is taking in the rest of the mine now: the wooden scaffold, holding up the yellow-white pitched roof; beneath, the sad grey-faced workers. They chip and heave the craggy gypsum through the endless dust and half-light. To either side of us are men filling barrels and hammering the lids in place. The air rings with the sound of people coughing, like a many-toned infirm orchestra.

'I'm going to cut that rope,' I say, nodding to a pile of barrels stacked on their sides and lashed together. 'They'll roll free and we can get away in the confusion.'

'It won't work,' says Jemmy with certainty. 'You'd need a narrow passage and this mine is too big. I don't know much about barrels, but I know that.'

'I thought you said your brother was a cooper?'

'Poetic licence. He's more of a smuggler.'

'Trust me. Just stop the foreman from getting in my way.'

I nod in the direction of a tall man with a whip in his hand.

Jemmy removes his sword. And before he can reveal any more doubts, I run at the mountain of barrels with my knife outstretched.

Men loading and shovelling halt, frozen in shock as they see me coming at them, black blade held high.

From behind me, a gunshot rings out, punching a bullet hole into the barrel I'm next to and spitting out little white dust puffs.

I grab the fibrous rope that holds the barrels in place and quickly saw through it. The hemp unravels in every direction and forty huge kegs of plaster roll free. Several cascade from the top, the gypsum shattering into a cloud on impact.

I look around to see rolling barrels and fleeing workers. Containers smash, spraying the dark ground with white rings of gypsum.

As I hoped, the air is thick with choking chalky mist. I grab Jemmy's arm. The dust cloud hides us completely. Somewhere in the haze, the miners are shouting in alarm, unable to see us.

'This way,' I say, coughing hard. 'If your compass is right, we'll come up near to the Café de Chevaleux.'

CHAPTER 80

WE REACH THE CAFÉ DE CHEVALEUX, A WOODEN-FRONTED building with a row of mullioned windows. Inside is deceptively large, with a number of wooden tables, most of them occupied.

From behind the fug of pipe smoke, a woman at a broad counter pours an oily brew from a copper kettle. Above her and to the side are panes of glass with caricatures behind them. A low bubble of acrid coffee and seditious talk fills the air.

'Can you see Danton?' I ask Jemmy, raising my voice against the general chatter.

'There.' Jemmy points and I follow the direction of his finger.

Danton is a large man, broad as well as tall. His face is one of the most unfortunate I have ever seen, his natural ugliness further marred by a motley assortment of pockmarks and scars.

The small eyes are pale and piggy between the great jowls of his face, which are at this moment sunk low in despair.

I glance at Jemmy and see he is as dispirited as I am.

Even from here, I can see Danton looks utterly beaten. There is no fight left in him.

He lounges with such drunken lack of caution on his small stool that his great bulk might topple off at any moment. One hand clutches the empty remnants of a red wine bottle. The table before him holds the evidence of many more. He looks as though he hasn't slept in days.

Jemmy strides across the coffee shop.

'Danton?' He places a hand on the large man's shoulder.

Danton swivels his blue eyes to look at it, trying to work out what's happening.

'Danton?' Jemmy pulls up a stool and sits opposite him. Danton lifts his empty bottle high, eyes glassy.

'The cause is lost,' Danton explains glumly. 'Those poor fools head to the Bastille, where Governor de Launay will put them down. The thing is over.' He sighs. 'The King has won.'

He shakes his great head again.

'*Ca ira, ca ira* ...' He drifts off into bad singing.

'Danton!' To my surprise, Jemmy slams his fist on the table, sending several empty bottles shattering to the floor. The large man's piggy eyes register him with the first glimmer of sobriety.

'Get a hold of yourself, man,' says Jemmy irritably. 'You've a war to win and you won't win it sat here. Robespierre plots against you.'

Danton's eyes flick wider.

'No, no,' he booms. 'I won't hear a word against Max. He's a strange fellow, to be sure, but I've known him since we were young men. His heart's in the right place and if you've come to deride my good friend, you may be on your way.'

I glance at Jemmy. He shrugs, then leans in closer.

'The protestors,' Jemmy says, speaking quickly. 'They hope to raid the gunpowder ...'

Danton breathes out hard, his face falling even further. 'And they'll die without even getting across the great moat. There is no way into the Bastille unless you have been invited by Governor de Launay.'

'What if someone were to lower the drawbridge?' I suggest.

Danton swivels his large head to look at me. His mouth broadens into a smile, revealing small pearly teeth.

'This is your mistress?' he asks Jemmy, never taking his eyes off me. 'Why, she is delightful!'

I swallow my annoyance.

'If there were a way to lower the drawbridge,' I ask him, 'would you fight?'

Danton pats my hand with his chunky fingers.

'Don't concern yourself with man's business, my sweet bun,' he says kindly. 'It's a lovely thought, but the governor will not simply lower the bridge, even if we ask him nicely.'

He shoots a conspiratorial glance at Jemmy, shaking his head and smiling slightly at my naivety.

Jemmy winces.

'I don't plan on asking nicely,' I explain patiently. 'I've an interest in forts and castles. I think I might know a way.'

'The Bastille is impenetrable,' he booms, something of the old Danton spirit returning. 'Walls as thick as a man. Don't let Robespierre's notions of equality run away with you, mademoiselle. No man in five centuries has breached it; a woman could hardly succeed at such a thing.'

I smile politely, stand and cross the coffee house. Danton barely notices. I feel Jemmy's eyes on my back as I approach the collection of satirical prints.

My eyes flick across them. They are mostly obscene pictures of Marie Antoinette, depicting her at orgies or attempting to rouse the sleeping King with graphic nudity. I see the image I was looking for – an artist's sketch of the Bastille with sad peasants being dragged inside – and lift it off the wall.

It's only when I land the wood-framed picture of the Bastille on to Danton's table, sending his bottle of wine flying, that he registers I might be worth listening to.

'The Bastille wasn't built as a prison,' I tell him. 'It was built as a fortress.'

I tap the drawbridge in the image.

'Forts constructed as long ago as the Bastille,' I continue, drawing on my knowledge of such structures, 'use rope, not chain, to lower their drawbridges.'

I raise the curved blade of my Mangbetu knife and stab it deep into the table, inches from his folded arms. 'With your help,' I conclude, 'I think I can cut the rope.'

Danton looks warily at my weapon then at Jemmy.

'Who is she?' he asks eventually, his voice strained.

'She's English,' says Jemmy with a shrug. 'I find it better to listen to her or she becomes aggressive.'

CHAPTER 81

I'M SAT, PEN IN HAND, DRAWING A PLAN OF THE EIGHT-SIDED Bastille. Danton has listened to our hopes to further his cause and rescue my cousin with growing interest.

'The Bastille protected this side of Paris,' I tell Danton, as I carefully ink the thick walls. 'The design was so successful I don't think it has ever been bettered.'

Jemmy brings me a plate of griddled sardines and a dish of eye-wateringly strong coffee.

'You need to eat something,' he says as I finish my rudimentary plan of the Bastille in pen and ink. 'Can't save your cousin if you're weak with hunger.'

He winks and I have a sudden feeling of elation. Jemmy believes we might actually do this. Danton, too, has an excited air. The drowsy drunkenness slid off him like snow from a sunny roof.

'Quite a talent for drawing forts you have,' says Danton, eyeing my detailed sketch with an uncertain note to his voice.

The fortress shape is etched in dark black lines. The deep walls are arranged in a traditional castle formation, with a tower on each corner. But extra turrets have been added, making eight in total.

'I was very interested in military forts as a girl,' I say, putting the final flourish on the moat. 'My father had a great library of books on war-craft. My cousin Grace and I used to replicate bastions in mud and besiege them.'

I realize they are both looking at me strangely.

'Don't most little girls play with poppets?' ventures Jemmy.

'I did play with poppets,' I reply. 'They guarded the ramparts. In any case,' I add, 'the Bastille is a classic. One of the best fortresses ever built. The style has been replicated throughout Europe. See that double drawbridge design? It's the reason the fort has never fallen in five hundred years.'

I point to where I've approximated the architecture.

'It's actually three separate bridges,' I say. 'A drawbridge connecting to Paris, another joining to the Bastille and a stone bridge in the centre, where both are attached.'

Jemmy looks closer.

'That is wicked,' he breathes. 'It's built to lure people, is it?'

'Get them across the first drawbridge,' I say, 'into that central stone section. Then raise both. Your attackers are trapped in the middle, ready to be picked off or fall into the moat.'

'The moat is dry now,' says Danton. 'Parisians used the water for their laundry.'

'That makes little difference to the defence,' I say. 'It really is masterful.'

Danton rubs his forehead. 'So what is the plan?'

'If I can get on to that stone middle bridge,' I say, 'I can climb up, cut the rope and lower the first drawbridge. If you have the people make a lot of noise and fire off a few shots it will create a distraction.'

Danton adjusts his black lawyer's coat uncomfortably.

'A distraction for what? I won't lead my people to be slaughtered.'

'I wouldn't ask you to,' I say. 'The Bastille has a weakness. It was built to repel invaders. When they changed it to a prison, large gridded bars were screwed to the outside of the windows to trap prisoners. At a certain height you can scale them like a ladder. And the top windows have no barricades.'

I tap the picture.

Danton is nodding thoughtfully.

'So you would climb in and lower the second drawbridge from the inside? But there is still a fair distance to ascend before there are bars,' he points out.

'I'll use this.'

I slip Atherton's secret weapon from the hiding place in my hair. The rubber slingshot.

'How can that get you up a tower?'

In demonstration I fit a cork and fire it across the coffee house. A wine bottle on the far side explodes in red.

'My apologies, friends!' says Danton, raising his hands at a table of wine-soaked men. 'We plan a revolution!'

The men seem to accept this and go back to their drinking.

Danton turns to me. '*Mon Dieu,*' he says, 'what is that thing?'

He reaches a finger and touches the rubber.

'It has incredible power and range,' I say. 'I'll use a skein of silk, a barb of some kind and fire it up and secure it to the first window. Once I climb that part, I'll be up on the bars.'

'I've never seen anything like that,' says Jemmy uncertainly. 'You're sure it will work?'

'It will work. Atherton made it.' I'm holding my catapult affectionately.

'I'll need the right person with me. Someone who could take down guards if need be.'

I say it as a question, my eyes moving to Jemmy, and I realize I've grown to like him as a comrade. He nods in a way that suggests such a thing was never in doubt. I feel a surge of warmth for him.

'How do you plan on finding Grace?' asks Jemmy.

'I'm not certain yet,' I admit. 'But if we can open the second drawbridge and Danton leads his people, there's a good chance any prisoners will be left unguarded.'

'Break the tower and rescue the princess,' rumbles Danton. 'Only the tower is a royal prison and the princess is a commoner. What revolutionary could resist such a task? If your plan succeeds, the French people will be freeing inmates, along with raiding gunpowder, you can be sure of it.'

Jemmy looks thoughtful. 'The Bastille is as large as a town,' he says. 'There are eight huge towers, endless walls and buttresses, rooms in the roof, dungeons.'

'And we will say we were there when it fell!' There is a sudden excitement to Danton, a vibrant energy about his bulky frame.

'It's a ridiculous plan,' he beams, rubbing his hands together, 'simply ridiculous. But, mademoiselle, I think it could work!' He frowns. 'You still have a problem,' he says. 'How will you get to that stone bridge to cut the first drawbridge?'

'I've been thinking about that,' I say. 'I think I could be lowered into the dry moat with rope. The next part is more complicated. Some sort of grappling hook, perhaps.'

'If I might bring some pirate simplicity,' interjects Jemmy, 'have you considered a plank?'

Danton and I look at one another.

'Why, that's excellent,' says Danton. 'A working man's solution.'

'I suppose there is a practicality to it,' I admit, sad not to have the opportunity to lay hold of grappling hooks.

'We have the will of the people,' says Danton, joy spreading across his scarred features. His ugliness is less apparent now; he looks more like a war-torn general. 'This could be a momentous day.' His excitement palpable. 'The Bastille is a sign of royal tyranny.'

'Danton,' I say, putting my hand on his shoulder, 'it's a good plan, but one of enormous risk. After I lower the first drawbridge, it is imperative you keep your people back. Do you understand? They must wait until the second bridge is lowered.'

He straightens his clothing and picks up his sword and pistol. 'Then we shall make a stand,' he says, attaching them to his belt. He finishes buckling his weapons. 'Today may be the day I die for my country,' he says. He frowns and places a hand on the table to steady himself, as though a wave of exhaustion has buffered him from an unexpected quarter. 'What day is it?'

'It's Tuesday,' I say. And then because he seems to need more clarity, I add, 'I think it's the fourteenth of July.'

CHAPTER 82

We marshal outside the Bastille in an atmosphere of great excitement. Frenchmen are arriving fresh from the Hôpital des Invalides holding raided muskets. Several hundred people are clustered around the prison and more join every minute.

I've retained Jemmy's shirt, now belted at the waist, with my culottes beneath. I have exchanged my satin shoes for a pair of soldier's boots courtesy of Danton.

'I like you dressed as a boy,' observes Jemmy.

'I always had my suspicions about a man who wore a purple cravat.'

My eyes track up to the Bastille itself, an edifice of fairy-tale proportions, twice as tall as its moat is broad. It is a forbidding citadel with looming bastions and walls that seem to draw out endlessly.

Several dark cannon muzzles are trained on the mounting crowd and there is an occasional flicker of movement at the ramparts. But for now, the mighty fortress only watches, keeping its counsel.

Jemmy follows my gaze. 'I'll wager there's a good view from the top,' he says.

'Buildings this large have been known to make their own weather.' Danton crosses himself. 'Lightning forks around it during thunderstorms.'

'Fortunate, then,' I say, 'we're here to take it down.'

Danton smiles and lowers his voice. 'The impossible fortress? Perhaps. But we will make a stand and that is all that matters.' His pale eyes light on mine. 'If we can get you inside to rescue your cousin,' he adds, 'we will have done a great good today.'

Danton comes alive as the long plank appears. He approaches a huddle of jobbing workmen manoeuvring it, rubbing his hands together.

'You got the plank, then, lads?'

They bring it, sweating, to the side of the moat and we go after.

'Jesus.' Jemmy crosses himself, as we reach the edge. 'I've never seen anything like it. It's more like an island in a lake than prison and a moat.'

I follow his gaze across the great open chasm dividing Paris from its notorious gaol. The bottom is spongy earth. Reeds and grasses grow.

'Enough land down there for several hundred cattle,' I say.

'I know a fair few peasant farmers who would be glad of such an enclosure,' agrees Danton.

A stone section rises from the centre, like a single tooth in a gummy mouth. It connects on one side to the Bastille and on the other to Paris by wooden drawbridges, but today these are raised.

'Raise those drawbridges and you can trap people in the middle,' I say. 'There is an art to such simplicity.'

Neither Danton nor Jemmy share my respect for the architecture.

'Where shall we put the extra muskets?' A tanner with ulcerated legs has identified Danton as their natural general.

'Make a row by the wall,' says Danton. 'Keep them upright and don't make a heap, mind. Those pensioners risked their lives to give us working guns; we must see they fire when needed.'

The tanner nods.

'We have shot, powder?' Danton is appraising the situation.

'Very little shot and even less powder,' says the tanner. 'Citizens are handing out what they have in private supplies. Some of us thought to buy bags of nails for bullets,' he adds with a gap-toothed grin. He slaps his musket, which jingles.

Danton raises his voice. 'Soldiers of France,' he announces, 'we have but little shot and powder. With God's will and our courage, it is enough. The rest, we will find inside the Bastille!' He points dramatically towards the prison.

The men turn to see Danton's massive frame, the barrel chest and scarred face. Meaty cheers go up. The people have been waiting for a leader.

'Three hundred barrels of gunpowder; the same of shot. Enough to charge every musket! And we must have it,' declares Danton. 'By God, we *will* have it. Comrades, this is a war. We are under attack by a foreign army!'

A crescendo of agreement reverberates around the crowd. The people are flushed, giddy with the excitement of what they have achieved.

More are arriving all the time, a steady flow through the markets of St Antoine. They come in twos and threes, alone or in a pack, drops of water making an ocean.

At the brink of the moat, the workmen holding the long plank let it drop. It falls towards the isolated stone section and slams loudly into place, forming a makeshift bridge. People shout and cheer. Their joy and hope is palpable. They are daring to breach Paris's infamous prison and no one is trying to stop them.

Without warning, a man in peasant's clothing makes a run for the plank. He jumps unevenly on to it and walks, hands aloft in triumph.

'That's the way, Robert!' shouts a woman from the crowd.

He's only halfway along when a gunshot cracks from the Bastille. The man stumbles, then slips and tumbles. He disappears out of sight into the cavernous moat.

'Shit!' Jemmy runs to the edge. 'No blood or bullet-wound,' Jemmy announces, 'but I think he's broken something.'

Danton shoulders in.

'We need to get him out,' he says. 'You men,' he points, 'get down there.'

Groans of agony can now be heard from deep in the moat.

'A warning shot,' says Danton, looking up at the Bastille.

A strange ratcheting of metal on metal echoes suddenly in the middle distance. We look up, alarmed. Slowly, on the ramparts, a gibbet rises up from the depths of the prison.

It swings, creaking in the breeze. Inside is a half-rotted corpse hanging like a hideous flag on the top of the battlements.

Danton swallows.

'One of the prisoners from the dungeons,' he says. 'They mean to frighten us away.'

The effect on the throng of Parisians is immediate. There is a dreadful hush as people cross themselves and look to the ghoulish spectacle. Mutterings and whispers go around of torturers and hidden dungeons.

'Better I get over that plank and cut the drawbridge,' I say, 'before the fight goes from the crowd.'

Jemmy puts a hand on my arm.

'It was never agreed,' he says, 'that you would be the one to negotiate the plank.'

'I have the sharpest knife.'

Jemmy fingers the hilt of his sword. 'You are better than me at many things,' he says, pushing a dark lock of hair from his face. 'Using long words, waving knives around,' he tilts his head, 'maybe even fighting, in certain circumstances. But at least let us both agree: pirates are good at walking planks.'

I hesitate. 'Very well.'

Jemmy makes towards the plank.

'Wait.'

He turns around.

I pull my knife from my dress. 'You'll need this.'

Jemmy's hand clasps around the handle of my Mangbetu blade. He holds it up wonderingly.

'I'll bring it back,' he promises. 'Get over your fear of guns and get yourself a musket. I might need covering fire.'

CHAPTER 83

GOVERNOR DE LAUNAY IS PACING THE INNER BASTIONS OF the Bastille with a frantic air.

There's an assembled guard, a handful or so of troops, awaiting instruction. Their opinion of Governor de Launay has been steadily falling since last week.

Adding to the general feeling of unease is the presence of a ghoulish-looking musketeer with a blood-red eye and a terrible metal hand. This Janssen fellow had simply *arrived* in the Bastille, in the early hours of the morning, bearing a letter from Monsieur Robespierre.

It reminds de Launay of the German play he once saw acted in the Versailles water gardens, back when the old King was alive. About a pact with the devil.

He never agreed for a man like Janssen to have access to the prison. But then, as Robespierre's letter cleverly insinuates, the small print was never exactly defined and a promise is a promise.

So now this musketeer is roaming the Bastille, unnerving guards. It really is intolerable, but de Launay has other things on his mind.

The ungainly roar of the crowd in the distance brings a strange feeling to the pit of his stomach.

'They have breached the first drawbridge.' De Launay turns to his guard, chewing the end of his finger. 'They mean to free the prisoners.'

'The second drawbridge is secure,' his guard assures him. 'It can only be lowered from inside the Bastille.'

'The inmates are locked in the dungeon?' confirms de Launay, his eyes lifted in some unspoken calculation.

'The last are being taken down now,' says the guard. 'We had to move the Marquis de Sade to another prison. He kept shouting to the commoners that he was being murdered.'

He frowns. 'Janssen was poking about there,' he adds, 'said he was looking for a prisoner, but wouldn't tell us which one. Said he had your permission to go where he pleases.'

De Launay feels his face redden, both at the affront and at the fact he cannot contradict it.

'Janssen shall have to wait,' he says, attempting to salvage some authority.

'He may not be happy,' says the guard ominously.

De Launay opens his mouth and shuts it again. Really it is quite impossible that a commoner might treat the Bastille with such freedom.

A blood-thirsty roar from outside the prison makes de Launay start. He smooths his lacy coat, trying to disguise the reaction.

'Fortunately,' he says, with a faint smile, 'the mob knows nothing about our little gauntlet.'

'A gauntlet?' The guard is confused.

'The courtyard,' says de Launay, his expression slightly manic. 'The courtyard for trapping and killing invaders.'

CHAPTER 84

Grace senses that time is running out. Prisoners are being moved. She hears them: asking questions, pleading. No reason is given, but Grace has read a good deal about the Bastille. She has heard how murders are done. Inmates are taken to the dungeons and discreetly strangled. There is a special room where it happens.

A sudden noise comes through the window: people cheering as though a significant victory has occurred.

She moves to the bars. Her eyes widen. There is a plank halfway across the immense moat. She can scarce believe it.

Her eyes scan the crowd. She can just make out a woman with long dark hair lifting a musket from a pile of guns. Recognition surges, then Grace smiles at her idiocy, shaking it away.

Just for a moment, she thought it to be her cousin Attica. That is what happens when you don't see a familiar face for so long, decides Grace, you begin making pictures in your head.

Even so, it occurs to her that perhaps Lord Pole or Godwin is trying to find her. If she is put in the dungeons they may never even know she was here.

Something else strikes her. The courtyard she was taken

into before entering the prison. It's lined on every side with weaponry. Grace doesn't know a great deal about warfare, but even she can recognize a killing ground when she sees one.

If those people get over the drawbridge and get through the door, they'll be gunned down by soldiers hiding behind their holes in the wall.

She hears footsteps again and knows her time has come.

Grace cups her hands and shouts as loudly as she can from the window.

'Don't cross the drawbridge!' she bellows in English. 'You'll walk straight into a trap!'

No one gives any sign of having heard. Her words are drowned out in the battle cries.

With a feeling of despair, Grace pulls the great diamond necklace from her dress. She hates it with a passion she could barely imagine in herself. The harm this dreadful symbol of greed and lust has done is incalculable.

An idea comes to her. Grace has read her fairy tales. If she is to be moved, perhaps she can leave a trail of breadcrumbs. Someone may realize she was here, in this room, and try to deduce where she was taken.

Glancing to the door, Grace breaks off one of the smaller diamonds from its silver casing. It gives her a malignant pleasure to damage this gaudy thing.

For a moment, she holds the glittering gem around the palm of her hand with her finger and wonders how much it alone is worth. She turns to the open window and puts the tiny diamond on the ledge, just out of sight behind the bars.

Tap tap tap.

Up come the footsteps, closer and closer. A wave of dread washes through her. The dungeon awaits.

CHAPTER 85

I WATCH, HEART IN MOUTH, AS JEMMY HOPS LIGHTLY ON TO the long plank. The soles of his leather boots flex with the wood. Beside me, Danton stares, fist held close to his face.

'He's fast,' concedes Danton, as Jemmy moves gracefully at speed. 'But it's a long plank.'

Jemmy is a quarter of the way along when a few of the crowd begin to cheer him. Seconds later, shots ring out.

I heft my musket. Danton has shaken down the assembled people for ammunition and powder. The result is enough for a handful of shots. Not much more. And I have to ration carefully. Too much and I'll soon run out, too little and the charge won't be sufficient to hit my target.

Another gunshot resounds, sending a shower of splinters from the plank. Jemmy ducks, wheeling on one leg.

'Attica!' His voice carries a note of accusation. 'Stop rationing your powder!'

I sight the man I think is firing and pull the trigger. The shot chinks harmlessly on a thick metal window bar, releasing sparks.

The guard on the other side ducks away, unharmed. I'm wondering if it's worth staying trained on this particular area when another shot rings out.

Jemmy is halfway across now. The plank sags and reverberates with his weight. His pace has slowed as he steps cautiously on the moving walkway.

I'm reloading when I hear a third, fired from another quarter of the prison.

Breathing to steady my aim, I shoot in one direction, then reload and discharge at another. I'm not managing to kill any guards, but it's slowing their attack, at least.

It's then I see the cannon, turning towards the moat.

'Jemmy!' I shout. 'Run!'

I see his head tilt up and recognize the dark muzzle now pointed square in his direction. He races, faster than I would have thought possible, along the final half of the plank.

'He's going to make it!' Danton's fists are clenched. 'He's going to make it!'

Jemmy is a few feet away when his makeshift bridge is simply obliterated, smashed into a thousand pieces by a cannon ball.

'Ah, but he was so close.' Danton's excitement fades. He rubs his chin thoughtfully.

'Wait!' I take his meaty arm. 'He's made it! Look!'

Jemmy pulls himself with great effort, up on to the stone midsection.

The people explode into cheers and applause. Jemmy stands before the raised drawbridge now. He moves to the side and begins to climb.

'He's in!' Danton can hardly contain himself. 'He's got to the mechanism.'

The crowd grows silent as we watch the looming drawbridge. Then its shape changes. Slowly at first, then faster.

'It's lowering!' I say to Danton. 'Jemmy has cut the ropes.'

There's a shriek of wood as the enormous drawbridge plummets directly towards us. The assembled onlookers flee as the foot-thick door free-falls.

Danton and I only watch as the great bridge smashes into the ground, driving up a cascade of loose soil.

'The impenetrable fortress has a chink in its armour,' says Danton with a grin.

We look out on the wide bridge now spanning half the moat. The remote prison door is suddenly a good deal nearer.

People are waving muskets, drunk with exhilaration.

Danton turns back to his people.

'One drawbridge down,' he grins, 'now for the second.'

We've bridged the gap to the middle of the moat, but a chasm of equal size to the first still stands between us and the prison entrance.

Danton sighs. 'There is a chance de Launay will see reason. He knows the people are entitled to bear arms at times of war. I doubt he keeps enough food in there for a long siege. Perhaps he will simply capitulate.' He smiles at me. 'Thanks to your pirate friend, we can begin ringing his doorbell, can we not?'

'Don't run away with that idea,' I say. 'The plan is to cause a diversion, remember? Let Jemmy and I open it from the inside.'

I see something wistful in Danton's small eyes. 'A dishonourable way to win,' he says. 'Ah, so be it.'

Jemmy returns to my side, sweat pouring from his face. The teardrop blemish by his eye is livid from exertion. He hands me my knife.

'Ready for your foolish plan?' he says.

I look up to the precipitous walls of the Bastille. At the very top, swinging gently in the breeze, is the iron gibbet with its cautionary corpse.

I nod to Danton. He sweeps a thick hand in the air.

'Those that have ammunition and guns, open fire!'

A cluster of men take up the cry. They point their muskets at the Bastille door and begin to discharge. We watch as gunshot peppers the centuries-old wood and nails embed themselves, crossing the void to lodge in the ancient entrance.

I turn to Jemmy. 'There's our distraction. Time to break the unbreakable prison.'

CHAPTER 86

FROM THE MARSHY BASE OF THE MOAT, I LOOK UP AT THE high heavy walls. Five centuries of tyranny, broadened and deepened over time. It's a fortress in the oldest sense.

I take out my catapult, an iron barb and a thick skein of silk, twisted into a strong rope.

It feels good to have it in my hand, despite my misgivings that Atherton has grown tired of my defying orders. I bring it to my lips and kiss it. I see Jemmy watching me. He rolls his eyes. I tie the projectile.

Fitting it to my catapult, I take aim and fire. The barb goes whistling through an upper-storey window taking my silk with it. I pull back, hooking the iron prongs tight against the bars. The rope flutters down, like Rapunzel letting out her hair.

I turn my head to check that Jemmy is in his position, crouched low at the outer wall, then I give him a nod.

Jemmy readies his pistol and eyes the ramparts. 'So far, your fool plan is holding water. Can't see any guards defending this part.'

I wrap the rope around my wrists, lean back and begin to climb. I winch myself up to the first set of bars, fixed with rusting bolts to the ancient stonework. Pausing for breath, I secure my feet then tie off the silk and let it fall.

Below I see Jemmy seize hold and start his own ascent. I wait until he appears next to me and we both climb together.

'You were right,' he says. 'It's like a ladder. Easier than ship's rigging.'

At the top of the bars, we're able to reach up and pull ourselves on to the next sill.

The summer air feels muggy, like the beginnings of a thunderstorm. But as we get higher, the closeness lifts. Now I'm above ground, the climb is less arduous. The square-barred iron is simple enough to assail and, in between them, window ledges provide helpful platforms. I'm almost to the third storey when the grille comes away in my hand.

I go swinging out, wide over the dry moat. Beneath me is the half-lowered drawbridge.

'Hold on, Attica!' shouts Jemmy. I feel the grating swing back into place and slowly, by welcome inches, I return to the relative safety of the wall.

'Thanks,' I gasp.

'You're sure you want to go on?' says Jemmy. 'The ironwork will be rustier the higher we go. If you fall, you'll break a limb.'

'I broke my arm in India,' I say. 'I was on my back for six weeks, strapped to a fracture box. I've never forgotten the lesson.'

I can still remember the crunching as the bone-setter tried to straighten it. I was only semi-conscious when my father arrived at my bedside. He sent the surgeon away and set the arm himself.

I start to climb.

'You were lucky,' says Jemmy, following. 'Break a limb aboard ship, and if it starts changing colour they'll saw it off. And there's no laudanum to float you through it.'

'I never take laudanum,' I say, putting one careful hand above another. 'I've seen bad things from excess.'

'You and I have a different idea of bad things,' gasps Jemmy through the exertion of pulling himself up.

We climb stoically, gaining height, sweating with the effort. I hear Jemmy stop climbing.

'Attica.' There's a warning in his voice I don't like at all. I look down to see his attention is towards the Bastille. We're high enough now to see something that couldn't be seen from the moat.

'So now we know why the Bastille is impenetrable,' says Jemmy. 'It has a false entrance.'

Cold fear grips me. I take in the vision of warfare.

The door to the Bastille opens to an interior courtyard. Anyone who breaches it will find themselves not inside the prison, but in a stone-walled space just outside the true fortress.

The three tall walls are lined with cannons and musket barrels.

'It's worse than that,' I say, calling to mind my study of forts. 'If the second drawbridge is lowered and the crowd enters that courtyard they'll be utterly defenceless. Those cannons will rip them to shreds in minutes.'

I swallow, looking to where the people heft their raided muskets. They've no idea what lies on the other side of the door.

I look down at Jemmy. 'If those people cross the second drawbridge they walk into a killing jar.'

CHAPTER 87

De Launay has removed his curled wig. He looks even older without it. There are wig-sores on his shaved grey scalp.

'I've called in the men from the upper towers,' he says. 'One of the traitors has got on to the central bridge by way of a plank. He has lowered the first drawbridge. Our security is compromised. We'll need to make a start now.'

He says it as if he's hosting a dinner party and some guests are late. He addresses the nearest guard. 'Lower the second drawbridge.'

The guard opens and shuts his mouth a few times. 'You mean to surrender?' he says finally, relief in his voice evident. 'Give the people the gunpowder?'

'We would think no less of you,' ventures another guard. 'A lot of your people are dying.'

A nasty expression forms on de Launay's face.

'Those are not *my* people,' he says. 'My people are in Versailles. Those filthy creatures out there are traitors against their King.' There is the slightest shake in his hands as he adjusts the jewelled sword at his belt. 'We will lower the second drawbridge,' he says. 'The mob will flood over the bridge like rats off a sinking ship. Into the courtyard ...' He pauses to let the image sink in.

No one answers, uncertain as to what response is expected. They are all picturing the courtyard: a broad enclosure, studded on every side by cannon holes, slots for muskets.

'You will take up arms behind the courtyard walls,' concludes de Launay. 'We shall have them all slain within an hour.'

One guard appears to be working up the confidence to ask something.

'What is it, man?' de Launay demands.

'You want us,' says a guard, 'to lower the bridge so we might lure them into a dead end to be slaughtered?'

'You have it exactly right,' says de Launay grandly. He privately wonders at how long it took the guards to understand his clever strategy. But that is the way with commoners, he muses. God appointed Kings and nobles to decide things for them.

CHAPTER 88

JEMMY AND I ARE HANGING HALFWAY UP THE BASTILLE, reeling from the discovery of the courtyard trap.

'We can still execute the plan,' I say. 'The courtyard stands between the drawbridge and the prison. If we open the door to the Bastille, people can flow through.'

'It's still a gauntlet,' says Jemmy uncertainly. 'Many more lives will be lost.'

I look up at the tower, defeat gnawing at me. The top window is within reach. I see it, glinting on the windowsill.

A tiny diamond. It takes only a few moments for me to work out what this means.

Grace! Grace was here.

I begin climbing sideways, heading for the jewel.

'Where are you going?' I hear Jemmy's voice.

'I think Grace was imprisoned in that cell.' I'm almost on it. 'Perhaps is still.'

I heave myself on to the edge of the bars, level with the open window.

If Grace is in that room, there might be some way to pull away the rusty iron, I decide, my heart racing.

We can get back down to Danton and explain the Bastille is deadlier than we thought. The armed courtyard might risk too many innocent lives.

Below us, Danton's men are on the half-lowered drawbridge keeping a steady attack on the entrance.

I concentrate on moving my feet carefully, passing one hand across one bar to the next.

A rush of wind blows a terrible waft of the rotting corpse, which swings still in the gibbet on the ramparts.

Gunfire starts up again from the front of the prison just as I reach the window. The little diamond winks at me.

I grasp the bars.

'Grace?'

The cell is dark and fear spirals though me. Surely they give the prisoners candlelight?

Unexpectedly, a figure emerges from the depths. A bloodshot eye appears inches behind the bars. In horror, I take in the battered musketeer's hat, the silver hand.

Oliver Janssen.

His face is set with dark intention. In his hand is a silver pistol. It's pointed directly at my chest.

Far beneath us, there's a sudden huge sound, loud like metal on metal, then a great thud of wood on stone resounds like a thunderclap.

The second drawbridge.

An icy chill running though my veins. Unless Danton can keep them back, those citizens will run straight into the enclosed courtyard to be slaughtered.

'Mademoiselle Morgan,' says Janssen, 'you didn't heed my warning.'

And he pulls the trigger.

CHAPTER 89

GRACE IS BEING HERDED ALONG THE BROAD CORRIDORS and down steep steps. All natural light has fled now and only torches show the way. Grace assumes they cannot possibly go any deeper. The air down here is so wet she can feel it on her skin. The walls are slick with slime and run with water in places.

She feels she has walked for miles. The guard leading her has kept a stoic silence at her increasingly desperate questioning.

'Please,' she manages, 'why are we in the dungeon?'

To her surprise, this elicits an answer. The gaoler, a broken-toothed man with dead eyes, gives her a lopsided smile.

'You're not there yet.' He grins.

They turn a corner and approach a vast circular chasm in the ground, a black shaft to oblivion, with a round brick-lined mouth like a Roman sewer.

At first Grace assumes it's a massive well, since there is a heavy chain dangling through its centre. The guard pulls a lever and with a deafening turning sound that rings around the stone walls, a contraption is hauled up. She finds herself standing on tiptoe to peer over the edge as a large swinging *something* is wrenched from the depths.

Not a water bucket. Grace tries not to panic, swallowing hard.

A cage: vast, metal, with a floor of bars, like a giant aviary.

The guard opens the door and gestures they step inside.

Fear is flowering in Grace's belly. She shuts her eyes. It plays with her conscience, telling her to give up the diamonds.

You could buy yourself protection, whispers a traitorous voice.

But Grace knows enough about the revolution to understand the consequences. In the wrong hands the necklace would mean certain victory for the King. She remembers the thin people on the streets of Paris. Women clutching paper-skinned babies.

She can't do it.

Grace steps inside, the cage swaying beneath her. The guard bangs on the bars. Someone beneath them releases the chain with a jerk. They descend fast through the gloom and with every foot, Grace feels sunlight and freedom slipping further and further away. And as the cage slams against the stone floor, sending her staggering, she knows in her heart there can be no escape from this underworld.

She is buried in a maze, beneath a hundred feet of solid rock and earth.

Her thoughts fly upwards, birdlike, to Godwin. Grace wonders whom he will marry when he eventually accepts she has vanished for ever. She feels as though she can see her former life branching away; causes she intended to champion, the children she hoped to raise. This dark prison has sucked it all away.

She realizes with a kind of numbness that it was never quite *her* life in any case. Things had been decided for her, chosen, picked out. She had just done what she was told.

Grace calls to mind the wild girl she had been growing up in Bristol. The one she has been trying to remodel into a well-behaved young intellectual. It was the dockside girl, Grace sees now, who stuck that man with a hairpin, who fought, who ran, who *survived.*

They reach a low door with a grille. The guard raps a complicated knock. Grace tries to remember it, but she is too frightened to hold it in her head.

An awful inhuman stink is rolling out from behind the door, the kind of fetid human filth that Grace knows from the docks.

The door opens to reveal a gaoler on the other side, a squat man who looks to have been out of the sun for many years. He has greenish skin and a slice of greasy hair across his balding head.

'The final prisoner for you,' says the guard. The gaoler looks at Grace for a little too long.

Behind him, Grace sees movement. She feels sick. Someone is chained to the wall. More than one person.

'What's happening upstairs, then?' he asks.

'De Launay wants 'em all down here.' The guard shrugs. 'Says someone will come. A musketeer. You're to let him in. No one else.'

No. Thinks Grace. *No.*

'De Launay's got plans to massacre all the people,' adds the guard nonchalantly. 'You're to be sure the gunpowder is kept safe, under lock and key.'

'Yes. Think he'll capture any alive?' he says hopefully. 'I've been working on some new tools. De Launay can be sure I'll have 'em bloodied and trembling so I might show them off to His Majesty.'

Grace never meant to do what she does next. It comes from nowhere. Her hand moves of its own accord. She reaches out and slaps the gaoler hard across the face. It is only after she's done it that the heavy feeling of regret settles on her.

She later considers, had the guard not looked so amused, the gaoler might have forgiven it.

He stares at Grace like a crow assessing carrion.

'This one,' he says, 'I might keep in the oubliette.'

Grace's French is deserting her. She has never heard of an oubliette. Sifting her memory, it translates as something like 'place of memories'.

This sounds very much like a torture chamber.

CHAPTER 90

As Janssen's gun hammer looses, I move my hand fast through the bars. As I expected, the musketeer is used to heavier rifles. It's easy enough to slam his arm upwards as the blast of gunpowder ignites. The rebound from the weapon does the rest.

He staggers back, shot discharging into the ancient Bastille ceiling, releasing a spray of mortar and dust on to his wide hat.

I momentarily let go of the bars so I might drop a few feet.

'Mind me head!' Jemmy's accent is notably more Irish than American when he's annoyed. I look down to see he has narrowly dodged my falling feet.

'Janssen,' I say breathlessly, indicating with my eyes in the direction of the prison window. 'With a pistol. Fortunately, he does that thing musketeers do when they've battled with older guns.'

'This thing?' Jemmy tightens his eyes in a wincing expression.

'Exactly that.' I glance up. 'We need to go down,' I say. 'We're easy targets out here. He's likely looking for us.'

We start climbing down the bars.

'I heard the second drawbridge,' says Jemmy. 'The protestors are nowhere near the mechanism. Someone inside must have lowered it.'

'Danton might be able to keep them back—' I begin.

There's a roar of cheers. Tramping feet and cries of victory.

I glance down. People are spilling over the second drawbridge, straight into the confined courtyard.

'There's no way out of that courtyard,' I murmur. 'And it's lined every side with guns and cannons. They'll all be massacred.'

'You think someone is deliberately setting a trap for the crowd?' says Jemmy. 'Luring them into the courtyard?'

I look down at Jemmy.

'De Launay isn't inviting them to breakfast,' I say. 'We need to get down there. The courtyard is joined to the main prison by a large door. If we can open it, the people will have an escape route. And I can get inside to look for Grace.'

'Open the door,' mutters Jemmy, shaking his head. 'You make it sound as though we simply turn the handle.'

'If my plans are so very bad, you might venture one of your own.'

'Maybe I do have a plan,' says Jemmy with a frown.

'Does it involve my taking my clothes off?'

Jemmy hesitates. 'No.'

'Then tell me.'

He's stopped descending now and has come to a halt around two storeys from the ground.

A line of thick wooden flag posts and flags have been driven into the wall here. Jemmy hops on to one, bouncing slightly on his heels, testing the strength. It's strong enough to take his weight.

The wind whips through my hair.

'The flag posts?' I say. 'You're certain they'll hold?'

'Those posts are hammered deep into the stone,' says Jemmy. 'They're wide enough to stand on and they run right above the courtyard.'

Jemmy points. Set into the inner courtyard wall at second-storey height are the flags, continuing in an unbroken line. The solid wooden flagpoles point out horizontally at intervals, royalist colours hanging down.

Jemmy jumps from one post to the next.

'Easier than climbing rigging,' he concludes. 'And even better,' he adds, jumping again and landing gracefully, 'they're out of range of the cannons.'

'If we can get to the courtyard door,' I say, 'there's a chance I could pick the lock.'

I follow Jemmy, springing across to the first flagpole. I teeter as I land, but it's broad and the solid post doesn't rebound even slightly under my weight. I leap to the next and the next, with Jemmy setting a fast pace in front.

Before long we've got close to the flag posts over the courtyard. It's screened by a haze of smoke, but we can hear the boom of cannon fire.

'Not far,' pants Jemmy.

Now we're nearer, the deafening gunfire gives way to another awful noise. People are screaming, I realize, my stomach tightening.

It's then I see the huge double doors barring the way to the Bastille. They're crushed tight with terrified people.

My heart sinks. I see immediately that the lock is too large and old to be picked.

CHAPTER 91

De Launay watches the crowd pour into the courtyard. He is surprised by how many people there are, how many women and children.

There is no way back now. Show mercy and the people would raid enough munitions for an army. The King would execute him as a traitor. Lose the battle and it would be his head on a pike.

The only thing left is to defend the Bastille.

Still, he hasn't been prepared for just how effective the courtyard is. De Launay had expected the people would beat a hasty retreat just as soon as they understood the deadly trap at the end of the second drawbridge. But the design forms a kind of funnel, creating an instant bottleneck. With so many people pouring through, the crush on the narrow entryway makes it impossible to turn and flee.

It is God's will, de Launay tells himself. Better there are no survivors to spread word of what had happened here. The next thing you know, you're pulled through the streets with hay in your mouth, thrashed with nettles.

Unfortunately, his indecision thus far has ramifications.

The hired Swiss guard have lost respect for him. And, to de Launay's amazement, are showing a worrying sympathy for the French peasants. They seem woefully reluctant to do their duty.

'They are unarmed civilians,' a guard is telling him. 'They could be deterred with musket. We do not need to blow them apart with cannon fire.'

'That one,' de Launay extends a shuddering finger, 'he fired a gun.'

'That's Lanac Baudin,' says a guard, 'he runs the tobacco stall in St Antoine.'

The other guards shuffle uneasily. They're all pipe smokers.

'Two weeks in Paris and you think you're native?' says de Launay. 'Do not fool yourselves for a moment that that mob will not rip you to shreds with their bare hands.'

No one replies.

'You're hired mercenaries,' rages de Launay. 'Do what you're paid to do. Load those cannons.'

Reluctantly the guards man their stations. The first cannon is lit. As it explodes into the crowd, several men avert their eyes.

A cannonball rips straight through the jaw of a young boy and smashes apart the chest of a woman standing behind him. Left and right people are being felled. Peppery blasts of shot are taking people down, one by one.

The joy of the rebellion has evaporated. They are being slaughtered. People try to escape and find they cannot. Panic surges. There's no way out.

CHAPTER 92

I SWING MY GAZE BACK TO THE DRAWBRIDGE.

Eager freedom fighters are surging towards the Bastille, with no idea of the deadly bottleneck that awaits them.

In the courtyard, people can't go back. They're trapped by the masses pushing them forward.

I see Jemmy's horrified expression.

We're on the part of the prison wall above the courtyard now. Close enough to see through the smoke. I make out a large square space, overlooked on all sides by defensive musket-holes and cannons. To the far end is a set of imposing double doors: the way into the mighty Bastille herself. But the wooden entrance is locked tight shut against the small army at the gates.

The courtyard is a deep enough drop to break a limb. For a moment I can't quite process what is happening. A greyish smoke obscures a thick crowd of people, packed tightly into the space. There are screams. They're being killed, I realize. Mercilessly. Women and children, too.

'It's a fortress design,' I say, my mouth turned down as I take in the carnage, 'let just enough of your enemy inside as you can slaughter at once.'

All below us is a bloodbath. I have seen worse things than most people, but even my heart breaks at the decimation of this unarmed populace.

I've made it to the final flag, just over the entrance to the courtyard. I can see the heavy double doors beneath me. It's even clearer to me now that there's no way to unlock them. The thick ancient mechanism defies modern lock-picks. The only way through is with a key, a cannon or a battering ram. And the protestors have none of these.

Hope is winging away.

I spot Danton's hulking form in the crowd. He looks up and sees me.

'We're dying down here, Attica!' he cries. 'If there's anything you can do, do it now.'

I open my mouth to shout back, but there's nothing to say.

Danton is bellowing fruitlessly in the direction of the blasting cannons.

'You Swiss who fire on us!' he shouts. 'We know you are not blind to our cause! We French are slaves to a tyrant. Cease your attack!'

I watch impotently as the French people, with their leafy cockades, are massacred. Another cannon booms and then another. I feel the post shift beneath my feet and I lose my balance. Jemmy lands next to me and stops my fall.

'Look at me,' he advises, fixing me with his green eyes, 'not at them. There's nothing you can do for them by dying.'

'Hey!' A sound from above makes me look up.

A man in Swiss uniform is leaning from the window over my head.

'We've been seen,' I tell Jemmy, reaching for my knife.

'Wait,' says Jemmy. 'Look.'

I look up again. The Swiss guard has something in his hand.

It's a key. 'Those Swiss are not such bastards after all,' says Jemmy. 'I'd say he's offering you the means to unlock the courtyard door.'

I look again to be sure my eyes don't deceive me. But it's true: the guard is holding a thick key. I watch in amazement as he waves it then throws it down.

I catch mutely, my eyes wide, standing precariously on the flag post. Hope blooms. I heft the great key.

Jemmy looks at the courtyard then draws his sword.

'Shall I show you a pirate trick to get down fast?' he offers, lowering himself to his knees above the royal crested fabric.

'The one involving a knife and a sail? I'm obliged to you, but most knife tricks I know.' I plunge my blade into the flag and streak down, leaving two sliced sections of fabric waving in my wake.

I hear Jemmy come down the same way on the closest flag to mine. Together we land in the mass of terrified people, crushed at Bastille's thick doors.

Quickly, I tuck myself in amongst them and push the huge key into the mighty lock.

Beside me, people are hammering fruitlessly against the door and pleading for mercy. A surge from behind crushes all in tightly.

Gritting my teeth, I turn the over-sized key. The massive doors creak slowly inwards. Then everyone is helping, pushing through the entrance to the unbreakable bastion, pouring inside.

As people realize what is happening, a cry of unbridled joy goes up. No one can quite believe it.

The Bastille, that looming impenetrable reminder of the King's ultimate power, is open to a thousand armed Frenchmen.

The ancient symbol of tyranny is theirs.

Jemmy arrives at my side as the shout is taken up and the people pour forward, away from the boom of the cannon fire.

'Long live France!'

'The Bastille has fallen!'

CHAPTER 93

GRACE KNOWS SHE CAN'T POSSIBLY BE BROUGHT ANY further underground. She is led to a dark corridor.

They approach a room filled with equipment that Grace understands only too well. She has been campaigning to stop its use in prisons. But nothing prepares her for seeing it. Thumbscrews and pincers are jumbled on a blood-streaked table, with manacles, pliers and a pointed little hammer.

There's a rack and a chair with leather restraints. Grace sees a single tooth lying on the stone floor. The sheer indifference of it, the casual scruffiness of the room, makes her feel sick to her stomach.

She pauses, but to her surprise the gaoler leads her past the open door.

Relief and trepidation play at her in equal measure. The dungeon comes to a dead end. Nothing but wall. For a moment, Grace thinks the gaoler has lost his way. He kneels and Grace frowns in confusion. The gaoler is busying himself with something at floor level. She tries to see, but it's dark.

In the flickering torchlight, Grace sees a circular metal grille in the floor.

Perhaps a drain of some kind, she decides, it is damp down here, after all.

The gaoler lifts the iron grating from the ground. Under it is a hole, the width of a man. Grace can't see how deep it is but it looks to go a long way.

The gaoler stands and pushes her forward. The gap yawns beneath her. She instinctively draws back, worried she will slip and fall into the shaft. A stagnant sewage-like smell wafts up. It's an old well, she tells herself, stomach fluttering, wondering why the gaoler is showing it to her.

'In there,' he instructs. 'Get inside.'

Grace's world implodes. The black depths seem to reach up to grab her.

'You can't mean ...' She is stammering.

'It's an oubliette,' says the gaoler. 'Get in.'

He has moved his candle over it now. She can see it is shaped like an upside-down sugarloaf. A narrow cone, drawing to a point at the bottom. Something deep inside moves. Grace takes a step back.

'Better you get in than I push you,' says the gaoler, as if it's all the same to him. 'Nasty place to be with a broken leg. You cannot stand easily,' he adds, watching her face to see the effect his words have.

Grace sits, feeling humiliation and fear wash over her. She dangles her legs into the abyss then levers herself down. It's still quite a drop and she can't see where to land. She falls awkwardly, twisting her foot in the wedge-shaped bottom.

There's no room in the pinched depths. Grace slides uncomfortably, pressing her ankles against the hard base. She comes to rest on pointed toes, one leg tight at the cold wall. She tilts her head up. The gaoler's face is a long way away.

Panic pushes away any semblance of dignity.

'The prison will be attacked,' says Grace, her voice high-pitched and frantic. 'You mustn't leave me here too long. I will be forgotten.'

The gaoler laughs.

'I thought you spoke French,' he says, replacing the iron grating. Grace is plunged into blackness. The slits in her metal roofing project strange shadows. The gaoler's candle burns far away then vanishes. She feels something slimy move over her feet and jerks in panic.

Grace hears a door clang and then nothing. Such a profound nothing, it slides icy fingers through her soul.

She remembers the meaning of the French word.

Oubliette: a place for forgetting.

CHAPTER 94

JEMMY AND I ENTER THE BASTILLE CAUTIOUSLY, AS PEOPLE rush past us on either side, waving muskets and calling for gunpowder.

We both stop simultaneously, taking in the vast interior.

'I suppose we might have expected it would be large,' says Jemmy.

My eyes are roving the tall walls dotted with small barred windows. The corridor stretching out before us is broad and seemingly endless. The flickering candles along the dark passages wink off into the black.

'A castle,' I say; 'it was built as a castle.' But I've never seen anything like this.

People are streaming past us, but the earlier mood of jubilance has vanished completely. They're not protestors any longer. The crowd have been trapped and tricked. They've seen their brothers murdered. There's a fury to them.

'Where are the prisoners?' asks a familiar voice.

We turn to see Danton, slick with sweat and flushed with victory. He holds a musket as a club, hefting it by the barrel.

'Perhaps it's true,' I say, looking along the deserted corridors, 'the Bastille is only for aristocrats and contains but a handful.'

'Or the governor is battening down the hatches,' says Jemmy, 'preventing his inmates escaping. In the case of attack, you take your valuables below deck.' He smiles grimly. 'If I were captain here, it's what I'd do.' His eyes meet mine. 'There's a dungeon.'

'An infamous dungeon!' declares Danton. 'Men rot for thirty years, iron masks on their faces, in the dreaded depths. If I could rally the people, perhaps we could find the gunpowder and blast our way down. Free those poor souls in the name of justice and liberty.' He sighs, watching people pelt past in all directions. 'There is no leading them now,' he says. 'The courtyard broke our cohesion. This rabble will do little more than make a mess.'

We're silent for a moment, thinking of the two hundred barrels of munitions hidden somewhere in the prison. None of us will say it out loud, but there is no way to remove it without an army. And these beaten-down peasants are anything but.

'Will the King's guards come to defend the Bastille?' I say, mapping escape routes.

Danton starts to shake his head and then something occurs to him.

'You have given me an idea,' he says. 'It could be there is a way to help the people after all.' He takes my hand and kisses it. 'I wish you the best of luck in finding your cousin,' he says. 'I have a mad kind of thought and if it works, God willing, I shall see you again.'

'If it doesn't?'

'Better not to dwell on such things. *Adieu.*' And he is gone, lumbering off like a great bear.

Jemmy and I exchange glances.

We begin walking down the broad deserted corridor. The ceilings form archways above us, the height of five men, and pillars dot our path.

I'm trying to create a mental image of the interior, based on the plans. The eight-towered structure. But it is suddenly overwhelming. I swallow, making the numbers.

'By my best calculations,' I say, 'there's a half-mile of corridor ringing this ground floor alone.'

'Seven storeys high,' says Jemmy. 'Eight towers. Though I think we can rule out the one where you had your friendly meeting with Monsieur Janssen.'

My hand tightens on my knife.

'Let's hope I have the pleasure of meeting him without a set of bars between us.'

We move deeper inside, passing grand medieval stonc fireplaces, long since abandoned for purpose.

'This is where some of the guards sleep,' I say, pointing. 'But there are none here now. Have they deserted?'

At one section of the corridor a big table has been laid out so the gaolers might take their meals and there's a leather wine flagon and some crusts of bread, all abandoned. An outsized pallet bed of plank strips has been festooned with simple rugs as bedding.

'All hands on deck,' says Jemmy. 'De Launay must have enlisted every last man to kill civilians.' But he sounds uneasy all the same and I notice his fingers are worrying at the little sack of gunpowder for his pistol.

The complete absence of guards and prisoners is unnerving us both now.

We walk on, coming to the first evidence that the building is used as a prison. Metal grilles have divided two sections of corridor, creating large cells. The iron doors are unlocked and hang ajar.

'Holding cells?' suggests Jemmy, eyeing the shreds of blanket scattered on the stone floors.

'Whatever they are, they've been cleared out,' I say. 'Not before last week either,' I add, pointing to some chalk graffiti, replicating a recent satirical poem.

My eyes track around, taking everything in. A feeling of intense claustrophobia is creeping over me, despite the scale of the prison. Something about the size of it all is getting to me. You could wander for days and not see a single soul. It's an entire dark town of loneliness and horrors.

I feel a lurch of despair. I've not the faintest idea how we might get to the dungeon.

A clot of people push past us, racing off into the maze-like depths. A woman in a striped skirt punches the air.

'Down with the aristos!' she bellows. 'By God's blood, we'll have de Launay's head!'

I turn to Jemmy.

'Grace will be dressed as an aristocrat. We need to find her before they do.'

Fear galvanizes my thought process.

'Up on the ramparts,' I say, thinking aloud. 'There was a gibbet, was there not?'

Jemmy nods.

'Gibbets connect directly to dungeons,' I say, 'so a gaoler might execute a felon and hoist them up to be displayed.' I marshal my thoughts. 'We don't need to locate the entrance to the dungeon,' I say. 'We only need to get up to the ramparts.'

CHAPTER 95

Jemmy and I stand at the door that leads inside Liberty Tower. The curving stone walls made it easy to identify one of the Bastille's bulbous turrets. The door is locked, but unlike the thick old door at the front it's a relatively modern construction.

A challenge, I decide, rather than an impossibility.

'The ramparts can be accessed by any of the eight towers,' I say, calling to mind the plans.

My hand touches the iron lock. I regard it admiringly.

'This is well before the time of three-tumbler locks,' I say, kneeling to put my eye against it. 'It's something of a puzzle,' I add, removing my picks and laying them out carefully on the floor, 'but not an unbreakable one, I think.'

'You don't have to sound so happy about it,' says Jemmy. He goes back to the window.

I fall to the business of opening the lock, humming to myself as I insert successive picks. It really is an impressive construction, made, I decide, by a genius or a madman. Or possibly both.

'Attica,' Jemmy's voice has a warning edge, 'how quickly can you get that door open?'

I glance over my shoulder. A group of uniformed guards have appeared at the other end of the long corridor.

'Perhaps they're friendly,' I say, only half paying attention. 'Distract them.'

The large lock is failing to reveal its secrets. I press my eye against it, trying to see what I'm missing. Behind me the shouts of the approaching guards grow louder.

'I need a few moments,' I say to Jemmy, turning back to the door and making an effort to tune out the danger.

'Wonderful,' Jemmy mutters. I hear the sound of a gun being loaded, gunpowder tapped and tamped. I glance back. One guard fires upwards.

'Surrender your weapons!' he shouts, as the air clouds with smoke.

Jemmy stands firm, pistol in one hand, sword in the other.

'Let's talk about this,' he says. 'None of you boys wants to die today.'

I work faster, lifting different picks, pushing them in, trying alternate weights and combinations.

I turn again to see two guards come at Jemmy from behind through the smoke. I'm about to issue a warning when he takes a backwards aim and fires. The first guard hasn't even hit the ground before Jemmy spins and jabs the second with his sword.

My lock-picking efforts are suddenly rewarded with the twang of a mortar rolling back.

'I've got it!' I shout.

Jemmy, whirling about with his sword, drops the attack and runs for the opening door.

Once he's through I slam it fast behind us, attracting the satisfying sound of gunshot spattering harmlessly on the other side. I slick the lock back into place, just as a body weight is hurled against it.

'This way,' I say, pointing to a curling stone staircase winding up.

We run up the stairs two at a time. After three flights, they change to something more like a wood ladder. It's stiflingly hot up here and we climb more slowly now, measuring our breath.

'You didn't learn to sword fight at sea,' I accuse, as we reach the top. 'Those were fencing moves.'

'A man I met in Granada,' says Jemmy.

'You're quite the man of secrets.' I can't keep the admonishment from my tone.

'You're one to talk.'

Jemmy lifts a trapdoor above our heads and we squeeze through and out.

The fresh air is glorious, a breeze rippling past. I catch my breath as I see Paris through the sturdy crenulations. Tiled and thatched city rooftops stretch away.

And rammed in the narrow streets between: thousands upon thousands of citizens, seizing their chance for liberty.

CHAPTER 96

DANTON STRIDES FROM THE BASTILLE, SHOULDERING aside French people who are pouring across the bridge.

He is met by a carpenter on the other side, clumsily bearing a musket.

'What's happening in the prison?' the carpenter asks Danton. 'Is it true de Launay slaughtered all the prisoners?'

Danton considers what he has seen: the strangely empty corridors.

'Yes,' he lies easily. 'He is a monster and we must take arms. But I'm afraid it is a shambles in there, my friend, and no order to the people at all.'

The carpenter absorbs this, chewing his lip.

'Better wait here.' Danton claps him on the back. The man sinks several inches into the mud under the force of it. 'The King's guard is only around the corner. I'm going to ask them for help.'

The carpenter looks at him as though he has lost his mind. 'They are royalist troops,' he says hesitantly.

'They may be,' agrees Danton, 'but they are also Frenchmen.'

Danton walks off, leaving the carpenter open-mouthed in his wake.

A few streets down Danton find eighty or so *Gardes Françaises* leaning against a wall with nothing much to do. As he approaches, they eye him suspiciously. A few drop their muskets from their shoulders.

'Brave *Gardes Françaises*!' booms Danton. 'Can you not hear the cannon fire?'

The guards look at him, their faces hard. A few more ready their guns, take steadier stance.

Danton lifts a hand to his face, overwhelmed suddenly with the exhaustion of the last few days. His great voice breaks.

'Governor de Launay is murdering our parents, wives and children,' he says, his voice strained with tragedy, 'who have gathered *unarmed*. Will you allow them to be massacred? Won't you march on the Bastille?' Tears are streaming down his face.

The guards look surprised. They huddle together. Minutes pass.

Danton waits. A few people have come out of their homes. Whispers are exchanged. They wonder what will happen. Most likely Danton will be arrested and they look forward to the show. Several men are already muttering that they will fight tooth and nail for the lawyer's freedom.

Finally the captain of the *Gardes Françaises* straightens his royal uniform and approaches Danton.

'We will march,' he says, 'if you will lead us.'

Danton agrees. He guides the militia through the streets, haranguing the locals in his great voice. More people join. Citizens hiding in their houses emerge and join them. Gunpowder and shot is handed around and shared.

When Danton arrives at the Bastille, the small guard has become an army.

The uncertain people milling about outside look on in awe.

'There are two hundred barrels of gunpowder in the dungeon!' announces Danton. 'Shall we take them in the name of France?'

The roar of ascent seems to reach every corner of the city.

Danton looks up at the Bastille, this mighty town within a town, its ten-foot-thick walls and insurmountable bastions. He paces a little at the side of the dry moat, wide as five houses, peering over like a bear nosing at a salmon river.

Danton eyes the turrets again, tilting his head full back to do so. He claps his great beefy hands together.

'*Allez*, lads,' Danton surmises, 'this thing is coming down today.'

CHAPTER 97

JEMMY AND I STAND ON THE RAMPARTS OF THE MIGHTY prison with Paris stretched before us. Immediately beneath us is the great dry moat – a yawning abyss of a thing where the swampy earth has cracked in zig-zags.

'I was right,' says Jemmy after a moment. 'It is a good view.'

I'm reluctant to tear myself away. Seeing Paris as this incredible sweeping vista is fascinating, not least because we can readily see how the crowd swarms and thickens, from the Hôpital des Invalides along to the Hôtel de Ville and then to the Bastille.

More and more people are coming. It reminds me of a swarming ants' nest. So many people are emptying on to the streets, seemingly from nowhere.

I focus my attention on the ghoulish task at hand. Finding the gibbet.

There's a great wide walkway, broad enough for five men to charge through, with broken stones underfoot where repairs have not been made.

'I don't see any guard,' I whisper, as I walk along.

Jemmy's face is lined in concentration, wary.

Up on the ramparts, preparations have been made to repel with force. But there's an unfinished air to it all: cannons lie in disarray; craggy piles of rock are roughly piled, in readiness to throw off the bastions; cannon balls are stacked in neat pyramids.

We creep along, expecting at any moment to be ambushed.

Jemmy stops short at a swinging cage which houses a decomposed body. Below it is a narrow tunnel descending to darkness.

Inside, the rotting skeleton swings in its gibbet, looking over Paris with empty sockets. A crawling feeling of unease is assailing me. There's something horribly familiar about this tiny enclosure. Virginian-plantation terrors are drifting back.

'You were right, this poor fellow will have been raised from the dungeons,' says Jemmy, looking at me. 'This is a disused chimney shaft by the looks of things, adapted to purpose.'

I walk closer to the gruesome display, an arm over my nose to ward off the smell. I feel my legs tremble slightly as I peer over the narrow edge. The tight dark space is the stuff of nightmares. I concentrate on noticing how the chain connects to a pulley-type mechanism.

'We only need pull that,' says Jemmy, 'to send you down.' His voice sounds far away. He's pointing to a long lever, furred with rust and joined to two equally orange-hued cogs. 'The gibbet will drop you down to the depths.'

I open my eyes wide.

'You're not suggesting I get *inside* it?' I swing my attention to the gibbet, appalled. I'd been planning to climb.

'It's the fastest way down,' says Jemmy.

'The jolt at the bottom would break my neck.'

Jemmy looks at the mechanism.

‘I think I can adjust it,’ he says, ‘use a belt attached to the chains to ratchet you down and stop you dropping too fast. I’ve used a similar thing for anchors in shallow harbours,’ he adds.

‘Have you ever broken an anchor?’

‘Never.’

I give him a hard stare.

‘Once,’ he admits. ‘Lot of seaweed swept in at Haiti. We couldn’t see the rocks.’

Damp terror pricks at me. I watch silently as Jemmy lifts the catch on the gibbet and stands neatly aside. The cage opens, dividing in half and the corpse plummets down. It’s a long time before we hear the thump of the dry remains hit some distant floor.

‘I didn’t know they opened that way,’ I say, hearing the words as though someone else is saying them. Fear is seizing at every part of me now.

‘Pirates are fairly familiar with gibbets,’ says Jemmy with a wry smile.

‘All aboard,’ he says, nodding to the two halves of the empty gibbet, ‘passage straight to the depths of hell.’

I have a detached sense that he’s making light of things to ease my obvious dread and am grateful. But my mouth is too dry to thank him. Unwanted thoughts are spooling like tentacles as I force my legs to take me to the metal cage and step on to the precarious grid at the base.

‘Don’t close it!’ I shriek as Jemmy reaches up to shut the gibbet.

‘I have to,’ he explains calmly. ‘It won’t fit down the shaft unless I do. And you’ll be safer this way.’

My heart is beating low in my stomach.

You're not a slave any longer, I tell myself. *You can free yourself from this cage any time you choose.*

But it doesn't stop the pounding nausea as Jemmy closes the gibbet over my face. He reaches in, takes my hand and squeezes it.

The fear abates slightly.

'This thing is as old as the prison,' I point out, eyeing the dry remains. 'Are you certain the chain won't break?'

'Chains like this can withstand a fair amount of rust,' says Jemmy, looking up at the rusty iron links that suspend the cage. He removes his belt, loops it around the lever.

'I'll follow you down,' he says. 'I can shin down the chain once the gibbet is dropped.'

'No,' I say. 'You have to find a way to take us out of France. You think you can find a ship?'

'My crew will have the *Esmerelda* at the docks,' says Jemmy. 'They're the fiercest pirates in the world and that boat is their home. Your English fellows might have reported it for capture, but they won't have succeeded.'

He has an expression that I can't determine is pride or wishful thinking.

'Very well,' I say. 'Then you must get to your ship and take us home.'

'If you make it out alive, I'll be at the cinque port. When word of the Bastille gets to the King, he will arm every river and dock. Get there before sundown.'

Jemmy pulls the belt, face contorted in effort as the old crank yields. There's a shriek of metal and the cogs start turning. And suddenly the cage plummets a few inches in a cloud of iron-coloured dust, then catches sharply, throwing me up in the air and painfully to my knees.

'Sorry!' says Jemmy. 'It didn't work quite as I expected. I've got it now.'

'I'm getting out,' I say, rising to my feet. 'I'll climb. Really it's better—'

I'm interrupted by a ghostly noise, a strange sort of cheering rippling up the chimney shaft. It takes me a few moments to understand.

'The rebels are in the dungeon,' I say, fear for Grace overtaking everything else.

Jemmy moves closer to the gibbet, the belt still looped in his hand.

'I'm sure I can rig something up, so you can climb down fast,' he says. 'But first I want to try something.'

There's a hint of dishonesty in his voice that I haven't heard before and I'm confused by what he's trying to hide.

Jemmy leans smoothly forward and kisses me through the bars of the gibbet. It's so unexpected I barely have time to react. Then he's saying something, mouth still against mine.

'I thought you might need the distraction,' whispers Jemmy.

It's only when I drop, cold air replacing the sensation of his warm lips, that I realize he's released the gibbet.

I'm free-falling down the shaft, my eyes screwed tight shut.

'You bloody *bastard*!' I hear myself shout it into the abyss, as deeper feelings of terror coil into my soul.

A few words float from above.

'*Takes one to know one, Lady Morgan!*'

CHAPTER 98

GRACE CAN'T BREATHE. SHE IS DRAGGING IN GREAT panicked gulps of air. Her heart is beating out of her chest. The sharp chain of diamonds is pressed against her ribs.

It is then, in the dark at her feet, she hears a horrible sound. Like a goblin clearing its throat. Something cold and slimy slips around her toes. She pulls up a foot and the noise comes again, more urgent.

It's only a toad, Grace realizes, giddy with relief. The realization of her own idiocy calms her slightly. She feels suddenly fond of the toad. Grace is ludicrously pleased to have a friend in the dark.

'I won't hurt you,' she whispers to it.

Grace tries to draw air in slowly, pulling in a thin stream. The panic ebbs but doesn't abate.

A door crashes open. Grace's heart leaps. She calls up. There are footsteps. Many footsteps and loud cries. There are people above, looking for prisoners.

Grace shouts and bellows. No one hears her. They're too far away. She's too deep underground. She screams until her throat is ragged. Something about this sugarloaf-shaped pit repels sound.

There's a splintering noise, as though someone is hammering at a wall, then an ominous trickling of water. Down in the dungeon they are the same level as a few old tributaries. It occurs to Grace something might have been damaged to cause a leak.

Feet run over her grating, but don't stop. And then, to her sinking heart, the people leave. All is quiet. Everyone has gone.

Grace returns to her breathing. It's the only thing she can do. And then she feels the first stream of cold water trickle in from above. It covers her ankles. Before she knows it for sure, the water is already at her hips.

CHAPTER 99

AIR IS RUSHING PAST MY FACE AS I DESCEND THE NARROW shaft, towards the dungeon. I realize I'm gripping the bars of the gibbet tight, my face screwed up in readiness for the impact.

The muggy summer heat of the prison flashes into damp cold. My free-falling cage slows, caught by some mechanism high in the ramparts. Relief blooms. Jemmy has done as he promised. There's a ticking kind of sound as I begin to drop more rhythmically. It's almost slowed to a stop when I feel the metal floor smash against something hard, sending a rictus of pain through my feet.

I stagger, still clutching the bars. I've landed on the gibbet corpse, I realize. The impact has smashed it to pieces, but likely prevented my ankles from breaking.

I peel my hands away from the bars. There are rectangular indentations in my palms and I rub them, wincing.

I'm in a large chimney breast and beyond is what can only be the Bastille dungeon. It feels completely different to the great deserted prison above. There is a cold dampness that immediately bites at your bones, a stench of mould and mildew strong enough to choke on.

I have an instant awful sense of entrapment. These unyielding walls seem to be shuffling in on me, whispering of a thousand poor souls who have died in the dark.

I reach outside the gibbet and loosen the catch, letting it open rather precariously atop its human buffer.

Taking out my knife, I assess my surroundings. There's a shout in the distance, a cry with a violence to it that is deeply disturbing.

Ahead I can see a meandering maze of dark tunnels. Bone fragments of the corpse I obliterated with the gibbet crunch under my boots.

The ceilings are so low I must stoop under the arching stonework. This is a dungeon in the truest sense, built so the old King of France might torture and terrify.

Doors have been opened in a pattern. A route. Someone was here before me, someone with a key.

I break into a horrid little chamber, the thick walls curved and rats running across the floor. My stomach turns. There's a smell I know only too well. The last time I encountered it was in the bowels of a slave ship.

Chained to the slimy brick are seven men. They are secured to the wall by their necks and ankles. Torture is all too evident on their starving bodies. Their wrists are worn to welts and pustulating wounds where their manacles rub.

Childish helplessness overwhelms me. I run to the first man, pulling at his chains. An animal instinct has overtaken me. I wrench and kick, I take out my knife and plunge it uselessly at the hard stone.

There must be rooms and rooms of such men. Where can I even begin?

Despair is sudden and paralysing.

A sudden explosion at the far end of the corridor smashes into my thoughts. A great ragged opening now stands where a wall once was. I stare in surprise. Through the smoke and tell-tale smell of gunpowder pour a legion of royal guards.

'Attica!' I hear a booming voice. 'Shouldn't you be looking for your little cousin?'

I turn, tears blurring my vision, to see Danton, complete with a small army of well-armed soldiers.

'We'll take it from here,' he says, 'you must be certain we shall have these men free. Jacques here found the gunpowder, barrels and barrels of it. So we are well resourced for a little *revolution*.' He grins, revealing small pearly teeth in his cratered face.

Danton advances on me and crushes me to his huge chest, kissing me on either cheek.

'The prisoners from upstairs are all in the east wing,' says Danton. 'That way.' He points back through the smoke. 'You can thank de Launay for the information,' he adds. 'He gave everything up when we cornered him. Not sure it will save him, though,' he concludes philosophically, rubbing his wide jaw. 'He's really pissed people off.'

CHAPTER 100

I MOVE DEEPER INTO THE BASTILLE DUNGEON. THE SLIMY walls and stink of unwashed prisoners are giving way to something else now. There's an unmistakable tang of blood in the air. I pass a strappado – a brutal crane-like hoist used to dislocate shoulders. A bench houses an array of bloody tools: boots for breaking the bones of feet, thumbscrews, pincers; there's something especially horrible about how they've been thrown together, as though some bored gaoler might rummage casually for their next careless infliction of agony.

I look around. All the doors so far are open. If people were contained here, they've already fled.

Despite the deserted feel, there's no mistaking this was once a very professional facility. All the latest devices, I think grimly to myself. No expense spared.

Another room houses a little bench and tools. It takes me a moment to realize this is an invention room, a place where some blood-soaked torturer experiments with ways to inflict pain. Several metal devices that I recognize from Russia and Germany have been taken to pieces. An iron chair with a brazier beneath the seat is half under construction.

I realize I've come to a dead end. Thinking I must be mistaken, I scan all the doors again. Open, every one.

I check a rising feeling of claustrophobia, a desperate sense that if a door were to clang shut in here, no one would ever find you again.

The silence is deafening. I notice another sound. Flowing water. I'm guessing this part may have been crudely connected to an underground tributary or similar, so gaolers might more easily wash away bodily fluids.

The thought sends a bolt of nausea through me. Under my feet, I see water streaming at a steady pace. My eyes fall to the ground. There's a grille set into it: a hole allowing the water to drain away.

I almost walk right over it. A horrible memory surfaces.

A small space beneath the earth. Fear and crushing heat.

I stop and look down.

Pushed up against the grille are blueish fingers.

I drop to my knees, staring down. There's someone inside.

A girl, still alive, her palms pressing helplessly against her confines.

My heart seizes.

It's Grace.

'Grace?' I can hardly believe it. There she is. The face of my lovely cousin pressed up against the grating.

'Grace!' I grab at the grille with both hands and pull with all my might. It won't budge.

Her face swims into view.

'Attica!' She manages a smile, but her words are weak and slurred. It's then I see she's up to her neck in freezing water. She must be on the verge of losing consciousness from the cold.

'Hold on,' I say, 'I'll get you out.'

I take out my knife, trying to dig it in the edge and lever up the thick metal. But it's no good.

'Attica! Look out!' Grace's eyes are wide in fear. It's only when I feel the weapon kicked from my hand that I realize I heard her warning too late. The next boot is to my stomach and throws me up and across the slippery flagstones.

I see my blade go spinning into a dank corner of the dungeon. My face is pressed on to a wet stone. I put a hand out to stand, when a third kick sends me back to the floor.

I breathe out, sickening pain filling my solar plexus. Through my swimming vision I see a pair of musketeer boots.

Oliver Janssen.

I curl up to sitting, back against the mouldy wall, hunched over slightly.

'How convenient,' growls Janssen. 'You've led me straight to the diamonds and now I can eliminate you and your troublesome cousin all at once. Perhaps Robespierre is correct, women do have their uses.'

The corner of his mouth tweaks in what could be a smile.

Janssen looms over Grace, assuring himself she is contained. 'A clean death, drowning,' he says. 'The Society of Friends will like that.'

He draws his sword and heads towards me, metal hand curled high like a weapon.

'Yours will not be quite so simple.'

Thoughts are flashing through my brain. From the oubliette I hear a gasping sound, as though Grace is trying to keep water from flooding her mouth.

'My knife,' I manage, breathing hard. 'Give it to me.'

Janssen cocks his head, red eye dilated half black in the gloom. 'What?'

'You say you are still a musketeer,' I say. 'Prove it.'

Janssen laughs, a horrible, grating sound.

'You think to fight me?'

'I am entitled to demand it from a true musketeer. Nowhere is it written that a woman hasn't the same right.'

Janssen considers. 'Very well,' he says, striding to where my knife has fallen. He tosses it into my hand. I stand, catching my breath, steadying myself against the wall.

Water has begun to bubble up from the grating where Grace is contained now. She must be entirely submerged.

'I'm sorry, Monsieur Janssen,' I say, 'perhaps you think yourself entitled to a heroic end. A grapple, a fight. I'm sure you would be an interesting opponent. But I simply don't have the time for you.'

I turn the curved knife easily in my palm.

Janssen's eyes follow it. He draws his sword.

'I can tell you have never fenced,' he says disdainfully. He extends his blade, relaxed, expert.

'Fencing is a sport and I'm a professional,' I say, circling away. 'I don't tinkle with blades, I kill people.'

There are several feet between us now. I'm flat against the wall, with no space to adopt a good sword-fighting stance.

Janssen laughs. 'Do you really think you can win a sword fight with a musketeer?' he says, shaking his head. 'I am larger, stronger, better trained and you have left yourself no room to–'

He stops talking suddenly. The black Mangbetu blade is buried deep in his blood-red iris. His good eye swivels to it, then flutters in spasm. I drop my hand from where I had raised it to throw the knife.

'Men are superior in every way,' I agree, as he falls to his knees, staring sightlessly at the dank dungeon, 'but for an unfathomable preoccupation with honour.'

CHAPTER 101

As Janssen flops lifelessly to the flagstone floor, I run to the grating where Grace is trapped.

Her cheeks are swelled, eyes screwed shut.

She's still alive, I tell myself. *She's still alive.*

I race to the strappado – an awful hoist for breaking limbs – and winch down one of its rope with a grunt of effort. I fasten it to the grille and turn the strappado's great winching wheel.

Slowly the grate lifts. I heave Grace's unmoving body from the watery hole.

'Grace?'

I grab her and drag her free. She's sopping wet, cold and stiff. Her dress is plastered to her body. For a moment I don't dare breathe.

Her eyes open.

'Attica,' she manages groggily through blue lips. 'Why are you dressed as a boy?'

I press her to me and hug her tight. She's coming back to herself now. I remember the feeling all too well. You get so used to being enclosed after a time, being back in the world feels like your skin is raw.

'How did you know I was down there?' she whispers.

'I've been put in something similar,' I say, 'as a girl.'

She coughs. 'Most people wouldn't think a prison could be under your feet,' she says.

'No,' I agree. 'They wouldn't.' I begin rubbing her arms and calves. My mother used to tell me I came out of the hotbox with the poise of a queen. It unsettled the plantation owners so greatly they abandoned the practice for a time. I'd forgotten that.

'Can you stand?' I ask Grace.

'I think so.' She tries, leaning on my arm, but staggers. Her eyes fill with tears and she throws herself into my arms.

'We can wait,' I say, hugging her. But she shakes her head rapidly.

'I wasn't down there very long,' she says, moving back and frowning at her weakness. 'I can do it. Besides,' she adds, 'I can't stay here another minute.'

I smile. This is the Grace I remember.

'Come on,' I say. 'Let's take you home.'

She stands steadily now. I look about and see some old sacking. I lift it up.

'Here,' I say. 'You can use this to disguise your fine clothes.'

She nods. Grace reaches into her dress and retrieves a great weight of glittering diamonds, strung piece by piece on to silverwork wide enough to be a belt.

'We are dead if anyone finds us with these—' She's halted by a boom from above.

'What's happening?' she asks.

'The Bastille has fallen,' I say. 'The people are storming the prison.'

'But that's impossible,' says Grace. 'This is an impenetrable fortress.'

'Times have changed,' I say. 'Let's go.'

CHAPTER 102

GRACE AND I REACH THE CORRIDOR ABOVE THE COURTYARD. We look through the window to see it is still teaming with people, more than I've ever seen in one place.

They've come from the streets, from the slums, the churches and the markets. They're lit up, charged with the chance to right the wrongs of their country. There are men and woman both, faces determined.

'It's like when a kettle boils over,' says Grace. 'There's no stopping them now.'

She sounds awestruck and a little envious. Grace has been relegated to the administration of social campaigning when she'd like to be on the frontlines.

People are rolling out barrel after barrel of munitions. Lines form and rebels queue to be given a portion of gunpowder and a handful of shot.

'Can we get through?' she asks me.

'There's too many,' I admit. The crush is dangerous. My eyes work around the courtyard. 'Perhaps if we stay to the edges,' I say. But I know it's not a good plan. We could lose one another or be trampled.

'Might I have your pistol, Attica?' asks Grace politely.

'It's no good, Grace,' I say. 'My gunpowder is long gone and even if it wasn't I wouldn't fire into a crowd of innocent people.'

'Nor would I,' says Grace, taking the gun from my purse and lifting out the necklace. Jewels flash and twinkle, so glitteringly ludicrously ostentatious it's difficult to imagine they're real.

In a deft movement, Grace drops them, turns the pistol and hammers the butt hard on to the gems. The silver casing breaks, sending diamonds spilling forth. She does it again, freeing more, then stands and stamps the heel of her foot into the broken metalwork.

'There,' she says, bending and scooping a handful of precious stones. 'Enough to cause a distraction, do you think?'

'I suppose we should find out,' I say, admiringly.

She smiles broadly and launches three diamonds into the crowd, making a wide arc. One hits a man in the face and he looks up, suspecting attack from above. Grace holds up another diamond and throws it straight at him. His hand rises and snatches it from the air on reflex. He stares at the jewel in wonderment.

A woman next to him sees the prize.

'Treasure!' she shouts. 'Bastille treasure!'

Grace tosses more, distributing them widely to cause the most chaos. There are so many, over a hundred tiny diamonds and a few larger ones. Grace hurls the remains of the silver metal.

By the time she's finished, the surging mob is on its knees, frantically searching for gems.

'Ready?' she asks me.

I nod.

We run through the courtyard and enter a small gatehouse. I'm sighing in relief to see the crowd are entering from the main drawbridge. We should be able to walk the circumference and get out on the north side, where the moat is shallower.

It's then I make the mistake that will haunt me for years to come.

I look back at the Bastille, taking in the great structure now fallen to the people. At the top, on the highest ramparts, I see a familiar man.

Robespierre.

He's a distance away, but something about the stiff way he stands is instantly recognizable. Robespierre is looking out on to the destruction, the glittering diamonds being passed around and dispersed.

I'm too far away to see for certain, but I think his fists are balled up so tightly the knuckles are white.

I scan the area for a spare musket. From this distance, I have a fair chance, I think. Even if I'm not near enough to kill him instantly, I might cause him to tumble from the ramparts.

As I'm deciding how to get a weapon, Robespierre sees me. He lifts a single hand in greeting.

For some reason, Jemmy's words come back to me: *You know countries are just fences put up by greedy men.* It's true, I think. Once we had forts like the Bastille, castles, knights. Now we have men of letters ordering horrors from their drawing rooms. Robespierre and Lord Pole. Perhaps even Atherton.

And me? I'm nothing but a finger on a trigger. A tool for calculating men.

A few days earlier I would have killed Robespierre without much thought. Today I'm of another mind.

There's more good to be done here, change is afoot. Maybe

Robespierre will be integral to it, maybe he won't. But it isn't my place to decide. Besides, I have the strangest feeling that killing Robespierre would be killing part of myself.

I turn to Grace, who's looking at me curiously.

'Come on,' I say, 'this way to the docks.'

If I had known then what Robespierre would become, would I have fired that musket?

Probably.

CHAPTER 103

GRACE AND I GET TO THE HÔTEL DE VILLE TO FIND EVEN more people have filled the streets.

'Who knew there were this many Frenchmen and women?' breathes Grace.

The whole area is clogged with confiscated carts and wagons and the city has come to a standstill.

'What can they be gathering here for?' I say, confused. 'The Bastille is the place to be.'

'I think I hear a reason,' says Grace, listening. 'That's Governor de Launay's voice.'

A reedy kind of plea is issuing from the very centre of the crowd.

'On my honour,' the governor is protesting, 'I never shot at the people. Gentlemen, you must believe me, I never shot at them.'

'How dare you say so,' returns a gravelly voice, 'when your lips are black with gunpowder from biting your cartridges? Come. You will face the justice of the people.'

'This way, Grace,' I say, pulling her firmly in the opposite direction. I couldn't spare her the underground ordeal, but

I can spare her this. I've a bad feeling the Bastille governor's end will be brutal.

'It's no good,' says Grace, 'we'll never get to the river. Better we wait until the trouble dies down.'

'I think we'll be waiting a long time,' I say, eyeing the surging crowd. 'And our ship to England leaves at sunset.'

Grace looks up at the sun low on the horizon and her face falls.

A few dead people lie on the ground. One corpse still clutches a burning torch and I wrench it from the tight fingers.

'I've an idea to clear a path,' I say, taking the reins of the nearest horse, still tethered to a hay wagon. 'Be ready to run,' I add, leading the animal carefully through the abandoned vehicles.

I hurl the flame into the cart. The contents smoke, then flares. I slap the horse hard on the rear and it goes galloping off, flames rising high behind it.

We watch as the fiery wagon heads towards the crowd, parting them as people jump to avoid the fire.

I pull Grace by the arm and we run on, into the path as it's made.

We reach the river and there, waiting as planned, is a ship. But as we near, my relief sickens and dies. It isn't the *Esmerelda.*

The vessel that has sailed to greet us is a French prison boat.

I take a step back, pulling Grace with me. But it's too late. Soldiers aboard have seen us. They raise pistols and order us to halt.

I look about to see if Jemmy and his crew are stationed upriver, perhaps escaping the ambush. But in my heart I know the truth. Jemmy has been captured and killed.

The troops march down the gangplank, weapons raised.

I grip Grace's hand tightly, trying to imagine a way to escape. But none comes.

All I can think is that Jemmy is dead and most likely so are we.

CHAPTER 104

The armed men make our arrest, seizing hold of us both and marching us aboard the ship. I grab at Grace, speaking in rapid English.

'Don't speak French,' I say. 'If they're obeying the law they'll have to consider an interpreter and that will confuse them. I'm going to create a diversion. When I do, jump overboard and swim to shore. Don't look back. Find Georges Danton. He might help you.'

I'm confident I can hold them off for long enough for Grace to get to safety. My own escape is unlikely.

Grace is frowning, her forehead crinkled.

'Why would I do that?' she asks. 'It's Lord Pole, isn't it? Come to rescue us.'

'Grace, there's a lot you don't know about Lord Pole,' I say, mentally sweeping the deck for guards I haven't accounted for, 'he's a politician who doesn't waste resources on expendables like us. This is a prison ship. A French one.'

The gangplank is drawn up behind us and we hear orders shouted to raise anchor.

'No it isn't,' says Grace patiently. 'This is an English vessel. I grew up by a port,' she added. 'I've always been interested in nautical things. This boat was made in Deptford,' she concludes knowledgeably. 'It has a lower stern because of the excellent deep dry-dock they have there.'

I hesitate, certainty rushing away. 'Are you sure?'

The sails billow and we begin drifting up river. It's only then the door to the captain's quarters opens and Jemmy steps out. He gives us a bow.

'How d'ye find my new vessel, Your Ladyship? Made by your countrymen.'

'So my cousin tells me,' I say drily. 'Didn't you think to warn us we would be accosted by men dressed as French guards?'

'A last-moment change of plan,' says Jemmy unapologetically, 'on account of the rivers now being under tight scrutiny. And I had a little help from that Atherton fella and your uncle. It seems Lord Pole isn't as angry with you as you thought.'

'What?' I'm blinking at the unlikeliness of this.

Jemmy only shrugs. 'All I know is his name was on the papers.'

'Which papers?'

'The ones that got me this ship and saved the lives of my crew.' He points to the armed guards and now I look closer, I make out some familiar faces.

'Lord Pole got French uniforms for your men?' I can scarcely believe it. This is exactly the kind of ill-conceived scheme Lord Pole routinely dismisses as a waste of money.

Jemmy nods. 'You'll excuse me a little trickery getting you aboard. I couldn't risk you being seen escaping by the wrong people.'

He tilts his head to look at me. 'Now that I know you better, I'm inclined not to think the worst of ye. Think you might ever feel the same way about me?'

'No,' I reply, smiling at him. 'Most likely not.'

CHAPTER 105

I'M LEANING AGAINST THE SIDE OF THE SHIP, LOOKING ON to the water of the Seine, when Grace arrives at my side.

She has lost the puppyish energy I remember about her as a younger girl and the nervousness that agitated her in the Bastille has also dropped away. She looks, I think, like a grown-up woman and I wonder if this is a good or bad thing.

'Did you know,' she begins, 'that it was Uncle Pole who put the diamonds in my trunk?'

I hesitate.

'Yes. How did you know?'

She follows my gaze out across the river.

'I didn't know for certain, until now.' She smiles. 'Perhaps something of you is rubbing off on me.'

'I hope not.'

To my surprise she reaches across and takes my hand in her little fingers and taps it comfortingly against the solid oak of the gunwhale.

'You always were too hard on yourself, Attica,' she says. 'You have a lot of good qualities to recommend you.'

I smile. 'Thank you.'

'In any case,' she says, 'I've decided to be more like you once I'm back in England.'

'What?'

'Oh,' Grace looks at me archly, through blue-green eyes, 'not entirely like you. I mean,' she frowns, 'I imagine I don't know the half of it, what you get up to.' She gives me an assessing stare then looks back to the water. 'But I'd like to be at the forefront of making things better for people, rather than just penning essays. Even if my family disapprove. You don't let anyone make your choices,' she concludes, 'even though a woman in your circumstances really should.'

I consider this. I suppose it is true.

'That's why I came out here, you know. Because I was doing what I was told,' Grace is pulling at a bracelet on her wrist. 'I had a bad feeling about it. I didn't want to come. But Lord Pole told me I should and I did. Girls like me,' she heaves up a deep sigh that makes her seem older than her years, 'we're not expected to question what our betters suggest for us.' Grace stops playing with her bracelet. 'But I think now I might.'

'You'll match your husband in that,' I assure her. 'Lord Godwin is creating quite a stir for his views against slavery. I think you seem well suited.'

'I think so too.' She looks out to sea. 'But I think I might delay the wedding for a time.' She casts me a little smile.

'Really?' I say. 'You don't want to marry on your return?'

Grace shakes her head. 'Not yet. I'd like to get to know my future husband better. Godwin expects me to have a great many children and settle down, but I don't think I'm ready.' She frowns. 'Godwin has some ideas about the natural state of the peasant classes. But I grew up close enough to those people to know that nursing eleven babies isn't as lovely as he might think.'

I laugh. 'You're worth waiting for.'

'Thank you,' she says with feeling. 'I had so many people tell me how lucky I was to snare Godwin and I must wed him immediately before he changed his mind. No one ever asked me if I were certain about it all.'

'If you do decide to marry,' I say, 'I'd say Lord Pole owes you a very expensive wedding trousseau. Be sure he pays you in full.'

Grace turns away, her hair shiny, loose and blowing in the wind.

I have a sudden rush of images of the life I might have led had Atherton proposed. But there's no sense in dwelling and I'm happy for my clever cousin.

CHAPTER 106

KING LOUIS XVI HAS UNDERGONE HIS USUAL RITUALS. His clothing had been passed to him in the correct order by the correct people.

He has consumed his breakfast, observed by the masses. Marie Antoinette sat at his side. She had eaten privately, earlier. A habit that had set tongues wagging.

Following his repast, the King strolled to his study, ready to fill out his diary for the day.

A minister enters. The King frowns. He is not used to interruptions.

'Your Majesty,' the minister bows low, 'I bring news from Paris.'

The expectant light in the King's eyes dims. Paris bores him. It has been so long since he has been in the city, he can scarce call it to mind. Besides, it is always bad news.

'What has happened now?' he says, trying to appear interested.

'The Bastille, Your Majesty, it has been stormed.'

The King nods at this.

'Parisians attacked it a few hours ago,' continues the

minister. 'They overcame the Swiss troops set to guard it. Somehow the word got out that there was ammunition in the prison,' he concludes breathlessly. 'They got in, got the gunpowder and are tearing the prison apart. There are forty thousand muskets and shot in the hands of the people, Sire.'

'Paris is a city of boutiques and servants,' says the King. 'It's only a small rabble that wants to cause trouble. Most of the commoners do very well by my reign, they love their King.'

'True,' says the minister, 'but there is ... ill feeling towards the Queen.'

'Go on.'

The minister swallows.

'The Bastille Governor, de Launay ... They cut off his head with a blunt knife, Your Majesty.'

The King sits pondering this for a long time. He holds the quill to write in his diary poised, as though to make some mid-air instruction.

'Is it a rebellion?' he asks, after a moment.

The minister hesitates. He wonders how much of the information he relayed has really gone in.

'No, Your Majesty,' he says patiently, 'it is a revolution.'

The King nods again.

'We intended to tear down the Bastille in any case, didn't we?'

'Yes, but ...' The minister is slightly dumbstruck.

'Perhaps I was hasty to send those Swiss guards.' The King leans back. 'The Queen and I are tired of all this bad feeling,' he adds. 'Let's just give them what they want. I'll travel to Paris and sign whatever needs to be signed.'

'If I may, Your Majesty, such complacence to mob attack would make you look weak. They have put Governor de

Launay's head on a pike. The head of your finance minister, Monsieur Foulon, is being toured around the city as a trophy.'

The King waves a hand. 'That will be all.'

He sighs as the minister leaves the room. His breakfast rolls are sitting rather heavily in his stomach. He must remember to ask his doctor about it.

The King realizes he still holds his quill. He shakes his head, dispensing with a troubling memory, then dips his pen to write.

Louis hesitates, face scrunched in thought. There is no hunting today, no parties he can recall and no meetings of an important nature.

July 14th, scribes the pen carefully. *Nothing.*

CHAPTER 107

GRACE RETURNS BELOW DECK AND I'M LEFT ALONE. As I turn back to the water, considering my next option, I feel someone arrive at my side. It's Jemmy. I find I am pleased to see him. More than pleased, if I'm honest with myself.

'Looks like your Uncle Pole put himself out on a bit of a limb,' he says. 'Got me a ship. Risked a few things on your success.'

I nod at this. Lord Pole still has the ability to surprise me. I can't help but feel he does it on purpose.

'And speaking of success, what of the famous jewels?' asks Jemmy, trying to sound casual. 'Were they with your cousin, as you hoped?'

I laugh.

'And here I was, thinking you'd come to celebrate my safe return.'

'Come now, Lady Morgan, you must know how happy I am to see you.' He says it gruffly, but looks hurt.

'I do,' I assure him. 'The diamonds ...' I hesitate. 'Let's just say there was some wealth distribution. I'm sure you'd approve, as a commoner from Hell's Kitchen.'

Jemmy looks less unhappy than I might have expected.

'Maybe they'll put some food in some young bellies,' he says wistfully. 'You never know. In any case,' he says, 'Lord Pole has more faith in you than you thought.'

'Perhaps,' I say, thinking this highly unlikely. 'More probably there's another political outcome he's considered.'

'Oh?'

'No one expected the Bastille to fall,' I say. 'Things have been set in motion. I imagine he has weighed up his options and decided a spy on the ground would be a useful thing. Particularly one who speaks fluent French and is, in many ways, above suspicion.'

'Strange you should say that,' replies Jemmy. 'I made something of a deal with your uncle. In return for the ship. He's not a man you play around, if you know what I mean. Even if you're a pirate.'

'Very sensible,' I say. 'But I thought you were a privateer.'

He shrugs. 'Times are changing. I fancy my luck in France. And I thought you might like to join me,' he adds.

'You and I working together?' The most surprising thing about the suggestion is it doesn't seem as terrible as I might have imagined.

'I've got a new trade: helping French aristocrats leave the country. It pays better than privateering.' My face must show my surprise because he laughs.

'*You're* shocked. At *me*?'

I try to explain how I feel about his new occupation and fail. 'I thought you were against the aristocracy,' I conclude lamely. 'These people sat at banquets whilst children starved to death.'

'One day in Paris and you're a revolutionary?' he taunts.

'I go where the money is, Lady Pimpernel. I'm afraid I can't afford your scruples.'

'So you want me to help you?'

His mouth twists.

'We-ell,' says Jemmy. 'You on land. I at sea. Rescuing people who want to flee France. We'd go by your name,' he says, his accent becoming more Irish the faster he speaks. 'Pimpernel. I thought we could use little flower tokens, so those we rescue might know us to be genuine.'

'Flower tokens?' I grin. 'A little romantic for a pirate, don't you think?'

I consider for a moment, remembering my time in Russia, in Europe, tracking the wrongfully enslaved and the kidnapped.

'A snake then,' he says. 'A curved knife.'

'It isn't only the symbol,' I say, moving a little nearer to him. 'All my life I've rescued people who deserve to be saved. Slaves. Not rich aristocrats who watch people starve.'

Jemmy thinks. 'Well, then, I suppose we'll only save the worthy.'

'My uncle won't approve,' I say. 'Or at least, he'll have a different idea as to what constitutes worthy.'

'Maybe so,' says Jemmy. 'Then we'll be fooling the English spies as well the French. What fun we'll have.'

He gazes at the Paris cityscape, where the smoke of gunpowder and the walls of the mighty Bastille can be seen. People are up on the ramparts and are pulling the hated structure apart, stone by stone.

'Atherton always told me the fight against slavery is not at the markets or on the ships,' I say, following his gaze. 'I never quite agreed. Perhaps now I understand him better. He'll help us,' I add, 'so long as we don't deviate too widely from patriotism.'

I notice Jemmy doesn't quite meet my eye at the mention of Atherton.

The outline of the great prison is already changed. Paris's dark stone fortress is becoming something else: a cloud of dust, a rapidly growing pile of rubble.

'A whole country of slaves,' I say. 'That would be something, would it not? To gain so many people their liberty?' I glance at Jemmy. 'Might take two people,' I concede, 'rather than just one. Perhaps we could help each other.'

It looks as though every last man, woman and child in the city has come out to complete the work. The despotic royal threat loomed over Paris for four centuries. By tomorrow it will be gone.

I find myself smiling.

'These are new and exciting times,' says Jemmy. 'Lots of gauzy dresses.'

'If we must go by the mark of the flower,' I say slowly, 'it should at least be red.'

'Scarlet?' says Jemmy. 'Like blood? I suppose that fits with a pirate better. Very well then, Lady Morgan. So it shall be. The Scarlet Pimpernels.'

Truth is stranger than fiction.

Which of these events really happened?

At least one of the following facts is false. Do you know which? Go to www.atlantic-books.co.uk/bastille to find out which, and unlock a secret history to *The Bastille Spy*.

1. The Bastille was thought to contain only a handful of prisoners, but in reality dungeons of secret inmates were found on July 14th.

2. A Swiss guard handed the key to the Bastille keep to a French commoner, just as the rebels were about to be massacred.

3. The Marquis de Sade was held in the Bastille, and his claim prisoners were being murdered was a catalyst to the people's attack on the prison.

4. Finance minister Joseph-François Foulon de Doué was accused of claiming peasants could eat grass, and was half-lynched before his severed head was paraded around Paris by the mob.

5. Spy weaponry of the period included carrier pigeons and dead-drops of the kind Robespierre utilises for his intelligence.

ACKNOWLEDGEMENTS

What an amazing book this has been to write, and how lucky I am to have had so much support along the way. First and foremost, the biggest thanks to my readers, who allow me to continue in this work that I love. Next, I should thank my brilliant partner, Simon Avery and my sister Susannah Quinn for their tireless feedback and amazing edits. There were times when I was in a very dark place with this book, so thank you both for helping me see the light, and generally putting up with me. Thanks also to my lovely dad, Don Quinn, for his great suggestions and vast historical knowledge – pencils and matches to name a few. And of course, to my mum, Jean Quinn, for all the stories.

Endless gratitude to my children Natalie and Ben for frequent uplifting visits to my desk to raid chocolate and watch YouTube.

Piers Blofeld deserves a medal for all the hard work he has put in on my behalf, and I'm proud to have him as my agent and friend. Heartfelt thanks go to my lovely publishers at Corvus, for their patience, belief and vision. Sara O'Keeffe for keeping the faith, and wearing great jackets, Susannah Hamilton for tireless spot-on edits and daring red shoes, Poppy Mostyn-Owen for being an early champion and reading until the small hours, Alison Tullett for considered copyediting and patience with my technology glitches, Kirsty Doole for having the mind-melting energy to commute daily from Oxford, Gemma Davis, for kind words and recognition of a neglected era, Patrick Hunter for getting digital book sales before it was rightfully possible, and last but not least, Will Atkinson for pouring a great deal of Champagne and rarely being thanked.

In terms of research, I owe a huge debt to my University of Leeds professors, Vivian Jones and Robert Jones, who were kind enough to have faith in me, and give me a lifelong love of history. I've not yet written a book I've been brave enough to send to such accomplished historians, but perhaps this will be it. Or maybe the next one...

Thanks to immensely talented cover designers, Richard Evans at Atlantic books, and illustrator Larry Rostant – I never dared dream I would have such an incredible cover, and I only hope the interior matches the exterior. Not forgetting proof reader Sarah Chatwin, for her eagle eye.

Thanks to the supreme generosity of author Sarah Hawkswood (whose historical mysteries everyone should be reading), for pointing out several historical errors in the eleventh hour.

I've also been fortunate enough to have a wealth of fascinating material come my way.

For first-hand accounts of the Revolution, I'd recommend *Journal of My Life During the French Revolution* by London socialite Grace Dalrymple Elliott, and Helen William's account of France during the time titled *Helen Williams and the French Revolution* (why complicate a title?).

For fascinating information on the 'real' Scarlet Pimpernel, Elizabeth Sparrow's *Phantom of the Guillotine: The Real Scarlet Pimpernel; Louis Bayard – Lewis Duval 1769–1844* makes enlightening reading.

How to Ruin a Queen: Marie Antoinette and the Diamond Necklace Affair, by Jonathan Beckman, provides a vivid account of the Queen's diamonds, their theft and the impact on the nation.

I've also enjoyed a number of interesting spy accounts, including: *Invisible Ink* by John Nagy, *Regency Spies* by Sue Wilkes, and *Secrets & Lies: Military Intelligence* by Jeremy Harwood.

Inside accounts of the Bastille have been aided by several first-hand memoirs, including *Secret Memoirs of Robert, Count de Paradès, on Coming Out of the Bastille and an Account of His Successful Transactions as a Spy in England* by Robert de Paradès, and *Escape from the Bastille: The Life and Legend of Latude* by Claude Quétel.

Always on my desk are Liza Picard's colourful accounts of everyday historical living, in this case: *Dr. Johnson's London*, and Professor Vivian Jones's *Women in the Eighteenth Century*.

Political fashions of the time have been elucidated by *Fashion in the Time of Jane Austen* by Sarah Jane Downing and *Georgians Revealed*, published by the British Library. Kitchen scenes and food, are informed by *Georgian Cookery* by Jennifer Stead and *Cooking for Kings: The Life of Antonin Careme* by Ian Kelly. The early history of hot air ballooning was detailed in *The Early History of Ballooning* by Fraser Simons.

And although a fictional work, Hilary Mantel's *A Place of Greater Safety* must be considered a work of fact in so many regards and a very great one at that.

Finally, big picture French Revolution accounts were gleaned from Christopher Hibbert's exhaustive *The French Revolution*, and probably my favourite of all, Stephen Clarke's hilarious and informative *The French Revolution and What Went Wrong*. If you read one book on the French Revolution, make it this one.

Read on for an extract from THE SCARLET CODE

[illegible]

[illegible]

[illegible]

dark fell a [illegible]

I am a[illegible] [illegible] k, hurrying [illegible]

the prow, and [illegible] sly across the [illegible]

[illegible] that [illegible]

[illegible]

CHAPTER ONE

Lisbon, 1789

IT IS NIGHT. THE DOCKYARD IS STILL, SAVE FOR THE CREAK of masts and tap of wood as boats knock against one another. From the crow's nest of an empty ship, I survey the shore. Guitar sounds and the occasional shout float on the air, mixed with a scent of garlic and frying fish from grills outside sailor taverns. As I watch, the last torch on a quay flutters out. The land guard is asleep. There is no time to lose.

I draw my knife; a great curved black blade. Placing it between my teeth I drop silently from the crow's nest to the deck, landing feet apart, balance perfect, taking the weapon into my hand. I wear assassin's garb – soft-soled dancing slippers, loose Arabic-style clothes, black silk trousers, a long-sleeved kurta cut short, tied with a thick scarf at the waist. My dark hair is braided up.

I slip across the deck, barely making a sound, step onto the prow, and jump easily across to the next ship. I assure myself the vessel is deserted, the crescent darkness of my knife invisible in the moonlight.

Looking out onto the water, I count the ships. Three to pass over until I reach the one where the captive is held. Her kidnappers have hidden her well; in an empty floating prison bound for Africa, to be filled with slaves.

Since there is no cargo yet loaded, there is a scant guard, but still I am careful. Assuring myself all is clear, I cross the deck, leap to the next boat. I'm in a rhythm now, running, jumping, checking for threats, knife held tight in my fist. I traverse a ship destined to take wool to England, a lumber transporter from Sweden, the smell of cut pine still fresh on deck. I arrive finally on *The Saint Jose.* A gilded diplomatic ship, old-fashioned, with a broad belly and shapely rear rising to a duck's tail of decorative carving and small windows.

Now my pace slows. There will be guards here. Quietly, I pad towards the captain's quarters at the back. As I suspected, the door is tightly secured from the outside. I need to open the padlock.

The first attack comes swiftly from behind. Feet strike the deck, then someone grabs my shoulder. My own hand sweeps back, locating my attacker's jugular, and I turn to face him. For a moment our stance is almost romantic, my fingers lightly at his throat, his grip still on my shoulder. With our faces only inches apart, his lips part in surprise. He hadn't been expecting a woman, and other instincts are befuddling him. Before he can resolve his confusion, my knife arrives at the artery my fingers have located. He drops soundlessly, blood filling his lungs.

The second man is only half-awake, a strong smell of drink pouring from him as he staggers to his feet. My eyes log the keys swinging at his hip. I close in before he can point his gun, since silence is imperative. His hand shoots out, grabs my chin. My knife is under his armpit, up and out before he realises. As he loses his grip on me, my knife comes up and around the base of his skull. The right eyelid spasms and he drops. I catch him before he thuds to the deck and lay him softly down.

I stand watching his twitching eye, still trained on me in disbelief. When the dying gaze clouds, I unhook first his set of keys, then the pistol from his belt and launch it through the air. It lands loudly on the deck of the lumber ship. A flurry of footsteps rings out on the adjacent deck. I listen, tense, making sure that any other guards are headed away. Then I approach a magnificent cabin door with its gaudy lock.

Always the way with Catholic countries, I think to myself as I fit the golden key, *to keep captives in finery.*

The door opens to reveal a woman, fashionably dressed in the latest French style of blousy muslin. She is sat at a table with a carafe of red wine and a silver plate before her. To her right is a bread basket and she holds a torn piece of its content half to her mouth as she stares at me in surprise.

'Am I being abducted?' she asks finally. 'How droll. Did the Duke sent you?' she adds hopefully.

Naturally, as a noblewoman, she reads a good deal to many romance novels.

'You are Fleur de Lucile?' I confirm, as she adjusts her dress to expose more of her shoulders.

She nods.

'You have already been abducted,' I tell her. 'It is only that you haven't noticed.'

She looks around the decorated captain's cabin.

'It is a jest?' she suggests, the slightest frown of puzzlement crinkling her smooth, white forehead. 'As you can see, I am very well cared for.' She gestures by way of explanation to the spread of food and wine, the finely set mahogany table.

'Silver forks do not ensure a host is trustworthy.' I walk to the window of tiny glass panes, assuring myself no warning torches have been fired on the docks. 'Your husband's stance against slavery has gained you powerful enemies.' I turn back to her. 'Did you ever question why your door was bolted from the outside? Why you are here alone, with guards placed to keep watch?'

'They said it was for my own protection.' She says slowly. 'The Portuguese ambassador . . .'

'Is in the pockets of the slave traders,' I say, moving closer to her table. 'You are aware how much money is made by slave trading every year?'

'Oh yes,' she says, rolling her eyes. 'My husband's friends are tiresome on the subject. But what has this to do with me?'

'Your husband is due to address the King, and convince him to sign the Rights of Man.'

Her mouth moves slowly, trying to match the words to a memory.

'The document written after the Bastille was stormed,' I explain patiently. She smiles in polite confoundedness.

'Agreeing that all men are equal,' I say, keeping my frustration in check.

'Oh that!' she claps her hands together. 'Why should plantation owners care if commoners and nobles are equal?'

'If the King signs the Rights of Man,' I tell her, 'he accepts that all men are equal. *All* men. Including the blacks in the French colonies.'

She does the thing with her mouth again, as though sounding out difficult words.

'Your captors are ruthless men; plantation owners, who will do anything to protect their business,' I tell her. 'Believe me, they have done worse than cut the throat of a lady and toss her in the sea.'

Understanding finally flickers over her features. She stands in shock.

'Who *are* you?' she manages. 'Are you Portuguese?' she adds, taking in the shade of my skin, and black hair. In reply I reach into my kurta and remove a letter from her husband. She takes it wordlessly.

'My name is Attica Morgan,' I say, as she reads. 'I'm an English spy. I have come to rescue you.'

CHAPTER TWO

FLEUR STARES FOR A LONG TIME AT HER HUSBAND'S LETTER.

Her eyes dart to me, something in her mind not matching.

'How am I to trust you?' she asks eventually. 'How can I be sure *you* are a friend?'

In reply I show her the slave brand, hidden under my hair at the back of my neck.

'My mother was African,' I explain. 'She died in Virginia when I was a girl, and we were enslaved together.'

Her eyes dart all over me now, looking for clues and inconsistencies. I often have this effect on people, since I am half of one continent, half of another. The medley of tawny skin and light eyes has been a great boon in my spy work, since I can pass for many nationalities.

'As soon as I got old enough to outrun my captors, I escaped to England and found my father. Lord Morgan,' I explain.

'You are Lord Morgan's *daughter*?' She says it that way people always do, when they know rumours of my bastard origins. 'I have heard of Lord Morgan,' she says slowly.

'Everybody has,' I say, unwilling to have the same tired conversation about my brilliant, yet erratic, father, and his brief awful decline into laudanum addiction. 'He is better now,' I add. 'Remarried. We should go.'

My family history has been enough to convince her. Fleur follows me onto the dark deck, and then grips my arm tight at the sight of the slaughtered guards littering the floor outside her cabin.

'They're dead,' I assure her, but it doesn't have the effect I hoped. I wonder briefly if I should have brought smelling salts, but Fleur manages to collect herself.

'This way.' I draw her to the prow, looking out onto the inky black water of the docks.

We creep along the edge of the boat. Moving to the side of the deck, I pull out my tinderbox and strike it. There's a pause and then across the docks another light flickers in reply. I count the flashes. Three times.

'That's the signal,' I tell Fleur, identifying the ship. 'Our rescuers are near. We will sail by night, and you shall be back with your husband by morning.'

'You surely will not attempt to sail us out of these docks?' says Fleur, panic rising. 'They are guarded. As soon as we raise anchor, they will gun us out of the water.'

'You must keep faith, Madame.'

I unwrap the scarf from my waist, and begin fashioning a makeshift grappling hook, tying the end to my knife handle.

Fleur watches the black curved blade in amazement.

'It is a Mangbetu,' I say proudly. 'Awarded to the fiercest fighters of the African Congo. My mother gave it to me.'

I send the blade winging over the side of the ship to lodge in a little yacht bobbing adjacent to us. Walking to the ship's wheel, I attach the other end of the silk and begin turning. Gripping with both hands, I haul on the scarf, winding it in.

There's a creaking sound as the little yacht begins drifting towards us. It's hard work and sweat beads my forehead, but I manage to pull the vessel close.

I allow the scarf to slacken. Our boats bob naturally against another. I put one leg over the prow and begin climbing down the rungs of the side of our larger boat, with Fleur following above me.

Once aboard I strike the tinderbox again. There is a pause, then a rope at the prow lifts clear from the water and tightens, and slowly but surely, we are pulled silently between the larger ships until we reach the hull of a large vessel waiting at the edge of open water.

A grappling hook lands loudly on the side of the ship and Fleur starts back with a cry of fear, then clamps her hands over her mouth. I can see the whites of Fleur's eyes in the moonlight, wide and frightened. Another hook lands, and another. A pack of swarthy men are climbing down to us.

'You mustn't mind their appearance,' I tell Fleur. 'They are here to help us.'

A figure hops nimbly onto deck, then emerges from the shadows. Jemmy Avery, almost invisible in his dark shirt and trousers, only his sword and flashy set of pistols glinting in the moonlight. He makes me a mock bow.

'Your ladyship.' Jemmy winks.

I give him a wide smile. 'Good to see you Captain Avery.'

'This is Jemmy Avery,' I tell her, noticing the fear in Fleur's eyes has deepened. 'He is ...' I decide to omit the word "pirate", 'a good sailor,' I conclude.

'Best sailor this side of the South Sea,' corrects Jemmy. 'And only that because we know of no land beyond it.'

'A humble man, as you see,' I murmur.

To Fleur, Jemmy bows low, taking off his broad-brimmed hat and rolling it smoothly along his forearm. I notice Fleur's shoulders relax, her expression soften.

'And this must by Fleur de Lucile? Do not fear, you are quite safe with me.' Jemmy is the very devil for charm when he needs to be.

Fleur's blue eyes widen. She is smiling coquettishly.

'My saviour,' she says, batting her lashes. 'How can I ever repay you?'

'A word, Captain Avery?' I interject, pulling him aside.

'Thank you, kindly,' mutters Jemmy, raising a dark eyebrow at me, and glancing back at Fleur. 'Anyone would think you were jealous.'

'Everything is as we planned?' I ask.

His eyes meet mine, their mongrel mix of green and brown masked by the moonlight. The tear-drop shaped burn at the side of his face looks more livid in the shadow.

'It is all as you wished it,' he says. 'The boys have been working hard. Lining below deck with barrels of pitch and brimstone, honeycombed. Brush and straw across the top. It goes against my boys' nature, to be sure, treating good ships that way. You're certain this will work, Attica?'

'I'm certain there's no other way out of this dock.'

His lips press together.

'I made a great study of naval warfare in my youth,' I assure him. 'So long as you can sail us where we need to be, it will work.'

'I can sail a horse trough through a hurricane, Attica, you needn't worry about that. She'll be where you want her.' He pats the prow then glances to Fleur who is standing a little apart from us now. Jemmy runs a hand over his shoulder-length black hair. 'Ready to blast the slave traders all to hell?' he says.

'Ready.'

Jemmy strides to the ships wheel, calling orders to his men. We are all action now, with no time for silence. Sails are trimmed, yardarms swing. The night breeze fills the sail. Shouts come from the shore. A torch lights.

'They've seen us now,' mutters Jemmy, turning the wheel expertly. 'Let's hope this old girl doesn't fall apart on us. There's a good tide once we're clear.'

The crew are cutting away the wrapping ropes, severing our connection to the smaller yacht as we drift free. It picks up the wind and begins a slow course inland.

Men are running along the quay, their voices raised as they near us, climbing aboard a man-of-war bristling with cannons.

Fleur is shaking her head, hands gripping the side of the boat.

'We'll never make it,' she whispers. 'They'll blow us to pieces.'

In answer, I strike a flint. It sparks on a little puff of cotton-flower kindling. I pick up the flaming material, lean overboard and drop it straight through the opening of the smaller yacht, drifting away from us. There's a silent moment before a crackling of ignition. Then smoke begins pouring up.

Moments later, flames lick upwards. The vessel continues to drift, headed straight for a cluster of moored boats that Jemmy's crew have already packed with tar and brimstone.

'We're not going to escape these docks,' I tell her, as Jemmy and his crew manoeuvre our rickety boat expertly towards the open ocean. 'We're going to burn them. Every last ship.'

Jemmy spins the wheel and the sails catch fully. Our boat begins to pick up speed, sailing fast from the Lisbon docks.

When I look behind us, all is blazing fury, as the fiery boat bobs benignly against the other moorings, spreading flaming cinders on everything it touches.

We enter the cool night-air of the ocean with nothing but smoke and flames behind us.